SAVAGE DESIRE

He remained atop her, bracing himself with his arms as he stared down into her eyes. She was surprised to realize that she could see him now. It seemed that only moments had passed since she'd awakened to find him there, and yet, as the images filled her mind, she realized that it had been much longer. Somehow, they had kept the wildness under control and stretched out time itself. One moment had spilled urgently into the next, filling their senses and blotting out all knowledge of time.

Perspiration covered them. She breathed in his distinctive musky aroma; it held within it the sharp tang of something primitive. He *is* a savage, she thought, meeting his amber gaze in the soft light. But, with him, so am I.

The Sorceress & The Savage

Saranne Dawson

LOVE SPELL BOOKS   NEW YORK CITY

A LOVE SPELL BOOK®

May 2000

Published by

Dorchester Publishing Co., Inc.
276 Fifth Avenue
New York, NY 10001

ISBN 0-505-52379-5

The name "Love Spell" and its logo are trademarks of Dorchester Publishing Co., Inc.

Printed in the United States of America.

Chapter One

Shera sat up in bed, chilled to the bone and sweating profusely. The dream receded—but her reaction to it lingered. She wrapped her arms around herself and willed herself to calmness.

Not a dream, she told herself. It was not a dream but a vision. She could no longer convince herself that what she'd seen was an ordinary dream, simply the nocturnal loosening of the bonds of reality. It would be impossible to make anyone who was not of her people—the Bacleev—to understand that, but she knew the difference—and had known it from the beginning.

She had to tell her parents. She should have done so the first time the vision came to her. Her only excuse was that there was so much fear among them now and she hadn't wanted to add to it.

Who is he? she asked herself, as she had every time the vision came. Was he from the past or the future—or both? And why was she the one receiving this vision? Why not the priests, or her parents, who were the leaders of her people? And yet she must be the only one to have had the vision, because surely if others had, they—unlike her—would have made it known.

And even as she thought about it, the vision returned, though with less clarity. A man, standing on a rocky ledge high above her, staring down at her and beckoning. A golden savage—that was how she thought of him. Dark gold hair, bronzed skin, and bold features all combined to give him a primitive, savage look. His rough clothing only added to that impression. He wore a sleeveless leather jerkin and short pants that revealed long, muscular legs, the lower part of which were encased in soft leather boots wrapped with lacings.

He is from the past, she thought, somehow nearly certain now that that was the case. But could he be from the future as well: a symbol of some sort rather than an actual man? Was his sudden appearance in her mind an indication that her worst fears were about to materialize: that she would be forced to leave her home?

"I've had a vision."

As one, her parents turned their dark eyes upon her, their attention sharpening. Shera knew that most of the time they regarded her as being little more than a nuisance. Once, they'd considered her to be a responsibility as well, but she was long past that now; at twenty-four, she had learned to care for herself.

Tasmun and Delora were the shegwas, the anointed leaders of her people, chosen by the gods for each other and blessed by the priests.

"Tell us," Tasmun ordered. He was never one to waste words, and his voice held the peremptory note of one who was accustomed to issuing orders that would unhesitatingly be obeyed.

She told the two about the man from the vision, watching them carefully to catch any hint of recognition. Unlike the rest of her tribe, Shera was convinced that her parents and the priests kept secrets: hidden knowledge that could unlock the mysteries of their past.

For one brief moment, she thought she saw a slight widening of her mother's eyes, but that was all. If her description of the man provoked any thoughts, her parents hid them well.

"What did you *feel?*" Delora asked, her voice only slightly less commanding than that of her husband. Her dark eyes bored into Shera's.

"Fear," Shera said simply. "Terrible fear, even though he did nothing that could be considered threatening. He only stood there, staring down at me."

"Where were you?" Tasmun demanded.

Shera frowned. She had given that part of the dream little thought, and now that she tried, she realized that she did, in fact, remember some details.

"I think it must have been in the mountains—strange mountains. There were many big trees." She hesitated, then recalled something else, although it seemed even stranger. "And there was a sound, like a roar, but not of an animal or a fire. I . . . I had the impression of a lot of water, but I don't remember seeing it."

She lapsed into silence again, trying to conjure up the setting without imagining the overpowering presence of the savage. "I'm sure it's a place I've never been," she said finally. "But I can't remember any more.

"I thought perhaps I was seeing the past," she said after a moment, once again studying them to see if her words had any effect. But it was as if she hadn't spoken. Instead, her father told her that they would pass her information on to the priests, who would probably wish to hear it from her own lips.

"Are we leaving here?" Shera asked. "I have heard rumors." They might be her parents, but she knew that meant little in this respect. They weren't likely to tell her anything before anyone else knew it. They never had.

"Perhaps," Tasmun said with a shrug of his thin shoulders. "The signs are not yet clear."

"I don't understand why we would leave here," Shera told him. "Even if this isn't our true home, it's a pleasant place to live—and the duke is happy to have us here."

"Nevertheless," Tasmun said in that end-of-discussion tone she knew all too well, "we do as the gods instruct us."

Shera nodded and bade them farewell, leaving them in the lovely garden behind their home. She herself lived in a small cottage at the outskirts of their village, which itself was located a short distance from the walled city that was the duke's stronghold.

She was certain that they *would* be leaving and that her parents already knew that. After twenty-four years, she knew how they ruled. They had almost certainly allowed those rumors she had heard to spread, as a way of preparing the people.

Not that they really required any preparation, she thought angrily. The Bacleev always did as their priests commanded. Her parents might be the anointed leaders of the tribe, but their authority extended only to those matters that the priests allowed. All else required the approval of the gods. They had always been a physically weak people—and they despised hard work, she thought. Of course they depended upon the gods. That was why she was different—she'd never feared honest labor.

She walked back to her cottage, where she paused to stare at the distant city with its high, dun-colored walls. The duke's castle sat high on a hilltop in the very middle of the city. He would be very unhappy to learn of their departure, though she knew he would do nothing to stop them from leaving. They had long been a part of his domain, although not native.

The Bacleev had arrived in the Trellan lands a century ago, but their history before that was a mystery—even to the tribe itself. No one—except possibly the priests—knew from where they had come or why they had no knowledge of their past. Still, the present duke's great-grandfather had welcomed them—especially when he learned of their magic.

The Bacleev had two great talents: they could summon rains for the crops, even in this arid land, and they were powerful healers. So the dukes of Trella treated them well, in return for which the Bacleev provided them with abundant crops and cured their ailments or healed their injuries.

All Bacleev could call the rains, and many some small talent at healing, but Shera, despite her young age, was one of the most powerful healers of her tribe. In fact, she was the object of some envy, and more than a little anger on the part of the priests and their most devoted followers, because the talents were believed to come from the gods, and Shera wasn't particularly devout. Still, she made her living by healing those who fell ill, and she had, earned a place—albeit small—in society.

As a child, she'd been taken to all of the many ceremonies that made up so much of her people's lives, but once she'd broken free from her parents' domination, things had changed. Now she went as infrequently as possible. There was, she thought, something wrong with those ceremonies, even though she could never quite explain what she meant. The rest of the Bacleev believed their gods to be wise and benevolent, but Shera thought differently. And she had since a young age.

As she had remarked more than once, to the consternation of her devout family and friends, "What kind of gods would rob people of their heritage?"

No one had ever had an answer for that, and once she began to ask such questions, most people had begun to avoid her—except, of course, when they had need of her talents.

That evening, after Shera had completed her daily walk about the village, checking on various patients, she was heading back to her cottage when she heard a familiar voice calling her name. She stopped, though dying to return home. Her arms ached and her head was throbbing as a result of plying her trade; she was in no mood to deal with Marcus now. But he was one of very few people who sought out her company, so she bit back her desire to shoo him away.

He caught up with her quickly, and she saw that his dark brows were knitted together in a frown. "I heard that you had a vision," he said, falling into step alongside her.

She nodded, having already guessed that was what had brought him to her. It might be worth telling him. In truth, Marcus had become almost a friend since she had firmly rejected his suit. She didn't want to talk any more about the vision, but she saw little harm in it. And he would pester her until she had. When she finished, he asked her what the priests had said about it.

11

"Nothing," she replied with a shrug. "Maybe they didn't even believe that it was a true vision. After all, I've never had one before."

"Yes, that is strange," he agreed. "But I think it unlikely that they would disregard it—especially now. Daren thinks we'll be leaving here soon."

Shera shuddered. Though Daren was Marcus's friend—and they had both pressed to marry her—she had never liked the other man. There was something about him that was cruel. "Do you think so, too?"

Marcus nodded somberly. "Glewena and several others have had visions of a long journey into great mountains. Many believe that the gods are preparing us for what we must do."

"I like it here," Shera stated. "Perhaps I will stay. I'm sure the duke would be happy to take me into his household."

Marcus gave her exactly the shocked look she'd expected. "You would abandon your people—and the gods?"

"Maybe. Of course, one could say that it is *they* who would be abandoning *me.*" And, she thought, Glewena's visions were nothing she put stock in. Like all Bacleev, the young priestess had a taste for wealth, but something about Glewena was different. She was . . . greedier. Marcus interrupted her thoughts.

"How can you jest about such a thing, Shera? I don't understand you."

How true, she thought with an inner sigh. "I'm not jesting, Marcus. I see no reason to leave my life here, regardless of what the gods have to say."

"Not even if we're going to our true home?" he asked.

"That might be different," she acknowledged. "But if the gods expect me just to pack up and leave without telling me where I'm going, then I see no reason why I should obey them."

He shook his head. "What I don't understand is how you came to have such talent though you mock the gods."

"Perhaps they're not quite as powerful as you and the others believe, Marcus."

* * *

But the next morning, as she set out for the city, Shera heard her words to Marcus echoing in her brain, mocking her. The vision had come again: the golden savage, the dark mountains, that strange roaring sound. And when she'd awakened in the middle of the night, she knew that she would follow her people. She might be very derelict in her worship of the gods, but she understood that there was a reason for this vision—and that the answer lay somewhere else, not here.

She passed through the open gate to the city and was met by the herbalist who always accompanied her on her rounds. Together, they visited the sick and the injured, with Shera laying on her hands and then instructing the herbalist about which potions would be most efficacious.

Wherever she went, she was greeted with pleasant smiles. The people of the duke's city all knew of her extraordinary talents, and they appreciated her generosity in coming here. The other healers in her tribe demanded that people be brought to them, which was often difficult. But Shera saw no reason why the sick and injured should be forced to travel several miles to see her, when she could easily come to them.

Besides, the Trellans were a happy and colorful people—unlike her own tribe. Her people looked upon them with carefully concealed contempt, since the Trellans were godless. Shera, on the other hand, was inclined to think that was why they were happy—another belief that had not endeared her to her people.

Late in the afternoon, as she was making her way back to the city gate, a young man wearing the livery of the royal household approached her respectfully.

"Milady," he said, bowing as though she, too, were royalty. "His Grace wishes to see you."

Probably the duchess was suffering from swollen joints again, Shera thought as she turned her horse and followed the page up the hill to the castle. Potions worked most of the time, but she'd probably ignored her prescribed diet again, as she was wont to do. Shera liked the duchess, but she had little patience with people who failed to take her advice.

However, to her surprise, it was the duke himself who rose to

13

greet her as she was ushered into his private quarters. Furthermore, he looked deeply troubled as he gave her a slight bow.

Shera did not curtsy, since her people, while grateful for the duke's kindness, did not regard him as their ruler. And such was their value to him that he treated the Bacleev as equals.

"I have just been told the news by Tasmun and Delora," he said unhappily.

"What news?" she asked, even though she suspected what it must be.

"You don't know?" He seemed taken off guard.

"I came to the city very early this morning," she told him, then added, "I'm afraid I didn't attend the ceremonies last night, either."

"They came to tell me that you will all be leaving—that your gods have decreed you must journey westward."

"I see." Shera wasn't really surprised, but she realized now that she'd still been hoping that it wouldn't happen.

The duke spoke hesitantly. "My dear Shera, I know that it is probably impossible, but I must ask anyway. Would you consider staying here? We would be delighted to have you live here with us."

Shera hesitated, too. The idea was very tempting. The Trellans were hardly strangers to her. She spent more time with them than she did with her own people, and spoke their language as fluently as they themselves did.

But she could not stay. She thanked the duke and explained that she must remain with her people. She even suggested that disobeying the orders of the gods could result in her powers being taken from her, although she didn't really believe that. If her past behavior hadn't been enough to warrant that, one more act of disobedience wasn't likely to make a difference.

The vision came again that night—but this time it was different. The place was the same, but instead of the golden-haired savage, it was a giant catlike creature that stared down at her from the high ledge.

Once again jolting awake, Shera sat up in bed, chilled and

drenched with sweat. The image of the great cat stayed with her, causing her to shiver with fear. It was huge—far larger even than the big dogs the duke raised. And its fur was a tawny color that was unnervingly close to the color of the savage's hair.

However, once the fear had passed, Shera began to question the meaning of this particular vision. The duke had told her that long ago, his grandfather had sent men out to explore the lands far to the west. Four men had gone, but only two had returned. The other two had been attacked and killed by huge wildcats in a mountainous region.

He hadn't described the beasts, but perhaps her imagination had filled in the details, then transposed them into her vision.

Or else, she thought, both the man and the cats are real and I am being given a warning.

The Bacleev set out on their journey one week later: nearly two thousand people, plue pack animals and livestock. As they passed through the small villages that dotted the great plain, people wept openly at losing their healers and the bringers of rain for their crops.

But the Bacleev remained dry-eyed—except for Shera, who felt guilty at deserting these people, many of whom had become her friends. The rest of the tribe, however, was hardened with resolve to obey the commands of the gods. Never had Shera felt less a part of her people, and several times she came quite close to turning back. The thought of being forced to spend the remainder of her days solely in the company of these fanatics—even if they were her own people— did not sit well with her.

Nevertheless, she followed them. Though loath to admit it, she, too, had been touched by the power of the gods the night before as the entire tribe had gathered to honor them and to seek their protection on the long journey. As always, she had shuddered at the darkness she felt in that power—but the power itself she could not deny.

She stared at the broad, empty plain ahead and the mountains beyond that and sighed. Perhaps if she had someone with whom to share her future, this exodus wouldn't have been so bad. But theirs was a small community, and she knew all the possible prospects. She could not summon up a true liking for any of them.

That first night, as they camped out beneath the stars, the vision came again to Shera for the first time since she had seen the great cat. This time it was the golden-haired savage once again, staring down at her from his ledge. But then suddenly he vanished, and in his place was the great tawny cat.

She awoke to the sound of her own cry, then quickly looked around to be certain she hadn't disturbed anyone. But they slept on. Apparently her shriek hadn't been as loud as it had seemed.

She sat up and peered into the darkness beyond the camp-fires. Guards were posted at regular intervals, carrying the rifles the duke had given them. She knew, from the duke's tales, that they were weeks, perhaps even a month or more, from the mountains where those long-ago explorers had met up with the beasts of her dreams. But she still imagined them out there, prowling the edges of darkness.

Was there a connection between the man and the cat—or was the feline a trick of her mind, an embodiment of her fear, stolen from the duke's stories of his childhood? And who was this dream man who seemed to belong to the wild land of her vision almost as much as the cat? She had heard nothing of the explorers encountering any signs of people.

The savage fascinated her, though she feared him, too. He looked so very different from her people, and from the Trellans among whom they'd made their home. Both the Bacleev and the Trellans were small, dark-haired people with refined features. The man of her visions was larger, more muscular, and rougher in appearance.

She lay down again, frowning. Why had no one else shared her visions? There were, among her people, many who regularly had dreams of the future—omens—but she alone had seen the man and the cat.

* * *

More than two weeks passed before they reached the mountains, and Shera knew, from the duke's story, that this was not the range where the explorers had been killed. Those peaks still lay far to the west, beyond yet another wide plain. Their progress now became agonizingly slow, as they sought out footpaths and passes, and were often forced to dismount and lead their animals over treacherous terrain. Each time they found a pass, Shera scanned the high ledges, searching for any sign of inhabitants, even though these mountains were far higher than any she'd ever seen, and they lacked the dark, jagged look of the land from her visions.

Finally, after another ten days of travel, they came down out of the mountains to a land of rolling hills and meadows. Two small streams meandered through the valleys, and there were berry bushes and nut trees that allowed them to replenish some of their food supplies.

Tasmun and Delora decreed a rest for the weary travelers. Their precious goats and cows had been giving far less milk, and the shegrias hoped that with time for proper grazing they could elicit more from the livestock. They set up camp between the two streams, with most of them choosing to sleep in the open instead of in the tents they'd brought along. Although summer was almost over, the days and nights remained warm.

After several pointed conversations, Shera learned that no one seemed to know about any great cats—or her vision. She found it rather strange, since word of her first dream had spread quickly. Also, the existence of the cats had been confirmed by the duke, who'd spoken of them to her parents after she had related her dream to them. Therefore, after camp had been set up, she approached Tasmun and Delora and inquired why the information was being kept secret.

"The priests have decreed that nothing be said about your second dream, or the cats," Delora told her.

"But why? Surely this is something everyone needs to know—in case we encounter them."

"That is their decision to make, Shera," Tasmun replied

rather irritably. "Surely you aren't questioning a decision of the priests?"

"But I *am* questioning such a decision. There are monstrous creatures about, beasts who killed two men."

"But not here. The duke said the explorers didn't encounter them until they reached the mountains far to the west."

"Will they tell everyone before we reach those mountains? Because if they don't, I will!"

"Shera!" her mother said sharply. "When you question the wisdom of the priests, you are questioning the very gods themselves!"

"Nevertheless, that is exactly what I will do!" Shera replied. She turned on her heel and left them there, no doubt shaking their heads and wondering how they could have produced such a child.

Shera had often wondered that herself. What was it in her that resisted the will of the gods? She certainly didn't doubt their existence. She'd felt their presence, and she knew that only the gods could have given her the magic she possessed.

Perhaps it was the result of her regular contact with the Trellans and her envy of their way of life. She'd long since realized that while those people owed the duke their allegiance, he didn't interfere much in the course of their lives. And the pagan Trellans didn't worship any gods except for the forces of nature. Yet the Trellans were happy people, much given to laughter and games and a joy for living.

The Bacleev, on the other hand, were dark and somber and always fearful of annoying their dark gods. It seemed like an unhappy way of life, yet she could not entirely cast off her heritage, any more than she could shed her skin.

After three days of rest and three nights devoted to the worship of the gods, the tribe moved on across the rolling hills and grass-covered valleys. It was a pleasant land, and Shera couldn't help thinking that the duke's ancestors had chosen badly. This place was far more suited for inhabitation than the flat, arid plains where the Trellans lived.

Suddenly she recalled a conversation some years ago with an elderly Trellan woman whose life was slipping away. Shera had been asked to ease her pain, which was the only service she could perform for one so old. She'd spent long hours with the woman, who was quite pleasant and full of tales.

What she remembered now was a story the woman had told that had its origins in the murky depths of antiquity. The woman had said that far to the west lay a terrible place where evil reined supreme, despite the beauty of the land. She'd said that was why her people had never ventured westward, but had instead chosen to settle on an outlet to the great sea in the east.

Shera had intended to ask the duke about the story, but instead she'd forgotten all about it. She hadn't before put much credence in it in any event; the Trellans were full of such myths.

Evil was a concept Shera couldn't grasp. She knew, of course, that some people were bad and that other basically decent people sometimes did bad things—but true evil was quite beyond her understanding. How could a land itself be evil? Surely the gods would not permit such a thing, even if they did seem to tolerate a certain amount of bad behavior.

As they began to travel again, the days stretched to weeks and then to a month. Gradually, the rolling hills and fertile valleys gave way to another arid plain that stretched to the horizon. Always, Shera rode with her gaze fixed on that horizon, seeking the mountains.

Finally, a little more than a month after they had come down out of the other mountains, she saw them at last: a faint, dirty smudge far to the west where the land met the sky. This was their destination.

Low murmurs arose from the long line of travelers. Shera thought wryly that if they'd been Trellans, there would have been whoops of joy. But then the Trellans would never have set out on this terrible journey in the first place, unencumbered as they were by dictatorial gods.

During the past few weeks, many in the tribe had begun to have visions of the mountains, and a few had seen a lush, green valley beyond them. None of them had seen the man or the cats, but Shera found it interesting that they *had* heard that roaring sound she'd heard in her own visions.

Some believed the sound to be that of a great waterfall. They'd already seen several falls in the mountains now behind them. But Shera thought that if that were true, the falls must be far larger than she could imagine.

The priests still remained silent about the visions—and about the cats as well. It made Shera wonder what other secrets they might be harboring.

It turned out that seeing the mountains and actually reaching them were two very different matters. Two more weeks passed before they even reached the foothills, where Tasmun and Delora called for a few days' rest before they proceeded.

These mountains were very different from the earlier ones. Jagged peaks seemed to be ripping at the very fabric of the heavens, and they were clustered so tightly together that it seemed impossible to pass through them.

When Shera learned that a small party was being sent out to scout for a way through the mountains, she approached the men as they were about to leave.

"Have you heard about what lives in these mountains?" she asked their leader, fearing that they hadn't been told.

The men nodded solemnly and fingered their long rifles. "The cats? The priests warned us about them. But we are not to kill them unless they attack."

She watched as the men mounted their horses and rode out of camp. Somehow, she knew they wouldn't be coming back. The knowledge settled onto her like a heavy, cold stone. But she told no one, because she didn't want to alarm their families. Perhaps she was wrong. Also, if she were right, there was nothing to be done. They would never believe her.

For three days, she waited anxiously for the scouts to return, and each night she feared that a vision of their deaths would upset her sleep. But there were no visions of any kind.

By the end of the third day, her own fears were being echoed by others, and by the fourth day, the uneasiness in the camp was growing. That night the priests consulted the gods and then announced that the Bacleev must move on into the mountains. Shera went to her parents.

"Why haven't you told everyone about what waits up there?" she demanded. "Those beast have killed the scouts, and now you would send us all to our deaths?"

"We must go through the mountains," Delora said simply. Her mother looked worried, yet remained firm. "And the gods have said nothing about the cats. They would warn us."

"You're wrong!" Shera spat, giving voice to a fear she'd held at bay for too long. "Those cats are a threat to *all* of us—and now I think the man may be, too. My visions were warnings!"

"We have nothing to fear," Tasmun intoned. "Can't you already feel the power of the gods growing stronger?"

"Come to the ceremony this night, Shera," her mother implored. "You will feel it, too."

Shera didn't *want* to feel it; that was why she hadn't been attending the services. Still, she nodded like a dutiful daughter. Her absence from the nightly ceremonies had become more obvious since they began their journey. And she no longer had the excuse of her work to keep her away. She could no longer escape.

She'd never spoken to anyone about her fear of the darkness she felt at the ceremonies. It was obvious to her that no one else felt the way she did. Always, instead, she heard people speak glowingly of the great power they felt of oneness with the gods.

But on this night—the last night before they entered the mountains—Shera decided that maybe she needed to feel some of that power herself. Perhaps then she wouldn't fear her vision—the cat or the man.

Just after the sun had set, the Bacleev formed their ritual circles within circles: twelve in all, with the priests at the very center. A waxing moon hung above them in a sky that was rapidly losing its light. The mountains were already nearly invisible, though Shera could feel their presence.

They began the ancient chants, the calling to the gods. At the

21

very center of the ring of priests, the sacred green fire glowed in its golden bowl, set this night on a large boulder that had been carried to its spot by several appointed men.

Shera murmured the chants automatically as she clasped the hands of those next to her. There was a certain soothing familiarity to the ritual for her this night, and she knew it was because of her fears and the fact that she had been cut off from everything familiar to her.

From where she stood, she couldn't actually see the bowl, but she could see the glow from the sacred fire growing steadily brighter. Finally, as the crowd fell silent and the priests alone continued the chant, she saw tongues of green fire leap high into the air.

Then she felt it: a low hum of power that passed through her. Many people saw visions at such times. Sometimes they were personal in nature—the answer to some problem. Other times they were more general. The priests, drawing on the forces within them all, were said to hear the actual voices of the gods.

Shera waited expectantly, hoping she would see something that would allay her fears. But instead she felt what she always did: a darkness beyond understanding and a bone-deep coldness. And for the first time, it was clear that she was resisting, fighting something nameless. She discovered it because, this time, the struggle seemed much greater.

When it was over and people broke the circles and began to mill about, she felt more alone than ever. In the light of the campfires, she could see their faces, and she could feel the power that lingered in them. But she still felt cold and in the dark.

Concealed within the thick, aromatic needles of a hundred-foot fir, Gar watched the foreigners break camp and begin their trek into the mountains. He had climbed the tree again just after dawn, having slept at its base after watching their ceremony.

Despite all the omens, he had been hoping that the Bacleev weren't returning, even though he knew it wasn't a hope shared by all. His people were badly divided, and that alone was sufficient reason for him to be concerned.

"You were right," Haydor said from his perch in the same tree. "The deaths did not stop them."

Gar merely nodded, his gaze still fixed on the long line of people and animals. Haydor claimed to agree with him about the negative effect the Bacleev would have on their people, but Gar thought he detected a hint of excitement in the man's voice.

"Perhaps they'll change their minds when they find the bodies," suggested Trega from a nearby tree. Gar knew that his best friend felt as he did about the return of the Bacleev.

"That won't stop them," Gar told him. "And there are too many of them for us to kill them all."

He had been hoping there might be fewer of them, that something might have happened to diminish their numbers over the past century. But it appeared that they'd not only survived, but thrived. He now deeply regretted the decision his great-grandfather had made not to go after them. If they had, they might well have succeeded in ridding this world of the Bacleev forever.

Still, he thought he knew why his ancestor hadn't pursued them. It was the same reason that his people were now so divided about their return: that unholy bond between them. For all that they'd now lived contentedly for a century without the tas-syana, the urge remained—even in him.

He began to climb down from the tree, followed by the other two. "I want to get closer, to see what weapons they might have. Perhaps we can at least reduce their numbers before they get to the valley."

Chapter Two

Shera reined in her horse, guiding it out of the procession as she stared around wildly. Marcus, who was riding next to her, quickly followed.

"What is it?" he demanded as he, too, looked around.

She didn't answer as she continued to study the encroaching trees. A few people glanced their way curiously, but most just plodded on, numbed by now to their surroundings.

Shera's heart was thudding heavily in her chest, and icy fingers of fear trailed along her spine. "I don't know," she replied finally, after Marcus had repeated his question.

She continued to run her eyes nervously over the hilly terrain. They were not yet truly into the mountains. Instead, the land around them at the moment was filled with thick fir and pine forests and huge rocky outcroppings, as though pieces of the mountain had come tumbling down to rest on the uneven land.

There were too many places to hide, she thought as she peered into the gloom of the forest to her right, then scanned the rocks to her left. Marcus fingered the rifle strapped to his saddle as he, too, gazed around them.

"Did you see something?" he asked nervously.

She shook her head. "No, I *felt* something. I still feel it. Someone is watching us."

"Go back to the others," Marcus said, untying the rifle. "I'll ride up into those rocks to get a better look."

"No." The sharpness of her voice startled even her. "I'll come with you."

Marcus hesitated, opening his mouth to protest and then closing it again. He knew better than to argue with her. In all things, Shera was her own woman. She would follow her own dictates regardless of what he said or did.

The horses began to pick their way carefully up the steep, rocky incline. Several other armed men made as if to follow them, but Marcus waved them back into line. They had few enough armed men to protect the people; he didn't want to draw any more of them away. He also relished the thought of having even a brief time alone with Shera.

When they reached the flat ledge at the top, they both looked around. A hundred feet below them, the tribe wound its way through the rocks, following a faint path that avoided the rocks and skirted the edge of the woods. The front of the line had disappeared around a curve in the trail, while the rear was hidden below the last hill.

Shera dismounted, then began turning in a slow circle, stopping when she faced a thick forest of dark firs that blanketed the hillside. The trees were very tall, and their thick clusters of dark needles made it impossible to see their trunks—or anything that might be hiding in them.

Something is there, she thought, chilled to the bone. *Something is watching us.* In her mind's eye, she saw the great tawny cat, but in the distance, she could see nothing.

Gar watched, fascinated—so fascinated that at first he paid scant attention to the man. She was staring straight at him, and yet he knew that she couldn't be seeing him. After a century away from the source of their power, the Bacleev couldn't have retained their talents—and yet she obviously sensed him there.

Crouched on a thick limb and staying close to the huge trunk, he stared at her. She was very beautiful, he thought, surprised that he could see beauty in any of his enemies. Her raven black hair flowed over her shoulders, curling slightly at the ends. In the bright sunlight where she stood, it had a faint bluish cast. She was nearly as tall as the man, though both of them were much smaller than he was.

She had a deceptively fragile look to her: delicate bones and a slim, lithe body. From this distance he couldn't see her eyes, but he knew they would be dark—as dark as her hair. "Black-eyed devils" was how his people frequently referred to hers.

With considerable difficulty, he dragged his gaze from her and studied the weapon the man carried. That it was, in fact, a weapon of some sort, he had no doubt. It was obvious from the way the man carried it.

Interesting, he thought. It seemed to confirm his belief that the Bacleev were, as yet, poorly defended. If only there weren't so many of them. . . .

He decided that he should find out just what sort of weapon his enemy held, and he reached out to pluck a heavy pinecone from a nearby branch. With a quick glance at his companions to let them know what he intended, Gar threw the heavy cone in a high, wide arc as far as he could. Immediately the man swiveled in that direction and raised the weapon to his shoulder to aim it.

A loud crack shattered the silence, and Gar saw a spark and then a wisp of smoke at the tip of the weapon. His keen hearing picked up the sound of something tearing through the branches near where he'd tossed the cone. The man began to scramble clumsily over the rocks to that spot.

Gar signaled his companions to stay where they were and climbed quickly down from the tree. In surefooted silence, he moved through the forest until he was directly behind the man, who was busy examining his surroundings. The weapon was now held loosely in one hand.

Gar's ears picked up the sound of the woman approaching, and then he heard her voice calling out to the man. But before the man could respond, Gar sprang.

"Marcus!" Shera called out again, both exasperated and frightened as she hurried after him. In the distance she could hear the shouts of others, no doubt drawn by the sound of gunfire.

She picked her way through the thick forest, where blackberry bushes grew beneath the tall trees in a nearly impenetrable tangle. She saw Marcus up ahead, visible through the dark forest only because of his red jerkin. She called his name yet again as she hurried toward him.

Then, suddenly, she saw movement: a flash of something tawny leaping out of the undergrowth. She drew a breath to scream, but even before the sound was released, Marcus had vanished from view. Behind her the shouts were louder, and she called out to the other Bacleev even as she pushed her way toward Marcus, now ignoring the thorns that tore at her hands and clothing.

When she reached him, she stopped. Her friend lay unmoving on the needle-strewn ground, and even in that first instant when she saw him there, she knew he was dead. An anguished cry poured from her lips as she staggered toward him; then she stopped, her eyes searching the forest for his killer. But the only sound was that of the approaching men.

She knelt beside Marcus and pressed her fingers to his throat, even though she knew the pulse was gone. But how had he died? There were no marks on him, none of the wounds she'd expected to find. She choked back a sob, trying to recall exactly what she'd seen. How could he have been killed so quickly—and without a sound?

Four armed men burst into the small clearing, rifles at the ready. Shera pulled herself together to explain what had happened, though even as she did so, she was blaming herself for his death. If only they hadn't come out alone to investigate her sense of danger . . .

One of the men knelt down and turned Marcus over, frowning. "There aren't any marks on him. What killed him?"

It hadn't been a cat, Shera thought, and an image of the man from her visions came back to her. "It could have been a native . . . a man," she told them. "He wore clothing the same color as an animal's fur."

The man who still knelt beside Marcus continued to frown. "But how did he kill him?"

"Maybe he broke his neck," another man suggested.

Shera forced herself to kneel again beside Marcus's body. Slowly she ran her sensitive fingers along his neck and the upper portion of his back, then shook her head. "No bones are broken."

"His rifle's gone—and so is his powder," one of the men pointed out urgently. "No beast could have carried them off. It had to have been a man."

They all fanned out in a circle to check the surrounding forest while Shera remained beside Marcus, quietly murmuring the ancient prayers for his safe passage into the other world. But all the while, her mind remained on that briefly glimpsed figure, and she was suddenly sure it was the man from her vision.

The other men returned and began once again to question her. How could a man of Marcus's size and strength have been killed so quickly and so mysteriously? they asked Shera over and over again, but she had nothing more to add. In the thick, shadowy forest, she'd managed only the briefest glimpse of his killer, and couldn't even guess at what weapons he might bear.

She thought about the man from her visions. He'd been standing far above her on a ledge, and she'd attributed the impression of great size to that, but she recalled as well seeing his powerful arms and legs. Even so, how had he managed to kill so swiftly and silently?

The men carried Marcus back to his horse and then they returned to the trail; the procession of travelers had stopped at the sound of gunfire. By now those ahead were streaming back as well. All was chaos until Tasmun and Delora arrived and ordered them to wrap Marcus's body and strap it to his horse until they could find a place suitable for burial.

Word spread quickly among the Bacleev. Now they had not only great cats to fear, but men as well—men who could kill an armed man quickly and without a sound.

Then, before the day ended, they found the scouting party. All four men had clearly been attacked by animals, and most probably at night, since they were in a makeshift camp. But their rifles were also gone.

Shera didn't see the bodies of the scouts, but she heard people talking about how they'd been killed but not devoured. It seemed strange. Didn't wild creatures kill only for food?

The journey came to a halt, and the tribe filled a deep ravine and the surrounding hillsides. It was decided that since they now had five bodies to deal with, they would bury them all in this place.

Shera attended the services, which were followed by the usual evening ceremony. This time, as the power of the gods flowed through her, she welcomed it. Instead of filling her with a bone-deep chill, the darkness soothed her; it whispered of safety and gave her a sense of protection.

Gar didn't hear the chants of the Bacleev because he was too far away—and also because he was too busy. After he'd killed the man and fled with his companions, they'd happened upon the bodies of the other four. They had taken their weapons as well, together with many pouches of the fine black powder they carried.

He had no feelings of guilt for having slain the Bacleev. Nor did he regret the deaths of the others, though he'd played no part in that.

What *did* trouble him was the woman. He could have killed her easily enough, and probably should have, even though she didn't possess a weapon.

Or at least, he thought nervously, she didn't have a weapon like these. He still recalled how she'd stared straight at him when she couldn't possibly have seen him. She likely had some power.

He'd let her go because she was beautiful—a foolish mistake. Unlike his own people, the Bacleev women were as dangerous as the males, which doubled their strength of numbers. And this one in particular he could tell would be very dangerous.

After a time, he left off his thoughts about her and concentrated on the strange weapons he and his friends had stolen. It didn't take him and his companions long to figure them out. The new weapons would be very useful; with luck, they could rid the world of a few more Bacleev before they reached the valley.

But it wouldn't be enough; he knew that, just as he knew that although his people would do his bidding, some were secretly eager to resume their old life. They hated the Bacleev—but they wanted what only the Bacleev could give them.

The line of travelers snaked its way through the narrow pass, now spread out over several miles, since they were forced to travel single file much of the time. The men with rifles were scattered among them, their eyes constantly searching ledges and hilltops and ravines. Their hands rested close to their weapons, as though to reassure themselves that they weren't completely defenseless against the unseen and unknown enemy.

If the priests knew anything about the identity of their human foes, they weren't telling the nervous Bacleev. Instead, they spoke of trials to be endured in order to reach their goal, interlaced with reminders that the will of the gods was not to be questioned.

Most Bacleev needed no such reminder. They believed implicitly that they would be delivered from this unknown terror, and even spoke of being rewarded by the gods for their long trials. There were rumors of visions: revelations of great, unimaginable power for the Bacleev, or of recovering something that had been taken from them.

Shera heard these rumors, but each time she tried to track them down, the people who'd supposedly had the visions were unwilling to confirm them.

Unlike the rest of the tribe, however, Shera *was* questioning the wisdom of the gods. Why were they subjecting her people to this—sending them ever deeper into what must be enemy territory? And if, as many were suggesting, the gods were directing them to their true home, why had they left it in the first place? Had they been driven out by the ancestors of the thing that had killed Marcus?

And when she wasn't asking herself those questions, she was wondering how it was that she'd survived. That question hadn't occurred to her until after Marcus and the others had been laid to rest and several people remarked that she was fortunate to have been spared by the gods from the same fate.

Given how quickly and easily he'd killed Marcus, their foe could certainly have killed her as well. Had he killed Marcus only to get his weapon, and let her live because she had none? Or had the sounds of the approaching men driven him away before he could attack?

She rode on, her eyes constantly scanning her surroundings, fearful in the knowledge that the Bacleev were being watched once again. She had become ever more certain that the man she'd seen in her vision had been Marcus's killer—and that she would encounter him again.

There were more attacks. Several armed guards were killed at night, apparently the victims of animal attacks, though no animal had yet been seen. On each occasion, the dead men had been unable even to fire their rifles before being felled.

But the attacks didn't come only at night. In the daylight, the attacks were clearly carried out by humans—though, again, no one was even seen. There would suddenly be the crack of a rifle, and somewhere along the line, someone would cry out and fall. In a few cases, Shera or one of the other healers had been able to save the victim, but more often than not, the targets were dead before they fell from their horses.

The Bacleev soldiers, who had been trained by the duke's men before their departure, were in awe of these unseen marksmen who could also apparently kill quickly and silently without rifles—and without leaving any marks. There were whispers of strange powers, and the Bacleev considered for the first time ever the possibility that another people might be favored by the gods.

The priests, of course, denied it.

On their fourth night in the narrow pass through the mountains, thunderstorms came. The Bacleev huddled as best they could beneath oiled skins, cold and miserable. Their food supplies were running low, and the torrential rains made it impossible to light campfires.

Shera was near the middle of the line. She had finally dropped off to sleep after the worst of the storm had passed, only to be jolted awake by shouts and cries from those ahead of her. She had barely managed to brush away the cobwebs of sleep and push aside the oilskins when she heard her name being called. A moment later, two mounted armed guards approached her.

"You must come with us now, Shera," one of them said. "The priests have sent us for you."

"Why?" she asked, feeling a sudden chill that had nothing to do with the cold and damp. "What has happened?"

"Come now," the older of the two guards ordered, reaching down to draw her up behind him.

They rode past the long line of people, all of whom were now awake and talking in hushed, excited tones. Dazed and frightened herself, she barely noticed their anxious glances.

When she reached the front of the line, she found the black-robed priests gathered there in a tight group. She searched for her parents but didn't see them. Then, suddenly, she knew the reason for her summons.

"Where are the shegwas?" she asked. She dismounted, still peering into the darkness in the desperate hope of finding them.

"They have gone to the gods," the high priest intoned.

Shera felt as though she'd been struck in the stomach. All the breath went out of her. Though they'd never been close, and more than once she'd wished for the kind of loving parents she'd encountered among the Trellans, the ties of blood were still strong. She immediately began to think of all the times she'd defied them and disappointed them.

"Wh-what happened to them?"

"They were attacked as they slept by . . . two creatures," the high priest replied.

"Where are they?" Shera demanded. "Surely their wounds can be healed."

"No, child," an elderly priest replied. He was an uncle of Shera's. "Mavissa was here with us, and she could not save them. Their wounds were too great."

"I want to see them."

The high priest studied her for a moment, then nodded to one of the guards. Shera followed him down a slippery slope into a narrow ravine. In the light of his torch, she saw two shadowy shapes on the ground, covered by oilskins. And as she approached, she could see dark stains on the skins.

The guard lifted the covers and Shera stuffed her fist into her mouth, to prevent a scream. She wasn't squeamish, having often dealt with bloody wounds. But those she tended had been strangers, and these were her parents. The bodies were barely recognizable. She turned away quickly, feeling bile rising into her throat. The guard covered the bodies again, then led her back to the priests.

"How could this have happened?" she demanded. "Why weren't they being guarded?"

"They *were* being guarded," the high priest said gently. "And we were only a few yards away ourselves. But no one heard anything until it was too late."

"Did you see the creatures?"

He nodded. "Two great golden cats." The tall, austere man actually shuddered. "I was the first to awaken, and they stared at me for several seconds before they vanished into the darkness."

"But why didn't they attack *you*?" Shera asked, guiltily wishing that the creatures had killed the officious priest instead of her parents. Oh, why hadn't she been a better daughter?

"Only the gods know," the high priest replied, but he lacked his usual self-righteousness.

Shera stared at him, thinking that for the first time she had heard a very human emotion in this cold, stern man: fear. That was very nearly as great a shock as learning of her parents' deaths.

But why had the creatures not attacked the priest? If her parents had been killed by men, she might have understood why they'd left the priest alone. Even savages might recognize a holy man. But creatures could not have known the distinction, could they?

Once again, there was a funeral—this time more elaborate, since the Bacleev were burying their leaders. As their only child, Shera would be required to play a role in the ceremony, so when she was once again summoned by the priests, she assumed it was to explain what she must do.

The storms had passed with the sunrise, and the priests had gathered alone, apart from the others, since before dawn. Shera knew they would be seeking the advice of the gods to choose the new shegwas. The announcement would undoubtedly be made after the funeral ceremony.

When she was ushered into their presence, Shera sensed a certain uneasiness within the group of twelve men and women. As the high priest explained her role in the ceremony, she wondered if he was still shocked at having been spared by the creatures. She could not imagine what else would give rise to such uncharacteristic behavior on his part.

Then, just when she expected to be dismissed, she was instead invited to join them around the golden bowl that held the sacred fire. Since she had never before participated in a funeral, she assumed that this must be some sort of private ceremony. But then there was a movement to her left, and someone else joined them.

Shera stared at the new arrival with disbelief and mounting horror. Before she could open her mouth, the high priest confirmed her worst fear.

"The gods have spoken," the high priest intoned. "You, Shera, and you, Daren, will become our new shegwas."

Shera froze. She wanted to run away, but she could not move. Neither could she bring herself to turn to Daren, though she felt his gaze upon her. Finally she found her voice.

"There must be a mistake! How could the gods have chosen *me,* when I pay so little attention to *them?*"

"Perhaps that is why you were chosen, Shera," the high priest said gently. "You cannot question their wisdom. See for yourself that they have chosen you."

He stepped back from the bowl, and a low chant rose from all the priests. Once again, Shera tried to force her legs to carry her away, but they still wouldn't obey. Then suddenly two tongues of green fire rose in the bowl and reached out toward her and Daren, enveloping them both.

What Shera felt in that moment was unlike anything she'd ever felt before. It was a heat that didn't burn. It was a power without limits. It was a warm promise. And then, as quickly as it had come, it was gone; the sacred bowl returned to its usual glow.

Daren reached out to take her hand, but Shera pulled away. "No!" she cried. "I refuse!"

There was a stunned silence, and then the high priest adopted a placating tone. "We understand that this is a difficult time for you, Shera. It would be appropriate for us to postpone the marriage ceremony until we have reached our home, which the gods tell us will be within a few days."

The paralysis that had gripped her faded away, and Shera turned quickly and walked off. She didn't even spare a glance for Daren.

Somehow she made it through the funeral ritual. She spoke the proper words and did the right things, honoring her parents in death as she hadn't always done in life. But throughout, a part of her was still lost in the touch of the sacred fire, its warmth and promise.

That feeling notwithstanding, however, Shera had decided that the gods were punishing her for her failure to honor them

35

properly. Not only were they thrusting upon her a role she didn't want, but they were giving her a mate who was the last person she would have chosen.

As the mountains rang with the chants of the Bacleev, Shera's gaze fell briefly on her betrothed, who stood in the first circle, facing her and the priests. She despised him—and she knew he knew that. He'd once paid court to her and she'd immediately rejected him. Even among a people not known for warmth and laughter, Daren was cold and humorless. His devotion to the gods was such that she'd often wondered why he hadn't been called to the priesthood.

Still, among their people, Daren was considered to be quite handsome—and he was greatly respected for his devotion to the gods. But Shera could not look at him without recalling the dark coldness she'd always felt during the ceremonies. It was in him, too.

The funeral ceremony ended, and Daren joined her and the priests as the announcement of their appointment was made. This time, when he took her hand, she could not break his firm grip. She stood, listening with some satisfaction to the murmurs of surprise that greeted the high priest's announcement.

When the Bacleev had sworn their allegiance to their new leaders and the crowd had begun to disperse, Shera tried to pull away.

"Let me go, Daren," she said in a hiss. "If you don't, I promise you I will create a scene."

He dropped her hand, but took her arm instead. "Come with me. We will find a place to talk."

She didn't want to talk to him, but he was already leading her through the crowd. People milled about to congratulate them and wish for them the wisdom of the gods. Hearing the ancient wish, Shera was tempted to respond that the gods weren't showing much wisdom at the moment.

As soon as they were alone, she faced him squarely. "I will not marry you, Daren! The gods have not chosen me. They wish only to punish me for my failure to show them proper respect."

"Then you will learn to show them respect, because you cannot deny that they have chosen you."

Her dark eyes blazed at him. "And do you think that you can force me to marry you, to spend my life mumbling prayers as you do?"

"How can you deny what the gods offer us? Can't you feel the power they would give us?"

"What power?" she scoffed, even as she shivered from the sensation she'd felt earlier. "We can't even protect ourselves from wild creatures or savages."

"But we will. They are but obstacles. When we reach our old home, we will know our true power."

"What true power?" she asked uneasily.

"Everyone feels it now, Shera. Our dreams are filled with a great roaring sound, a rushing of water. It is there we will find our true power."

"In a *waterfall?*" she scoffed. "And exactly what are these powers, Daren? Will we be able to kill without a trace?"

"You will see. And we *will* be married when we reach our destination."

Then, without waiting for a response, he turned on his heel and walked away.

Gar watched the lengthy proceedings from his treetop concealment. He'd learned of the earlier attack only just in time to reach the scene as the ceremony was beginning. The victims had apparently been their leaders, since the ritual was very elaborate.

Though he hadn't played any role in the killings, he was not displeased about it. In fact, he and his companions had been trying to catch the shegwas away from the priests and kill them with their new weapons. They'd always been surrounded by the black-robed priests, though, and Gar had not been willing to risk hitting one of the holy men. He was not above defying the dark gods in small ways, but that didn't include killing their priests.

His gaze homed in now on the accursed clerics—and the

woman with them. He squinted, trying to see her better. He was nearly certain that she was the same woman he'd seen before. Her presence among the priests was significant. Perhaps the dead shegwas were her parents.

Gar felt a moment's sympathy for her. If it *was* the same woman, she'd probably lost her mate and now her parents. But his sympathy was fleeting. She was Bacleev—and therefore his enemy.

They'd become quite adept at using their new weapons and would probably be able to kill a few dozen more of them before they reached the valley. But unless they managed to sieze their enemies' supply of black powder, their weapons would soon be useless. Worse, he feared that once the Bacleev regained their powers, his people would no longer want to make war on them—even if they were able to do so.

He left off his bleak thoughts abruptly as the chanting died away and a silence fell on the crowd. He was too far away to hear the words, but he could tell that the high priest was now addressing the crowd once again. The woman remained beside him, and now a man joined her.

Gar frowned as the two held hands and the crowd began to chant once again. Were these two the new leaders? If he was right about the identity of the woman, he could not believe that even the Bacleev were heathen enough to remarry so quickly.

He narrowed his eyes, studying the distant figure of the woman. He could sense defiance in her. The new male leader raised his arm to the crowd, but she remained frozen. Then, as the ceremony ended, she pulled her hand from his and seemed about to walk away, but the man seized her arm. He led her off, out of Gar's view.

Gar was curious. There'd been no marriage ceremony, as far as he could tell, and shegwas were always wed. Still, he was convinced that the two of them had been chosen. He pondered for a few moments, then climbed down from the tree and began to make his way through the woods with the agility of one born to the mountains.

* * *

Shera walked through the ravine, determined to stay as far away from Daren as possible. She continued walking when she reached the limits of the camp and the ravine had narrowed to little more than a crevasse. From time to time, she glanced up at the sheer rock walls that pressed close on both sides, but her thoughts for now were on her predicament, not on the danger of her surroundings.

Everyone knew what she herself knew; she'd seen it in their eyes even as they professed loyalty to her. She was not suited to lead. In fact, it was difficult for her to think of anyone *less* suited to such a task.

The gods *were* punishing her; she was sure of it. But how could they care so little for the Bacleev that they would force upon them an unworthy leader?

This situation reminded her of other times when she'd felt that the gods were capricious—even wicked. She'd never said such a thing, of course. There were limits even to *her* sharp tongue.

And as if choosing Shera to lead her people were not bad enough, they had chosen as her mate the least desirable man in the whole tribe, as far as she was concerned. If Marcus had been chosen, she might have set aside her doubts about him and accepted him as her mate—albeit reluctantly—but she would never accept Daren.

She shuddered, recalling that moment when the sacred fire had reached out to them. For all that she'd felt the heat and the power of the gods, she'd still been left with that same coldness and darkness.

Lost in thought, she continued to make her way over the rocky ground. Behind her, the multitude of voices faded away. Then the ravine ended abruptly with a further narrowing and then joining of the rock walls on either side. After pausing to scan her surroundings, she sank onto a broad, flat rock that jutted out over a tiny pool. A thin trickle of water seeped from the rocks and gathered there, then spilled out into a small stream. It was a lovely spot, fragrant with the scent of pine and rich, damp earth—but in her misery, Shera barely noticed.

Did she have the courage to rebel against the gods? What would the priests do if she did? Such a thing had never happened before—or at least not as far as she knew.

She drew up her knees, wrapped her arms around them, and stared down into the clear pool. For one brief moment, it seemed that she heard the strange roaring sound that Daren said others now heard. But within it there were voices, calling to her.

Gar saw her through the trees as he made his way silently down the hillside. She was completely alone, which surprised him, given the havoc he and his people—and the chezahs—had been wreaking upon the Bacleev.

The closer he came to her, the more certain he became that it was indeed the woman he'd seen before: the one who'd sensed his presence. He stopped for a moment, studying her. If she were the new shegwa and he killed her so soon, it would surely strike terror in the black hearts of his enemies. They might even panic and turn around, leaving his mountains forever.

Strangely indecisive, he began to edge closer, staying behind her as she continued to stare into the pool. She seemed vulnerable, hurt. There was none of the defiance he'd seen earlier when he'd watched her during the night's ceremony. He grimaced at the thought of her vulnerability; he needed to retain his blind hatred if he was to be effective against them.

He was some thirty feet above her, and he moved laterally along the rock wall until he reached a ledge just beyond her peripheral vision. There he paused, still uncertain.

Shera felt something—something that caused her to turn to her left even before the thought had quite registered. And as she did, she knew—even before she saw him—that her vision had come true.

The golden-haired savage stood there, staring impassively down at her from a ledge. She could see him more clearly now than she had in her visions. Every detail was burned indelibly into her brain: his thick, tawny hair, his rugged face with its cleft chin, his tall, powerful body.

She knew she could not hope to escape. Before she could scramble over the rocks and get within shouting distance of the others, he could easily reach her. She was trapped and she knew it. For one brief moment, she took some heart from the fact that he carried no weapon, but then she remembered that it was this man—or one like him—who had killed Marcus swiftly and silently.

She got to her feet warily, her hand sliding into the pocket of her loose trousers to touch the small, bone-handled knife she kept with her at all times to cut clothing away from the site of a wound.

But the cold hardness of the knife failed to reassure her. It would be nearly useless against such a man.

He still didn't move, though his powerful body seemed poised to leap upon her at any moment. And then, suddenly, he addressed her in her own language.

"Are you the new shegwa?"

Shera was too stunned to answer immediately. How could this savage be speaking her language? She let his deep voice echo in her brain for a few seconds before she finally nodded.

"My name is Shera," she told him, trying to keep fear out of her voice.

He stared at her for a moment, cocking his head to one side. "Is it that you don't want to be shegwa—or is it that you do not wish to have that man as your mate?"

She drew in a sharp, audible breath. How could he know to ask such questions—unless it was true that he possessed some magic powers? Should she answer him? If she didn't, he might attack and kill her.

"It is both," she said honestly.

"The man I killed—was he your mate?"

"M-Marcus?" she asked, stammering, unable to believe that he was casually admitting to having murdered him. "No. He was a friend."

And even as she said it, anger was welling up in her. Without giving any thought to the wisdom of her words or actions, she reached into her pocket and withdrew the knife.

"You murdered him!"

His expression didn't change, and he didn't move. "I killed him. There's a difference."

"Who are you?" she demanded.

"My name is Gar. I am chief."

"Chief of what?"

He frowned. "Of the Walkens. Do you not know your history, Shera?"

His tone was mocking, but she ignored it as she weighed the danger of once again speaking the truth. Then she shook her head.

"I know nothing of you—or of the Walkens."

He stared hard at her for a long moment, then began to climb down from the ledge toward her, casting one quick glance back toward the camp. He moved easily, with a singular feline grace. He paid no attention at all to the knife she continued to brandish.

She stood her ground as he stopped less than ten feet away. She was even more trapped than before. Only a few feet behind her was the edge of the rock, with the small pool some twenty feet below.

His silence was unnerving, and he continued to study her. She could see now that his eyes were amber and deep-set beneath straight brows. Frightened as she was, Shera still felt a fascination with this savage. He was compelling in a way she couldn't begin to explain.

"How can you not know your people's history?" he demanded, clearly believing that she'd lied.

"I don't. None of us does." Except, possibly, for the priests, she amended silently. She still wasn't certain about them.

"Then why are you here?" he challenged.

"Because the gods told us to come here."

He said nothing. She wondered if the silences were deliberate—intended to unnerve her—or if this was just his way. Her arm had grown tired from the effort required to hold the knife out before her, and she let it fall to her side. His gaze flicked briefly to it, and then back again to her face.

"Turn around. Go back to wherever you came from. If you don't, more will die."

"But why? We mean you no harm. We wish only to live in peace, as we have been doing."

His wide mouth curved into a sneer. "No harm?" he echoed derisively. "Perhaps you don't know your people's history, Shera—but I think you will soon learn it."

"We do only what the gods tell us to do," she replied. "We are a peaceful people."

"Your first words belie your last," he stated coldly. With that, he turned abruptly. Within seconds, it seemed, he had vanished into the forest.

Shera still didn't move, though she knew she should run back to the camp before he changed his mind and returned to kill her. All her instincts told her that her life had been hanging by a thread while she talked with him and that, for some reason, he might even now be regretting that he'd decided not to kill her.

And it was the second time he'd made that fateful decision, she realized. He'd spared her when he'd killed Marcus, although he'd believed her to be Marcus's wife.

What had he meant by his final words? If she understood the cryptic statement, he was saying that her people couldn't possibly be peaceful because they did what the gods told them to do.

Shera drew in a shaky breath, her thoughts returning to the dark coldness she felt after any encounter with the gods. Could he be a mind reader; was he playing on her doubts about the wisdom of the gods?

She shuddered. There had always been those among the Trellans who'd believed her people to be capable of such magic. They'd sometimes thought that of healers like herself, because healers could sense the source of an illness even if the victim hadn't explained it. But she'd thought, as did all her people, that only the gods could see into the minds and hearts of people.

She turned and fled back to the camp, slowing down only when she could see people gathering kindling for the camp-fires. He hadn't read her mind—he couldn't have—but he *did* seem to know far more about her people than she did. Or had he been playing mind games with her to try to persuade her to leave?

This man Gar was clearly a savage, but she could not afford to underestimate his cunning. And neither could she forget the strange effect he had upon her.

Chapter Three

Shera lay down on the thick quilt and pulled a blanket over her. The camp was silent now, except for the crackling and snapping of the nearby fire. Exhausted by their long journey, most people slept. But Shera remained fully awake.

After her encounter with Gar, she'd returned to the camp and issued orders she hoped would protect them better. She'd requested more guards and suggested that they each be equipped with torches, as well as rifles. A small group of armed men remained near the center of the encampment, where they could watch the perimeters and be ready to move if a torch was dropped or extinguished. She'd also issued orders for everyone to stay close, forsaking privacy for the added protection.

Even though she hadn't yet fully accepted her new position as shegwa, the orders had flowed easily from her. Furthermore, it hadn't occurred to her to consult Daren before issuing the instructions. When she returned after her encounter with the savage, she'd seen Daren at the edge of the encampment with the priests.

She'd started in that direction, to tell them what had happened—but then, for reasons she still didn't understand, she'd stopped and turned her attention instead to the safety of the camp.

Later, after he'd discovered what she'd done, Daren had reminded her coldly that such decisions should be discussed before orders were issued. When she'd asked what he might have done differently, he'd had nothing at all to say.

Shera shuddered, thinking about the coldness in her soon-to-be husband. Warmth was not a trait associated with any Bacleev—but she could think of none colder than Daren, except possibly for one of the priests.

Her meeting with the savage had temporarily driven away her unhappiness over her situation and her guilty grief at the loss of her parents. But now, as she tried to find sleep, it all came back, overwhelming her.

She could not marry Daren. If it were possible for them to be the leaders of their people without also being husband and wife, she could accept that, even though she didn't want it. But she knew that neither the priests nor the people—nor even Daren himself, in all likelihood—would ever accept such a departure from their traditions.

Bleak as her situation was, however, her thoughts could not stay on Daren for very long. Soon, as she drifted closer to sleep, she was once again focusing on the man called Gar. Why hadn't he killed her? She couldn't believe that the knife had frightened him—but how was she to understand the mind of a savage? Perhaps the knife *had* scared him. He'd carried no weapon himself that she could see. But he hadn't needed a weapon to kill Marcus, who was far more able to defend himself than she was.

She slid down into sleep, where she was met by Daren and Gar and a huge cat, all of them circling her warily. She kept turning, spinning about to keep them all in sight, sensing that each of them represented a terrible danger. Daren, then Gar, and then the cat. They passed before her closed eyes, moving faster and faster. And she was so cold—so very cold.

* * *

She awoke abruptly, and for a moment the spinning seemed to continue, though the three images had faded. Her heart was thudding noisily in her chest as she sat up and looked around at the quiet, peaceful camp. The small group of armed men at the center of the camp were the only ones awake, and as she caught sight of them, she also saw one of them raise a torch and wave it back and forth for a few seconds. When she turned and looked behind her, she saw a guard at the edge of the camp respond in a similar fashion. They had obviously devised a system to signal that all was well.

Knowing that she wouldn't be able to sleep now, Shera got up and began picking her way carefully past the sleeping bodies to the guards at the center. Then, when they had assured her that all was indeed peaceful this night, she made her way through the large camp, still thinking about her dream and especially about the savage chief.

She thought about his sneering remark that she would soon learn the history of her people, then about the priests' statement that their journey was nearing an end. Abruptly, she recalled the roaring waterfall—if indeed that was what it was—and she belatedly realized that the sound had filled her dream.

She knew that she had to tell the priests and Daren about her encounter with Gar, and she turned in that direction. Earlier, when she'd visited the guards at the center of the encampment, she'd heard the low sounds of chanting coming from the area where the priests and Daren had set up camp. They had invited her to join them, but she'd chosen to stay with her mother's family.

The chants, though low, grew more distinct as she made her way across the camp. Then she could see a very faint glow from the sacred bowl, though not the bowl itself, because the priests and Daren had chosen a spot just on the other side of a small hump of land that now blocked her view of them. It wasn't the safest place for them to be, but the priests always preferred to be by themselves. After escaping harm when her parents had been killed, they now apparently believed they had nothing to

47

fear. In any event, the armed guards were circling the camp beyond them.

There was a dark spot of perhaps a hundred yards or so between the campfire closest to the gathering of priests and Daren and their own campfire. Shera stopped there, thinking that perhaps she should make herself a torch. But when she found nothing from which to make one, she moved on. It was only a short distance, even though it was very dark, and at no time would she be out of sight of the guards.

She was halfway across the dark space and wondering how she was going to explain her failure to tell them about her encounter earlier, when she suddenly sensed something. She had no more than a fraction of a second to register fear before a large, hard hand was clamped over her mouth. In the next instant, she felt fingers press against the base of her skull. After that, she felt nothing at all.

Shera awoke groggily. Her head hurt and her limbs tingled in a strange way, as though a million pins were pricking her. She was surrounded by darkness. She struggled into a sitting position, ignoring the pain in her head, and couldn't see a single campfire or torch. As she drew in a shaky breath, she smelled the damp, aromatic odor of a pine forest, even though they were camped on open ground.

Her thoughts spun muzzily. Hadn't she gotten up at some point to go tell the priests and Daren about her meeting with Gar? Or had she dreamed all that?

Then, abruptly, she recalled the hand over her mouth and the pressure on the base of her skull, and she cried out involuntarily.

"I've done you no harm—yet," said a low voice from somewhere nearby.

"Gar!" She gasped, staring into the darkness from where his voice had come. She could now make him out, but just barely, although he was only a short distance away. She struggled to her feet.

"Don't wander off," he warned. "You'll only get lost and we'll be wasting time."

She hated his tone, the certainty of his control of the situation. "Where are we?" she demanded.

"What difference does it make? You don't know the area."

Then she could see movement as he got to his feet. She refused to back away as he came toward her. What choice did she have? He was right; she'd be lost within seconds if she ran.

"I just stopped to rest for a time," he said, pausing a few feet from her. "You're a heavier burden than I'd expected, but at least now you can walk."

"Walk where? What do you think you're doing, Gar? Where are my people?"

"Your people are where they were before—sleeping the night away. In the morning, a few more guards will be dead and their weapons will be gone."

"They'll be caught this time," she countered.

"You mean because of the torches? Was that your idea? It's helpful—but not helpful enough, though it may keep the chezahs away."

"Chezahs?" she echoed.

"The cats. The fire will probably keep them away—but maybe not. Let's go. We have a long journey and I want to be home before dawn."

"Where are we going?"

"I already told you," he said impatiently. "To my home."

"Take me back to my people, Gar!"

"No. Instead of trying to provoke me, you should be glad that I haven't killed you. Must I remind you that I could have done that three times now?"

"Then why haven't you?"

He was close enough for her to see him fairly well now in the pale light of the stars and a waxing moon. After one of his characteristic silences, he shrugged.

"I don't know—and if I were you, I wouldn't ask that question again—or you may force me to rethink it."

Was that a trace of humor she heard in his voice, and perhaps a slight smile on his lips? Before she could give that unlikely possibility much thought, he reached out and seized her hand, then began to drag her along with him. She struggled to free herself from his grip, but he merely tightened it until her fragile bones threatened to break. She stopped resisting and he immediately loosened his grip, though he didn't let her go as he set off through the woods.

"I can't see!" she protested.

"I can. There's a path. Just stay with me and you'll be fine."

She did as ordered because she had no choice, but she wondered how he could see where he was going. There'd been at least a little light in the clearing, but now that they were under the trees, the night was as black as any she'd ever seen. And yet he kept moving at a rapid, sure pace.

Did he have magical powers? The question hammered at her. She didn't want to believe in such a possibility, but she couldn't quite discount it, either. The thought that he might possess unknown powers terrified her—and then made her understand how the Trellans must have felt about her people.

But there's a difference, she reminded herself. *Our powers are good. They save lives and help crops grow.*

Her headache began to fade and the prickling sensation was now gone from her limbs. She thought about how he'd captured her, and broke the long silence between them.

"What did you do to me?" she asked.

"I just put you to sleep for a while, that's all."

"How?" she asked, then held her breath, waiting to see if he would admit to having magic.

Even in the darkness, she could feel him turning to her briefly.

"Would you like me to show you?" he asked.

"No, I just want to know what you did."

He dropped her hand and raised his to the back of her neck, touching her lightly at the base of her skull before she jerked her head away. Her flesh there was slightly bruised.

"I touched you there. Pressure in that spot puts you to sleep—or kills you."

He couldn't possibly have seen her expression, but he must have guessed at it because he chuckled. In spite of everything else she was feeling at the moment, she didn't fail to notice what a pleasant sound it was.

"The trick is in knowing exactly how much pressure to apply."

"Is that how you killed Marcus?" she asked, the question out before she could consider the wisdom of it.

"Yes."

She waited, hoping he might say he was sorry for her friend's death, or at least make some excuse for why he'd done it—but he said nothing. Only a savage could kill without regret and without excuse, she reminded herself.

And she knew that she *needed* that reminder, because Gar continued to fascinate her. He was so different, both in his appearance and in his demeanor, from any man she'd ever known.

Shera had no idea how long or how far they walked. At first, the journey had been on relatively level ground, but now they seemed to be going steadily uphill, though the path had dipped a few times. And slowly, the sky was beginning to lighten above the thick canopy of trees.

She was by now too exhausted to speak, and Gar seemed disinclined to do so. It took every bit of her energy to keep up with him as the way became ever steeper; it was a steady uphill climb now, without the welcome respite of level places.

But tired as she was, her confidence was returning with the light, and she began to consider the possibility of escape. But what good would it do, when she had no idea where she was? Furthermore, if daylight gave her the chance to flee, it would make it easier for him to find her as well.

At one point, as she was struggling up a particularly steep portion of the path she could now see, she cast a glance over her shoulder—and screamed!

Two of the great cats were walking only a few yards behind her! They stopped when she screamed, remaining where they were as she began to back up the steep path until she collided with a solid wall of flesh.

Saranne Dawson

Gar's long arm slid around her waist to steady her. "They won't harm you. They've been following us for some time."

"Why?" she asked as his arm dropped away, again leaving her feeling very vulnerable.

"They often follow us in the woods," he said with a shrug.

"Don't they ever attack you or your people?" she asked curiously.

"No," he replied, and turned to begin climbing again.

She cast the chezahs one last look, then hurried to stay close to him. "They've killed *my* people," she told him, then added, "But they didn't eat them."

"Chezahs don't eat human flesh," he replied.

"Then why do they kill? Animals kill only to eat."

"You'd have to ask them," he responded with that wry humor she'd heard before from him.

Although she had no intention of posing the question to the creatures, Shera turned, only to find that they were gone. She told Gar, who didn't even bother to look. They might have been harmless squirrels or rabbits for all the concern he showed.

The footing became more difficult—for her, at least. Gar continued to climb easily. The track they were following had many small pebbles underfoot now, and suddenly she slipped and then began to slide down at an angle. She lunged for a small tree and missed, and the movement sent her sliding inexorably toward a ledge, where she could tell the drop must be hundreds of feet!

A scream had barely passed her lips before Gar was there, grasping first her upper arm and then her waist as he hauled her back to safety—away from the ledge and against his hard male body.

She clutched his arms, shaking at her close brush with certain death. Then she looked up, her lips already parted to thank him. No words came out. His amber gaze dropped slowly from her eyes to her mouth, and his grip on her tightened—just before his mouth was on hers.

Power surged through him and into her, roaring through her veins, setting fire to her loins, awakening something she'd never known existed. His kiss was not gentle. It was harsh,

52

demanding, all-consuming. And without realizing what she was doing, Shera responded in kind, arching against him and threading her fingers through his thick, tawny hair as their tongues curved sensuously in an erotic dance.

A wildness came over her. She forgot who she was, who he was. It didn't matter. She wanted only for it to go on and never stop.

But it did stop. He withdrew, then stared down at her for a long moment and finally stepped away, leaving her swaying on her feet, in danger of sliding down the mountainside once again. But he reached out and seized her hand and began to haul her up the mountain with him.

Shera was too stunned to be angry. Her lips still tingled warmly from his kisses. Her body still bore his powerful imprint. And a hunger for what hadn't happened still burned within her.

She was no innocent. The Bacleev, unlike their former hosts, the Trellans, believed that sexuality was a normal part of life, like sleeping, eating, and breathing. Very few ever went to their marriage beds without experience.

Yes, Shera had known lovers, but only a few—and those had been years ago when she'd been caught up in adolescent crushes. As she'd grown older and grown into her talents as a healer, she'd become a very private person, not given to sharing any part of herself with others.

With one kiss, this savage had broken through those formidable walls of reserve. Shera had fended off many carefully planned seductions, but she understood now—too late—that seduction was not Gar's way. And she knew that this made him even more dangerous than she'd previously supposed.

Still confused by what had happened, Shera reached the mountaintop only to face yet another shock. In fact, what she'd believed to be the top as she'd labored up the path turned out to be only a broad ledge, a sort of giant step below yet another sheer rock face composed of many more ledges. And on those ledges sat a series of dwellings almost indistinguishable from the surrounding mountain.

"This is your home?" she asked in amazement. She'd never seen anything even remotely like this: an entire village of homes set one on top of the other, connected by wooden steps like ladders, which were anchored between the levels. The houses themselves were made of cut stone the same color as the mountain, with wooden shutters in the windows.

Behind them and off to the left the sun had risen, and it bathed the entire mountaintop in a ruddy glow. But nowhere did she see any people.

"Yes," he said, staring up at the village. "My people have always lived here."

He led her up the series of ladders, which proved to be much thicker and sturdier than she'd at first thought. They climbed from one level to another, going higher and higher, until she thought she could go no farther. And to make matters even worse, the wide steps of the ladders were obviously intended for people with much longer legs than she had.

Finally, just when she was about to protest that she could not climb another ladder, she realized they had reached the top, where a single house sat alone. She'd seen it from below and now, remembering that he was the leader of his people, she realized he would merit the highest home's extra degree of privacy.

She turned to ask him if this was, in fact, his domicile, but before she could speak, he gestured off to the right.

"There is your valley."

She turned in the direction he indicated. The mountain dropped away sharply—and beyond it lay a long, narrow valley of incredible lushness. She moved closer to the edge, her tiredness temporarily forgotten as she stared down at her people's home. And then she became aware of a sound that had undoubtedly been there all along, but had been masked by the wind and perhaps ignored because of her tiredness and her surprise at this strange place.

The roar was low and distant, but it was unmistakably the same sound she'd heard in her vision. She moved as close to the edge as she dared, ignoring the dizziness that hovered at the edge of her consciousness. The sound seemed to be coming from a spot off to her left, somewhere beyond a curve in the mountain that hid a portion of the valley from her view.

But as she studied the valley, the sunlight pierced its depths and she saw it reflect off a stream that flowed out from the unseen portion. And now she could see something else: small stone cottages, clustered together at the base of one mountain, barely visible through the thick forests.

"Is that where we lived?" she asked, having heard him come up behind her.

"Yes." His tone was noncommittal.

"What is that sound? It seems to be coming from over here." She pointed to the curve in the mountain.

There was silence for a moment, and then he confirmed her belief. "It's a waterfall."

"It must be very large."

"It is."

She turned to him. "Why did my people leave this place, Gar?"

The question came out naturally, because she couldn't imagine why her ancestors could have given up such a beautiful home. But when she saw the look in his eyes, she immediately regretted her words.

He said nothing as he stared first at her and then at the valley. They were very close to the edge. If he were to push her over, she would not be able to save herself.

Through her mind ran a warning she'd ignored: *This man is a savage, and just because he kissed you doesn't mean he won't also kill you.* She sidestepped a few paces, fearing that he would grab her at any moment and fling her to her death. But he continued to stare at the valley, paying no attention to her movement.

After she had retreated to a place of relative safety, he gestured to the house. "This is my home. You will stay here."

He offered her some food, but she shook her head. She was

too tired to eat. So he led her deeper into the house, carrying with him a thick candle to light the way.

"You can sleep here," he said, indicating a tiny room half-filled with a thick straw mattress covered by colorfully woven blankets. She needed no further urging. Seconds after her head hit the soft pillow, she was fast asleep.

Gar carried his breakfast outside, where he ate staring down at the valley. He'd made a mistake by bringing her here. Instead, he should have captured the high priest. It was now apparent to him that she really did know nothing of her people's history.

He supposed that he would let her go when her people reached the valley. But he didn't want to do that. The memory of her soft lips and her warm curves pressed against him lingered, taunting him. He wondered if such a thing had ever happened before. If so, it had been kept secret.

The distant roar of the waterfall intruded into his consciousness. The sound was always there, of course, but only with the return of the Bacleev had he truly become aware of it. He hadn't gone down there in years, though, as a child, he'd made the trip many times with his companions. They'd all stood there, feeling its power and thinking about the stories they'd all been told.

Now it would happen all over again. Only a foolish, irrational part of him believed that it could be different. He closed his eyes, thinking about the boy who'd stood staring at the waterfall and wishing, as all boys did, that the Bacleev would return and offer their gift to the Walkens.

But those were the dreams of a boy. The grown man feared what was to come.

Shera awoke to confusion. At first she thought she was back in her old home. But that comforting thought lasted no more than a few seconds. Then it all came back to her in the form of the image of her captor, followed all too quickly by the memory of his kiss. Before she could stop herself, she had touched her fingers to her lips, reliving that moment and wondering once again how one kiss could have invaded her very soul.

She raised herself up in the bed and peered around. The windowless room was dark, but a tentative light spilled in from the open doorway to the hall. She listened carefully, but heard nothing other than the distant, barely audible sound of the waterfall. So she threw back the covers and got off of the comfortable mattress with some regret. It had been a long time since she'd slept in a real bed.

Thoughts of her long journey prompted her to thoughts of her people. What would they be thinking? A brief smile curved her mouth as she decided that some of them, at least, might think that she had chosen to disappear. It was possible that Daren and the priests might even be relieved.

She smiled again. Perhaps Gar had unwittingly done her a favor. The priests might well beseech the gods to choose someone else to rule beside Daren—and perhaps they would do just that.

The heavy wooden outside door stood open, and Shera paused in the archway, half expecting to find Gar just outside. But there was no one in sight, though she could hear voices drifting up from the terraces below. She also noted from the angle of the sunlight that it must be late in the day. That didn't surprise her, since they'd arrived at dawn.

She was very hungry, so she turned away from the door and found the bread and fruit he'd offered her earlier waiting for her on a small table near the hearth. A kettle suspended over the dying fire was still warm, and she found the makings for tea, an herbal concoction much like one she often made for herself.

She cut a slice of the thick, crusty bread, and as she devoured it hungrily, she looked around the cottage with interest. The interior was dim and cool, though it was quite warm outside. But the darkness of the large main room was brightened by boldly patterned rugs and the gleam of copper pots hanging near the hearth. The furniture was large and sturdy, made of wood and intricately tooled leather.

Putting the fruit into her pocket, Shera picked up the tea and carried it outside. She walked over to the end of the walkway and stared down once more at the valley. Most of it lay deep in shadow now, an undulating green carpet of forests and mead-ows, with the stream curving through it all.

At this time of day, the wind had died down, and she could hear far more clearly the distant thundering of the waterfall. She listened to it, imagining what it must be like, feeling the sound seep into her body.

When she raised the mug to her lips again, the tea was cold. She frowned. Had she drifted off into some sort of trance? She wasn't aware of the passage of more than a few moments, and yet she knew she must have stood there much longer. All of the valley now lay in shadow, and the wind was picking up again.

Vaguely uneasy, she moved away from the view of the valley and instead went over to peer down at the terraces below. They jutted out unevenly, so that she could see only some of them, but on one several levels down she saw children playing a game with a brightly colored ball. They all had the same burnished gold hair that Gar had.

Then she gasped as a huge cat—chezah, she corrected her-self—got up from a spot not far from the children, stretched its powerful body, and started toward them. Shera was horrified, but before she could scream a warning, the children saw the creature and one of them pounced on it.

The chezah was nearly as tall as the child, but as she watched in horrified fascination, it allowed itself to be dragged into a wrestling match by the child, whose companions soon joined in. The game went on for some time, until the chezah finally cast them all off and walked away. It made its way gracefully down the ladder to the next level and disappeared. A short time later, Shera heard a woman's voice call out, and the children vanished as well.

Shera was nonplussed. Were some of the chezahs kept as pets? How could these people trust their children with such a creature? Images of her parents' ravaged bodies came to her mind, and she shuddered. Could the chezahs that had attacked them and others have been acting under the orders of the Walkens? Could the one she'd just seen also kill on the orders of its master?

Far below, at the bottom of the vertical village, she saw four men emerge from the woods carrying large sacks that undoubtedly held game, together with rifles they had obviously taken from her dead soldiers.

The men were all tall and muscular and blond, dressed much as Gar had been. From this distance, she couldn't tell if he were among them. As they crossed the open space below the first level of cottages, five chezahs appeared, coming from the village. The men passed within a few yards of them, with no interest shown by either group. The chezahs vanished into the forest, and the men passed from her view as they climbed the ladder to the first level of the village.

Shera retreated back into the cottage and made herself another cup of tea. As she sipped it, she thought about her predicament. Escape was clearly impossible in daylight and far too dangerous at night. The only way down from her lofty prison would take her past all the other cottages, where she would surely be seen and stopped. Besides, there were the chezahs to consider. They hadn't harmed her when she was with Gar, but who knew what might happen if she were alone?

And then there was the question of where she would go if she did mange to escape. Finding the path wouldn't be difficult, even at night. She had seen the men arrive on it. But she couldn't be sure it would lead her back to her people. There was a large gap in her memory of the journey because of the time she'd been unconscious.

She reached up and touched the spot at the base of her skull. It was still slightly tender. Maybe he hadn't used magic, after all, but that didn't lessen her fear of someone who could disable—or kill—so quickly and easily.

She sighed, knowing that escape would be very risky even if she managed it. She might well end up lost in the forest—and at the mercy of the chezahs. It would be much better, she thought, to persuade him to let her go. But why had he captured her in the first place?

She went outside again and began to pace along the walkway, staring down at the other terraces and wondering if there could be a path somewhere that led directly down into the valley. It seemed likely, since there was obviously some connection between the Walkens and her people. If she could find it, she would simply go down to the valley and await their arrival.

She peered down at the valley again, narrowing her eyes to try to see the cottages. That would be a good place to wait, since they would immediately be seeking shelter.

Then she thought about what lay ahead. The priests had said she would marry Daren when they reached the valley. A terrible desolation came over her. If she stayed here, she risked being killed by a savage who could not be trusted—and if she returned to her people, she faced a marriage she did not want.

She was still gazing at the valley when she suddenly sensed his presence. She spun around quickly to find Gar stopped near the ladder, staring at her. He held two sacks in his hands, and Shera realized that he must have been one of the men in the hunting party.

"Dinner," he said, setting down the sacks. "I know you don't eat meat, so I did the best I could. Did you sleep well?"

She nodded, startled by his display of politeness and concern, as though she were an invited guest, rather than a prisoner. For all that he looked like a savage, it seemed that he could be very civilized—when he chose to be. She reminded herself that this man had killed Marcus—and had undoubtedly played a role in other deaths as well.

"Why did you bring me here, Gar?" she asked.

"To learn of your people's intentions." He shrugged. "It was a mistake. You know nothing."

"Then what do you intend to do with me?"

"I don't know." His gaze slid away from her as he reached down and opened the sack, extracting a piece of fruit.

Fear slithered along her spine. Could he really kill her? He'd killed others, but . . .

"Let me go," she spat.

He had been about to bite into the fruit, but he stopped, and his eyes grew hard and cold. She might as well have been staring into the eyes of a chezah.

"Don't start issuing orders, Shera!" he said in a low, threatening tone that sent chills along her spine.

Shera stared at him in shock. She had the strong sense that something beyond her demand had triggered that reaction. She backed off a few steps and raised her hands in a placating gesture.

"I'm not your enemy, Gar—and neither are my people. All we seek is a place to live in peace."

He flicked a glance toward the valley, then returned his gaze to her. The coldness was still in his eyes. "That may be true now—but it will change when you reach the valley."

"Why?" she asked, turning to glance briefly at the valley.

"Because then you will learn who you really are."

"What do you mean?" Once again she was aware of the distant roar of the waterfall.

He said nothing for a moment. Then he began to walk toward her. She stepped aside and he continued on until he was standing at the very edge of the walkway, just above the place where the mountain dropped away to the valley. He spoke without turning.

"The Bacleev are evil!" he said in a low, cold voice that just barely carried over the sounds of the wind and the waterfall. "For centuries they held everyone around them in thrall!"

"That's ridiculous!" she cried. "My people aren't like that! We lived for a century among the Trellans, and there was never any problem."

"We drove you away from your 'gods,' " he said, his tone betraying his contempt. "And without them you had no powers."

"That's not true! We *do* have powers. We can heal and we can bring the rain for the crops."

"Your accursed gods didn't give you those powers," he said dismissively. "The Bacleev have always been able to do those things."

"Gar, I am the leader of my people now. Whatever we may have done in the past, it won't happen again." She didn't believe his story, but she was desperate to prove to him that her people meant his no harm.

"To do that, you will have to kill your priests—and even that might not make any difference once you reach the valley."

"I couldn't kill the priests," she said, appalled.

He gestured to the two sacks. "Eat your dinner. I will see you tomorrow."

He walked hurriedly away and soon disappeared down the ladder. Shera picked up the sacks and carried them inside, but food was the last thing on her mind at the moment.

Everything about this encounter had left her badly shaken: Gar's solicitousness, followed so quickly by his coldness; the story he'd told; even his parting words had sounded like a threat. Did he intend to kill her tomorrow?

The fire was nearly out and the cottage had grown cold. She built up the fire, using the logs he'd left near the hearth, and then she sank into a comfortable chair and stared at the flames, going over and over everything that had been said.

What had he meant when he'd said that her people had held everyone around them in thrall? Since leaving the duke's lands, they'd encountered no one except for the Walkens. Were there other people around, in the lands farther to the west—or the north or south? Or had he meant only his own people?

And why was he so certain that her people would change when they reached the valley? What was there that could change them?

Suddenly she became aware once more of the low, distant rumble of the waterfall, barely audible now over the rising wind outside and the crackling of the fire inside. The waterfall! Yes, she thought; that must be it. People had been dreaming about it, hearing it as she had, sensing its power.

The Bacleev are evil! Gar's words came back to her as clearly as if he were standing there now. And with those words came the memory of that impossibly cold, dark feeling she'd had at her people's ceremonies.

What if he'd spoken the truth? an unwelcome voice inside her whispered. Could the priests be leading her people back to an evil past—back to a source of dark power?

It can't be true! she told herself. *Perhaps he really does believe it, but that doesn't make it so.*

The Sorceress & the Savage

She went back outside. The valley lay in total darkness now, though there was still some light up here on the mountain. The waterfall roared. A sudden vision came to her. She saw a huge wall of water cascading down from unimaginable heights, shaking the very ground beneath her feet and driving from her mind everything but its presence.

Then, in that roar, she could hear voices chanting seductively, drawing her toward them, making her long to hear what they were saying. Without conscious intent, she moved closer to the sound until she stood at the very edge of the walkway, just above the chasm.

And then the image began to fade, and when she saw just how close she had come to falling to her death, Shera backed away and fled into the cottage.

Gar, too, was listening to the waterfall. The sound enveloped him as he perched on a high, thick branch of a tall fir. From his vantage point, he could see the shadowy peak where it started, though he could not see its base. The last light from the heavens reflected off the water as it began its headlong plunge into the valley.

He wanted to think that she had the strength to resist—that even if the rest of her tribe reverted to their old ways, she would remain as she was. Perhaps that might have been possible if she hadn't become a shegwa.

He knew that she hadn't yet married the man who'd been chosen, and he wished he'd asked her about that. Had she resisted—or had the priests simply decided to wait until they reached the valley?

His need to possess her was strong, and grew stronger with every moment he spent in her company. That was why he'd left her. How could he want such a woman? There were certainly women within his tribe who pleased him, and he should have chosen one of them as his mate long before this. Unlike the accursed Bacleev, leadership of his people was solely hereditary, and he knew he should be producing an heir.

63

Saranne Dawson

He thought about Ruwen, his dead wife. They'd married at twenty—and she'd been dead before her twenty-first birthday, along with his newborn son. He'd loved her, but he'd never wanted her as badly as he wanted Shera now.

He continued to sit there in the tree as the last light leaked from the sky and the stars came out. And he was still sitting there when the moon rose. The war within him raged. In his mind's eye, he saw Shera in his bed, her black hair spilling over his pillow. With a cry of anguish, he stood and stared off into the night.

Chapter Four

The dream was familiar. Shera stood in a twilit place filled with the sound of a waterfall. First Gar appeared, then the chezah—a much larger one than those she'd seen before. And then Daren was there. She stood in the center of the triangle they made, wary and frightened and confused. And then she began to spin helplessly, their images moving in and out of focus as the din of the waterfall grew ever louder.

She awoke to total darkness and a pounding heart. The waterfall's roar had receded to a faint, distant drone. And then, suddenly, she knew she was not alone.

"Gar?" she asked, her voice husky as she sat up and peered into the darkness.

For one brief moment, she recalled his kiss, the feel of his body against hers. But then fear sliced through her, driving out the desire. Had he come to kill her, perhaps finding the act easier to perform in darkness?

Her knife was in the pocket of her trousers, out of her reach now. When he'd said that he wouldn't return until the next day, she'd taken off her filthy clothing, washed up as best she could, and then had put on one of his soft, worn shirts.

"Gar?" she repeated, her voice stronger now.

"I'm here," came the reluctant response.

"I wasn't expecting you. I . . . borrowed a shirt." She spoke rapidly, fearing that her only hope of avoiding death lay in reminding him that she wasn't just an unknown enemy, but someone he knew—someone he'd kissed. His reluctant tone seemed to indicate that she might have a chance.

"If you want your bed, I'll sleep by the fire," she said, staring into the darkness in the direction of his voice.

"No."

She heard sounds: cloth against cloth, the creak of leather. "Gar, talk to me—please!" She added that last as she recalled how he'd suddenly turned cold when she'd ordered him to let her go.

"What would you have me say, Shera?" His voice was closer now, and she could feel his presence, as though his body were sending off waves of heat.

She took a deep breath. "I'd like you to say that you aren't going to kill me."

She still couldn't see him, but she had the sense that her words had frozen him. A faint hope seeped into her.

"Is that what you thought?" he asked, clearly surprised. "If I'd wanted to kill you, I could have done that many times."

Now, with her eyes accustomed to the darkness, she could see him—or at least his outline—as he stood beside the bed. And suddenly she knew that he hadn't come here to hurt her.

"I want you."

The words echoed through her brain endlessly, turning fear into desire with breathtaking speed. It coursed through her, throbbing with its intensity. She didn't even try to speak. He knelt beside the bed.

"Do you want me, Shera?"

The question was soft, taunting—as though he already knew the answer, but had to hear it from her. She wasn't surprised that he knew. Every fiber of her being cried out for his touch.

"Yes, I want you, Gar." And with those simple words, she felt the heavy burden of her desire lighten and spread out to meet his hunger, making the space between them vibrate with anticipation.

He lowered himself onto the bed, and with one quick, impatient movement, he tore the shirt away from her. Even as his mouth covered hers, his hands were busy molding her to him, digging into her soft flesh as though demanding that she become a part of him.

He was not gentle, and she sensed that was his intention. And he paid no attention to her hesitancy, her desperate attempts to keep something of herself from him.

With lips and tongue and teeth and fingers, he took her body away from her and made it his. But the wild hunger was in her as well, and she staked her claim, too, letting all her senses fill up with him.

And then, for the first time, he became gentle. He parted her legs and entered her slowly, but she no longer wanted gentleness. She writhed beneath him, then wrapped her legs around him and drew him still deeper into her molten core.

The faint, distant roar of the waterfall was punctuated by their cries of pleasure as they moved against and with each other in an ancient, pulsing rhythm. Her body slipped through the final attempt by her brain to exercise control, to remain herself. Instead it became a wild thing, a primeval embodiment of the female need for a man.

Her fingernails dug into the taut skin of his back, and her teeth sank into his muscled shoulders. His fingers bruised her soft flesh as he lifted her and thrust still more deeply within.

She shuddered and cried out, and her cries were drowned out by his deep groan. Together they found perfect oneness, a unique balance of give and take.

He remained atop her, bracing himself with his arms as he stared down into her eyes. She was surprised to realize that she could see him now. It seemed that only moments had passed since she'd awakened to find him there, and yet, as the images filled her mind, she realized that it had been much longer.

Somehow they had kept the wildness under control and stretched out time itself. One moment had spilled urgently into the next, filling their senses and blotting out all knowledge of time.

Perspiration covered them. She breathed in his distinctive musky aroma; it held within it the sharp tang of something primitive. *He* is *a savage*, she thought, meeting his amber gaze in the soft light. *But, with him, so am I.*

She looked away, suddenly unable to accept what had happened—how quickly the thin veneer of civilization had been stripped from her by her own powerful, savage desire: a passion that had sprung full-blown out of a certainty only seconds before that he intended to kill her. How could such a thing happen?

He levered himself off the bed, then reached out a hand to her. "Come. We will bathe together."

"Where?" she asked. She hadn't seen baths of any kind. The only thing she'd found was a pump in the crude bathroom where she'd washed herself earlier.

He said nothing as he pulled the cover from the bed and wrapped it around her. Then, still naked himself, he led her from the house.

She followed him down the ladder to the next level. No one was about in the pale predawn light. He led her along a narrow space between two of the cottages and then down yet another ladder, helping her descend as she struggled with her wrap.

Before they had reached the bottom, she could hear the sound of water: not the roar of the falls, which she couldn't hear from this spot, but rather a musical, tinkling, bubbling sound. The breeze blew to her a strange but not unpleasant scent.

At the bottom of the long ladder, a narrow path led around a huge boulder, and there before them lay a large pool, its bubbling surface barely visible beneath a layer of mist. High stone walls surrounded the pool on all sides, and when they reached the edge, the air had become noticeably warmer.

Gar pulled off her covering and drew her into the water. She gasped with shock at its warmth, having been prepared to accept the cold in exchange for feeling clean again. "How is it heated?" she asked in amazement.

He shrugged his wide shoulders. "It's a hot spring. There are many of them here."

She cast a nervous glance around them. "Will anyone else be coming?"

"Probably not until later. Why? They know you are here."

"Do you all bathe here together—men and women?" she asked, suspecting now that that must be the case.

"Of course. And children, too."

He drew her down into the warm, scented water. Their bodies flowed together and she felt him grow hard against her. The pool wasn't deep—at least where they stood—but the water still came almost to her shoulders and made her balance precarious. With his feet planted firmly on the stone bottom, Gar lifted her and slid into her before she quite realized what was happening.

Shera gasped. "Gar, we can't! Someone might come!" Her body was throbbing with a wild excitement, but her eyes were darting around the edges of the pool, which she could barely see because of the mist.

But he ignored her, and within seconds she was swept away on a tide of rekindled passion. The warm water lapped at them as she clung to him and wrapped her legs around his waist, all too quickly sliding into a sensual oblivion. What had she become, to be so swept away by this passion for her enemy?

There was a fierceness in his eyes as he watched her succumb to her desire. Golden flames leaped in their depths. His wide mouth curved into a smile that was knowing, though not tender—there was no tenderness in this man. He wanted. He took. He enjoyed. And he knew that she felt the same pleasure as they exploded together in the culmination of their lust.

Then he let her go and began to swim, striking out for the far side of the pool, bypassing the spot in the center where the bubbling waters spewed up into a fountain. She followed him without giving any thought to the fact that she couldn't swim—and to her amazement, her arms and legs moved as surely as if she'd been walking.

Finally they both climbed out and wrapped themselves together in his bedcover, letting their combined body heat dry them as the first rays of sun found the pool and began to dissipate the mist.

As they made their way back along the path between the cottages, a man and a woman appeared, both of them naked, with bronzed skin and golden hair like Gar's. They greeted Gar and stared at her with a wary interest as she unconsciously drew her bedcover wrap closer around her.

Two more couples appeared before they reached the steps that led up to Gar's house. Shock vied with a hint of envy in Shera. These people were completely and unself-consciously naked, totally at ease with their bodies. On one level, it reinforced her impression of the Walkens as being savages—but she had only to recall what had happened between Gar and herself to feel that distinction blurring.

Shera watched as Gar paced around the cottage, then went outside to resume his pacing on the ledge pathway. Then, when she didn't see him pass by the windows, she went to the door and found him standing at the far end of the path, staring down at the valley.

The day had been a strange mixture of fierce lovemaking and brooding silences on his part, with occasional brief conversations. Once, after their passion was temporarily spent, she'd fallen asleep, awakening to find him standing by the bed, staring down at her with an expression she couldn't decipher.

If it weren't for her questions, there would have been no conversation at all between them. Sometimes he answered her, other times he seemed not to have heard her at all. She asked about the chezahs, believing that it should be a safe topic, but even then his answer had been guarded and wary.

The chezahs weren't pets, as she had suggested. They were wild creatures that came and went as they pleased. When she expressed shock that they would be permitted near children, he said that they would never harm any of his people, child or adult.

But when she'd brought up the subject of the waterfall, he had ignored her completely. He'd just sat there, honing the long blade of a knife against a stone.

She thought now, as he resumed his pacing outside, that he reminded her of the chezahs: lithe and powerful with a barely concealed savagery moving just beneath the surface. Perhaps that was why the Walken got along so well with the creatures.

She wondered what he really thought of her. It was the first time in her life that Shera had ever given any true consideration to how a man might feel toward her. She told herself that it was only because he was, in spite of what had happened between them, still her captor. But deep inside, in a place she didn't want to examine too closely, she knew that she cared what he thought, and that it had nothing to do with her being his prisoner.

That he delighted in the coming-together of their bodies she knew beyond question. Gold fire lit his eyes when he saw the effect he had on her, and he responded encouragingly to her clumsy attempts to please him.

He was a study in contrasts: boyishly eager and joyous in his lovemaking, then silent and brooding when the fires of the flesh were temporarily banked. She found herself craving small signs of affection and wanting to give them to him as well: touches, hugs, light kisses—even a loving glance. But that didn't seem to be part of his nature, and since it had never been part of hers, either, she didn't indulge this new desire.

Earlier, she had washed out her only clothes, then spread them out to dry outdoors. Now, clad in one of his shirts that reached to her knees, she went outside to retrieve them. He was staring down at the valley again. He turned briefly, indicating his awareness of her presence, then resumed his study of the valley.

She gathered up her clothes and went back inside to the bedroom. She had just peeled off his shirt when she felt his presence, and turned to find him standing in the doorway.

His gaze ran over her nakedness slowly, lingering upon each curve and swell. She drew in a shaky breath, unable even now to believe the effect he still had on her. With no more than a look, he could make her throb with need.

71

Saranne Dawson

"I will see you in the morning," he said, then abruptly turned and walked away. By the time she had recovered from her shock enough to go after him, he was gone.

What was it she had seen in those amber eyes? Contempt? Shame? Regret? It seemed to have been all of them, and perhaps more.

Shera crept stealthily past the row of houses on the terrace below Gar's home. Night was just beginning to give way grudgingly to the coming day. She knew she had very little time. Even if Gar didn't come home until later, the others would soon be stirring.

The discovery of the passageway that led to the bathing pool had given her some hope that there might also be another path she hadn't seen: one that led down into the valley.

She grew increasingly desperate as she ran along the terraces and down the ladders that joined them. Twice she wasted time following pathways that turned out to lead only to other bathing pools. Then, as she reached the bottom of yet another ladder, she saw a chezah ascending stairs a short distance away.

She froze. Surely the creature would know that she wasn't a Walken. They must be able to tell the difference, since they'd already killed more than dozen of her people. The animal reached the top of the ladder, paused a moment to stare at her, then padded soundlessly toward her. A scream rose in her throat, then died away to a gurgle as the chezah brushed past her, actually flicking its long tail against her legs as it climbed the ladder she'd just left.

It must be because I'm here in the Walkens' village, she thought as she continued her desperate explorations. *It assumes that I belong here, even if it can sense my otherness. Surely it would be different if I encountered it in the woods.*

Then, just as she was about to give up her attempt to flee down to the valley, she came upon a set of narrow stone steps that led down into a thick forest. By now the light was growing stronger, and she knew that she had run out of time. If the steps led only to more houses, she would be fortunate to make it back

72

up to Gar's home before the village awoke—or Gar himself returned.

The steps didn't descend in a straight line; instead, they began to spiral around the mountain, becoming wider and then narrower and even vanishing for a short distance when the ground was level. Her progress was slowed by the fact that, like the ladders, the steps had been designed for longer legs than hers.

But before long, she knew that the staircase was taking her down into the valley, weaving its tortuous way along the mountain. And then she realized that the roar of the waterfall, an ever-present background noise she'd almost learned to ignore, was becoming louder and louder.

After a time, the steps went up again, but only briefly. And when she reached the top, she was momentarily out of the forest. Shera stopped and stared with awe at the scene before her.

Perhaps a mile or so away stood the tallest mountain she'd yet seen, and tumbling from a spot near its jagged peak was a cascade of water that shimmered in the morning sunlight that illuminated the top third of the mountain.

She could follow the progress of the waterfall only a little more than a third of the way down, because the hills in between blocked her view. But when she let her eyes seek out the base of the mountain, she saw another gleam of water: a lake, or at least a pool. She could see only a tiny portion of it from where she stood, but she was eager to see it all.

Ahead of her, the steps plunged down in a straight line for some distance before making an abrupt turn. She ran down them as fast as she could, her thoughts on the sheer beauty of what must lie ahead. She had completely dismissed the notion that the great waterfall could be the source of something evil. How could anything so spectacular and awe-inspiring be bad?

Covering the remainder of the distance to the valley floor took her longer than she'd anticipated—or perhaps it was merely her eagerness that made her impatient. But she was nearly there now, following a narrow, curving path that wound down in a gentler fashion, when she came around a corner to find a chezah and two cubs on the path ahead of her.

The mother turned to stare at her as Shera came to an abrupt halt, her eagerness to see all of the waterfall now buried beneath her terror. She knew that no creature was more dangerous than a mother with her young in tow. Even normally harmless animals could turn vicious under such circumstances.

She didn't move, but her eyes darted about, seeking a tree with low branches she could climb. She wondered if the chezah could climb, too.

But the chezah turned away from her, emitting a low growl at one of the cubs that had strayed from the path. It came reluctantly to her, and all three trotted off.

Shera slid down against a tree trunk as her trembling legs threatened to give out. Why had it not attacked her? Could it have seen her at the Walken village earlier? But she'd seen no mother with cubs.

Gar had said that the chezahs were wild creatures that followed their own ways—but now she knew he must have lied. If that mother with cubs hadn't attacked her, it must be because chezahs, left to their own devices, didn't attack people at all. And that meant that the attacks on her people must have been directed by the Walkens—by Gar, who was their chief.

She didn't know why this revelation bothered her so much. After all, she knew for a fact that Gar had personally killed Marcus and that he or his people had killed the guards.

Then she understood. He'd never denied those killings—but he'd lied about the chezahs. It was that lie that troubled her. For all that she didn't understand him, she had believed in his honesty.

She felt betrayed by her own body, shamed by the wantonness that had overtaken her. And she began to wonder what other lies he might have told her.

After waiting for what she hoped was long enough to prevent another encounter with the mother chezah, Shera got up and once again set out on the stairs. She was even more eager now to see the wondrous waterfall, because she was convinced that

74

Gar had lied to her about her people—and that if the waterfall held any secrets, they were surely benevolent in nature.

With each step, it seemed, the roar of the waterfall became more deafening. The path no longer descended the mountain, but instead wound its way along the valley floor. And soon the very ground beneath her feet began to shake.

Her first complete glimpse of the falls came suddenly. The path climbed a small rise, the forest fell away, and there it was, wholly visible now in all its great height—except for the base, where she could see a mist rising into the clear air.

The sight dazzled her, bringing her to a stumbling halt. Even though she'd known it must be huge, she was totally unprepared for the sight that now lay before her.

A veritable wall of water shimmered before her eyes, reflecting the morning sun. In the fine mist created by droplets of water flung off during its plunge, hundreds, perhaps thousands of tiny rainbows gleamed like colorful jewels.

Shera had no idea how long she stood there, overwhelmed by the beauty of the scene and the great power displayed before her eyes. But after a time, she dragged her eyes away and resumed her journey.

For the next hour, she caught glimpses of it again and again, though there was no point at which she saw it in its entirety. And then, after the sun had passed its zenith, she came to the end of the path—and to the lake.

Now, for the first time, she saw it all: the mountain, the wall of water, and the large lake at its base, from which a swift-running stream flowed off into the forest.

What she felt in that first moment was the great age of this place. The trees were taller than any she'd ever seen before, and their trunks were twisted and gnarled. Vines as thick as her arm climbed their trunks and hung suspended between their branches. Strange flowers bloomed on the floor of the forest, and as she watched, a butterfly lit on one of them. Shockingly, the lovely petals snapped shut around the butterfly, revealing for one brief second what looked to be bloodred teeth.

Saranne Dawson

Shera gasped, all the more startled because it had happened here, in this most beautiful of places. The episode sent a chill through her, but it vanished quickly as she turned her attention back to the lake. The huge wall of water that poured into it stirred the surface even near where she stood, on the opposite bank. And close to the falls themselves, the waters churned and foamed in a frenzy beneath a fine mist.

Exhausted from her long trek down to this place, Shera sank down onto the grassy bank and opened the small sack she'd brought with her. It contained only a few pieces of fruit and the end of a loaf of bread: the last of the food Gar had brought her the evening before. She was hungry, but she knew that she had to eat sparingly as she waited for her people to arrive. So she leaned over and, cupping her hands, drank from the lake, then ate a few bites of bread.

She decided to rest for a time before she set out toward the village, which shouldn't be far away. Her people had had orchards and large gardens and various nut trees in their Trellan village, so she hoped she might find food when she reached their old homeland. In any event, she knew the others would quickly find their way there, too.

She had no way of knowing how long it would take them, since they were coming by a different route, but she wasn't in any hurry to see them again. As one accustomed to spending a great deal of time alone, she wasn't troubled at the thought of being alone now, here in the valley. Her only concern at the moment was that Gar might follow her.

His face hovered in her mind's eye, taunting her. She was truly hurt that he'd lied to her. Somehow it made what had happened between them shameful. And yet, even now, she could easily close her eyes and relive those moments in his arms.

The vibrations from the falls began to make her sleepy, and now that the sun had risen high enough to warm the valley, within moments, her eyes closed.

* * *

76

The Sorceress & the Savage

Gar stayed away from her for as long as he could, but his desire drove him back to his house before midmorning. Even as he climbed the ladder, he was throbbing with need.

At first he could not quite believe that she had gone. He went down to the bathing pool, thinking that she must have gone there. Then he asked about her, but no one had seen her. It wasn't until he returned again to the house that he saw she'd taken the food from the night before and one of his leather sacks.

Anger surged through him, mixing explosively with desire. How could she leave him when she wanted him as much as he wanted her? And where could she have gone? She wasn't foolish enough just to wander off into the woods, not when she couldn't hope to find her way back to her people.

And then he knew. She must have found the way down to the valley. For one brief moment he considered going after her and bringing her back. But he guessed that she had probably left at first light—before anyone could see her. She would have reached the falls by now.

He stared down into the accursed valley. It was too late. The evil that she called her gods would have claimed her by now. They would meet again—but she was lost to him forever.

Shera awoke feeling very strange. She could tell from the position of the sun that she hadn't slept long—perhaps two hours—but she felt refreshed. Still, her sense of well-being didn't quite mask a deeper feeling that seemed to stir at the very core of her being.

She stood up, and without conscious intent began to strip off her clothes. The shallow water at the lake's edge had been warmed by the sun and she stepped into it. Her naked skin tingled from the combination of the sun's warmth and the light breeze.

When the bottom dropped away sharply after a few dozen yards, she began to swim. She had gotten quite proficient, and her smooth strokes soon carried her to the center of the lake— and closer to the falls. Swimming became more difficult as she was buffeted by the currents, but she continued to swim toward the falls with no thought of danger. The water was cooler as it lapped against her body, but it felt good—deliciously sensual.

Then, abruptly, she was caught up in the churning, foaming water and tossed about like a piece of driftwood. The fear she should have felt much earlier consumed her, and she flailed about wildly, trying to get back to calmer waters.

The great roar of the falls was so deafening that she could barely think, and she could no longer see anything as wave after wave washed over her. She was certain that she was going to die, and in that moment it was Gar's face that came to her mind, his amber eyes sparkling with passion.

Then suddenly she was in calm water again. Even the sound of the falls was muted. She blinked and looked around her in confusion. She was in a dimly lit cavern, and it took several seconds for her to realize that she had somehow been drawn through the falls into a calm backwater pool.

She dragged herself from the water onto the ledge that ran along the perimeter of the basin. Exhausted from her attempts to fight the currents, and chilled by the coolness of the cavern, she wrapped her arms around herself and peered at her surroundings.

The first thing she noticed, once her eyes had adjusted to the dim light, were the old torches, affixed to iron brackets along the stone walls. Scanning the length of the walls, she saw that there were many of them, burned down to blackened twigs. Then she saw a deeper shadow at the back of the cavern. Was it an opening of some kind?

Not yet ready to think about how she could possibly get out of this place, she nonetheless got up and walked along the ledge to the rear; it was indeed an opening into a narrow corridor. Furthermore, the air that flowed from it was much warmer than the air in the cavern itself. That itself was enough to persuade her to see where it led.

That it turned downward became quickly apparent. No more than four or five feet wide and perhaps ten feet high, the corridor snaked its way deeper and deeper into the mountain, until

78

the roar of the falls became nothing more than a distant, barely audible sound.

She had no idea how far she'd gone before it occurred to her that there shouldn't be light in the passageway—and yet there was: a faint illumination that seemingly had no source. She stopped, and for the first time considered the wisdom of her actions.

An uneasiness came over Shera. She was not wildly impetuous by nature, and yet she'd recently acted twice without thinking: first when she swam into the falls, and now that she was following this mysterious corridor.

When first she heard it, she thought she was imagining the chanting. It was low and indistinct, blending with the distant sound of the waterfall. But as she listened, it seemed to grow slightly louder, though the words were still indecipherable. Still, she recognized the rhythmic rise and fall of the voices.

She frowned. Could her people possibly have arrived in the valley before her and found another way into this cavern—a back entrance? It seemed unlikely, and yet she was certain that she was hearing her people's evening ceremonies.

She turned first one way and then the other, and decided that the chants were coming from somewhere ahead of her. She set off again, moving more quickly this time as the voices grew louder.

The corridor ended abruptly, and Shera found herself standing at the entrance to another large cavern, this one many times the size of the cavern with the pool. The same diffuse light filled the place, and once again she could find no source of that glow.

The chanting stopped the moment she reached the cavern. It didn't fade away gradually, as it would have done if she'd been mistaken about the direction. Neither had it come to a natural end. She had not recently been a regular at evening ceremonies, but she still knew them well enough to know that the hymns had ended prematurely.

She became more and more frightened as she stared at the

cavern. It was perfectly round, and in the very center of the stone floor was a small pool that bubbled like the hot spring where she'd bathed with Gar. Wisps of steam hung in the air above it. But the odor that tickled her nostrils now was different from that other pool: acrid and unpleasant.

And then she knew that she was not alone. The light was dim and her eyes darted about, trying to seek substance in the shadows. The feeling of a presence grew ever stronger, sending a chill through her.

"Who's there?" she called, then shuddered as her voice echoed over and over again, seeming to mock her.

"Shera! Shera!"

"Where are you?" She whirled around, seeking the thing that hissed her name.

Something brushed against her with a featherlight touch. She spun about, but found nothing. The sibilant whisper came again, calling out to her.

Then she felt cold fingers touch her bare skin. Once she'd moved away from the chill of the first cavern, she'd nearly forgotten her nakedness. But now she felt more vulnerable than she ever had in her life; the ghostly fingers continued to touch her, prodding at her, urging her toward the bubbling pool.

"No!" She shouted the word, then was forced to listen to its echo.

She struck out blindly at the unseen force and refused to give in to its urging. Despite the warmth of the place, she was now shivering with cold—a cold that penetrated to her very soul.

And then she knew. It was the same cold she'd felt at the ceremonies: a coldness with darkness at its center. It began to reach into her mind with dark whispers and sensual promises.

"Power!" it whispered. "Power beyond imagining. Riches beyond your dreams. All can be yours."

Images floated through her mind: a palace far more lavish than the duke's castle, richly furnished, herself clad in garments of great luxury, dripping with glittering jewels.

And all the while, the invisible fingers stroked her, their

touch growing less cold, more sensual, until she was damp and aching with desire.

But the heat of desire brought a memory of Gar, and no sooner had his image invaded her mind than the unseen force withdrew—and for one brief instant, she could feel its loathing—and its fear.

Trembling with her own fear, Shera turned and fled back to the narrow corridor, back to the other cavern with the pool, back to the splashing tumult of the waterfall. And after only a second's hesitation, she dove into the pool and swam out into the churning waters.

Once again she was at the mercy of angry currents and the pounding cascade of water. Exhausted from her previous encounter with the waterfall, Shera still found the strength to struggle on. As she was tossed this way and that by the violent waves, she managed to catch brief glimpses of the lake beyond the falls, and she kept herself moving in that direction, sometimes swimming against the currents and sometimes letting them carry her.

And then, at last, she was free of the falls and buffeted only by small ripples. She could see the far shore—and safety. With her last reserves of strength, she dragged herself through the water and fell onto the grassy shore. She lay there, exhausted, as the sun's rays drove away the last of the cavern's chill.

When she awoke, she was shivering. But this time the chill was from the evening breeze that swept down from the surrounding mountains. The sun had gone, and as she rolled over onto her back, she could see a few stars already glittering in the dark heavens.

She dressed quickly, then devoured the remainder of her food as she sat staring at the waterfall. Her mind and body felt bruised and sluggish, not quite under her control.

Her memories of the waterfall and the caverns were clear enough—but she didn't trust them. In fact, if it weren't for the aching of just about every muscle in her body, she might have been able to convince herself that none of it had happened.

But obviously something had happened. At least she knew that she must have gone swimming in the lake and ventured too near to the falls. But why would she have done such a thing? As she sat there, staring at the roiling waters of the lake beneath the falls, she simply could not imagine herself taking such a foolish risk.

She let her mind dwell on that thought for a long time, unwilling to move on to a consideration of what had happened next. She tried to recall getting into the water, perhaps intending only to go for a brief swim in the calm portion of the lake. But what she remembered was a compulsion to swim into the waterfall. Even now, it continued to beckon to her in some strange, seductive way.

She shuddered as she remembered cold fingers touching her, repulsive at first and then . . . "No!" she cried aloud. She could not have welcomed that touch. It hadn't happened. Perhaps there was a cavern in there with a calm pool, and she'd fallen asleep beside it, exhausted from her struggles. But she'd dreamed the rest of it.

A nearly full moon rose above the mountains, bathing the lake and the falls in a sheen of ghostly silver. She heard once again the faint chants of her people at evening worship. When she concentrated on the sounds, they seemed to slip away, merging into the roar of the falls.

I must get away from here, she told herself, putting action to her thoughts by scrambling to her feet. But where could she go? The moon was bright enough to guide her if she were familiar with this place, but she wasn't. She couldn't hope to find her people's village at night.

She turned to her left, thinking about the path she did know: the one that led back up the mountain to Gar's village. She could find it, and once on it she couldn't possibly get lost.

She hesitated. Would Gar take her back—or was he glad to be rid of her? He hadn't come after her, though he must have guessed where she'd gone.

Go back to him, she told herself. *He alone has the answers you need. He knows about your people's past. He can help you.*

She set off, skirting the edge of the lake until she found the path. Then she began the long, tortuous climb back up the mountain. Very little light filtered down through the trees, but it was enough. Several times she thought she heard the chanting again, but when she stopped and listened, all she could hear was the sibilant roar of the waterfall.

Once, she heard a rustling in the woods, followed by the snapping of twigs, and she thought she saw something moving in the deep shadows. But whatever it was, it came no closer to her.

Then she was climbing the last set of stone steps that led into the mountainside village of the Walkens. Hungry and tired, she stumbled along the walkway, then dragged herself up the ladder to Gar's house. Without bothering to knock, she pushed open the door.

The warmth of the fire enveloped her. A bowl of fruit sat upon the table, next to a half-eaten loaf of bread. She fell upon them, even though she was nearly too tired to eat. She had just bitten into the fruit when he appeared.

Tired as she was, Shera still felt the soft pulse of desire steal through her as they stared at each other. He was naked, and the firelight flickered over his lean, hard body. She wanted so much for him to welcome her, but instead he just stood there, his expression unreadable.

"Please don't send me away," she said, too exhausted to care that she was begging.

"Where have you been?" he demanded.

"Down in the valley." She continued to eat, fearing that he would order her to leave before she could fill her stomach.

His brows arched in surprise. "You went down there—and then came back up here?"

She nodded and reached for the bread, wondering why he seemed so shocked. Was it only the distance—or something more? "I didn't want to stay down there."

"Why not?" he demanded. His tone was still disbelieving, and he continued to keep his distance.

"I don't know—but I think *you* do," she replied, somehow summoning up the energy to challenge him.

He stood there for a long moment, staring at her as she continued to eat as fast as she could. She didn't understand his wariness. Surely she couldn't represent any kind of threat to him. But then she thought about what he'd said earlier, about her people being evil. She'd denied that, and then he'd told her that things would change when they reached the valley.

She shuddered involuntarily, recalling those moments in the cavern. But she reminded herself that he had lied to her about the chezahs, and had probably lied about the rest of it as well.

"What happened?" he asked, his amber eyes boring into her.

She told him all of it—and in far greater detail than she would have if she'd been able to think more clearly. And as she forced herself to relive those moments, she suddenly remembered something.

"It all ended when I thought about *you*," she said slowly, not really looking at him as she recalled the moment when the unseen force had withdrawn. It was when she'd begun to be aroused that she'd suddenly thought of him. Embarrassed now, she kept her gaze averted as she continued.

"Then I ran back to the pool and swam through the falls and back across the lake."

He said nothing, and she forced herself to look at him. His gaze quickly became a mask again, but for one brief moment she thought she saw pain there—and perhaps even sympathy.

"What is in that cavern, Gar? You *know*, don't you?"

"I've never been there," he replied coldly.

"That's not an answer. You—"

"Come to bed, Shera. You need to rest."

She was too tired to protest his failure to give her an answer, and too grateful that he had decided to let her stay. In the morning, when she was more herself, she would demand some answers. She struggled up from the chair, then swayed slightly, unable to control her aching legs.

Gar made a sound of disgust, then picked her up easily and carried her back to the bedroom. She began to fade away the moment he deposited her on the bed, and was only vaguely aware of his hands on her as he undressed her. Before he had finished, she was fast asleep.

Gar stood beside the bed, staring at her in the shadowy light. She whimpered several times and curled herself into a tight ball.

He clenched his fists helplessly, trying to quell the rage that rose within him. Why had he brought her here in the first place—and why hadn't he forced her to leave? He wanted her more than he'd ever wanted any woman—but she was one of *them,* even if she didn't seem to understand that yet.

Her candor about what had happened in the cavern surprised him, but he assumed that she would have been far more circumspect if she hadn't been so exhausted.

Or *had* she been honest? She seemed so innocent, but it could all be a trick. And the more he thought about it, the more he became convinced that it was a trick, even if he couldn't yet see the reason for it. She would never have been chosen by the priests to be one of her tribe's leaders if they suspected there was any rebellion in her.

He turned to leave, intending to sleep by the hearth. But then she whimpered again, and he thought she might have spoken his name. He hesitated, then returned to the bed. She murmured again, and this time he knew she'd called out to him. Hating himself for his weakness, Gar reached for her and she came into his arms easily, her silken black hair fanning softly across his chest.

Chapter Five

Shera awoke to find a soft, golden light illuminating the room. But she had only a few seconds of peace before the events of the previous day came crashing down on her, leaving her once again confused and frightened.

She listened for sounds that would tell her whether Gar was still there, out in the main room. As she listened, she breathed in his scent that lingered in the bed. Had he shared it with her, or had he slept in the outer room? She had a vague memory of being enfolded in his warmth, but that might have been only a dream. It was becoming more and more difficult for her to separate dreams from reality.

She got up and dressed, her thoughts on the bath she'd shared with him. How she'd love to go there now, but she feared asking for any privileges. She knew that whatever claim she had on his hospitality was tenuous at best, and based only on his desire for her, not on any feelings of affection.

Still, she knew she had to risk his wrath by demanding some answers. Very soon—perhaps even today—her people would arrive in the valley, and sooner or later they would find their way to that cavern, as she had.

She drew in a sharp breath, realizing that she was all but accepting his story that her people were evil—or would soon become so. And whatever was in that cavern, it was definitely evil: seductive and powerful and wrong.

She swallowed hard, remembering just how close she'd come to surrendering herself to that unseen force. But surely the priests could persuade her people to resist, even if she herself couldn't. Surely they, too, would recognize that place as being evil. And the key to her being able to persuade the priests of the danger lay in the knowledge she was certain Gar had.

She found him outside, at the far end of the ledge path, once again staring down at the valley. Her bare feet made no sound as she approached him, but he turned anyway, when she was still some ten feet away.

His expression was again cold and wary, and she decided that she'd only dreamed of sleeping in his arms.

"Gar," she said firmly. "you *must* tell me what you know of my people's history, and of that cavern behind the waterfall. I can't protect them from it if I don't know what it is."

"You are foolish to believe that you can protect them from it," he said dismissively. "They will welcome it."

"Not if the priests order them to resist—and they will if I can tell them the truth."

"The priests?" he scoffed. "The priests will have your people go there as soon as they arrive."

"What do you mean?"

"Your priests *worship* them, Shera. They always have."

"No! You're wrong, Gar! Our priests worship the gods!"

"And what do you think was in the cavern?" he taunted her.

"It was evil!" she replied. But she was remembering how she had felt that same cold darkness at their ceremonies.

"All right. You want the truth, so here it is. Many centuries ago, the Bacleev worshipped that which lived in that cave—the gods. They believed, and rightly so, that they were favored.

87

They alone had the power of healing and the magic to bring rain, and they used it to help everyone.

"But then it all changed. There was rumbling in that great mountain and the land shook for miles around. Somehow, evil had taken up residence in the mountain, but the Bacleev denied that. And then, soon after that, they began to change.

"Instead of helping people, they enslaved them and took from them everything they had. They kept the rains coming for the crops, but they demanded all of the harvest for themselves. This was once a prosperous land, filled with happy people. But people began to starve, and the sicknesses that the Bacleev had once cured they were now unwilling to cure. Many died.

"Finally, a little over a century ago, your people went too far. They enslaved every able-bodied male, forcing them to begin building a great palace for them. Many men died as they struggled to build it. With so few people to tend the crops, there was a famine. But the Bacleev didn't care because they had already filled their storehouses.

"Finally, though your kind were the favored of the gods, the people rebelled—and they succeeded in driving you out of the valley."

Shera listened in silence—and increasing disbelief. "How could my people have enslaved so many—and where are these other people now?"

He waved an arm. "They live in the hills and plains beyond here. And they were enslaved by magic—the evil magic given to the Bacleev by the Dark Ones in the mountain."

"I don't believe you, Gar. There may be evil in that cavern, but I am Bacleev, and I resisted it." She knew herself to be on shaky ground, because she knew how close she'd come to being seduced by what he called the Dark Ones. Still, she did not want to believe her race had acted so cruelly.

He looked away from her, down at the valley. "Yes, somehow you did resist, if your story is true. Perhaps there were even those who resisted centuries ago, but they gave in in the end—and so will you."

His tone was so bleak that for a moment she thought maybe

he really did care about her. But then she thought about his story and wondered if his anguish stemmed from another source.

"Were *your* people enslaved, Gar?"

His silence went on for so long that she thought he wouldn't answer. But then, without looking at her, he shrugged. "In a different way."

"What do you mean?"

Again he hesitated, and when he spoke she could tell that he was choosing his words with great care. "There are different ways to enslave people. Sometimes it can be done by giving them what they want most."

"And what is that?" she asked, perplexed. She'd seen no sign that his people had any great riches.

But he ignored the question, gesturing instead to the house. "I have brought more food for you. Your people will arrive in the valley before day's end. Go join them. You will find a path that leads to the valley's entrance near a large rock by the lake."

He started to walk away, stopping with reluctance when she called out to him.

"Gar, why did you lie to me about the chezahs? You said they acted on their own, that they aren't pets."

She saw him stiffen as he glanced over his shoulder at her. "I didn't lie."

"Then please explain to me why a mother with cubs didn't attack me. If ever there was a time for these beasts to attack . . . I think they attack humans only under the direction of you and your people."

With obvious reluctance, he turned back to face her. "When did this happen—when you were returning from the valley?"

"No, it happened when I was on my way down there."

He frowned. "Are you sure?"

"Of course I'm sure. Why does it make a difference?"

He studied her for a long moment, then left without saying another word.

Shera watched him descend the ladder and then disappear

from view. Her story had shocked him—but why? Did it mean that he'd told her the truth about the chezahs? But if so, why hadn't the mother attacked her?

She went back inside to eat her breakfast, thinking about his story. At first she wanted to dismiss it out of hand, but the more she thought about it, the less she could bring herself to do that. She *had* felt evil in that cavern.

As she ate, she examined his tale piece by piece, seeking something wrong—or some missing piece. It didn't take her long to find both.

If her people had enslaved everyone around them with magical powers, then how had those slaves managed to rise up in rebellion and drive out their masters? That seemed highly improbable, especially if the Bacleev had all the power he claimed they'd had.

She remembered those seductive whispers from the cave, promises of great riches and even greater power. Did those not lend credence to his story? Except that she'd told him about her experience before he'd told her his story. He could easily have used her own injudicious words against her.

And then there was what he'd said—or *hadn't* said—about his own people's role. He'd said that there was more than one way to enslave a people, and that it could be done by giving them what they wanted most. But what could her people have offered? And why would the Bacleev have treated the Walkens any differently from the others? Obviously, that was what he'd seemed to be implying.

A short time later, with the unanswered questions still in her mind, Shera left Gar's house. She'd hoped that he might return, and she was surprised at her reluctance to leave him. As with everything else right now, her thoughts about Gar were far from clear.

She wanted him—but she didn't trust him. Furthermore, she knew he felt the same. But still, she left the village of the Walkens with great reluctance, wondering how it was that her body could so betray her—and for an untrustworthy savage at that, a man who could sometimes seem more like the beasts that lived with him than like any other man she'd ever known.

This time, as she made her way back down the staircase into the valley, Shera did her best to block out the roar of the waterfall—and at least her memories of what lay behind it. Still, when she reached the bottom, at the edge of the lake and gazed across the water, she felt something stir within her, and for one brief second she thought she again heard those low chants.

She turned her back on the lake and quickly spotted the huge boulder Gar had said marked the path that would take her to the valley's entrance. The path was overgrown but still easy enough to follow. It wound its way through the valley, for a time following the narrow, swift-running stream that was fed by the lake. Then it veered off through meadows and woods, up small hills and down again.

As she walked, Shera forced herself to consider her coming reunion with her people—and, specifically, with Daren. Somehow she'd managed to forget that she would be expected to marry him now.

There would be no marriage; of that she was very sure. No one—not even the priests—could force someone to marry against their will. Or so she believed. Actually, no one had ever defied the priests before.

Still, Daren was nothing more than a minor problem. What occupied her thoughts as she headed toward her people was the priests' reaction to her story. She didn't wholly believe Gar's tale, but she suspected that there might be at least a kernel of truth in it, as there so often was in folktales handed down over the ages.

It was possible, certainly, that her people had become greedy and had demanded payment for their services—perhaps even exorbitant amounts. That could have been enough to cause a rebellion that resulted in the Bacleev being driven from the valley. But she didn't believe his story about her people enslaving the entire surrounding area. There were so few Bacleev.

Perhaps her people and Gar's had waged war a century ago—and her people had been the losers. The Walkens surely were even fewer in number than her own people, but if she was right about their control of the chezahs, they could certainly have wreaked havoc upon the Bacleev—as they were doing now.

The path continued, and she realized that finding the pass into the valley wasn't as easy as she'd thought. The land was hilly here, and she saw that she was already several hundred feet above the valley floor. So she stopped to rest and look around—and when she did, she saw a sight that sent a chill through her.

On a low rise some distance away, she saw a huge stone structure. It swept upward into a partially finished tower, and the remainder was a series of walls of varying heights. She actually blinked a few times, hoping it was nothing more than an unusual rock formation that resembled a castle—in the way clouds could sometimes take on the appearance of various objects. But she knew she was being silly. It remained what it clearly was: a partially completed castle of huge proportions.

Even confronted with this corroboration of Gar's tale, Shera could not accept it. No doubt he'd seen this many times and had simply woven a tale to fit his purposes. Her people might well have been building a castle, or a fortress—that made sense, especially if they had been at war with the Walkens. Its existence proved nothing. And yet it made her very uneasy as she considered his claim that slaves had been driven beyond their endurance to create it while their crops went untended and their families starved.

Then, when she dragged her gaze from the huge structure, she discovered that the village she'd glimpsed from Gar's home was visible from here as well: a collection of modest stone cottages nestled in a hollow against a steep mountain. The thatched roofs had rotted away long ago, but otherwise the homes appeared to be in good condition.

She stared at the deserted village, thinking what a lovely place it could be. Not far from the village she could see neat, precise rows of trees that she knew must be an orchard, and she'd already seen that the valley was filled with various berry bushes and nut trees of several varieties.

All in all, the valley was a place of great beauty, and unless the Walkens were determined to make war on her people, the Bacleev could be happy here. Surely, in the midst of all this plenty, her people could resist—as she had—whatever lurked in that cavern. They had only to be warned by the priests about it, and they would stay away.

Your priests, worship them, Shera! They always have!

Gar's words came back to her, echoing all their original disgust, and she wondered what she should do if he'd actually spoken the truth.

An hour later, just when she was thinking about going into to the village herself to look around, she saw the Bacleev approaching. First came the black-robed priests, together with another figure she assumed to be Daren, and then the others. She was standing on a hilltop and waved at them. The procession halted for a moment, then began to move steadily toward her.

As the long line began its slow descent into the valley, Shera's attention was caught by movement on a distant hilltop far above her. It was a group of Walkens, together with several chezahs. She couldn't tell if they were armed, though she was sure that the distance was too great for them to fire at her people.

They didn't attack. Instead they stood, looking down at the homecoming of the Bacleev, then vanished into the forest. Shera wondered if Gar was among them, and she felt that treacherous heat steal through her that the thought of him never failed to evoke.

"He lied, of course. What else could you expect from a murdering savage?" Daren had barely waited for her to finish her story before he spoke up to dismiss her fears.

She paid scant attention to Daren. Instead her full attention was focused on the priests. But each one of the clerics wore expressions of nothing more than curiosity. Daren started to speak again, but she cut him off, her attention still on the holy men.

"There is more." She told them about the cavern and the presence there. "Gar said it is an evil place. He called its inhabitants the Dark Ones. In that, at least, he is right: whatever is in there *is* evil!"

Glancing around, she still saw nothing in the faces of her audience. But when he tried to speak, this time it was the high priest who cut Daren off.

"You were frightened and confused, Shera. That is understandable. But that is a sacred place. There can be no evil there."

"How do you know it's a sacred place?" she demanded. The one thing she'd left out of her recounting was Gar's statement that the Bacleev had always worshiped the Dark Ones. "Are you saying that you already knew of the existence of that place?"

For just a moment, the high priest seemed uneasy—or so she thought. But he quickly adopted a placid expression and replied in a somewhat soothing tone. "From the moment when we first heard the waterfall, we all knew that it was sacred to our people. But it may be that the cave you describe doesn't even exist. You yourself admitted that you thought it might be nothing more than a dream."

"I said I thought that at first, but not now. You must warn people to stay away from there. I'm fortunate to be alive, after swimming through the falls."

"The gods kept you safe, Shera," he intoned piously. "And yes, you are quite right. If there is evil, the people must be warned. But everyone will be busy getting the cottages ready for habitation now. If there is danger coming, the gods will warn us. We must trust them. We must go now to find a suitable place for the evening ceremonies."

"Where is this castle you saw?" Daren asked as the priests walked off to follow the others to the village.

Shera gave him a speculative look. She wished that she could gain an ally in Daren, but she trusted him even less than she trusted Gar—and even less than she trusted the priests at this point.

Perhaps I've misjudged him, she thought. She did need an ally. Deciding to take a chance, she led him up to the hilltop where she'd first seen the castle. She pointed, and he made a sound of surprise as he stared at it, shading his eyes from the glare of the setting sun.

"This savage, Gar, must have known of its existence," he said, echoing her own thoughts. "He probably knew you would see it, and he included it to give credence to the rest of what he said."

She nodded. "I thought about that, too."

Daren continued to stare at the structure, and then his gaze flicked briefly to the village. "It might have been intended to be a fortress. A village would be difficult to defend. Perhaps you're right, Shera, and there was some truth in his tale. Or maybe these Walken savages were at war with us."

Once again his words confirmed her thoughts. Shera still didn't like him, but she began to think that perhaps he could help her.

"What was this man Gar like, and why do you think he didn't kill you?"

"I'm not sure he wouldn't have killed me if I hadn't escaped," she replied. She had edited her story somewhat, leaving out details and not admitting that she'd gone back to Gar after her first journey down here. And it was true that she really wasn't sure how safe she had been.

"It's . . . difficult to describe him."

"But you called him a savage?"

"He is. There is something about him that is . . . wild, untamed. He kills—or orders that people be killed—without any guilt. He shows no emotion. He and his people live side by side with those cat-beasts—the chezahs—even though he says they're wild creatures, not pets."

She could have said more: that he was a relentlessly demanding lover, not a gentle one; that in bed he had an air of barely leashed savagery about him. But she didn't say any of those things, though thoughts of Gar made her shiver with remembrance.

"How many of them are there?" Daren asked, his thoughts obviously still on the defense of their people.

"I'm not sure. Certainly not as many as we are. But if they control the chezahs as well . . ."

"Yes. That is a problem. It's too bad that castle was never completed. We would be much safer there."

Days passed as the Bacleev worked to establish their new home. They were not a people accustomed to hard physical labor, but the long journey had toughened them. Still, there were many complaints as they worked long hours to make the old cottages habitable.

Shera understood and even sympathized. When her people had arrived in the land of the Trellans, they'd carried with them a considerable quantity of gold; it had allowed them to hire Trellans to build their houses and then furnish them luxuriously. They still had plenty of wealth, but now they were forced to do the work themselves.

More than once, as Shera labored alongside her people, she thought about the whispered promises in the cavern and about Gar's story. Even though she was unlike her people in many ways, she, too, wished for someone else to do such work.

The Bacleev had always considered physical labor to be demeaning, as had the upper ranks of Trellan society. Shera, on the other hand, had spent considerable time among the Trellan peasants, and had grown to respect their capacity for hard work. Nevertheless, even she was not happy about the aching muscles and the calluses that quickly developed on her soft hands.

She did her best to keep track of the priests, who, of course, demanded that the others prepare their homes. The holy men spent most of their time in worship, but as far as she knew, they didn't attempt to swim through the waterfall to the cavern. Shera thought that most of them were too old for such an arduous undertaking, anyway.

And they *did* warn everyone about the waterfall, although the warning came in the form of prohibiting people from intruding upon that sacred place. People swam in the lake, but they stayed well away from the roiling waters beneath the falls. And if anyone felt the compulsion she had, or heard voices chanting in the roar of the waterfall, they kept it to themselves.

Shera returned to the lake herself, but she felt nothing of what she'd felt before. After venturing into the lake several times, she was forced to conclude that it *had* all been a dream—brought about by exhaustion—and that Gar's story had been simply an old myth.

Nevertheless, Gar continued to haunt her dreams, coming to her at night in a sensual assault, causing her to awaken with a heaviness in her loins and a longing that would also surface during her busy days.

As for Daren, he was unfailingly polite to her, and spent as much time with her as their busy schedules permitted. The priests had decreed that their wedding could be postponed until the end of their labors to reestablish themselves in the village. Shera thought it rather strange, but she didn't protest; it gave her more time to think of a way to prevent the marriage.

She and Daren agreed that a twenty-four-hour guard should be kept at the entrance to the valley, but Shera didn't tell him about the other entrance to the valley, the path that led directly to the Walkens' village. It was invisible from the lake, and as yet, no one had the time to go exploring.

She couldn't really explain—even to herself—why she kept it secret. Obviously, if the Walkens intended to attack them, they would use that route. She soothed her conscience by insisting that not only the entrance to the valley be guarded, but the perimeters of the village as well. It was unlikely they would be surprised, even if their enemies did use the secret route.

Nearly two weeks passed with no sign of either Walkens or chezahs. Given the new abundance of prey in the valley, this made Shera even more certain that the chezahs acted under the instructions of the Walkens. Why else would they stay out of the valley, when stalking deer and other prey among the tall grasses and thick forests must surely be easier than finding them in the mountains?

Then, on a sultry afternoon, Shera decided to pay a visit to the partially completed castle. Daren had already been there, as had the priests and many others, but she had yet to visit the place. Even though she now discredited Gar's lurid tales, enough of her horror at that tale had lingered to keep her away until now.

But her curiosity finally got the better of her. She'd listened to Daren and others talk about it in reverent tones, saying that if it could be completed, it would be more splendid even than the duke's castle had been. Daren also continued to think of the place as a fortress, even though they had not been attacked for some time.

They planned to send a scouting party into the regions beyond the valley as soon as they were settled. Daren had reminded her that she herself had agreed that there could be some truth to Gar's tales, so it behooved them to discover whether there were other people nearby—and what threat they might pose to the Bacleev.

There was no actual road that led from the village to the castle, but by now so many people had visited it that they'd worn a track through the tall grasses of the meadow that lay in between. Shera followed it, then plunged into the thick forest that surrounded the hillside leading up to the keep.

When at last she reached the hilltop fortress, she paused, turning to see the view spread out around her. She was surprised to see that the entire lake and the waterfall were visible from this point, while the village was hidden from view. She had to agree that it was a splendid spot for a palace—or a fortress—commanding views of both the entrance to the valley and the secret path that led up to the village of the Walkens, which was closer than she'd expected. The path itself couldn't be seen, but because she knew where it ended, in a rocky area not far from the lake, Shera was able to trace its path up the mountain. The Walken village was hidden by a bulge in the mountain into which it had been built.

She thought about Gar, and wondered uneasily what he was doing. Daren and the others seemed to have all but dismissed the Walkens as a threat, but Shera was not so sanguine. If he'd told the truth about there being other people in the region, she considered it quite likely that the Walkens might even now be stirring them up against the Bacleev.

She turned to study the far end of the valley, where none of them had yet ventured. It was as Daren had said: dark, steep cliffs rising in an unbroken line—a highly unlikely place for an invasion, even by people accustomed to mountains.

She was so lost in thought about her people's safety and the possible trouble the Walkens might cause that she was slow to recognize the feeling that came over her. She whirled around, looking up, and gasped.

Gar stood above her. He was no more than fifty feet away, and with him was a chezah. Both of them were standing on top of a partially completed wall about fifteen feet high. The sun had turned his hair to a burnished gold, and it was nearly the same shade as the chezah's fur.

She gasped again as he leaped from the wall and landed in a crouch, amazingly unhurt. The chezah followed. What amazing athleticism this man possessed!

He straightened up, then stood there silently, his amber eyes intent upon her. The huge cat remained at his side, motionless except for its long tail, which twitched impatiently.

"What are you doing here, Gar?" she asked when it became evident that he intended to say nothing. Already she could feel her blood heating and coursing through her veins.

"I came to see you. It took you long enough to decide to come up here. Does it bother you to know that this was built at the cost of so many lives?"

"I don't believe your story."

"No?" He arched a golden brow. "The bodies are here—what's left of them. The Bacleev wouldn't even permit people to come and bury their dead. Instead they sealed them up inside these walls. Come. I'll show you."

She hesitated, still not believing him, but unwilling to be proved wrong. But when he turned and walked away, she followed. He stopped near a corner of the wall, which was many feet thick, and began to remove the stones, easily hefting the heavy cut blocks.

Shera watched him uneasily, feeling ashamed at the way her gaze lingered on his bare, muscular arms and his powerful legs. After having removed perhaps a dozen stones, he stopped and beckoned to her.

Beginning to feel sick to her stomach, Shera walked over to him. She backed away quickly when she caught a glimpse of the grisly display. Skulls and bones filled a gap between the inner and outer wall. She had no idea how many were there, but it seemed that the entire space was filled with them. What a strange idea—that such a beautiful structure might be filled with evil and death.

Gar studied her with satisfaction, then turned and began to replace the stones. Shera sank down onto a nearby pile of stones that had been cut but not yet fitted into place. There had to be another explanation! Despite the evidence, she still could not believe his story.

He finished his task, then came to stand before her. "There are hundreds, perhaps thousands in these walls."

"Stop it, Gar! There must be some explanation!"

"You already have the explanation, Shera—and soon your priests will order that construction resume. How many more deaths do you think it will take to complete this?"

"That won't happen! I won't allow it!"

"You can't stop it. The priests and your mate have already been visiting the cavern, listening to the Dark Ones."

"No, they haven't! Everyone was warned to stay away from there, and I've been watching the priests. And Daren isn't my mate!"

"Oh?" He arched a brow in disbelief.

"I . . . that hasn't happened yet."

"Why not?" he asked, staring at her intently.

"The priests said that we will wait until everyone is settled."

"That will be soon."

"I'm *not* going to marry him."

"You would disobey the priests?" he asked, incredulously.

"Yes." She didn't want to talk any more about that. "Why do you think the priests and Daren are going to the cavern?"

"I *know*. They're using the back way, not swimming through the waterfall."

"The back way?" she echoed.

He nodded. "And they knew exactly where to find it."

He left hanging the very clear implication: that the priests did in fact know her people's history—and that all was just as Gar had claimed.

"I don't believe you," she said with more conviction than she felt.

"It's still true."

"And this is what you came to tell me?"

He was silent for so long that she finally raised her head to meet his gaze, only to have him look away.

"No," he said softly. "I also came because I want you."

His words came out reluctantly, and their impact was all the more devastating for that. The very air between them seemed to shimmer with heat as he turned back to her. Shera drew in a breath, then held it, as though to hold on to the moment. To hear this man admit that he, too, was in the grip of something beyond his understanding both frightened and tantalized her.

"I want you, too, Gar, but—"

She never had the chance to say that it was dangerous—and wrong—because he swept her up into his arms and carried her into the half-finished castle. He lowered her to the ground in a spot where soft grasses had sprung up amid the clutter of the bailey. The chezah followed them, watched for a moment as Gar began to tear at her clothes, then flicked its tail and wandered off.

The wildness swept through her body, consuming her. She tugged ineffectually at his clothes until he shed them himself; then he fell upon her, his hands and mouth claiming her, demanding a response.

She let her own hands, explore the texture of him: taut muscles, rasping hairs, and unexpected softness. She breathed in his

101

scent and tasted his flesh as she rained kisses over his neck and shoulders and chest. And when he shuddered with pleasure, she murmured with satisfaction. The murmur changed to a cry as he slid down her body and parted her legs to bestow that most intimate of kisses.

"Please!" she cried out when she could take no more. He had built her to a crescendo of desire, and though her mind wanted to grasp the moment and hold it, her body demanded the ultimate satisfaction.

Gar was quick to comply, lifting and thrusting into her. She could feel her eyes reflect back to him the raw, primitive need that had taken her over.

Shera saw the triumph glitter in his golden irises as she slipped over the edge, then felt the heat of his own release filling her. She clung to him, trying desperately to hold the moment as the tremors rippled through them both. Spent, they both collapsed.

Their ragged breathing punctuated the silence between them, and as reason returned, they avoided each other's eyes. Shera told herself that what had happened between them could not be wrong, but she still felt the uncomfortable sting of shame.

Gar got to his feet and began to dress. She saw that his fingers trembled, but it gave her little satisfaction. He cast her a quick glance.

"You should clothe yourself. Someone might come."

His tone wasn't harsh, but it still felt like a slap in the face. "That didn't concern you a few moments ago," she stated coldly.

"No, it didn't." He sounded matter-of-fact.

She dressed hurriedly, then faced him squarely. "This will not happen again, Gar."

"Yes, it will. We want each other."

Is that all this is? she screamed silently, her eyes searching his face for some sign of affection, some hint of tenderness. He turned away, seeming to scan the valley below them.

"Do not seek the impossible, Shera," he said without turning. "Be glad for what we have."

She was stunned, not only by his words, but also by what she thought she heard beneath them. Did he regret that there couldn't be more?

"I don't understand you, Gar."

"No, you don't." He swiveled his head sharply to the left, and a moment later the chezah reappeared.

"Someone is coming. I must leave. Meet me here again when the moon is full."

"No!" she said it defiantly, but he merely turned back to stare at her for a moment, then loped off into the forest, trailed by the great cat.

Shera clenched her fists helplessly, angry and hurt in equal measure. How dared he assume that she would be at his beck and call? She vowed that she wouldn't come back, but the oath rang falsely in her mind. Already she wanted him again.

She walked around the wall and saw a group of people approaching, just now emerging from the forest that cleared about a hundred yards from the castle walls. She frowned. How had Gar known they were coming? He couldn't possibly have seen them from behind the ten-foot wall.

A chill raced through her as she remembered that he'd made his announcement when the chezah reappeared—almost as though the creature had somehow warned him. But she had seen nothing in its behavior that could have signaled the approach of strangers.

He knows them well, she thought. *There must be something I missed.* But at the very least, it seemed to her to be further proof that the Walkens did indeed control the great cats.

She cast a glance back at the corner of the wall where Gar had re-covered the skeletons. She wanted to demand an explanation from the priests, but how could she explain her knowledge without betraying Gar's presence?

The group had reached her by now, and she stayed for a time, talking to them. It was becoming clear to her that her people were obsessed with completing the great castle, though no one as yet knew how it could be done. Great physical strength was not present among them. Even their labors to rebuild the village had not produced the kind of strength it would take to lift the blocks of stone into place, and Shera was glad about that. She could not imagine living in such a place.

She left the others there and returned to the village, lost in thought about the other information Gar had given her: that the priests and Daren had been back to the cavern. She didn't want to believe it, but she could no longer convince herself that everything he told her was a lie.

Nor could she convince herself that she didn't want to see him again. Even now—despite the lies, the deaths, and his prophecies of doom—she ached for his touch, yearned to have him fill her again and make her whole.

Chapter Six

Shera froze as a twig suddenly snapped beneath her foot. The sound was, to her ears, as loud as the report of a rifle. Her heart thudded noisily in her chest, and even that seemed loud enough to draw their attention to her.

But none of them turned; none hesitated. She continued to hear the low murmur of their conversation as they moved through the woods ahead of her.

She relaxed, realizing that the roar of the waterfall had likely masked the sound of the twig. There was no place in the valley where the waterfall's sound couldn't be heard, and she'd grown so accustomed to the din that most of the time she forgot about it. But they were close to it now, though the falls were out of sight around a hill—it would have been invisible anyway in the dark of this night, for the clouds were covering the moon.

She began to follow again, wishing that she could hear the conversation. She was very certain that the group was headed toward the cavern. Their path was taking them around a hill to one side of the lake and the waterfall. Gar had been right.

Until he had told her that the priests and Daren were going to the cavern by a secret back route, she had kept herself apprised of the priests' activities only during the day. She had paid no attention at all to Daren's whereabouts.

But after her meeting with Gar, she had begun to watch them at night as well. Most of the village went to bed, or at least retired to their homes after the evening ceremonies, so it was easy for the priests and Daren to slip away unnoticed—except, of course, by her.

She continued not to attend the ceremonies, even though she knew that people were talking among themselves about her lack of devotion. Although they'd done that before, there was more talk now because of her new position in the community.

Fortunately, though, people were also accustomed to her preferring her own company; no one ever came to the small cottage at the edge of the village that she'd chosen for herself. To work unnoticed would be easy. She had only to light a lamp, and anyone looking in that direction would assume that she was home.

Twice before tonight, she thought she'd seen the priests and Daren moving off into the woods, but both times she'd lost track of them before they had gone very far. She'd tried to find a path herself during the day, when she could manage to get away from her responsibilities, but as she discovered this evening, there was no true path. They were simply making their way through the woods.

She peered up at the heavens, wishing that the clouds would disperse. There was some light, but so little that she had to stay very close to them in order not to lose them. Tonight, she told herself, she was determined to find the secret entrance to the cavern—if only to confirm that they were indeed going there.

Suddenly they disappeared from her view, and as she hurried after them, she saw that they'd gone down a short, steep hill. She saw them clearly for a moment; then they vanished again, into the dark shadows at the base of the mountain.

Concealing herself behind a thick clump of bushes, Shera watched the spot where they'd vanished. When several minutes had passed with no sight of them, she followed their path down the hill.

The opening was nearly invisible, and probably would be so even in daylight. To reach it she had to wend her way past several huge boulders, then down a short, steep slope to the low opening. She crawled through on her hands and knees, then paused to listen.

Back here, with rock between her and the waterfall, its sound was muted. She could hear the priests' voices somewhere up ahead. She crept all the way through the tight opening, hoping that the cave would amplify their sounds and let her hear what they were saying.

She discovered that only a few yards inside the opening, the ceiling rose to a height of perhaps ten feet—and here, as in the other cavern, a pale, diffuse light illuminated the passageway. She stood up, straining to hear voices that were growing steadily less distinct.

Suddenly they were gone completely; they had likely turned down another passageway. Now the only sounds she could hear were the faint rumble of the waterfall and the steady gurgle of water as it trickled down the cave's stone walls.

Shera wanted very much to follow, but she didn't want to risk another encounter with the terrifying unseen spirits that Gar called the Dark Ones. It might be possible to conceal herself from Daren and the priests, but surely the Dark Ones would be aware of her being there.

Finally she decided to risk going partway, hoping that she could stay away from the evil presence while still being able to hear Daren and the priests. She hurried along the narrow, twisted passageway, her heart thudding noisily in her chest.

There was no doubt in her mind now that something was very wrong. The very fact that Daren and the priests were coming here in secrecy told her that much. But wasn't it possible that they were only trying to find some way to placate whatever thing lived in this mountain?

Shera had never much liked the cold, arrogant priests, and

she hadn't ever liked Daren either—though she had to admit that he'd been quite pleasant to her lately, and they were sharing their responsibilities comfortably—but she simply could not imagine either the priests or Daren worshiping evil—not even an evil as seductive as the one that she'd encountered.

The passageway twisted sharply to the left and Shera paused, checking to be certain there wasn't an intersecting corridor. But the stone walls were seamless, so she continued on, and a few moments later she heard a faint, familiar sound.

It was the priests—and presumably Daren as well—chanting the prayer with which they began evening ceremonies: the same prayer they'd spoken back in the village only a short time ago. The words were ancient, and so deeply ingrained in every Bacleev as a child that Shera, at least, paid them scant attention.

The prayer thanked the gods for protecting their children, the Bacleev, and begged for their continued blessing. It also spoke, in eloquent and rather elliptical terms, of the good fortune the gods had bestowed upon the tribe and of the powers that had been granted to them by the gods—the power to heal and to bring rain for the crops.

As Shera listened to it now, her mind filling in the barely audible words, a chill crept over her. The familiar, distant chant became all mixed up with Gar's warning about her people and the words whispered into her mind by the spirits in the cavern. Was it possible that the power they spoke of could do more than heal and bring the rains? Were the priests really coming here to beg the Dark Ones to restore to them other, darker powers?

The prayer ended and the lone voice of the high priest began to exhort the gods. Shera could hear only a few words and syllables, but she knew that this was not a prayer she'd ever before. Some of the words she *could* hear were unfamiliar.

She had stopped, but now she found herself moving closer and closer to the source, which must be the cavern she'd visited. Up ahead, the light seemed brighter, and it flickered, throwing strange, dancing shadows on the rock walls.

The voice insinuated itself into her mind, a low whisper

humming beneath the droning voice of the high priest. It spoke her name and urged her to come forward.

And then came that touch again, as though someone were brushing her lightly with feathers, drawing them across her body in a slow, sensuous caress. With the stirrings of her desire, an image of Gar came once more unbidden into her mind—and she felt the feathering caress vanish. She thought she heard a low hiss of anger.

She turned to flee, only to freeze as she saw figures blocking her path. It was Gar and his chezah—but a different, much larger chezah than the one she'd seen with him. Shera knew almost instantly that what she saw wasn't real. The vision shimmered slightly, blurring at its edges.

Suddenly it began to change. Before her astonished eyes, the man and the animal merged into one being: a chezah with Gar's face. And then it faded and was gone.

Shera ran, and for one brief instant, as she passed the spot where the strange vision had been, she thought she smelled Gar's distinctive scent. But she didn't stop until she reached the opening to the cave, and there she paused only long enough to drop to her hands and knees and crawl through the opening.

Safely out in the woods, she decided to wait for the priests and Daren to exit the cavern. This time perhaps she could move close enough to overhear their conversation. So she sank down against the thick trunk of a huge pine tree and waited for her heart rate and her breathing to return to normal.

She shuddered at the memory of that seductive touch and that low, compelling voice. But it was the image of Gar and the chezah that tormented her most. What did it mean—or was she wasting her time seeking any meaning? Perhaps her subconscious had deliberately conjured up a memory of Gar to free her from that evil presence, and the last time she'd seen him, a chezah was with him.

But it was the merging of the two that disturbed her most. It gave rise to a wholly irrational fear, something so deep and cold that she couldn't begin to understand it.

* * *

It was at least an hour before her quarry appeared, and then they came terrifyingly close to discovering her presence. She hadn't been watching the entrance, assuming that she'd hear their voices. But suddenly they were there, passing within a few feet of her hiding place.

Shera held her breath. The clouds that had earlier covered the moon had now dwindled away to a thin veil that only barely diminished its glow. If any of them had happened to look in her direction, they would probably have seen her, despite the screen of bushes. But none of them did, and so, after a moment, she began to follow, curious about their silence.

They were not far from the village when she heard Daren break the silence, though she couldn't make out his words. Now that they were out from behind the mountain and passing along the edges of the lake, the noise from the falls was once again stifling.

Shera had been maintaining a careful distance, but now she hurried to get closer to them. She heard the high, nasal voice of the high priest, apparently responding to something Daren had said.

"There's no need to worry about the Walkens. They will do as they are told."

"But they . . ." It was Daren's voice, but the rest of his protest was lost as the group disappeared over the top of a small rise.

Shana ran now, not caring if twigs snapped beneath her feet. The waterfall would mask the sound.

" . . . a difficult lesson. It is only a question of keeping greater control over them. After all, they want what we alone can give them." It was the high priest's voice.

"Shera—" Daren's voice began, only to be cut off abruptly as the group reached the side of the lake directly opposite the waterfall, and their voices were lost in the roar.

Shera stopped at the tree line. She could not risk crossing the open space near the lake. If any of them turned, they would see her. By the time she caught up with them again, they were

110

entering the village, where they went their separate ways with no further talk.

She hurried back to her own cottage, confused and frightened. The final words of the high priest rang menacingly in her ears: *They want what we alone can give them.* She remembered Gar saying much the same thing, when he'd described his people as having been enslaved in a different way.

For the first time in her life, Shera felt the terrible weight of loneliness. There was no one to turn to for advice, no one to comfort her. She had set herself apart from the others long ago, and now she was paying the price. Only Marcus had been her friend, patiently enduring her rebuffs and her silences—and he was gone.

Gar was not a friend. Their intimacy did not extend beyond a joining of bodies. He would listen to her, as he had before—but he would reveal little or nothing. And as for comforting her . . . She shook her head sadly. Either he wouldn't understand her need or he would be incapable of providing for it. Gar was nothing more than a splendid savage whose mind she could understand no better than she could fathom the mind of a chezah.

Fighting the solitude that engulfed her like a cloak, Shera tried to decide what to do.

Gar looked into the eyes of the men around him and saw fear, mixed with a carefully veiled hatred. But he'd expected that. He really hadn't hoped to persuade them to take up arms against the Bacleev. Instead he'd come only to warn them—and to reestablish contact after so many years.

Communication with them was difficult. The Bacleev had forced everyone to learn their language, and had even forbidden the teaching of any other. But a century had passed, and now these people spoke a mixture of the Bacleev tongue and their own ancient language.

Furthermore, the situation was made even worse by Gar's disdain for these people. They were weak and passive, making

111

them easy prey for the Bacleev. He forced himself to conceal his distaste.

"Are ye sayin', then, that ye won't hep 'em this time?" one old man asked, speaking slowly as he struggled to form the correct words.

It was the question Gar least wanted to hear. "I will try to prevent my people from joining them."

"Ye will eventually join them, though," the man said, nodding his grizzled head.

Gar said nothing. His struggle with his people was not for their ears. "There is a woman," he said finally. "One of their shegwas, who may prevent it from happening. She is resisting."

The men looked at him with undisguised disbelief—and he couldn't blame them for that. He stayed for a while longer, sharing food with them—even drinking a small amount of the strong spirits they made, though he disliked anything that affected the mind, as did all his people. It brought back too many unpleasant reminders.

Finally he left, riding his borrowed horse back to the first village he'd visited, and returning it to its owner with thanks and some money. Then he set off on foot for the mountains. No sooner had he entered the low hills at the edge of his ancestral lands than three chezahs appeared and trailed along after him.

Gar had made this journey alone, deciding that one Walken would be less threatening than a small band. It had been a risky move, but apparently the people's old fear of his people outweighed their hatred.

Night fell and he pressed on under a full moon. He wondered if Shera had gone to the fortress to meet him, and if she had, what she had thought when he wasn't there.

It was possible that she hadn't shown up, or even that she'd brought along others to ambush him. Despite what he'd told the people he'd visited, he didn't really believe that she would be able to hold out against the Dark Ones. The desire to serve them was in her blood, as the hunger for tas-syana was in his people's blood.

He stared up at the sky, imagining her in the half-completed moonlit fortress. His fingers itched to trace the soft curves of her delicate body. He ran his tongue over his lips and could almost taste her as she writhed in pleasure beneath him.

Mostly, when he thought about her, it was these images that came to him. But occasionally, as now, there were other images: the wounded, vulnerable look in her eyes he'd seen, the way she'd slept that last night in his bed, curved against him, murmuring his name.

Gar willed away all those images as he began to climb hand over hand up the nearly vertical face of a mountain. He took carnal pleasure from Shera, and she found pleasure with him. There was nothing more—and never would be.

"Shera, it is time for you to face up to your responsibilities."

"And in what way have I *not* been responsible, Daren?"

"It's time for us to marry. We have put it off too long, and you know that as well as I do."

"I have no intention of wedding you, Daren. I never did. I never asked to be shegwa; I was *told*."

"You were *chosen*, not told."

She tilted her head and arched a brow. "Have you ever wondered why the gods would have chosen one like me—someone who is less devoted to their worship than just about anyone else among our people?"

"Yes." His gaze slid away from hers.

"And?"

"I don't know. The gods have not seen fit to explain themselves."

"But you *do* believe that they had a reason to make me their choice?"

"Of course. They always have a reason."

"Well, then, it seems to me that they must also have a reason for my refusal to marry you. We are taught that the gods know always what is in our hearts, and if that is so, then they surely knew that I won't marry you—or anyone else, for that matter."

"Your desire to remain unwed is *unnatural*, Shera!"

She shrugged.

He reached out to grasp her arm painfully. "You *will* marry me, Shera."

She pivoted and struck out with her leg, catching him on the back of his knee. With a cry of surprise, he let her go and fell hard. She stood over him, her hands fisted against her waist. "Don't ever touch me again, Daren!"

She turned and walked away, not even trying to restrain her smile of satisfaction. Suddenly she was glad she was so different. If she hadn't been different, she wouldn't have spent as much time with the Trellans—or learned to defend herself.

She'd learned from a young Trellan woman whose mother Shera had treated. The girl worked as a barmaid, and when Shera had asked her if that wasn't very dangerous work for a woman, she had shown Shera several tricks for self-defense.

Shera's pleasure was short-lived. It was obvious that Daren's careful, polite treatment of her had come to an end. She was sure that she would soon be subjected to a lecture by the high priest. Despite feeling a certain desire to give the pompous cleric the same treatment she'd given Daren, not even Shera would consider such a thing.

It had been a week since she'd first followed Daren and the priests to the cavern. They had gone each night since then, but she'd given up following them. She would not risk being caught, and she doubted that she would learn anything in any event.

Instead she had spent the week discreetly questioning people, trying to determine whether anyone else might be privy to what was taking place in the cavern. As far as she had learned, no one else had gone there, but she couldn't be sure.

There was, as she'd expected, a great deal of curiosity about the waterfall and what lay within the mountain. The fact that the priests had forbidden people to go there was sufficient to arouse their interest—but it appeared that no one was willing to disobey the priests. And if any of the particularly devout knew anything, they concealed it very well.

But what would her people do if the priests attempted to draw them into some evil scheme? That was the real question, and Shera feared that she knew the answer. They would obey the priests even over their own consciences. Taught from birth by the priesthood that it wasn't always possible to divine the reasoning behind the gods' instructions, they would simply assume that their evil actions masked a greater good.

Then, too, there was the dissatisfaction she saw among them. Their life here was a far cry from the life they'd had in the land of the Trellans, and nearly all of them longed for luxuries, for an end to the menial chores they were now forced to perform. She couldn't blame them for that. There were times when she, too, regretted leaving behind her comfortable life. But the difference for her was that as she had moved among the Trellan poor on her healing missions, she'd learned that one could be content—even happy—without such luxuries.

She wandered through the village and on to the lake, where a number of people had gathered to while away an unusually hot fall afternoon. Children were splashing about in the shallows, watched over by mothers in heavy cotton chemises and fathers in knee-length shorts that functioned as bathing suits. Even the heavy chemises seemed a wild departure for her people, who were normally so strict about prohibiting displays of nudity. But her people were changing. From what she'd heard, some of the younger couples had come down to the lake at night to frolic without their bathing suits.

She sighed, recalling the pool in Gar's village and that glorious morning of nakedness she'd spent there with him. Tonight the moon would be full, and he would be expecting her to meet him at the castle.

Shera knew she would go, however much she tried to tell herself to the contrary. When night fell and the moon rose, she would be drawn to the castle—to him—like a moth to a flame. Her body would overrule her brain, as it always did for him.

The question wasn't so much whether she would go, but what she would tell him. How she wished she could trust him! But even if so much of what he'd told her had proven to be true, there were still things she knew he wasn't telling her.

He is very like me, she thought, surprised to be realizing that

115

only now. *He keeps his own counsel, follows his own dictates, and cares little what is thought of him.*

But she *had* been open and honest with him, even if her initial candor had come about only because she'd been too exhausted to consider the wisdom of it. Perhaps it was time to remind him of that—and demand that he reciprocate.

By this time, a clear path had been worn through the meadow and the woods between the village and the hilltop castle. Shera had not been back since her meeting there with Gar, but everyone else made regular trips to the spot, and there was much talk about how wonderful it would be to complete work on it one day.

Secretly Shera hoped that day would never come, because as shegwa she would be expected to live there, together with the priests and Daren. Not only did she not want to live in close proximity to them, but she could not imagine living in a place where the walls held such a gory secret.

She had waited an hour after the evening ceremonies, which she had begun to attend. Though she didn't believe that the priests would begin exhorting the people to do evil without first trying to convince her, at this point her distrust of them was so great that she had decided to keep a close eye on them.

Now she was walking through the moonswept meadow, pausing every few minutes to turn and check that no one was following her. She had done nothing to arouse any suspicion, but her own clandestine activities had made her wary.

She was determined that this night, she and Gar would do nothing more than talk, but as she made her way up the hill, she felt those all too familiar stirrings. Why, she wondered, did he have such a hold on her? Hadn't she always wanted tenderness from her lover? True, she had never seen it among her own people, but she had observed it often among the Trellans. How could there be such a difference between what her body demanded and what her heart wanted?

She would never talk to Gar about it, of course. Not only would he not understand, but she herself found it difficult to speak such words, raised as she had been in a culture that frowned on talk of feelings.

She reached the outer walls of the castle, glanced one more time behind her, then called out to him. There was no answer, except for the soft sighing of the breeze.

She waited for hours, wandering around the hilltop, expecting to see him appear at any moment. Then, when it became clear that he would not be coming, she grew angry. But the anger was followed quickly by fear. What if something had happened to him?

Gar seemed so strong, so totally sure of himself, that it was impossible for her to imagine anything that could have happened to him, but the longer she thought about it, the more she feared that Daren and the priests had somehow gotten hold of him. How and why they would do such a thing she couldn't begin to imagine, but that didn't stop her from worrying.

She continued her lonely pacing, thinking about the broken skeletons, invisible within the walls, and about unseen forces in the darkness that might even now be working to turn her people into evildoers.

The strength of her fear for Gar made her acknowledge for the first time how much he had come to mean to her. It was, she thought, a sad irony that a man she couldn't trust had somehow come to mean more to her than any other. Neither did she like the fact that she needed him so badly, and not just for the pleasure he gave her, but because he was the only one with whom she felt she could be honest—even if he didn't reciprocate.

She waited until the moon was close to setting, then trudged tiredly back down the hill and through the meadow, wondering if she should risk going back to his village. She could not.

Shera returned to the castle the next three nights, hoping that something had merely delayed him and he would show up. She was sure that it hadn't been coincidence that he'd appeared that other time, that he surely had some way of spying on her and her people. But she saw no sign of him, and began to consider once again making the long journey up to his village. It would be very risky; she would have to wait until dark and then wouldn't be able to return before dawn, which meant that she might be seen. And the journey would be made even longer because she would have to avoid the area around the lake, since there were likely to be night swimmers there.

When she returned from the castle the third night, it was well after midnight. As she approached her cottage, a form detached itself from the shadows near her door and moved toward her. Gar's name was on her lips because he was in her mind, and relief flooded through her—only to be stopped abruptly when she saw that it was Daren.

"Where have you been?" he demanded.

"Why should that be any concern of yours?" she asked coldly.

"We need to talk to you," he replied in a somewhat softer tone. She'd noticed that every time she asserted herself, he backed down, and she wondered why.

"*Who* wants to talk to me, Daren?"

"The priests and I."

"What about?"

"It is time that you understand some things, Shera."

"Such as?" She looked him in the eye. "I already said that I won't marry you. There's no need to discuss that any further."

"It isn't about that, though it's related."

"Well, if you want me to renounce my position so that you can marry someone else and make her shegwa, that's fine with me."

"That isn't it."

"Then what is it, Daren? Can you not speak for yourself?"

Even in the darkness, she could see the anger in his face and feel a barely controlled violence within him. She was a little overwhelmed by the force of his anger, and surprised by it.

"You should never have gone into that cavern alone, Shera—or listened to that savage's tales. You don't understand what is there."

"Oh?" She felt her heart begin to race wildly. *So this is it,* she thought. *The sneaking around has come to an end.* "And what do *you* know of that cavern?"

"The gods are there. They have been waiting there for our return. Now they would speak to us—and restore all our gifts."

"What is in that cavern is evil, Daren—and you have obviously allowed it to seduce you. I will have no part of it—and if you try to involve our people, I'll tell them what is *really* there."

"No one will believe you, Shera. Why should they, when you have never been like us? They will believe the priests."

She knew he was right. But then she thought about the skeletons in the walls. "I can prove that the story Gar told me is true, Daren."

"How can you do that?" he scoffed, but he seemed nervous at her reply.

"I will do it if it becomes necessary. Good night, Daren."

She turned away and walked into her cottage, shutting the door and then bolting it quickly.

"Tomorrow, Shera," he called. "Tomorrow you must talk to the priests. And if you disobey them, you will be shunned!"

She bit off the sharp retort that sprang to her lips. What would banishment mean to one who was already an outsider? Instead, she listened with her ear pressed to the door until she heard his footsteps fade away.

Shera spent the next day trying to avoid the priests and worrying about Gar. Should she go to his village? The risk was great. Daren might even have her followed. His questioning her whereabouts last night seemed to indicate that he might already be suspicious.

But as worried as she was about Gar, she was even more concerned about what was happening to her people. It was obvious from Daren's words last night that the priests were about to draw the Bacleev into that evil in the cavern. And Daren was right: no matter what she said—even if she showed them the skeletons—they would believe the priests and not her.

She avoided the situation by setting out early in the morning to explore the valley. Most of her people were still busy finishing new homes for themselves, so few had ventured out into the rest of the long, narrow valley after the initial foray by soldiers had established that it was uninhabited. The tiny cottage Shera had chosen for herself had required little work beyond rethatching the roof, which had been done for her by several of her cousins, and a thorough cleaning, which she had accomplished herself.

It was just past dawn when she passed through the old orchards, where late peaches and early apples were ripening. Beyond that was a large grove of walnut trees. The waterfall and the village sat near one end of the valley, and at the far end, sheer cliffs rose hundreds of feet into the air. The swift-running stream that led from the lake bisected the land, flowing through the valley's thick forests and large meadows.

What a beautiful place this is, Shera thought as she stood at the edge of a forested hill and gazed down at a field where mist hung over the tall grasses. After a lifetime spent on the arid plains of Trella, the valley seemed lush and welcoming. And yet she feared it held darkness at its very heart.

She continued to roam, paying scant attention to where she was going because it was impossible to get truly lost. She could easily get her bearings whenever she wanted because of the steep, forbidding cliffs at one end, and the half-finished castle on the high hill near the other.

Occasionally she came across overgrown paths, but when she tried to follow them, they always vanished into a tangle of undergrowth or stands of young trees that had likely sprung up since her people left the valley.

It was well past midday when she finally reached the base of the cliffs. She'd never seen anything quite like them. The mountains they'd crossed to get here were sometimes quite steep, but none of them had been solid, sheer walls of rock like this.

She had been more or less following the course of the stream, and now she saw that it veered off into an area of huge boulders at the base of the cliffs. Curious about where it went, she spent the next hour climbing carefully over the rocks above it, only to see that it vanished into a cavern below. She considered climbing down there to see if it was possible to go into the opening, but she decided against it. The descent would be very difficult, and she now disliked caves. Her experiences had soured her to them.

Instead she turned back, this time choosing a route that would take her along one side of the valley, instead of down its middle. She was about halfway home when she came upon yet another old path, this time one that appeared to be easy to follow. Since it was headed in the direction she was going, she followed it along the base of the mountain.

After a short time, the path began to climb steeply, now ascending the mountainside instead of winding around its base. In no hurry to get home and possibly find the high priest waiting for her, she began to climb the mountain.

The path ended abruptly only a short distance up the mountain. Beyond its end lay a dense tangle of berry bushes and some young saplings. Finding it strange that it should end this way, Shera made her way laterally along the mountainside to get past the thorny bushes. And then she saw where the path had led.

Like the back entrance to the cavern behind the waterfall, the mouth of this cave was low and almost invisible behind a pile of rocks. But unlike that other cavern, this one was barred. A gate composed of thick wooden slats stretched across the opening, and a rusty hasp and padlock hung from it on one side.

Shera got down on her hands and knees and tried to peer beyond the wooden slats, but could see nothing in the darkness. She thought she heard something, though: the distant roar of a waterfall? It was impossible for her to be sure what she was hearing from inside the cavern, however, since she could hear the waterfall from the valley itself. But could this cavern be connected to that other one?

The wooden gate was badly rotted, and it took her only a few minutes to pry it apart. The old padlock held, but she managed to break through the door's middle, then edged her way cautiously into the cavern on her hands and knees.

Once inside, she discovered that the waterfall could definitely be heard inside, and that the sound was traveling through the cavern itself. But before she had much time to consider that, her attention was caught by what lay before her.

A little light entered the passageway from the outside, and it was enough for her to make out the shapes of perhaps a dozen or more huge old trunks. As in the other cavern, once she'd crawled through the entrance, she found she was able to stand upright.

The trunks were not locked, but the hinges were old and rusted, so she tugged and pushed until she managed to get one of them open. She gasped at the dimly lit contents.

Inside was jewelry, finely wrought ewers, plates of gold and silver, and gold coins in rotting leather bags. She began to open more of the trunks and found that they all contained the same things. Finally she picked up some of the jewelry and carried it back to the mouth of the cave in order to examine it in better light.

It was beautifully made, but unfamiliar in design, and when she brought some of the coins to the light she saw upon them writing in an unfamiliar language.

Shera frowned. There were artisans among her people, of course, but she knew that none of this could have been created by them. The designs were exotic, completely unlike anything she'd ever seen.

She returned the items to the trunks, then closed them and turned her attention instead to the cavern. It was very dark at the back, but she soon discovered another opening—one that, this time, led deeper into the mountain. It also was sealed off by a heavy wooden door and padlock, and both of them were in far better shape than the outer door.

Then, as she was making her way along the wall back to the entrance, she came upon skeletons. In the darkness, she tripped over something that she at first thought must be a rock. But when her foot struck what seemed to be sticks, she bent down to examine the debris. Her scream echoed through the cavern, finally swallowed up by the mountain as she fled back into the daylight.

Once outside, surrounded by the placid beauty of the valley,

Shera found it nearly impossible to believe what she'd just seen. But impossible or not, it was there. She was sure there were also three or four other skulls besides the one she'd tripped over.

She moved farther away from the mouth of the cave, then sank to the ground, recalling Gar's accusations about her people. He'd said that they had stolen riches from their neighbors—and now it seemed that he'd spoken the truth about that as well. Nothing she'd seen in there had come from Bacleev artisans.

On the other hand, she thought, still resisting such an awful truth, her ancestors could have bought those items, then stashed them there for safekeeping, especially if they feared an attack.

With a sob, she shook her head. That might explain the presence of the treasures—but it could not explain the skeletons. The only explanation for them that she could think of was something too awful to contemplate. The owners of those riches might have been forced to carry them in there, and were then sealed in as well. That was the only answer that could explain why the bodies would be padlocked inside.

She shuddered at the thought, unable to believe that any of her people—even Daren—could be capable of such a thing.

It was late in the day and the sun had deserted the valley by the time Shera set out again, this time grimly looking forward to a confrontation with the priests and her loathsome fiancé. She could not admit to knowing about the skeletons in the castle walls without also revealing her relationship with Gar, but now she had a proof of evil that she had found on her own.

Chapter Seven

"And everything there was stolen by our ancestors," Shera declared when she had finished her description of the cave and its contents.

"The things you saw were undoubtedly payments made to them for their services," the high priest replied with a shrug. "Perhaps they were stored there because our ancestors feared an attack."

"And what about the skeletons, Jawan?" she demanded, deliberately breaching etiquette by using his given name.

"Perhaps you were mistaken," another priest suggested. "You said it was dark in the cave."

"I wasn't mistaken. There were human skulls and bones. I think they belong to men who were forced to carry it all there, then were killed to keep its location a secret."

"Even if that is so," the high priest said, "you must remember that our people were at war—perhaps in the midst of the battle that caused them to flee the valley for their very lives."

Shera glared at him. "I believe our people were driven from

this valley because they were *evil*, Jawan! And now you seek to bring back that evil."

The high priest's eyes became cold. "We seek only to do the work of the gods—and that means restoring to our people all that is ours."

"I will find a way to stop you, Jawan!"

"If I were you, Shera, I wouldn't count on help from your savage friend," Daren said with a sneer, speaking for the first time.

Shera whirled on him, suddenly terrified that they'd somehow managed to kill Gar. "What do you mean?"

"We learned how to deal with him," Daren stated smugly.

Shera was about to ask him to explain himself when one of the other priests spoke. It was Menan, her uncle. Shera disliked him less than she did the others—but only marginally so.

"Come back to the cavern behind the waterfall with us, Shera. You were frightened when you were there before, and that is understandable. You yourself said you weren't really sure what happened."

"But I know what I felt," she insisted. A terrifying part of her wanted very much to believe him.

"Isn't it possible that you misunderstood what you felt?" her uncle persisted. "After all, you'd only just escaped drowning."

Somewhat belatedly, Shera realized that she wasn't supposed to know how they'd been going there. "It's too dangerous. We'll all drown if we try to swim through the falls."

"There is another way—around the side of the mountain," Jawan told her. "The gods themselves showed us the way."

"All right," she agreed. "I'll go." Excited, they assured her that she would be safe with them, and that if she chose not to stay, she could leave at any time.

"Meet us after evening ceremonies," the high priest said. Shera nodded, but as she did, she felt a spasm of fear tear at her insides.

Shera spent the intervening hours pacing about her small cottage, wondering if there could possibly be truth to what they'd said. If she hadn't long ago set herself apart from her people, would she give any credence at all to Gar's version of their history?

It was true that her first venture into the cavern had come on the heels of a near-death experience. And it was also true that she herself hadn't been completely certain about what had happened. It was also the case that at least part of what she'd felt in there had been similar to positive feelings she'd had during worship. Was it possible that the wrongness was within *her*—that for some reason, she simply refused to accept the presence of the gods?

But what she'd felt when the sacred fire reached out to her, when she'd been made shegwa, was different, she reminded herself. Then, she'd felt a glorious warmth unlike anything she'd ever known before or since.

Perhaps it was her. Perhaps she'd set herself so far apart from her people that she could not feel what they did. But then why had she been made shegwa?

Then there was their explanation of the treasure-filled cavern. Shera had no direct knowledge of battle but she'd listened to the tales of men who had fought in the duke's wars. She recalled one such man—a kindly, doting grandfather who had boasted of having killed more than twenty men in one battle. He'd cut off the thumbs of each, and his proud wife had fashioned the shriveled, ghastly things into a necklace.

So she knew that in war men were capable of terrible acts they would never do in times of peace—and that could explain the skeletons in the cavern. But she failed to see how it could explain those other skeletons: the ones in the castle walls. If the castle had been under construction at the time war broke out—as it must have been, since it was left unfinished—the fighting would surely have ended the work. So the skeletons must have already been in there when the laborers quit.

She sighed, knowing that she could not demand an explanation for that without revealing how she'd made the discovery. And she would protect Gar, at least until she knew his people's true role in all this.

Then she remembered Daren's cryptic remark, and she wondered if the answer would come when she accompanied him and the priests to the cavern.

By the time she left her cottage to attend the evening ceremonies, Shera had decided that even if the presence in the cavern was evil, she still needed to go there. She would fight that evil when it became necessary; in the meantime, she might learn something that could help her in that battle.

The soothing chants of the ritual were still ringing in her ears as she followed the priests and Daren through the woods. Daren was back to being very solicitous of her, helping her when she stumbled over an exposed root, telling the others to slow their pace to accommodate her own.

They were nearly to the hidden entrance when she remembered to ask a question that had occurred to her during the ceremony. "Why have you not brought the sacred bowl?" she asked the high priest, referring to the golden vessel that held the fire of the gods.

"Because it isn't necessary, child. Their presence exists without it in this place."

Shera remembered the bubbling pit at the center of the cavern, but she said nothing. She still had her doubts, though with each step she wanted more and more to believe them.

They crawled through the opening, then stood up, their eyes gradually becoming accustomed to the soft glow. Shera asked where the light came from, and the high priest replied, as expected, that the gods had provided it for the mortals who required light in order to serve them.

As they made their way along the narrow corridor, Shera remembered the gated passage in the treasure cavern and how she'd thought it might connect with this one. She hadn't mentioned that when she'd told her story. At the time, it had been nothing more than an oversight, but now she decided to keep it her secret. Perhaps she would find where it connected.

She'd expected to feel something as they approached the cavern with the bubbling pit, but she felt nothing beyond her own fears. And then they were inside, and the high priest was inquiring whether this was the place she'd visited.

"Yes," she replied, her gaze fixed on the pit. She gestured into the shadows on the far side of the huge cavern. "The way is over there, where the sound of the waterfall is loudest."

"We have already seen it—and the pool just behind the waterfall. The gods indeed blessed you, child, to have kept you safe from harm that day."

It *was* the gods—or the Dark Ones—who drew me there in the first place, Shera said silently, her gaze still on the pit as they all moved toward it, their footsteps echoing loudly in the open cavern.

No sooner had they arranged themselves around the pit and begun the ritualistic call to the gods when the dark water inside began to bubble. It boiled in a frenzied manner that made Shera gasp and step back. Daren glanced over and made as if to stop her, but then he dropped his arm.

The dark waters began to churn even more wildly, spewing both water and mist high into the air. Their chant ended and they all fell silent. Shera found herself edging forward to the pit, drawn by shadowy forms she saw there: forms that might have been human, or nearly human. Nothing like this had ever happened with the sacred fire—at least not that she was aware of.

And then she felt it again: a feathery touch, a light brushing against her skin. First her face, and then her body, registering even through her clothing. She cast sidelong glances at the others and saw that their eyes were closed and there were faint smiles on their faces.

It did feel good: warm and sensuous and soothing. Last time she'd been naked and frightened, but this time she was better prepared. So she stood as they did, her eyes closed and her mouth slightly curved in appreciation of that seductive touch.

The whispers began, but they were different this time. The voice that wasn't a voice murmured of her people's special closeness to the gods, of how they had been chosen to lead those less fortunate than themselves.

Over and over, the same message in different words. Shera

stood there, swaying slightly, shuddering with pleasure as the presence caressed her.

Soon, said the whisper. *Soon I will show you how to use the Walkens, how to turn the savages into your servants. . . . The gift they . . .*

Shera didn't hear the rest of it. Something in her mind began to resist. It had been the mention of Gar's people, and his image sprang into her mind. And once again she sensed anger as the presence withdrew.

She opened her eyes. The cavern had grown dark as the swirling mist from the pit diffused the glow. But she could see Daren and the others still swaying with their eyes closed and with those same smiles on their faces.

She backed away from them, and then, when she had reached the passageway, she turned and fled back to the world outside. Twice she looked back to see if she was being followed, but she was alone.

She sat down on a rock near the entrance and waited. Why was it that the mere thought of Gar so angered the gods—or whatever they were? She was no longer convinced that the power in there *wasn't* that of the gods—but neither was she as certain as the others that it was.

There had been none of the coldness this time, the sense of evil. Instead it had felt dark and sensuous. Even now she could feel that throbbing awareness, the pleasant ache that heretofore she'd felt only with Gar.

For a moment it crossed her mind that the force in there was competing with Gar, trying to win her away from him. But she quickly dismissed the thought as being foolish. She and Gar didn't belong to each to each other; in fact, it seemed likely that she'd never see him again. How could the gods—or whatever things were in there—see Gar as a threat?

She didn't see Daren until he had crawled through the mouth of the cavern and gotten to his feet. He came over to her and took her hand—a strange, unnatural gesture, she thought though she didn't pull away. For a brief moment, she felt a sort of connectedness to him that shocked her.

"Why did you leave?" he asked. There was no hint of disapproval in his voice.

Shera withdrew her hand, unnerved by the difference in him.

"I left because it withdrew. It left me," she replied honestly.

"It? You refer to the gods as 'it'?"

"I'm not convinced that what I felt was the gods, Daren."

"So you still believe that savage's story?" he asked, his voice closer to its usual cold quality.

She ignored the question. "What is this 'gift' we can give the Walkens?"

"I don't know—yet. The gods have not seen fit to explain. But the Walkens are not human, Shera. I know that much."

"Not human?" she echoed. "You forget that I spent time with them, Daren. Their ways may seem strange to us, but—"

"They are less than human," he insisted. "And they are dangerous. They must be controlled."

"I will have no part of any attempt to control them. Since we reached the valley, they have left us in peace."

"Because they fear the gods—and what the gods might have given us."

Shera stood up. "I'm tired of all this talk, Daren. We have found our home, and it's a beautiful place. We're safe here." But her final words rang hollow. They *weren't* safe—not as long as whatever was in that cavern whispered to them.

She left him there and started back to the village, but his statement about the Walkens followed her. She wasn't as certain as she'd sounded, although it made her angry to hear him refer to them as less than human. Gar *was* different—but he was still a man. She could certainly attest to that.

She reached her cottage in the midst of a debate with herself over the wisdom of going to see Gar. If it were only that she wanted him—which she surely did—she would have ignored that hunger. But she needed to talk to him. He alone seemed capable of telling her the truth, even if he hadn't done so yet.

When she pushed open the door, her dilemma still unresolved, a movement in the shadows near the fireplace froze her in the doorway. But the fear that welled up in her was cut off as the shadowy figure materialized.

"Gar!" She stared at him in shock, then quickly glanced back out the door, fearful that Daren might have followed her. No one was in sight, so she closed the door and spun about to face him.

"What are you doing here?" she asked. He stood there, his amber eyes glinting in the reflected light of the fire.

He ignored her question. "You were in the cavern."

She saw no reason to lie. If he'd managed to find her home, he had probably discovered for himself where she'd been. "Yes."

He studied her for a long, uncomfortable moment. "But they haven't gotten you . . . yet."

"The priests say that it is the gods who come to us in the cave," she told him.

He snorted and made a dismissive gesture. "They lie, Shera. And you must know that, or you wouldn't resist."

"I . . . don't know what I think," she said with a sigh. Then she faced him squarely, ignoring the rekindling of a desire that was uncomfortably close to what she'd felt in the cave.

"What is this 'gift' that my people can give yours? You spoke of it yourself."

He said nothing. It occurred to Shera that one of the qualities that made him so different was his uncanny ability to be absolutely still. At such times it almost seemed as though he stopped breathing.

"Daren, the other shegwa, says that the Walkens are less than human." She flung the words at him, seeking a response—anything other than that calm, implacable stare.

"I'm a man," he said finally. "You know that."

The words hung there between them in a space filled with memories and anticipation. He didn't move, but with each beat of her heart she felt his maleness reach out to her—and into her.

"Tell me about this 'gift,' Gar. If I am to help my people—and yours as well—I must know."

131

But the moment for talking had passed. Shera knew that even as she spoke. The flames of passion were licking at her reason, driving it out, replacing it with a wild, nameless hunger she could not fight.

"I want you, Shera."

A small part of her still wanted to resist that statement that was, in reality, a command; Gar was laying a claim to that which he knew was his. What came from her parted lips was a small sound of surrender. Before all reason was banished, she wondered why it was that she could resist the forces in the cave but she could not resist this man.

And then she stopped thinking, because thinking had no place in this. Followed by his eyes, her fingers moved to undo her buttons, then tear away cloth until she stood naked before him.

Instead of removing his own clothing, he closed the space between them and reached out as a blind man might, tracing the outline of her. She shuddered, remembering that touch in the cavern—but this was different. Gar's hands were hard and callused. He held a breast in each hand, teasing the hardened nipples, then moved down, across her flat belly and down still farther until she gasped with pleasure.

"I dream of you," he said in a low, husky voice. "I dream of you, hot and damp and waiting for me. I want no other woman, and I will not let *them* have you."

He slid his hands down, forcing her against him as his mouth came down on hers, hard and demanding. He abruptly let her go, then, and tore off his own clothes before carrying her to the thick, soft rug near the hearth.

Then Gar possessed her. He laid claim to her with a ferocity that stopped just short of pain, stretching the taut leash on his self-control to its limits. But she fought his restraint, wanting, needing, demanding all that he could give.

Joined by the molten heat of their passion, their bodies shuddered in unison, then became still except for the tiny aftershocks that quaked through them both. When he began to move off her, she tightened her grip on him. It was a mute plea for the tenderness they couldn't seem to find with each other.

He broke her grip easily, but remained propped above her, studying her face intently. Then, with one long finger, he gently traced the outline of her lips. She pressed a kiss into his hard palm, waiting and hoping.

"I will stay," he said, then got up and lifted her easily, carrying her to the bed.

He held her gently, his hands moving slowly over her as his lips brushed against her hair. There was an awkwardness to his movements, all the more obvious in a man who seemed so sure of himself.

She closed her eyes and smiled as she fitted herself against him. Something had changed. He'd found that tenderness within him, even if it was, as yet, very tentative.

"Gar?" she murmured sleepily, not at all certain what she wanted to say.

"Sleep, Shera," he said softly as he continued to stroke her.

Gar didn't want to leave her. In the pale light of earliest dawn, he watched her sleep and was surprised by the feelings that were inundating him: feelings he'd never known before. He started to lean over to kiss her, then backed away. He didn't want to awaken her. If he did, she might start to ask questions he didn't want to answer.

He slipped quietly out of her cottage into the fog that covered the valley. After assuring himself that no one was about, he started toward the path that led to home, ignoring the hunger for her that had awakened the moment he had.

Gar knew he shouldn't have come. With each passing day the risk became greater. It was only a matter of time—and probably not much of that—before the priests succeeded. And yet it seemed that he could not stop himself from seeing her.

His grandfather had known tales of the time of the battle that had driven the Bacleev from their valley, and when Gar himself was a child, he'd listened to stories of those long-ago times. He could still recall the wistfulness in the old man's voice as he spoke of those days: a wistfulness that seemed to be the exclusive province of those approaching the end of life.

Then, Gar hadn't understood the love-hate relationship his people had with the Bacleev, but now he thought that maybe he *did* understand it, at least a bit—especially since he'd come to know Shera.

His grandfather had said that the Bacleev were not truly evil, but had rather been weak: too weak to resist the dark spirits that whispered to them.

Shera wasn't weak, for all that she was a woman. And if the Dark Ones *did* capture her mind, as they surely would, sooner or later, he knew he could never consider her to be evil.

"We were weak, too," his grandfather had told him. "The Bacleev couldn't resist the temptations set before them by the Dark Ones—but our people could not resist what the Bacleev offered. So, little Gar, who do you think is weaker?"

It was a question Gar had never answered—and he couldn't answer it now.

He reached the edge of the woods. Before him lay a mist—shrouded meadow, and then the lake. The waterfall roared in his ears, a far more menacing presence down here than it was up in the mountains. Gar paused and peered into the mist, then crossed the broad meadow.

His path took him close to the shore of the lake, and when he reached it, he stopped again to look up. There was a brightness up there, above the layer of fog. The sun might even now be touching the top of the falls.

Just as he lowered his gaze again, he felt something. It sent shivers down his spine and pricked his skin, making every little hair stand on end.

Shera awoke to the soft gray light of early dawn. The smile that had hovered about her lips vanished in a flood of disappointment. Gar was gone.

She sat up in bed and breathed in the cool, damp air, finding in it his distinctive scent. So it hadn't been a dream. For a moment she'd doubted his visit, even though her body told her he'd been there.

She got up, wrapped herself in the bedcovers, and went to the door. Fog drifted over the valley, but at the edge of her vision she saw something moving away in the woods. So he'd just left. That must be what had awakened her.

She stood there for a few seconds, wondering if she should go after him and demand answers to her questions. Then suddenly she felt a great rush of warmth, a certainty that she *must* go after him.

So powerful was the urge that she didn't even question it. Instead she turned away from the door, flung on her clothes, and ran out into the fog.

She was nearly across the meadow when she saw him. He was standing motionless on the shore of the lake. Then, just as she was about to call out to him, he began to wade into the water. At first she thought that he merely intended to go for a swim, but she dismissed that thought quickly. He wouldn't go into the lake, and in any event, there was something wrong about his movements. As she ran toward him, calling his name, she knew with a cold certainty what was happening.

She paused only to kick off her moccasins before plunging into the frigid water. She could see him about twenty yards out, swimming in a straight line across the water—directly toward the falls.

Shera swam hard, and when she paused and raised her head as she treaded water, she could see that she'd narrowed the distance between them. He wasn't swimming hard. His strokes had that same sluggishness to them that she'd seen as he walked into the lake.

By the time she reached him, they were already in the churning waters near the falls. She screamed his name, but was engulfed in the roiling waters before she could see if he'd responded.

Shera lost all sense of time as she struggled not to drown. She pushed herself against the water currents, getting almost close enough to touch him, then being swept away again. Once, she saw his face, but it seemed that he didn't see her. There was no point wasting her breath to call out to him again. The roar of the falls would swallow her voice as it seemed to be swallowing them.

The pounding, foaming water totally engulfed her, tossing her about like a feather—and then, as before, it all ended abruptly and she was in the backwater pool of the cavern. She tossed her head back to fling her hair from her eyes and saw him climbing out of the pool.

"Gar!" she shouted, her voice echoing off the stone walls as she swam toward him.

He had started to move along the ledge, toward the back of the cavern, but at the sound of her voice he stopped, then turned slowly as she heaved herself out of the pool.

She ran over, cold and trembling, and wrapped her arms around him. He didn't resist, but neither did he reach out to her. She gripped his upper arms and shook him.

"Gar! Wake up!"

He stared at her blankly for a few seconds. Then a shudder passed through him and he suddenly gripped her so tightly that she could scarcely breathe. At the same time, he began to look around wildly.

"Gar, we're in the cavern behind the falls!" she shouted, trying to make herself heard over the roar. "They're trying to get you!"

He was now staring at the passageway that led to the deeper cavern, and she grabbed his face and turned it toward her. "No, Gar! You can't go in there!"

Gradually the light of awareness came back into his eyes and he loosened his grip on her slightly. His brows knitted together into a frown.

Shera waited for him to ask what had happened or how he'd gotten here, but he remained silent as he looked about the cavern. She belatedly realized that he wouldn't ask, because to question what had happened would betray a weakness he didn't want her to see. Gar was a prisoner of his belief in his own invulnerability.

"Can you swim back through there?" he asked, gesturing toward the falls.

"I've done it before," she reminded him.

His gaze swept over her, as though measuring her physical capacities. He nodded reluctantly. "Let's go."

They leaped into the pool and began to swim toward the wall of water. Twice before they reached it, he looked back at her and she saw the fear in his eyes, but she didn't know if he was frightened by what had happened or worried about her ability to get through the falls.

As they swam into the torrent, Gar reached out and grasped her hand, and he somehow managed to hold on to it as they were both swept into the angry waters.

It seemed this time that only moments passed before the falls released them and they were holding each other and treading water outside in the lake. Then they both swam for the far shore and stumbled out onto the grassy bank. The fog was already lifting and the sun had risen.

"You must go, Gar. People will be coming." She spoke the words reluctantly.

He merely nodded, staring down at her for a long moment. Then he ran off toward the path, where he was quickly swallowed up by a lingering patch of mist that clung to the base of the mountain.

Shera walked slowly back to her cottage, shivering in her wet clothes. Only now, when she knew he was once again safe, did she let herself think about what might have happened.

The moon was rising, bright and full, above the valley as Shera set off for the meadow near the lake. When she reached the edge of the forest, she paused, staring at the circles that were already forming. Over the years, it had become an informal tradition among her people for those who were the most devout to arrive earliest, then create the smallest inner circle, closest to the priests. In fact, first-circle was a term used regularly to describe someone who was particularly avid in his or her worship of the gods.

It was also traditional for the shegwas to be in that first circle, but Shera had continued to stay in the outermost circle, generally composed of artisans and others whose worship of the gods tended to be rather less devout.

She walked unhurriedly across the meadow, her gaze fixed on the upper heights of the waterfall that were still touched by the glow of sunset. And when she reached the outer circle that was just forming, she turned and stared at their castle on its distant hilltop.

Would Gar come tonight? She hadn't seen him since his visit to her cottage and their journey through the falls. There was no real reason for her to think he would come this night, except that he'd promised to come during the last full moon. Still he hadn't actually appeared until several days after that.

The chanting began and Shera's voice joined the others. She was apprehensive about this night. The priests had sent word earlier in the day that the evening ceremonies were to be moved to this spot. When she'd questioned Daren about it, he had merely shrugged and implied that it was a priestly whim.

Priestly whim, indeed, Shera thought. Never in her life had she known a priest to act on a whim, and Daren's casual treatment of this departure from the norm only served to further her fear that something momentous was about to happen. So, too, did the fact that it was a full moon.

Those around her had their eyes closed, but Shera kept her own eyes wide open, her gaze fixed on the base of the waterfall, which she could barely see in the gathering darkness.

The ceremony continued as she watched the churning waters; the silver-tipped waves were ghostly in the moonlight. Though she tried to pay attention, her mind began to wander. Would Gar come to her? Should she risk going up there after the ceremony? For some reason, she was certain that Daren would keep a close eye on her tonight.

Still, she knew that she would go, dangerous or not. Just thinking about Gar made her heavy with desire, and besides, she was still determined to force him to talk. For the past few weeks she'd had the strange certainty that something was about to happen—something very bad. She'd had no visions of any kind, but the feeling was there, settled into her bones with a certainty.

Visions of Gar, memories of his hard body against hers, his golden eyes intent upon her face as he moved inside her: all of this swam in her mind as she clasped the hands of her neighbors and swayed in unison with them.

Then, abruptly, something drew her out of her reverie and made her pay attention to the chants of the priests. Something was different. The words had changed. She glanced at those on either side of her, but they continued to sway, eyes closed, giving no indication that they'd noticed.

The changes in the priests' chants were subtle, and given her usual lack of attention to the rites, it was surprising that she'd even noticed the difference. But there were now words she didn't understand and had never heard before.

The rows of people between the priests and her seemed to be swaying more frantically, and now, in a sort of ripple effect, the frenzy caught even the outer circle where she stood.

She wanted to scream, "Stop!" She wanted to let go of the hands that clasped hers. But she did neither. Instead she kept her gaze fixed on the ghostly churning waters beneath the falls.

The dark coldness didn't move slowly this time. Instead it invaded her all at once, as though she'd been plunged into icy water. And then, a second later, it was gone, and she felt a not-unpleasant tingling that extended throughout her body.

At the center of the circle, the priests raised their hands in a final supplication to the gods, and Shera gasped as she saw haloes of greenish light around their hands. Then everyone else raised their hands as well, in the final act of the ceremony—and the meadow was suddenly glowing with thousands of green haloes.

Shera stared at her own hands in mute horror as the haloes brightened, then faded away. She lowered them and flexed her fingers and stared at them as though they weren't her hands at all.

The circles dissolved and people began to speak, at first in low tones and then more excitedly. She didn't have to listen to

139

individual conversations to know that they had all felt something different.

She pushed her way through the departing crowd to the group of priests, but before she reached them, she was suddenly struck by another difference she hadn't noticed. How could she have failed to notice that tonight they hadn't brought the sacred bowl? True, she couldn't have seen it on the ground from her vantage point, but why hadn't she—or apparently anyone else—noticed that the green flames, which always leaped into the sky, were missing?

"Where is it?" she demanded as soon as she reached them. "Why didn't you bring it?"

The high priest looked down his long, thin nose at her. "What are you speaking of, child?"

"The bowl. Where is it?"

"It is where it has been since we arrived here, Shera."

"Why didn't you bring it? And why did you change the ceremony?"

"This night was dedicated to the recovery of our heritage," he replied. "And that has been accomplished."

Shera felt her stomach churn as she saw the small smile that touched his lips. She had never seen this man smile before.

"What did you do, Jawan?"

"We are now all that we are intended to be," he replied with another satisfied smile. "And that includes even you, Shera." And with that he swept away, surrounded by the other priests.

Shera started after them, but her way was quickly blocked by Daren. "There is nothing you can do, Shera. We are whole again."

"Whole?" she echoed contemptuously. "Just what does that mean, Daren?"

He raised his hand, and for a moment she thought he was going to strike her. What happened instead was even more terrifying. The glow returned to his hand. Then he made a gesture, and a burst of green fire surrounded it.

"Power, Shera! Power to destroy our enemies—or to make them do our bidding!"

Shera was so horrified that she couldn't speak. Finally he seemed to tire of his demonstration, and he closed his fist. The green fire died away. The smile on his face was exactly like that of the high Priest.

"You *will* use it, Shera. And then you will see that we are right, and you will become my mate."

He turned and strode away across the meadow, leaving her standing there, still speechless.

Chapter Eight

Shera slipped out of her cottage and into the woods, circling the village. Normally most people would be asleep by this time, but tonight lamps glowed and faint voices could be heard behind every window. Two hours after the ceremony, people were still talking in excited tones about the transformation that had taken place.

She had visited the home of one of her cousins and had seen for herself the great change that had occurred. Wenda's dark eyes were glowing with pride: more than pride, she thought. Arrogance.

"Isn't it wonderful, Shera?" she's asked, laughing. "We have all our powers back again."

"But don't you care how you got them—or what they're going to be used for?" Shera had asked.

"The gods gave them to us, of course. And we can use them for whatever we wish. Everyone is talking about completing the castle. Won't that be wonderful?"

Shera had simply walked out, unable to stand any more of

her cousin's smugness, the same that she saw on the faces of others.

Now she plunged into the forest and hurried on to the castle, praying that Gar would be there and could help her make sense of this. But she knew with a cold certainty what he would say. Her people were evil, and she was only now seeing it.

Still she went, seeking sanity in the midst of what was surely imminent madness. Gar could help her understand it and fight it. He was the only one she could turn to now. And if he wasn't there, she would go to his village, dangerous or not.

She was partway up the hillside to the castle when she suddenly sensed something behind her. She spun around, fearing that Daren had followed her, but no one was there. She scanned the dark woods fearfully, already trying to think of an excuse for her trip here.

Suddenly not one but two figures emerged from the forest, moving soundlessly: two chezahs. She looked around wildly for Gar, certain he must be with them, but he was nowhere in sight. The chezahs continued to move toward her up the hill in their loose, agile way.

They were walking side by side, but when they reached her they moved apart and passed by her, then continued up the hill toward the castle. She breathed a sigh of relief, and, filled with a renewed hope that Gar would be there, followed them around the wall.

Indeed, Gar stood there, now flanked by his giant cats. He said nothing and made no move toward her. There was something in his stance that troubled her. Was it hostility?

"Gar?" she asked.

When he still said nothing, she moved closer to him. "Gar? What is it? What's wrong?"

And then, suddenly, she knew. He had seen the ceremony. The meadow and the lake were plainly visible from here. "You saw it."

He nodded. In the moonlight his eyes looked cold.

"Gar, tell me what happened. I don't understand. The priests changed the ceremony and moved it to the lake and—"

"And the Dark Ones have taken you," he said, cutting her off with a voice as frigid as his eyes.

"No! I—"

"It's too late, Shera—too late for all of us. It was already too late when you returned to the valley."

She stared at him, badly shaken by his cold, unemotional voice. Was that the sound of despair? It was so hard to guess what he might be feeling. She reached out to him, then withdrew in shock as an unearthly green glow surrounded her hand. He flinched, then took a few steps back. The glow vanished.

Tears sprang to her eyes. "Gar, help me! What has happened?"

For one brief moment, she saw in his eyes the tenderness she had wanted so much to see. But it was gone quickly.

"So they haven't told you yet about us," he said, searching her face carefully, as though seeking the truth through her confusion.

"I don't know what you're talking about," she replied, brushing away the tears. "I want you to tell me how to rid myself and my people of the evil in the cavern."

He shook his head. "I can't do that. If I could have gotten rid of it, I would have done so long ago—for *my* people's sake, not for yours."

"Why?" she asked, sensing that he was treading carefully around some terrible truth. "Gar, what is this *gift* my people can give yours?"

His gaze slid away from hers, and then he shook his head. She thought he was refusing to tell her, but it seemed that he'd been holding some discussion with himself.

"I didn't want to tell you," he said. "I . . . It doesn't matter now. You would have found out soon enough. The priests must even now be making their plans."

He swept a hand toward the mountain behind them where his village was. "Many centuries ago, when the gods chose this valley for their home, these mountains were already filled with chezahs. They live nowhere else but here.

"The gods were very fond of them, believing them to be the

noblest of creatures. When the gods withdrew from the valley, they left behind two creations: the Bacleev and the Walkens. They gave the Bacleev the power to heal and the power to bring rain, so that the valley would always be fruitful. And they gave the Walkens a gift as well: the gift of being able to communicate with the chezahs, to understand how truly noble they are.

"For centuries we lived in peace—the Bacleev in the valley and the Walkens in the mountains. But then the earth shook and the Dark Ones took up residence in the mountain. You began to worship them, and before long your people offered the Walkens a gift they couldn't refuse. The Bacleev seduced us with dark whispers, offering us a chance to truly know what it felt to be a chezah. And when we accepted that gift, they began to use us to subdue the people beyond the mountains."

"I don't understand, Gar. What *is* this gift?"

"We are no longer human, Shera. Now we are part cat."

Shera felt shards of ice prick her spine. Into her mind came the vision from her last visit to the cavern: Gar and a chezah, blending together. She swallowed hard, unable to ask the question whose answer could change everything.

He watched the play of emotions across her face in stoic silence. "We are part chezah, Shera. When the Bacleev gave us their gift, the desire to mate was overwhelming. We bred with the chezahs. Then, when we finally drove the Bacleev from the valley, we were returned to our human form. But the hunger remained—the hunger for the freedom to roam these mountains as chezahs. We call the transformation the tas-syana: shape-changing. But that doesn't quite describe it, because more than our shape changes. Our minds change, too. A part of us becomes chezah, and only a part remains human."

Shera staggered back against a wall, a hand pressed to her throat as she shook her head. "No!"

"Yes! That is what your people did to us, Shera! Even now, after a century, when there is no one alive who can remember what it was like. We are not the same. And we hunger for it. It is as though a part of each of us is sleeping and dreaming, remembering what it was like.

"The Bacleev can kill easily with their fire—or steal away men's minds. They did that many times, but they often used the Walkens because people were somehow even more frightened of us than they were of the Bacleev."

Shera felt sick. She thought of all the times when she'd seen that differentness in him, the times when she'd thought that he seemed more like an animal than like other men. Nothing he had told her about her own people affected her as powerfully as this. For all the terrible powers her people had, they were still human. But the Walkens were not. Bile rose in her throat, and she choked it back as she tried to think of what to say, what to do.

"The priests will call us soon," he went on. "Some of us will resist—but others will welcome the tas-syana. It will do no good for me to order them to resist; they cannot. The hunger is growing already."

"Kill our priests!" she cried, shocked to hear herself speak the words. "You have rifles. You could do it."

"It would do no good, Shera. Others would quickly take their places. It is the Dark Ones who need to be killed—and I can't do that. If it weren't for you, they would have killed me already."

She thought about that morning. "Why did they want to kill you?"

"Because they know I am resisting."

"But I have resisted, too—and they haven't tried to kill *me*." She started to reach out to him, then dropped her hand. "Gar, maybe they *can* be beaten! Maybe there is something we can do together."

Gar looked at her sadly, then abruptly shifted his gaze to a spot behind her. She turned to see the two chezahs.

"Someone is coming," Gar said. "I must leave." But they were standing near a corner in the outer walls, and before Gar could slip away, a lone figure appeared around a corner.

"Daren! How dare you follow me?" Acting purely on instinct, she moved quickly to put herself between the two men.

Daren barely glanced at her before turning his full attention to Gar. "So this is the reason you find the castle so fascinating, Shera. I take it that this savage is the *man* called Gar."

He gave her a smile that was filled with scorn. "Has he told you yet just how much of a beast he really is? Has he told you that he isn't even human? But perhaps you enjoy that."

"Get out of here, Daren. Leave him alone!"

His smile merely widened and he raised a hand that began to glow brightly. Shera saw Gar draw back. "No!" she shouted, and raised her own hand.

An arc of green flame had just left Daren's fingers when it was intercepted by one of her own. Night briefly turned to day as the air crackled with an unholy fire. A sharp pain traveled through Shera's arm, and Daren cried out and fell to the ground. The glow from his hand flickered and died.

Shera closed her fist, barely knowing what she was doing. The pain left a numbness in her arm, and she clutched at it as she turned from Daren to Gar. The green glow around her hand had vanished, but Gar was still staring at it.

He sees me the same way I see him, she thought suddenly. *To him, I have become evil—and to me, he has become inhuman.* The pain of the knowledge was far worse than any physical agony.

"Leave, Gar, before he recovers. I don't know if I can stop him again."

But Gar ignored her. Instead he walked over to Daren as he was struggling to get up. With one hand Gar picked the man up off the ground and held him so that his feet dangled several inches above the ground.

"Take this message back to your damned priests, shegwa," he said, shaking Daren as though he were nothing more than a rag doll. "Tell them that I will fight them. Tell them that they will not be safe from me as long as I live."

Then he threw Daren back against a wall. "And if you harm her in any way, I will hunt you down and tear you limb from limb."

Gar then turned to her and reached out to grasp her hand. He held it for one long moment, then dropped it and disappeared without another word.

Shera ignored Daren's whimpers. She stared at the space Gar had occupied, still feeling the power of his presence; then she lifted the hand he'd held: the hand that still tingled with power. Had he taken it to show her that he wasn't afraid of her?

"Help me, Shera," Daren called out, obviously in pain. "He broke some bones."

She turned to face him, but didn't move to help. "And what would you have done to him, Daren?"

"I wouldn't have killed him. I just wanted to . . . teach him a lesson."

She knew he was lying. And if he hadn't intended to kill Gar originally, there was no doubt in her mind that he did now.

"I will send someone else to heal you, Daren," she said as she turned her back on him and walked away, knowing that she was violating the rules of her profession. Healers did not make judgments; they used their talents whenever they were requested to do so.

But something in her had changed.

Shera sat, legs crossed and feet tucked under her, in a pretty wooded glade several miles from the village. A small branch of the stream that flowed from the lake gurgled and babbled nearby as it rushed over mossy rocks. Huge old hemlocks dipped their branches into the cold, clear water.

At the age of twelve, when her healing talents had been discovered, Shera had been taken in hand by an aunt, who was then the greatest healer among them. The first lesson she'd learned—a very difficult one for a twelve-year-old—was the art of self-hypnosis. It was essential, her aunt had told her, to be able to reach deeply into oneself in order to find the source of one's talent and then learn to use it to its greatest advantage.

Over the years Shera had become very adept at sending herself into a trance as a means of achieving inner peace and self-awareness. She'd even tried teaching her methods to a Trellan woman who had seemed to have some healing talents herself. But, for whatever reason, the woman had never been able to manage it.

It was difficult for Shera to explain to anyone how to accomplish it, or even to describe how the process felt. She lost all awareness of her body, except for a part she always thought of as being a warm, glowing ember somewhere deep inside her. The only time she'd come close to experiencing that feeling when she wasn't in a trance had been the time when the sacred fire had leaped into to her. She shuddered at the thought.

Deep in a trance now, she found the peace she sought and was able to examine her situation with an objectivity she couldn't have found without it. The thoughts and memories that flowed from her mind now seemed to be part of someone else's life.

It was the day her encounter with Gar and Daren at the castle. She had left the village just after dawn, stealing away in order to avoid the priests. She would have to face them sooner or later, of course—and Daren as well—but before that happened, she wanted desperately to find a small measure of peace in a life that had become nearly intolerable.

Her thoughts centered on that moment when, without any conscious intent on her part, she had summoned the fire to save Gar from Daren. With the trance having cleared away all the emotions she'd felt at that moment, she saw now what she hadn't considered before, she was obviously more powerful than Daren.

The thought caused a sort of ripple that threatened to break the trance until she firmly pushed it away. It was true. Daren had been rendered nearly unconscious by the clash of their magic fire, while she had suffered only some pain in her arm that quickly went away.

What that suggested to her was that the magical powers given to them by the Dark Ones were not equal. After pushing aside the question of from where those powers had come, she thought about that. It made sense, she realized. The powers given to them long ago by the gods were not distributed equally among them. Not everyone could heal, and among those who could, some were better than others—and no one now was as strong as she was.

The same was true of the bringers of rain. Not everyone

could do it, and among those who could, some were definitely more talented than others. Shera had a secret she had kept for many years now. As far as she knew, she was the most powerful among her people at both. She'd kept it secret because by the time she discovered that she could bring the rains, she had already become aware of how different she was from the rest of her tribe, and she hadn't wanted to admit to anything that would only make that more obvious.

She'd made the discovery one day when she was visiting a small and very poor village far from the Trellan capital. She had gone there as a healer, knowing that the people couldn't possibly make the long trek to her village, and during her stay there she had seen how the crops were withering away from lack of rain. No Bacleev was willing to make the long journey—especially to a village so poor that it couldn't afford to pay for the services.

After making her rounds, she'd looked at the dying crops, thinking that these people would starve when winter came. And before she realized what she was doing, she was raising her arms and whispering the words that begged the gods for rain. Within moments, as she stood there in shock, the dun-colored sky had begun to darken. In less than half an hour, the rains had come.

When she had made her next visit to the village, she'd found the people harvesting the greatest bounty they'd ever known. They told her that the showers had lasted three full days—though they had been gentle. It was a shock, since the best of the rain-bringers among her people could produce no more than one day's rain without once more beseeching the gods.

Now, deep in her trance, Shera wondered if there could be a connection. Her power made her laugh, given the fact that she neither worshiped the gods properly nor paid homage at all to the Dark Ones. And yet, it was hers.

Her thoughts turned to Gar, and immediately his image came to her. She saw him standing there, holding Daren as though he were no more than a child, then hurling him against the wall.

Even now she could feel the primitive rage in him, the raw power he wielded.

She saw again the moment when he'd taken her hand, and she knew that it *had* been an act of defiance: his way of telling her that he did not fear her magic. But was it part of the same act of defiance that he'd demonstrated with Daren—or was it his way of saying that he knew she would never harm him? It was an important difference, but she didn't know the answer.

Gar was half man and half chezah. Once again, the emotions that she'd held at bay threatened to disturb her trance, and this time she was barely able to contain them.

She thought about Daren's claim that he hadn't tried to kill Gar. Perhaps he'd spoken the truth. Perhaps he, too, had sensed something in Gar, some power beyond their understanding, or held a primeval fear of all things inhuman.

Shera felt that—and yet she also felt that same longing for him, for the warmth and power of his body next to hers, the hard-driving force of his lovemaking.

Gar filled her mind, the images swirling about as she thought of her times with him and thought, too, about how reluctantly he'd told her about his people's history. She knew that he wouldn't have told her at all if he hadn't known that she would soon find out.

He knew it would change things between us, she thought. And yet had it? Maybe she'd always known, deep inside, that Gar wasn't what he seemed to be. The truth had probably been there all along, but she hadn't wanted to see it.

She went still deeper into her trance, trying to forget about Gar and about the Dark Ones and about the change in her people. And then, just when that wonderful sense of peace came to her, so, too, did a vision.

She'd never had a vision in this trance state, but she knew instantly what it was. She saw the Walkens—all of them, she thought—gathered in a large cavern. At first she thought with horror that it was the cave of the Dark Ones, but then she saw that it was different. The ceiling was lower and the floor was uneven, covered with strange formations. The same strange shapes hung from the ceiling as well. They seemed almost like rocks—but as if rocks had melted and then reformed.

Gar stood in the very center of the gathering, and although she took note of his surroundings, her full attention was drawn to him. He paced back and forth in the space created for him, looking, she thought with a shock, very much like a caged beast. He gestured as he spoke, and she saw the corded muscles on his arms tense. The glitter of gold fire raged in his eyes.

But she could not hear what he was saying. Instead she heard only the roar of the waterfall. Did that mean they were in a cave near it?

She tried to focus on him, hoping to break through the invisible barrier that was preventing her from hearing him. Suddenly he stopped speaking and seemed to be staring directly at her. Shera drew in a sharp breath—and then the vision faded away.

She brought herself out of her trance. Had Gar sensed her presence? How could that be possible? What had he been doing? It was obvious that he was exhorting his people to do *something*—but what could it be? Now that her people had their magic fire, the Walkens wouldn't attack them. Would they?

Then she recalled what he'd said about some of his people wanting the tas-syana: the transformation. And suddenly she knew that he had been trying to persuade them to resist.

Shera got up and started back to the village. She didn't know how her people used their magic to allow the Walkens to turn themselves into chezahs, but she was determined to find out. Instead of avoiding the priests, she was now ready to confront them.

The priests lived in a cluster of cottages set off from the main village by a wooded copse, and Shera went directly there. In the center of the group of homes was an open space, a meadow, where the Bacleev had been gathering for the evening services until they went to the meadow near the lake. Shera stopped as she saw the sacred golden bowl, set atop a large boulder that had undoubtedly been used for that purpose when the Bacleev had lived here before. The glow of the fire was low, barely visible above the rim of the large bowl.

That's strange, she thought. She'd never seen it like that. Even when the tribe wasn't worshiping the gods, the fire still rose higher than the rim. She started to walk toward it, ignoring the proscription against anyone but the priests approaching the bowl. She stopped as she heard the high priest's peremptory tones.

"Shera, where have you been? It is necessary that we talk!"

Shera dragged her gaze from the bowl and faced the priest, who waited for her to come to him. When she did so, he looked down at her with eyes that seemed to her to be made of black ice.

"Explain yourself, Shera! How long have you been meeting with that savage?"

Shera knew that he expected her to grovel before him, but she met his piercing gaze steadily. "I've met him several times since I stayed in his village. Why is that any business of yours, Jawan?"

His eyes grew colder still. "You have never shown proper respect, Shera—and it is time you do so now. You have met secretly with that savage, and worse, you walked away from Daren when he was in great need of your healing."

"Did Daren tell you what happened?" she asked curiously, since he hadn't mentioned their sorcerous battle.

"He told me that he followed you up there. The Walken sneaked up behind him and attacked. That you refused to heal him."

That's interesting, Shera thought. She wondered what the high priest would make of the truth. "He didn't tell you the truth, then—and I wonder why."

"You're accusing Daren of *lying?*" he asked incredulously.

"Gar did not sneak up on Daren. He was standing with me when Daren arrived. Daren tried to turn the magic fire on him—and I stopped him."

"Y-you *stopped* him?" Jawan said, actually stuttering in shock.

Shera described exactly what had happened. "My arm tingled a bit, but Daren was left nearly unconscious. It seems that his power may not be as great as mine," she finished, affecting a casual shrug. "That's curious, isn't it, Jawan? And I suppose I should tell you that I have always been able to bring the rains as well as heal better than anyone else. Why do you think that is?"

Jawan took a few steps back. His mask of icy anger dissolved into the simple face of an old man who had just received a very bad shock.

"You lie!" he cried.

"If you think so, then bring Daren here and let us both tell our stories. I'm not lying, Jawan. How is it that the gods I've never worshiped and the Dark Ones I despise have given me such great powers?"

"Do not blaspheme!" he thundered, having recovered from his shock. "Do not call the gods by the name given to them by those savages!"

"They are *evil,* Jawan! We must resist."

"Go away! I have nothing else to say to you."

"But I have something more to say to you. I want to know how you plan to bring about the tas-syana."

He sneered. "So the savage has told you. Did he tell you all of it, Shera—that he is not human?"

"Yes, he told me, and it makes no difference. Answer my question, Jawan!"

"How dare you demand anything of me?"

"Tell me, priest!" Shera spoke the words softly, and she felt her mind pushing at his. It was a strange and frightening sensation, almost as if she'd reached out to move him with her hand.

That he felt something was very clear. His eyes widened in shock, and then he abruptly turned and walked away as fast as he could while still maintaining some semblance of dignity.

Shera started back to her home, still unnerved by that strange sensation. Gar had said something once about her people taking away minds. Was that what she'd been about to do: destroy the will of the high priest? Could such a terrible thing be so easy?

She was very uncomfortable with herself. What other powers might she have that she knew nothing about? She hadn't intended to harm Jawan, only to persuade him.

She still didn't have an answer to her question, and as she saw Daren's cottage ahead, it occurred to her that he was likely to know as well. She still had some reservation about using any powers she might have acquired upon the priests—but she had no such compunction where Daren was concerned. She walked up to the door and knocked.

Daren answered, holding himself like a man in pain, even though she knew he must have been given an herbal anesthetic as well as receiving the attention of a healer.

"Have you come to apologize?" he demanded coldly, though she thought she saw a flicker of fear in his eyes.

"No. I have no need for that. I came to tell you that Jawan now knows you lied to him about what happened. Why did you lie, Daren? Were you ashamed to admit that my powers are greater than yours?"

"They aren't! I just didn't expect you to . . . attack me."

"Oh?" she asked archly, moving closer to him and forcing him to step aside to let her enter. "Did you think I would stand by while you killed Gar?"

"I told you that I had no intention of killing him," he replied sullenly.

"Why not? You obviously regard him as an enemy."

"We will need the Walkens—and he is their leader."

"And just how do you intend to use them?" she asked. This conversation was right where she wanted it to be.

"They're not human, you know," he said with a sneer, watching her reaction.

She shrugged. "I already knew that. Gar told me their history. Answer my question, Daren."

"You know that he's part animal?" Daren asked, obviously hoping that Gar had lied to her.

She nodded. "I've known that for some time," she lied. "It doesn't matter. How will the tas-syana happen, Daren—and when?"

155

This time she felt the beginning of that mental push and reined it in slightly. Daren's face lost all expression. His eyes, which had been flashing with anger, grew dull.

"Tell me," she ordered softly, still nearly unable to believe that this could be happening.

He told her in a voice devoid of any emotion. The ceremony would take place at the dark of the moon—about two weeks from now. The priests would call for the assistance of the gods, and the Walkens would be changed forever, transformed into chezahs.

She released his mind and Daren staggered backward, then sank into a chair. "Leave me, Shera. I am tired. Scella will come to heal me and take away the pain."

Shera left, stunned by what she had done, but already wondering how she could use her newfound powers to prevent her people from succumbing to the seductions of the Dark Ones. There were limits to her powers, she knew. She'd unconsciously used far more on the high priest than she had on Daren, and yet the priest had been able to resist.

She spent the next few days trying discreetly to learn if others possessed the same power to influence others. Her position as shegwa allowed her an access to other people's lives that she would not have otherwise had. Among the many duties of her position was to ensure both individual welfare and the general welfare of the tribe. This could mean settling everything from disputes within families to establishing rules for all. It also often meant simply providing a sympathetic ear for complaints large and small. Although she had held herself apart from her people, Shera reasoned that most people would prefer to come to her, rather than to Daren. She had learned that he was widely regarded as being incapable of either empathy or sympathy. Besides, he was still recovering from the attack by Gar.

It seemed to her that if everyone—or even a few people—possessed the power to force their will upon others, she would soon be hearing about it. In a close-knit, isolated tribe like theirs, there were always grudges, often carried on from one generation to the next. Sooner or later it seemed certain that when someone discovered that he or she had such powers, they would soon be put to use.

But she heard of nothing. Instead she heard only more complaints about how difficult their lives were now, with no servants to assume the menial chores of daily life. It had been common practice among her people in their previous home to accept service in lieu of payment when they cured the sick or brought rain for farmer's crops. Shera herself had done so, though only when the family in question had insisted that they be allowed to repay her in this manner.

People also wanted luxuries that their present lives did not afford. Their cottages were crude, lacking the indoor plumbing they'd had in their other village. And they were unadorned by the thick rugs, fine porcelains, and other objects they'd been forced to leave behind.

More and more, people spoke of abandoning the cottages altogether and enlarging and completing the great palace on the hill. But to accomplish that, they needed workers—many workers.

One of Shera's uncles told her that it was time they found out if there were other tribes living in the hills and valleys beyond their new home. "We can use them to build our home—and to provide us with the other things we need," he said as she sat in front of his cottage one morning.

"We haven't enough gold left to pay them to build our palace and provide these other things, Uncle," she told him

"Pah! Why should we pay them? We are the favored of the gods. They *owe* us these things."

It was a sentiment she heard echoed over and over as she made her rounds of the village. Many people also told her that it was time to send out a small contingent to round up these other tribes.

She also tried her best to keep an eye on the holy men, who had avoided any contact with her since her confrontation with the high priest, Jawan. It didn't take long for her to discover that the clerics were spending a great deal of time in the cavern of the Dark Ones. No longer sneaking there at night, they were now going in daylight as well.

Then, one week after his encounter with Gar, Daren showed up one morning at her cottage, looking very much himself.

"We need to discuss sending out a party to explore the region beyond the valley," he stated as she reluctantly let him into her cottage.

She asked why, though she knew the answer.

"You already know the answer to that, Shera. I know you've been going about among the people. You've heard their complaints. It is our duty to see that our people's needs are seen to.

"The priests agree that we should complete the construction of the palace, and enlarge it so that everyone can live there. No doubt that is what our ancestors intended, but they didn't make it large enough."

"Come with me, Daren. I want to show you something."

"Come where?" he asked suspiciously.

"Up to the castle. You need to see something there."

He followed her, though with some reluctance. "Are you trying to trap me?" he demanded. "Is that savage up there again?"

"Not as far as I know. I haven't seen him since that night, and I don't think he'll come back."

"He'd do well not to," Daren muttered darkly.

Shera ignored him as she thought about Gar. She knew that guards had been posted in the castle around the clock since the attack on Daren. Gar wouldn't go there again, but she'd been hoping that he would come to her cottage, as he'd done once before. True, there were guards stationed around the village, but that hadn't stopped him then.

Still, she thought, those guards now have magical powers they didn't have before, and Gar wouldn't take such a risk just to see me—especially if he now has doubts about me.

She would have to go to his village—and soon. He needed to be warned about the ceremony scheduled for the dark of the moon—now less than a week away.

She slanted a glance at the angry, silent man beside her. She couldn't really prove it, but she believed that he'd assigned a small group of men to watch her—others much like him who were fanatic in their devotion to the gods and the priests. They seemed to be too much in evidence wherever she went, and several times she'd looked out at night and thought she'd seen someone lurking in the shadows.

"The priests say that it is past time we marry, Shera," Daren said, breaking a long silence as they emerged from the woods and started up the hillside to the castle. "And the people are demanding it as well."

"We've been through this before," she replied coldly. "I will not marry you, Daren!"

"It's him, isn't it?" he demanded angrily. "You've lain with that savage. I saw the way he looked at you, and I heard his threat to kill me if I harmed you. He regards you as his!"

That, Shera thought uneasily, wasn't so far from the truth. Gar didn't love her, but he undoubtedly did believe that she belonged to him.

"I belong to no one, Daren—and I never will!"

"We could just have the ceremony. I wouldn't force myself upon you—unlike that . . . creature."

"He never forced himself upon me, Daren." She gave him a sidelong glance, wondering why he was suddenly so eager for them to be married when he hadn't raised the issue for some time. He certainly didn't want *her*. Daren wanted nothing except to please the gods. Neither could he believe that by marrying her, he could change or control her.

"It seems to me," she said, "that the gods wouldn't look favorably upon a fake ceremony."

"It wouldn't be fake," he insisted. "We are already joined as shegwas, and marriage is more than a union of bodies."

They had reached the top of the hill, and now she faced him, searching his face for some hint of the truth behind his insistence that they be wed. What she saw in his eyes certainly wasn't love—or anything even close to that. In fact, she was quite sure that she disgusted him as much as he did her. His next words proved it.

Saranne Dawson

"I have no desire to take you to my bed, Shera—certainly not after you've dirtied yourself with that beast."

Ah, she thought, so *that* is it. She was now unclean in his eyes. She would have liked to laugh it off, but her own thoughts on that particular subject were confused at best.

"In that case, I will consider it," she told him. Perhaps it wouldn't be such a bad idea. It was true that her people expected them to marry, and her continued refusal could weaken her position with them at a time when she badly needed their respect—especially if she was to counter the nefarious schemes of Daren and the priests.

She led him through the maze of walls and piles of cut stone to the corner where Gar had shown her the skeletons. "What I want to show you is in there," she said, pointing.

"I see nothing."

"That's because they're in the walls. Gar showed me. We will have to remove some stones."

He looked at her askance. "I can't lift them."

"Surely we can do it together," she said, then turned as she heard footsteps. "And they can help us."

Two guards had come around the corner. Shera motioned them over and told them to remove some of the blocks. When they glanced uncertainly at Daren, he nodded perfunctorily. Shera did not miss this indication of his power. Both were men she knew to be sympathetic to his views, just like the ones she suspected were following her.

It took them much longer than it had Gar, but they finally removed enough of the stones that they could see what lay within. Both men backed off quickly.

"What is it?" Daren asked, moving up to have a look himself.

Shera waited as he peered into the space between the inner and outer walls. Unfortunately she didn't see his initial reaction. By the time he turned back to her, his mask of indifference was firmly in place. Or maybe it wasn't a mask. Maybe he truly didn't care about the grisly discovery.

"Gar says that those are skeletons of men who died here, that

160

they worked themselves to death—under the orders of our ancestors."

Daren shrugged. The guards remained impassive. "Accidents happen. No doubt men died building the duke's castle as well."

"It wasn't an accident, Daren. They were worked to death, and their families weren't even permitted to come and claim their bodies for burial."

"When they worked for our ancestors, they were working for the gods," Daren intoned piously. "Their families should have considered their entombment here to be an honor."

He turned back to the guards and ordered them to replace the stones. "No doubt some may die as well when we begin working on this again. But that is the will of the gods."

Faced with that kind of self-serving statement, Shera simply turned and walked away, wondering why she'd ever thought she might find a scrap of humanity in him. And he had the nerve to refer to Gar as a savage?

Shera was learning that savagery took many forms. Gar's people might not be fully human—but apparently neither were hers.

Chapter Nine

Shera extinguished the lamp, then sat in the dark cottage to wait. She was hoping that this would signal whoever was out there that she had gone to bed. Surely Daren and the priests weren't forcing someone to sit out there all night to keep an eye on her.

There were now only four days left before the dark of the moon and the ceremony that would transform the Walkens into chezahs. The past two nights had been cloudy, but tonight was bright with stars and the rapidly waning moon. The trip up the mountain to the Walken village would be difficult even so, but she had no choice. Gar had failed to show up at her cottage as she'd hoped, and there was no time during the past three days when she could have slipped away. She was being watched very carefully, though the spies were taking some pains to hide their interest.

It was her hope to persuade Gar to take his people away from their home, at least for the night of the ceremony. Surely if they weren't close at hand, they would be safe—assuming, of course, that they *wanted* to be safe.

She sat there thinking about Gar and wondering if he could resist the tas-syana—or if he wanted to resist. She couldn't pretend to understand the allure of being transformed into an animal—even one as magnificent as the chezah. But she was certainly seeing clear evidence of how easily her own people could be seduced by their desires.

Her need to warn Gar had taken on an even greater urgency because tomorrow a small group of men were setting out to explore the region beyond the valley, hoping to find people they could force into slavery. How this was to be done, she didn't yet know, but she suspected that the Walkens were intended to play a role. Daren and several people were already busy with plans to enlarge the unfinished castle, and Shera didn't have to see those plans to know that they would require hundreds, if not thousands of men to make their dream come true.

She got up and peered out between the curtains. Then, seeing no sign of anyone, she went to the other windows. Finally she opened the door quietly and stepped out into the warm night. She had dressed all in black and had even darkened her face with ashes from the fireplace.

At first the night seemed so dark that she despaired of even finding the path up the mountain, but as she slipped into the woods near the cottage, her eyes began to adjust and she found that she could see well enough.

Every twenty feet or so, she stopped and listened for the telltale sound of footsteps or twigs snapping. But the night was silent except for the roar of the waterfall. It was strange, she thought, how they all had come to ignore that sound.

She reached the edge of the woods, where it gave way to the broad meadow that bordered the lake. It would cost her precious time to avoid the open meadow, so, after one last glance behind her, she began to cross it.

This side of the lake was serene. No swimmers were out at this late hour. The mist that hovered above the lake in the mornings hadn't formed yet, so she could easily see the churning waters and the great falls. Then, halfway across the meadow, she saw movement along the shore. Dropping quickly into a crouch that she hoped would hide her in the tall grass, she peered at the moving shapes.

Deer. She breathed a sigh of relief and moved on. Twice she stopped to look back, and once she thought she saw movement in the grass behind her. She guessed that it was probably an animal, but still, when she reached the area where the hidden path led up the mountain, she crouched behind a rock and watched.

The moment she had come into view of the falls, Shera had been prepared to encounter the Dark Ones. She knew they had grown in power with the worship of the Bacleev. But nothing had happened, and so she was unprepared for any confrontation now that she felt safer.

The darkness slipped into her with a seductive whisper, sending tremors of desire through her. She throbbed with want, but fought that aching need as she had before: by conjuring up an image of Gar.

This time, though, the presence didn't withdraw. Instead it hovered there, waiting, taunting her with an image of Gar transforming himself into a chezah. Fascinated and repelled in equal measure, Shera saw him lose all that was human until only his amber eyes remained.

She felt her will slipping away, being subsumed into something much greater. But just when it seemed that she'd lost herself, she recognized the terrible coldness that lay at its center—and suddenly she was free again.

She sat there trembling for a moment, then got to her feet and hurried on to the hidden path, wanting to put as much distance as possible between her and the waterfall. And as she ran through the rocks and bushes, then up the path itself, she wondered why Gar's image hadn't driven it away this time.

Is it because I feel different about him now? she asked herself. *Did I love him before—but not now?* She didn't know because she had no experience of love, but she suspected that might be the case. The Dark Ones had spotted a weakness in her, then exploited it by showing her that terrifying image of Gar's shape-changing. Even now, she could not get it fully out of her mind.

She was halfway up the mountain when she decided to rest. Instead of conserving her strength for the long, arduous climb, she'd been hurrying, both to get away from the waterfall and to reach Gar. She sank down against a huge pine and rested her head on her drawn-up knees, hoping that seeing the real Gar would drive away that image.

Too late she heard the footsteps behind her. Before she could do anything more than lift her head, a heavy cloak was thrown over her and her arms were quickly pinned to her sides as she flailed about. Someone had followed her after all! Frightened by spirits, she'd failed to keep checking for human foes.

There were two of them, and they lifted her to her feet. Then, still grasping her arms, they began to propel her blindly down the path, back toward the valley. If there had been only one of them, she could probably have gotten away. Neither one of them was much stronger than she was. But she could not break two grips.

Shera was more angry than frightened. They remained silent despite her repeated orders for them to identify themselves. But she knew they would do nothing more than return her to the valley—most likely to Daren or the priests.

Her rage burned inside her—and suddenly exploded! Even afterward, she was never certain just what happened. But suddenly she had cast off the hands that were gripping her arms, then thrown aside the cloak. The two men, whom she now recognized, had both stumbled back and fallen.

They began to get to their feet. Shera raised her hand. Immediately twin arcs of green fire lit the night—and both men fell heavily without a sound, their faces briefly consumed by fire.

Shera stood there, stunned, the green flame now reduced to a glow around her hands. In her mind's eye she saw their expressions, the fear and shock on their faces as they had died. And she knew they *were* dead.

She closed her fingers into fists and the fire vanished, leaving only a faint warmth in her fingers. Then she knelt beside the two men to confirm her suspicions. She got up and staggered back, a fist pressed to her mouth to prevent a scream. She hadn't intended to kill them. She'd wanted only for them to let her go.

Unable to stare at their lifeless bodies any longer, Shera turned and fled up the trail, seeking comfort, even though she knew she wouldn't find it with Gar.

The small amount of light provided by the crescent moon was gone by the time she reached the long set of steps that led up to the village. Shera was exhausted, her mind still filled with horror at what she'd done. She hurried past the closed and darkened homes of the Walkens and stumbled up the final ladder that led to Gar's house.

Consumed by a sudden fear that he wouldn't be there, she pushed open the door. The embers of a fire glowed in the fireplace, and the air was pungent with the smell of cooked meat—an odor that Shera, like all her people, found very unpleasant. And now it also served to remind her of what Gar was.

She called his name as she stumbled across the threshold, her voice scarcely more than a hoarse whisper as she gasped for breath after the long climb.

He appeared almost immediately as she sagged against the door frame, temporarily unable to take another step. He was naked, and firelight bathed his great, muscular body in a ruddy glow. His golden hair was slightly longer than it had been and tangled from sleep. He ran a hand distractedly through it as he stared at her.

"Shera. Are you hurt?" He stepped toward her, but she could see that his movements were cautious, wary.

"No, I'm just tired from the climb," she replied, then burst into tears.

He still didn't move to her. Instead he frowned as though he'd never seen anyone cry before. It made her angry. Why couldn't he care? She'd come here to save him and his people.

Her anger grew; then she saw him stare down at her hands and begin to edge backward, and she looked down to see the green glow again. Horrified, she closed her hands and it promptly vanished.

"I didn't mean to do that," she said, choking back a sob.

"Gar, I just killed two men—and I didn't mean to do that, either. Help me!"

He took a few steps toward her and she saw his face contort with rage. "You killed two of my people?"

"No! They were my people. They followed me up here."

His expression changed to a frown of disbelief. "How could you have killed two Bacleev?" he scoffed.

"With the fire." She raised her hands briefly, then let them fall again as she told him what had happened. He didn't take his eyes off them, and she knew that he saw them not as hands, but as weapons—which they were.

"I didn't mean to do it," she finished. "I was just so angry with them and I wanted them to let me go."

She walked over and sat down in his big chair, then buried her face in her hands and sobbed. She couldn't help it. When she finally got herself under control, she looked up to find him still standing in the same spot—and still wearing an expression of disbelief.

"It couldn't have happened that way."

She gestured toward the path. "If you don't believe me, go down there and see for yourself. They're *dead*, Gar—and I killed them!"

He sat down on the hearth rug. She kept her gaze averted. This was no time for her to be thinking what she was, but at least she knew that that much hadn't changed. There was some comfort in that, she supposed.

"Why do you say that it couldn't have happened that way?"

"Because no Bacleev can use his or her powers on another member of the tribe. They only work on . . . others."

"You're wrong, Gar. This isn't the first time I've used them. You know that. I used them against Daren when he tried to attack you. I've used other powers as well," she told him, then went on to explain what she'd done to the high priest and then to Daren.

"That's why I came here—to warn you to take your people away before the ceremony."

"Are you telling me that you actually had some effect on the high priest?" he asked.

"Yes, I know I did—though not as much as I did on Daren." She couldn't understand why he seemed more interested in this than in the news she'd brought him.

"And no one else seems to have that power. Or if they do, they're keeping it a secret, and I doubt that very much."

"They have it," Gar stated flatly. "I told you that the Bacleev could rob people of their minds."

"But then why aren't they using it, Gar? If they—"

"It doesn't work that way," he stated, cutting her off. "They can use it only against outsiders—like the fire."

"The stories you heard must be wrong, Gar."

"They're *not* wrong. My people know everything there is to know about the Bacleev."

"Well, then, how do you explain it?"

"I can't."

She got up and edged past him to check the kettle hanging over the fire. It was still hot, so she lifted it from its hook and carried it over to the table, then rummaged around until she found a pot of herbs and a mug.

"I'll have some, too," he said.

She bit back a desire to tell him to get his own tea and found another mug instead, then handed it to him.

"Why is your face dirty?" he asked.

"I blackened it so it would be more difficult to see me if I was being followed. I'm followed all the time now—and there are guards at the castle, too."

"I know."

"You went down there?" she asked, sitting down again and still struggling to avoid looking at him.

"No. The chezahs told me."

She had lifted the mug to her lips, but she set it down quickly. He frowned at her.

"I told you we can communicate with them." He got up and went to the door, which was still open. She watched as he stepped out to the edge of the walkway, stood there for a moment, then returned.

"What were you doing?" she asked as he resumed his place on the rug.

"Calling them."

"How? I didn't hear anything."

"We reach out to them with our minds," he said with a shrug.

"Why are you calling them now?"

Before he could answer, two chezahs suddenly appeared in the doorway. Gar stared at them for a moment; then they turned and vanished into the night. Shera tried to suppress a shudder. Given what she herself was capable of now, she didn't understand why his ability to communicate with the chezahs should trouble her.

"I sent them to take care of the two men."

"Take care of them? But they're already dead."

"Yes, but when they're found, it will look as though they were killed by chezahs."

Shera choked back her nausea. "Why?"

"Because it would be better if no one knows you can kill."

"You really believe I have powers that no one else has?" she asked.

He nodded, staring into the fire. Suddenly she recalled the vision she'd had of him in a cavern with his people, and how he'd seemed for one moment to be aware of her presence.

She described what she'd seen. "Was it real?"

"Yes. The cavern is deep in the mountain here. I was trying to persuade my people to fight the Bacleev. And I thought I felt something for a moment. I wasn't sure what it was. It was *you*."

"Will they fight?"

"I hope so, but I don't know. We cannot prevent the tassyana, Shera. Nothing can stop that, and I knew it would happen at the dark of the moon. But that doesn't mean that we can't still fight."

"I don't understand."

He didn't answer her. Instead he got up and walked back to the bedroom. She couldn't resist looking at him, at his long, lithe body that moved with such uncommon grace, at the

169

bronzed skin that covered smooth, powerful muscles. But she also couldn't help thinking about what he was—or wasn't.

She raised her hands and stared at them. They looked so ordinary—more ordinary than he did—and yet they were deadly weapons, weapons she didn't quite control.

Neither of us is what we seem to be, she thought painfully—and neither of us can accept that.

He returned fully clothed and she wondered if he'd been aware of her discomfort with his nakedness. Certainly *he* hadn't seemed to be uncomfortable with it. Such was her state of mind that she cherished this one indication that he cared about her feelings. But then his words took away even that as he started toward the door.

"I'll be back in a few minutes. I need to get some help to move those bodies back down to the valley."

"No!" she cried, getting up quickly. "I asked you a question, Gar. I'm tired of your ignoring me. I risked a lot to come up here to warn you—and I want some answers!"

He turned to face her as she stood there, clenching her fists to prevent the fire from returning. His gaze lingered on them for a moment, and then he walked back over to the hearth. She sat down again.

"After the tas-syana, we will be chezahs in body—and partly in mind. But something of our human minds remains—or so I've been told. It's that combination that makes us so valuable to the Bacleev: animal strength and power and cunning—and human intelligence.

"What I told my people is that we must hold on to our human minds and not allow any of the chezah mind to take over. Somehow my ancestor, who was the leader of my people when they drove out the Bacleev a century ago, managed to do that.

"He hadn't been human in his lifetime. Our people had been living as chezahs for centuries—but they still retained something of their human nature. Now that we've been human for a hundred years, we should be able to do it better."

He paused and looked away from her, into the fire. "I think we've learned a lot about what it means to be human in the past century—but maybe not enough. There is much I don't understand, Shera—and it is you who makes me aware of that."

He shook his tawny head. "How strange that a Bacleev could show me such a thing."

By the time he'd finished, Shera was actually holding her breath. It was the first time he'd ever spoken this way to her— probably the first time he'd ever spoken to *anyone* this way. But she sensed that this was not the time to push him further. It was obvious that he was uncomfortable.

"How did the Bacleev use your people?" she asked.

"They used us as a very effective army. We would be sent into the villages to round up slaves and to terrorize people so they wouldn't try to fight. People were more afraid of us than they were of the Bacleev."

Yes, she thought with a shudder, they undoubtedly were. She could understand that. The Bacleev could kill with their fire, and if Gar was right, they could rob people of their will, but horrifying as that was, it paled beside the threat of a powerful beast with teeth, claws, and human intelligence.

She told him about the scouting party that was to depart the next day to find the people beyond the valley.

"I've already been there, to warn them and to tell them that we will try to help them." He paused and glanced at her. "That's where I was when I promised to meet you at the fortress."

Shera managed to restrain a smile of satisfaction. He hadn't bothered to explain his failure to show up that night until now, and she considered this to be a triumph of sorts—another attempt on his part to consider her feelings.

"You could kill the scouting party," she suggested, even though it sickened her to be thinking such a thing. But he shook his head.

"It's too dangerous now. I couldn't risk lives like that. You can be sure that whoever is sent, they wouldn't hesitate to destroy us."

"Maybe not. Daren swears that he didn't intend to kill you that night. He said he was only trying to teach you a lesson."

Gar nodded. "That's probably true. He knows I'm the leader

of my people. Perhaps the scouts might not kill anyone I sent after them—but they would still hurt them badly, and the result would be the same; they will find the villages."

"Then what can we do?"

"I don't know yet. But there *are* some differences this time. We are different from our ancestors. We have learned much. And then there is *you*. As long as you can resist the Dark Ones, there is at least a chance that history will not be repeated."

Shera thought about her encounter with the Dark Ones on her way here. She hadn't told him about it, but she did now.

"Before, they withdrew when I thought about you. I could feel their anger, but they still left me. This time it was different. Thinking about you didn't work—exactly. They withdrew only when I felt that awful coldness that no one else seems to feel."

Gar gazed at her steadily, his expression neutral. "The difference is that you now know what I am—and that has changed your . . . feelings toward me."

"Yes," she said softly. "It has."

He got up again and started toward the door. "There is nothing I can do to help you, Shera. You must fight that battle alone."

His words echoed over and over in her mind after he had vanished into the night. It wasn't what she had wanted him to say—but it was the truth. And she understood now what she should have known before: what she felt for Gar was all that was keeping her safe from the Dark Ones. If she couldn't accept what he was, she would be lost.

If only he would tell her or show her how he felt, she thought miserably. She needed desperately to know that he cared for her, too. Maybe he *had* shown that, in his own way, but it wasn't enough.

Do I love him? she asked herself. *Do I really love this man who isn't a man?*

Before she had even begun to find the answer to that question, Gar returned with another Walken, who seemed to be about Gar's age. The two looked very much alike, but there were subtle differences that made Gar, to her mind at least, more attractive.

"We should leave now," he told her without introducing his friend. "It will be daylight soon."

Reluctantly Shera got up, thankful that at least the journey back down to the valley would be easier than her climb up. It wasn't likely that they would encounter any more of Daren's spies. The two dead men wouldn't be missed yet.

Gar and his companion picked up two large folded pieces of heavy, rough cloth that they'd apparently left outside the door. Shera was about to ask what they were for, when she realized, with a sickening lurch in her stomach, that they must intend to use them to wrap her victims' bloody bodies.

They set off down the mountain, the two men adjusting their pace to match hers, though not without a certain reluctance, she noted. From time to time Gar's unnamed companion cast curious glances her way, and she noticed that more than once he looked at her hands.

"Tell me about the chezahs that are . . . just chezahs," she said, breaking the long silence. "Will they continue to follow your orders after the . . . transformation?"

"As much as they do now," Gar replied. "We can't control them, but they listen to us and generally do as we ask."

"Why didn't that mother with cubs attack me?" she asked, since he'd never given her an answer to that.

Gar shrugged. "Probably she was aware of your connection to me. They can communicate with each other. That's how we learned that the Bacleev were returning. They passed the message along among themselves until it reached us."

"A chezah wouldn't attack a Bacleev," Gar's friend said, speaking for the first time.

"This happened before they had regained their powers," Gar told him.

The man frowned. "It did? A mother with cubs?"

Shera nodded.

"Hmm," he replied, still frowning thoughtfully.

"There is another explanation," Gar said after a few moments. "It could be that she knew there was something different about you."

"What do you mean?" Shera asked.

"The chezahs are the favorite creatures of the gods, and I think they know that. The Bacleev and the Walkens were also favored, but the Bacleev strayed. Maybe the chezahs know that evil hasn't taken you. . . ."

Yet, she added, hearing that word at the end of his sentence.

"It won't happen, Gar," she said, impulsively reaching out to touch his arm. He didn't flinch, but he did look down at her hand. So did his companion.

"But I certainly couldn't be favored by the gods, either," she went on, removing her hand. "I've never worshiped them as others do."

They continued on in silence. At one point, where the path was narrower, Gar's hand brushed against hers and she seized it. Once again he looked down, but he didn't pull away. Then, after a moment, his strong fingers curled around hers. She smiled at him, and was rewarded by a gleam in his eyes that told her all she needed to know.

She thought about his cottage—about the big bed that held his distinctive scent. She wished they could have stayed there longer—long enough to find temporary oblivion with each other. She ached with desire for him, and if they were alone now . . .

Gar stopped suddenly and Shera saw the bodies on the trail ahead of them. She felt ill. Even from here she could see their torn clothes—and the blood. The chezahs had done their work.

The two men moved on, but Shera stayed where she was. She'd never liked either of the dead men, but they were still her people—and she had killed them, then allowed their bodies to be desecrated by the chezahs.

Gar and his friend spread out the pieces of cloth, then lifted the bodies onto them and rolled them inside. She forced herself to join them, wondering how much more death she would be seeing. How could they hope to stop it?

The two men hefted the shrouded bodies onto their shoulders

easily, and they set off again. Shera asked if it was safe for them to go all the way down to the valley.

"There are no guards around that area," Gar replied. "We know where they are. The chezahs keep track of them."

"I wasn't thinking of guards. If you go all the way into the valley, you will be near the waterfall."

"We'll be careful. I don't want them to be found near the path. Since they were following you, that would tell Daren and the priests that you came up to see me."

"They don't know about the path."

"But if they're found near it, the priests will probably discover it."

Shera understood and accepted his reasoning, but she still grew tenser and tenser as they reached the valley. The sky was beginning to lighten, and a thick fog hung over the valley, so thick that it even muted the sounds of the waterfall.

"We'll leave them over near the lake," Gar said. "That way, if you're questioned, you can say that you went for a swim."

Shera nodded as she tried to peer through the fog. What was she looking for? If the Dark Ones put in an appearance, they wouldn't be seen, but instead be felt—and by that time it could be too late.

They plunged into the fog. She had no sense of where they were, but Gar and his friend seemed to be moving purposefully. She'd always heard that cats and other creatures could see in the dark, and she wondered if Gar might have preternaturally good night vision as well. She recalled how easily he'd moved through the woods when he had kidnapped her.

The two men came to a stop and set down their burdens, then began to unwrap them. Shera averted her gaze; then, as a breeze shifted the fog a bit, she saw that the lake was only a few yards away. If she'd been here alone, she would have walked into it before she could see it.

She wondered what questions she would face when the bodies were discovered. Or would they be unwilling to admit that they'd set spies on her? It did seem to her that Daren and the priests were attempting to avoid any confrontation.

Could Gar possibly be right? she wondered skeptically. Could the gods be protecting her from the Dark Ones? It seemed highly unlikely to her, given her disregard of them.

She was still pondering it when suddenly she felt that dark presence in her mind. Immediately she turned toward Gar and his friend. But they were gone! All that remained were the bloodied bodies and the now blood-soaked shrouds.

"Gar!" she cried, desperately scanning the fog for any movement. Surely they hadn't just left without saying anything. She glanced back at the bodies. No, they couldn't have gone. They would have taken the shrouds with them.

A breeze sprang up again—and now she could see them for one brief moment before the fog closed in again. They were wading into the lake! She ran after them, staying silent now because she knew that people in the village might be nearby.

She kicked off her shoes and ran into the cold water. They were already waist-deep, and if they began to swim she wouldn't be able to catch them. She risked calling out again, but neither man responded.

Gar was slightly ahead of the other man, so she reached his friend first. She grabbed his arm and forced him to stop. He tried to pull away from her, but she hung on desperately as she called out to Gar again.

The other man shook her off, but he didn't move. And then Gar stopped and slowly turned back to her. In her head, Shera could hear and feel the Dark Ones' anger, like a swarm of angry bees. The noise drowned out even the roar of the falls, and she clapped her hands to her ears, an instinctive gesture that did no good.

"Shera!"

Gar grasped her shoulders and shook her— and the noise died away. All that was left was that deep, terrible coldness.

"Are you all right?" he asked. His voice and his eyes were full of concern.

She nodded, then shuddered. "They were angry. They sounded like a hive of bees."

Gar wrapped an arm around her waist as they all began to walk to shore. "It happened too fast," he said, his deep voice slightly shaky. "I thought it would be different this time because I was aware of the danger."

They stepped out onto the grassy bank. The sky was growing steadily lighter and the fog was already beginning to dissipate. Shera found her shoes and Gar offered his arm for her to cling to as she put them on.

"I'm going to walk with you back to the path," she told him.

She expected him to protest, but he merely stared at the lake and the falls that were just now visible through the remaining fog. Then he nodded.

The trio walked back through the meadow and into the woods. Shera was still frightened about what had nearly happened, though she also felt a sense of triumph that she'd once more somehow managed to drive away the Dark Ones. But she knew that she'd feel far more triumphant if she understood how and why it had happened. She was still very reluctant to accept Gar's explanation that the gods were protecting her.

Gar was walking silently beside her, and when his hand touched hers, she thought it was by accident. But then his fingers curved warmly around her hand, and when she looked up at him, he was actually smiling at her. It was a tentative sort of smile, the kind that might have seemed unnatural if it weren't for the accompanying light in his eyes.

They reached the rocky area that hid the path up the mountain. Gar's friend continued on, but Gar stopped, still holding her hand. She stretched up on tiptoe to kiss him, and for a moment she thought he would resist. But then he suddenly drew her against him, surrounding her with himself and awakening the hunger that was always there when she was with him.

His kiss was gentle—or it tried to be. But she could feel him stretching the limits of his self-control as his lips met hers and his tongue began to probe hers.

It lasted for an eternity—and only a moment. Then he stepped back, though he still held on to her hands.

"Will I see you again, before—" She stopped, unable to finish the sentence. How would she even know him if she encountered him after the tas-syana?

"I will try to come to you," he said, then abruptly dropped her hands and turned away.

Tears filled her eyes as she watched him hurry to catch up to his friend. Just before he was lost to view, he stopped and turned to stare at her for one long moment. She saw him through the haze of her tears: tall and golden, a man, but not a man. And then he was gone.

The bodies were discovered an hour later by some early swimmers. Shera had returned to her cottage and fallen exhaustedly into bed, only to be awakened by an insistent pounding at her door. She opened it to find four men there: the group that had made the bloody discovery.

Tired from a night without sleep and a very long walk, she nevertheless managed to feign shock when they told her that the two men had obviously been attacked by chezahs.

Unfortunately one of the men who found the bodies was the younger brother of one of the victims, and his anguish tore at Shera.

Daren was quickly summoned, and she was forced to accompany him back to the lake. Seeing the two men now in bright daylight, their torn bodies lying beside the lovely lake, Shera felt sick all over again. She had killed two people, who would never have truly hurt her. And then she'd permitted their bodies to be mauled by the chezahs. For the first time, she wished for Gar's unemotional temperament that so annoyed her.

"Why did it happen now?" the younger brother cried. "No one has been attacked by chezahs since we came to the valley."

"It is not for us to question the will of the gods," Daren intoned, setting her teeth on edge and providing no solace at all for the distraught young man.

"I am sorry, Klaya," Shera said, reaching out impulsively to touch his arm. "But you must be strong. Your nephew will need your strength and guidance now."

His look of gratitude for her sympathy cut through Shera like a cold knife, laying bare all her guilt. She turned to Daren.

"Why were they out here at night?"

The question was a mistake, and she knew it—but she could not stop the words.

He contrived to look shocked. "Why do you ask *me?* I don't know what they were doing here."

But her question had drawn the grieving brother's interest. "Youri told me that he was working for you," he said accusingly. "I invited him over last night, and he said that he had to do something for you."

Daren's face flushed crimson as everyone present stared at him. "I never asked him to do anything," he insisted, then quickly strode away.

Klaya glared at his departing back, then waited until the others had moved beyond earshot. "Youri told me that Daren wanted him to follow you, Shera. Daren said that you were refusing to marry him because you'd taken a lover."

Shera managed to keep her surprise hidden. "Then that could explain why they were at the lake," she told him. "I went swimming late last night, after everyone else had gone. But I saw no chezahs."

"I don't like Daren—and I don't trust him," Klaya said impulsively. "I know that's wrong, but . . ."

"I don't like him much either," Shera said.

"There are some of us who question the wisdom the gods showed in choosing him," Klaya went on.

"And also many who question why *I* was chosen," she said with a smile.

"Yes, that's true. Everyone knows you never paid much attention to religion. But we all know that you're a good person—and that's what is important."

Shera was shocked by his words, but she had little opportunity to dwell on them as the widows arrived, together with a large crowd from the village.

* * *

Later, when Shera had finally managed to return to her cottage and tumble once again into bed, she thought about Klaya's remarks. Perhaps she'd been wrong to believe that all her people would allow themselves to be led so easily. It was just possible that she could have some badly needed allies.

Chapter Ten

Shera stood helplessly, listening to Daren fan the flames of hatred against the Walkens. Already the high priest had done his work, explaining that the Walkens weren't human at all, but were rather half beast. And she'd seen how her people reacted to that news: with much the same revulsion she herself had felt.

Now Daren was insisting that the chezahs that had killed so many of their people—including two in this very valley—had done so at the behest of their bestial neighbors.

She now knew that bringing the two men's bodies back to the valley had been a mistake. People were willing to accept the deaths in the mountains as being part of the price they'd had to pay to reach their ancestral home; the priest had convinced them of that. But the deaths in the valley had shocked them and fueled their rage.

There was nothing she could do. If she spoke up and admitted that she herself had killed the two men by accident, it would make no difference. An ugly thirst for revenge was demanding to be satisfied—and Daren was pointing the way, telling them that the Walkens and their kin, the chezahs, could be controlled only by means of the tas-syana.

Standing silently beside Daren and the priests, Shera scanned the crowd and knew that nothing she could say or do would change their minds. Furthermore, seeing how easily they were being led, she knew that, when the time came, they would also easily accept the enslavement of the people beyond the mountains.

They were gathered in the large meadow near the lake in the early evening, just before dusk and the evening ceremonies. Daren and the high priest had to shout to make themselves heard over the waterfall, and Shera thought that its power lent an even greater authority to their words.

When Daren had finished, Jawan, the high priest, took over again, his deep, powerful voice ringing out over the meadow.

"The gods have decreed that we are to be their representatives in this world. Those who live beyond the mountains are an evil, godless people. It is our duty to conquer them and use them as we see fit. The inhuman Walkens and the chezahs will help us to do this."

He went on, drawing pictures of a people he'd never seen, accusing them of evil practices, but Shera tuned him out. She saw now with certainty that the thing from the mountain was evil. They had lived for a century among a godless people, but no one had suggested that the Trellans should be conquered. True, her people had been contemptuous of them in private— and sometimes in public as well, if they were peasants—but no one had ever suggested that they should be enslaved.

Slowly and painfully, Shera was also reaching the conclusion that the evil wasn't just in the cavern behind the waterfall, but in the hearts of her people as well. While it was true that there were those among them she didn't like, she had never once considered that her own kin could be truly bad. But how else could they be led so easily?

And why was she different? Was it really true, as Gar had suggested, that she was somehow being protected against the evil

that had infected her people? For what purpose? Even if a few
people agreed with her, what could they hope to accomplish?

The exhortations by Daren and the high priest ended and the
evening ceremonies began. She moved with Daren to the first
circle, which she'd always avoided in the past. His hand
grasped hers, while her other hand was taken by one of his
henchmen, an obnoxious man who could have been Daren's
twin.

As the chanting began, a thin crescent moon rose over the
waterfall. Tomorrow night would be the dark of the Moon—
and the tas-syana ceremony.

Shera felt a chill that had nothing to do with the cool breeze
blowing down from the mountains. She had hoped that Gar
would come to her. She wanted desperately to see him one last
time, to feel his hard body against hers and feel their passion
ignite once more.

But she'd also feared his coming. The deaths of the two men
had not stopped Daren's spies. Standing in the darkness of her
cottage, she had seen them out there, moving in the shadows,
and she didn't want Gar to risk his life.

Now she accepted that he would not be coming ever again.
Seeing the looks on the faces of her people this night, Shera
knew that the only way she would ever see Gar again would be
if the Bacleev were either dead or once more driven from this
valley.

Lost in her pain, she was slow to sense the Dark Ones' presence entering her far more powerfully than ever before. For one
brief moment, she no longer wanted to fight it.

The stealthy, dark presence crept through her body and mind,
leaving her eager for more. She tried to cling to an image of
Gar, but this time it refused to come. Instead she saw a chezah
staring at her with Gar's amber eyes.

But then she heard his voice. *There is nothing I can do to
help you, Shera. You must fight the battle alone.*

And she began to fight—not by using his image this time, but
by using her own will. She found the deep, quiet place within

her that was strong and impregnable. As before, she imagined it to be a glowing ember—but now she envisioned that ember suddenly bursting forth into a bright green flame, like the fire of the sacred bowl.

The darkness vanished, leaving her with nothing but a cold reminder of its presence that also disappeared beneath a spreading warmth. The warmth reminded her of that moment when the sacred fire had leaped out to choose her as the shegwa.

When the ceremony had ended, she saw Daren watching her closely. And when she started back to her cottage, he followed her.

"Did you feel the power tonight?" he asked eagerly. "You've never joined the first circle before."

"And I will never do so again. That power is evil, Daren! How can you not know the difference between it and the power of the gods who chose us to be shegwas?"

She saw what appeared to be genuine confusion on his face. "What do you mean? It is the same."

"It *isn't* the same, Daren. I don't understand it, but I know it's not the same."

Daren stared at her, and for just a moment she saw confusion in his eyes. She pressed on.

"I've always felt both—even when we were still in our old home. I think there are two forces warring over us."

"That's ridiculous—blasphemous!" he stated coldly, having quickly reverted to his usual self. "How can you—who have never worshiped the gods properly—dare to claim that you know more than the priests?"

"I know what I feel!" she replied, meeting his angry gaze squarely.

"And you alone feel this?" he jeered.

"Perhaps so. Good night, Daren."

She turned to enter her cottage, but he reached out to seize her arm. She spun around, her anger rising, and, obviously remembering before he quickly let her go.

"What about us?" he asked, his voice slightly uncertain. "You agreed to marry me in name only."

184

"No, I didn't. I said I would think about it. I have—and I won't." She walked through the doorway and slammed the heavy door shut behind her.

"You'll regret this, Shera," he called.

She tossed another log onto the fire and sank down onto the thick rug. She wasn't at all certain where those words had come from about her people being caught in the midst of two warring forces, but now that she'd spoken them, she felt their truth. When they'd lived among the Trellans, far from the waterfall and the Dark Ones, perhaps the gods had had the upper hand. But now that they were here, the Dark Ones had become much more powerful.

She wrapped her arms around herself and shivered. She'd always wanted to believe in good and gentle gods—and she'd welcomed the wonderful warmth she would feel at the ceremonies. But always, she'd also felt the coldness and darkness.

She thought about the sacred bowl that was never brought to their ceremonies anymore, but instead sat amid the cluster of cottages occupied by the priests. And she remembered how low the fire had been burning the last time she'd seen it.

I must go there, she thought. *I must see for myself if it is truly the fire of the gods.*

The priest permitted no one but themselves to approach the sacred bowl, except, of course, when it was time to choose new shegwas. But the priest were old and they retired early. She could risk discovery and their wrath, for what did she have to lose?

She waited for night to settle in, and periodically, she peered out through the curtains to see if Daren's spies were in evidence. Once, she thought she saw someone hiding among the trees.

The tiny cottage had no back door, but it did have a window that faced the rear, where the trees grew close to the cottage. Shera put on black clothing and smeared her face once more, then crawled out the window and slipped into the woods.

Most of the lights were out in the village, and when she came at last to the circle of homes belonging to the priests, all the windows were dark. Still, she stayed hidden behind some bushes and watched for a time. From her vantage point, she couldn't see the sacred bowl atop its rock in the center of the circle of houses, but she could see most of the houses themselves and part of the clearing at the center. Nothing moved.

She crept along behind the cottages until she could see the bowl, visible only because of the softly glowing fire within it. It seemed to be burning somewhat brighter than it had been the last time she'd seen it, but that had been in daylight, so she couldn't be sure.

She studied the dark windows. Every house faced the stone-paved circle where the bowl sat. If anyone was awake in there, they would certainly see her, even in the darkness. The stones were light in color, and even on this relatively dark night she would be plainly visible.

Furthermore, it was even possible that the priests would know through some supernatural means that someone approached the bowl. They'd always claimed that they alone could approach it because of their special relationship with the gods.

Her mouth was dry and her hands were clammy as she began to creep between the cottages toward the circle. Failing to worship the gods properly was one thing; disobeying a prime tenet of their faith by daring to approach the sacred fire on her own was quite another.

She reached the circle and, after one last look around, crossed swiftly to the bowl. At any moment she expected to hear the stentorian voice of Jawan commanding her to stop.

Then she was standing before it, staring into its depths, where the green fire restlessly moved. She shuddered as she thought about the green fire that had surrounded her hands and killed the two men. Was it the same fire? Was she wrong in her belief that there were two forces at work?

She edged closer, nearly hypnotized by the swirling, glowing fire. And then it began to rise within the bowl!

Shera stepped back involuntarily as a tongue of flame flickered toward her. But it reached out still farther and enveloped her like a soft, warm blanket.

There was none of the dark sensuality she'd felt earlier. Now she felt only the warmth and gentleness of love—and she knew that she'd been right.

The tongue of fire withdrew from her, but the flames rose high above the bowl. And then, in their flickering light, she saw two familiar images: Gar and a chezah. They barely had time to register on her brain before the fire died down to its previous faint glow.

Shera fled across the circle and back between the cottages to the woods. There she waited for a moment, but she saw no lights come on. Then she began to make her way back around the village to her own home at the far end.

She was both pleased and frustrated: pleased because her guess had been correct, and frustrated because the gods had given her no instructions. The image of Gar and the chezah meant nothing; she'd had that vision before, and for all she knew, she'd conjured up that image herself because the tassyana was so much on her mind.

By the time she reached her cottage, she was feeling very disappointed. She didn't doubt their presence in the sacred fire, or their essential goodness—but why weren't they providing guidance? She had been hoping they would tell her how to prevent the ceremony tomorrow night.

It irritated her greatly to realize that in one thing, at least, the priests were correct: the gods were inscrutable. They might be offering her some special protection, but they weren't offering her any help.

She crawled back through the window into her cottage, tired and dispirited. She'd left no light burning because she'd wanted to create the impression that she'd gone to sleep. So now, after stopping long enough to wash away the soot from her face, she made her way in the dark to her bedroom and stripped off her clothes.

There was no sound—but suddenly Shera knew she was not

alone in the cottage. Instantly she thought of Daren. She'd finally driven him to violence! She whirled around to face the bedroom door, her hands already beginning to glow.

"Shera, it's me."

The voice was low and familiar—and so was the tall form that she could just barely make out in the doorway.

"Gar!"

Shera rushed to him, reaching out, the green fire still surrounding her hands. Gar backed away, but he could take only a few steps across the narrow hallway before he collided with the wall behind him. Shera tripped over his feet, and the two of them tumbled to the floor in a tangle of arms and legs. Too late, she realized that he was trying to avoid the lethal touch of her hands.

"I'm sorry. I didn't think. I thought you might be Daren."

He stared at her hand, which still gripped his arm. The fire was fading away on its own.

"Did I hurt you?" she asked when he said nothing.

"No." He shook his head and reached out to take both her hands.

"What is it, then? What's wrong?" It was obvious to her that something was troubling him.

He continued to hold her hands as she lay sprawled half on top of him. "I felt nothing," he said in a wondering tone.

"You mean that you *should* have felt something?"

He nodded. "When Daren tried to attack me and you loosed your fire at him, I felt something, even though it didn't touch me."

"Maybe it's because the fire wasn't directed at you. I thought you were Daren."

"Maybe," he said doubtfully. "Do it again." He was still holding her hands.

"I . . . I don't know if I can. It just happens when I'm angry or frightened."

"Try," he insisted.

She concentrated reaching down to that deep place within her, and within seconds her hands began to glow again. She tried to extricate them from his, but he merely tightened his grip. Then, finally, he let her go and she closed her fists, extinguishing the fire.

"You can't hurt me," he said, his voice still full of wonder.

She scrambled off him and got to her feet. "Did you think I would?"

He got up, too. "I thought you *could.*"

"How long have you been here?" she asked, not wanting to carry this discussion any further.

"Not long."

"I didn't think you'd come. It was risky."

She'd hoped that he would say he'd come because he wanted to see her, but instead he asked where she'd been. In the shock of finding him here, she'd nearly forgotten about her nocturnal journey to the sacred bowl. She told him about it—and about her belief that her people were under the influence of two warring forces. When she had finished, he nodded.

"But the Dark Ones have captured them all now—except for you."

She thought about how close they'd come to getting her as well, but she said nothing. They were standing close together in the darkness of the little hallway, and every fiber of her being was crying out for his touch.

"I'm glad you came," she said, her voice embarrassingly husky.

"I cannot stop myself. I want you too much."

As before, his declaration came out grudgingly. Shera wondered if the time would ever come when he could speak those words—and more—without regret. But for now it was enough. She wrapped her arms around him and pressed her face to his smooth leather jerkin, feeling the strong beat of his heart and breathing in his scent.

His hands moved restlessly, impatiently over her, and then he lifted her and carried her to her bed, where they both fumbled eagerly with their clothes.

Their hunger swept them away into a wild tangle of arms and legs and hard muscles pressed into soft curves. But for the first time Shera felt him fighting for self-control, trying to draw out the moment. He whispered her name over and over again hoarsely as he kissed every part of her—from her lips to her taut nipples to that part of her that needed him most.

She followed his lead and felt him tremble beneath her touch, from the corded muscles of his shoulders to his long, hard shaft. He groaned with pleasure and seethed with impatience, and she knew that this was something new for him, this holding back.

But holding back became impossible for them both. He lifted her atop him and she took him into herself. He bucked wildly beneath her and she rode him into that all-too-brief place of perfect oneness.

She collapsed on top of him, but he lifted her off, then settled her against him, stroking her with his long, hard fingers.

"I try to be gentle," he said softly.

She smiled against his chest. "I know."

Then, after a small silence: "Gentleness is not my nature—not our nature as Walkens. Always we have to struggle to be human."

Shera felt tears springing to her eyes and moved her head so he wouldn't feel them. "And after tomorrow you will have to struggle still harder."

He stroked her hair, which fanned out across his chest. "Yes, but thinking of you will give me that strength." He paused for a moment, then asked in a slow, tentative voice, "Is this what it means to be in love, Shera?"

She swallowed hard to rid herself of the huge lump in her throat. Then she nodded. "Yes, I think so."

"I had a mate once. She died giving birth—and I lost my son as well. We . . . pleased each other. But this is different."

She raised herself up and looked down at him in the dim light. "Yes, Gar, this *is* different. I've never loved anyone, either—but I know that I love you."

"I want to protect you—but I can't. And after tomorrow night . . ." His voice trailed off and he looked away from her.

The full horror of what was about to happen struck her then, and she realized that she'd been avoiding it.

"Is there a way to reverse it?" she asked, struggling against her tears.

"It happened before only when the Bacleev were driven out of the valley—away from the Dark Ones."

"There *has* to be a way to end this!"

"Perhaps we are that way," he replied carefully.

"But how? The gods aren't helping me find any answers."

In the eerie half light of predawn, with fog once again blanketing the valley, she walked with him to the door. Her body ached pleasurably from their lovemaking. His scent lingered on her skin.

"I'll walk with you past the lake," she said as he reached for the door latch.

"No. I'll stay away from it and go through the woods. I don't want to risk being seen together."

"What does it matter now?" she asked bitterly.

He reached out to touch her face gently. "It matters. You cannot hope to influence your people if they know about us."

She knew she couldn't influence many of them in any event, but she didn't tell him that. Instead she nodded, then wrapped her arms around him one last time, trying not to think how he would soon be leaving the body she held so tightly.

"I won't even know you if I see you again," she cried.

"Yes, you will. I'll make sure of that." He kissed the top of her head, then gently removed her arms and opened the door.

After taking a few steps outside, he stopped and turned to her. "I love you, Shera. That won't change."

The chanting rose and fell as it drifted across the twilit meadow. Shera remained in the forest, watching and listening. Where before there had been a certain beauty to the ritual chanting, now there was an ominous feel to it. First the voices of the priests could be heard, and then the people would repeat the words.

She couldn't hear the words from where she stood, and she didn't want to hear them. But neither could she stay away, since

191

there remained in her one last, desperate hope that it wouldn't work—that the gods would rise up and strike all the Bacleev dumb.

She had spent the day searching for allies, hoping to find others who would be willing to stand with her to oppose this. But not even Klaya, the brother of the man she'd killed, would listen to her pleas. Of course, he had good reason to hate the chezahs; he believed them to be responsible for his brother's death.

The last of the light leaked from the sky, and the stars came out, their numbers and brightness greatly increased without the moon—and still the chanting went on. Shera had never before felt so alone.

Then she saw the priests raise their hands high, followed by the people in the circles. Suddenly the night was filled with green fire. The glare was so bright that even from this distance, Shera had to shield her eyes. When again she risked a peek, it seemed as though the group had been consumed by it. The flame was so brilliant that it lit the waterfall and the mountains around it.

As she covered her eyes again, she felt the dark presence seep into her. But unlike before, this time she fought it off easily, driving it from her with a trembling rage. She continued to feel its presence hovering near her, but there were no voices, no sensual whispers. She thought that what she'd felt might have come from the people, and not from any spirits.

The brilliant light died away slowly, retreating back to the hands of the participants. The chanting began again. Shera turned away. She knew it was done—and Gar was lost forever.

The next day, the talk in the village was all about the great power of the magic they'd created, and the fact that they no longer had any reason to fear either the chezahs or the Walkens. Shera walked among them, saying nothing. She saw the uneasy glances that were cast her way. Everyone knew that she'd refused to participate.

She tried to avoid Daren, but when she returned to her cottage late in the afternoon, he was waiting for her. She had to close her fists tightly to prevent the rage she felt from compelling her to strike out at him.

"Your lover is gone, Shera," he said with a sneer. "Now he's an animal in body as well as in mind."

"He is more human than you ever were, Daren."

"He will do as he is told by us."

"Don't be so certain of that."

She was rewarded by a brief look of uncertainty in his eyes, though his thin-lipped mouth continued to sneer.

"The Walkens have grown much, Daren. This time they may be able to hold on to their humanity and their free will."

"Is that what he told you?" Daren laughed nastily. Then he made a dismissive gesture. "I haven't come here to listen to such nonsense. I've come to tell you that our marriage ceremony will be held tomorrow night—in the cavern. The gods have decreed that the ceremony should take place there."

"No."

"You *will* be there, Shera. If necessary you will be brought there by force. And don't try to run away, because I have men watching you."

"I will *not* marry you, Daren!" she stated coldly, but as she walked into her cottage and closed the door, she felt a brief tremor of terror.

Several hours later, Shera came out of her trance to be mocked by the echoes of her final words to Daren. She *would* marry him—because she had no choice.

In the self-detachment afforded her by her trance, she understood that Daren's threat of force had been real—and that it represented desperation on his part and the part of the high priest, who had surely condoned his threat. She could counter his power easily, of course, but to do so would so anger her people that she would never be listened to again—and might even be banished.

Her people were completely in thrall to the Dark Ones now, and her only hope of changing that lay in choosing her battles very carefully. If she continued to refuse to marry Daren, the priests might well declare that she had forfeited her position as shegwa. Only by appearing to accede to their wishes could she maintain any power at all.

She wasn't particularly worried that Daren might renege on his promise that it would be a marriage in name only. He had seemed genuinely disgusted about her relationship with Gar, and if he overcame that disgust and made any attempt to touch her, she would deal with it quickly. She doubted it would come to that, though. Daren was afraid of her. He knew her powers were greater than his.

Neither did she fear going to the cavern of the Dark Ones. For reasons she couldn't understand, she knew that they couldn't capture her, though of course they would try.

Perhaps, she thought, *I should pretend that I have finally accepted the Dark Ones. It may be that the priests and Daren would believe me.* Daren had hinted on more than one occasion that she'd fallen under Gar's influence, and she could now use that belief against him. Gar was gone and could no longer "influence" her.

The next morning Shera was awakened shortly after dawn by her aunt, who brought with her a wedding dress that had been worn a year ago by Shera's cousin. And so it was that she learned that the whole village knew about the impending ceremony.

"Everyone is so pleased." Her aunt smiled. "It was unnatural for the shegwas not to be married. People were beginning to say that you should not be shegwa, and your Uncle Menan told me that the high priest was considering asking the gods to choose another."

Listening to her, Shera felt the dubious satisfaction of knowing that she'd made the right decision. The high priest wouldn't have truly asked the gods to choose another—but he would have pretended to do so. Furthermore, Shera was certain that her uncle had asked her aunt to come here, in order to find out if she intended to make any trouble.

"I've just been very confused," Shera lied.

"Of course, dear. We all understand that. It is a great burden to have thrust upon you when you've just lost your parents and then been kidnapped by a savage. But the gods have faith in you."

Do they? Shera wondered. *I'd be happy for a little less faith and a little more in the way of guidance.*

"What a happy time this is for us!" her aunt went on as she began to pin the hem of the gown, which was slightly too long for Shera. "The gods have restored our powers to us, and soon we will be able to complete the work of our ancestors."

"You mean finish the castle?" Shera asked.

Her aunt nodded. "The plans are complete. All we need now are workers— and Menan says those will come soon."

The fact that those workers would be slaves seemed not to trouble her aunt at all, but Shera kept her silence. She knew that she would have to become very adept at holding her tongue.

Her aunt was still happily chattering on about the wedding celebration, the hastily prepared feast, and Shera's cousins, who had left at first light to find the loveliest wildflowers for her wedding.

Not once, however, did she mention Daren. It was as though he didn't exist. Shera knew that while her uncle thought Daren was a fine, devout man, her aunt didn't like him. And, in fact, Shera was certain that her aunt didn't like her uncle very much, either. She had married him for the same reason many Bacleev married: because the priests had decreed it. Among the Bacleev, if someone desired to marry, that person sought the blessing of the gods through the priests, and when that blessing was given—as it most often was—the other person acquiesced, even if his or her feelings were not that strong. It was the will of the gods.

Shera had always thought it strange that none of her would-be suitors had obtained such a blessing. She wasn't even sure that any of them had actually sought such a blessing, but if they had, it apparently had never been given.

Finally her aunt departed, still talking about the coming festivities. Shera walked her to the door, then stood there for a moment, lost in her thoughts. She was about to go back inside when a movement at the edge of her vision captured her attention. She turned—just in time to see a chezah vanish into the fog beneath the trees.

She ran after it, keeping her voice low as she called Gar's name. Once, as she ran through the woods, she thought she caught a glimpse of it again, but when she came out to the meadow, the fog had lifted enough for her to see better—and it was gone.

Crouched low on a high ledge, hidden by bushes, Gar watched the procession move toward the cavern. First came the accursed priests, and then the man Daren—with Shera. After that came the others, but he paid no attention to anyone but Shera, in her long white dress.

He knew what was happening, and the human part of him was enraged. Only the other part—the chezah mind—kept him from rushing down there.

He was learning already to live with the duality. So far it was easier than he had expected. He had the advantage of the chezah's great power and agility and keen eyesight and hearing—and yet he had retained his capacity to think.

Unfortunately the human side of him was at the moment veering between anger and despair. Had the Dark Ones succeeded in capturing her as they had him? Or was she marrying Daren for another reason?

Gar still didn't understand the concept of love very well, though he thought he might have if there'd been more time. And because he didn't fully understand it, he also didn't trust it. Shera might have loved him—but he was gone, and perhaps she lacked the strength to fight the battle alone.

He watched from his hiding place until everyone had disappeared into the cavern. Then he began to climb the mountain. While he waited and watched the procession, he'd felt his mind being brushed by one of the others. There was news of some sort—and it probably wasn't good.

If it had been possible, he would have smiled grimly. The

Bacleev didn't know that his people could communicate with each other this way. Shera would know, because she knew he could communicate silently with chezahs when he was in human form. But she would keep the secret. Perhaps her love for him had been nothing more than a jecana—a beautiful flower that lasted but one day—but she would not betray him.

When the Dark Ones made their presence known, Shera mentally swatted them away with no more effort than would have been required to dispense with a pesky insect. She sensed that the attempt had been halfhearted at best, as though they knew there was no hope of success, but were nevertheless compelled to try to overpower her resolve.

The cavern was filled nearly to overflowing, and the songs and chants echoed off the stone walls, swelling the size of the crowd still more. The pool at the center of the cavern bubbled and churned, like a huge cauldron of dark, boiling water. In the steam that rose from it, all the way to the vaulted ceiling, one could easily imagine strange, twisted, semihuman shapes. Shera wondered why no one but herself seemed to find its acrid odor offensive. And she wondered too why no one seemed to question why they were here, instead of being gathered around the sacred golden bowl. How did the others accept all this so easily?

The answer, of course, was the priests. Shera swept her gaze over them as they stood in a circle around the pit, their eyes closed as they chanted. The Bacleev were long accustomed to a blind obedience to the priests, and people always found it easier to continue familiar ways than to consider change.

She stood facing Daren, a long silken cord loosely binding their hands together. His touch sickened her, but she kept her expression smooth. She must do this if she was to have any influence at all over the future of her people—and Gar's.

Little was required of her right now, so her thoughts strayed to Gar. For one brief moment, when the procession was wending its way through the forest to the cavern's entrance, she thought she had felt his presence. She didn't dare stop or even look around, lest she draw attention to him if he was, in fact, there.

Could he have been there—or had her feeling been nothing more than a final, desperate hope that he'd somehow escaped the tas-syana and had come to rescue her?

Foolishness, she thought. He had not escaped—and even if he had, he could not save her. As he'd said himself, she must fight this battle alone. Besides, she'd never in her life relied on anyone—not even the gods.

She returned her attention for a time to the long ceremony and intoned the proper words, trying not to think about Daren's soft hands against hers. Like other Bacleev, Daren eschewed physical labor. The only reason she gave it any thought now was that she had been thinking of Gar's strong, callused hands.

With her part of the ceremony now over, she let him fill her mind again. She wondered if he could have been there. If he was, then her unique ability to sense his presence hadn't been lost with his transformation. She didn't know what to think about that possibility. How could she face him when he was no longer a man? Wouldn't it be better not to know?

The final song, beseeching the gods to grant Daren and her a long and fruitful life together, swelled and filled the cavern. Shera shuddered inwardly, sending up her own silent declaration that it would be neither.

If Gar was there, and if he knew what was happening, did he understand—or did he think that she had betrayed him and cast her lot in with the Dark Ones?

She turned her gaze on the bubbling pit, and for one long moment that seemed to hang suspended in time, she was staring into the darkest, coldest, most evil force imaginable. But she neither blinked nor felt threatened. Instead, she sent it a silent message:

I will return here one day and I will see you destroyed!

The celebration lasted the remainder of the day and into the evening. Shera smiled a lot and avoided Daren whenever possible. Everyone bemoaned the lack of proper foods and appropriate gifts for their shegwas, while expressing the satisfaction that they would soon be living well again.

At one point, Jawan, the high priest, announced that as soon as they had workmen to remove the stores of treasures from the hiding place that Shera had discovered, they would be brought to Daren and Shera to take from, then distribute what remained as they saw fit.

Shera covered her disgust with a polite smile. She had no intention of enjoying wealth bought with the blood of its owners. And since she alone knew the location of the treasure cave, neither would anyone else have them. She would simply claim to have forgotten where it was.

The celebration ended with the evening ceremonies in the meadow near the lake. Standing with Daren in the first circle, Shera once again easily shielded herself from the Dark Ones, countering their icy presence with her own cold determination.

After the ceremony came the most difficult part. Shera's belongings, paltry as they were, had been carried to Daren's much larger home near the center of the village: the cottage had obviously been the home of earlier shegwas. Surrounded by the good wishes of all, they walked hand in hand to her new home.

She had considered insisting that she remain in her own home, but in the end she knew that she must maintain the appearance of being Daren's wife in order to be fully accepted as shegwa.

She didn't fear that he would try to take her to his bed, but she detested the thought of being forced to share living quarters with him, however spacious they might be.

As soon as the door had closed behind them, she pulled her hand from his. He contrived to look surprised—or perhaps he truly was.

"What is wrong, Shera?"

She planted her fists against her slim waist and glared at him. "Understand this, Daren! I have married you because our people expect it—and for no other reason. You swore that this would be a marriage in name only, and I intend to hold you to that oath."

199

"But you can't still want that savage! He's not even *part* human anymore."

"Gar has nothing to do with this. If he'd never existed, I would still hold you to your promise."

"I want nothing to do with you after you have . . . lain with that creature," he sputtered, but Shera thought, to her horror, that she saw a very different message in his eyes.

"Good. But remember what I can do to you, Daren. My magic is stronger than yours."

"Perhaps not anymore," he muttered darkly.

"Oh? Would you like to find out?" she challenged. "Even in the cavern, before that noxious pit, they could not touch me."

"You lie," he scoffed, but he seemed uneasy.

"If I were lying, we wouldn't even be having this discussion, would we? Instead I'd be pleased to be your wife.

"There is a battle going on, Daren—a battle for the very souls of our people. You fight on the side of the Dark Ones— and I fight on the side of the gods."

She knew she should have kept quiet, but she could not stop the words from coming out. It was as though some force greater than herself were compelling her to issue this challenge. Even as she spoke, she felt a touch of that wondrous warmth she'd felt at the sacred bowl.

"How could you fight on the side of the gods, when you have always ignored them?"

"Apparently they haven't ignored *me*. Would you like to go to them now—to the bowl?"

He blanched. "We can't do that. No one is to approach the sacred fire—not even the shegwas."

"But I already have, Daren." She gestured toward the end of the village where the priests' houses encircled the bowl. "Let's go there now. Get Jawan and the others if you wish."

"No."

"You won't do it because there is still some fear left in you: fear of your masters' displeasure. I have no such fear because the Dark Ones have no sway over me."

"The Dark Ones, as you call them, do not exist. Because you

200

have never worshiped the gods properly, you do not understand them as I do."

"No, Daren, it is you who do not understand. I've never liked you much, but I don't believe that you are truly evil. It's just that you and the priests and everyone else who is devout have been worshiping both all along.

"Even as a child, I felt that duality: the gentle warmth of the gods and the cold darkness of the others. That's why I rarely went to services.

"When we lived among the Trellans, the gods held sway, though the Dark Ones were still present. But now that we are here, the Dark Ones have gained ascendancy, and the sacred fire burns low."

"There are many gods," he countered. "If you'd ever studied them as I did, you would know that."

"I *do* know that—and some of them are evil!"

"That savage filled your mind with nonsense! I have nothing more to say to you, Shera. Good night."

He turned and walked into the hallway that led to the three bedrooms. Shera sank into a comfortable chair in front of the hearth. She wasn't very happy with herself at the moment. She'd tipped her hand, though she doubted that Daren would tell anyone other than Jawan, and it was possible—even likely—that the Dark Ones had already communicated to them her treachery.

Still, by marrying him, she had secured her place as shegwa. Not even the priests could keep her from exercising her authority now. Perhaps she could not stop what was to come, but surely she could exert *some* influence.

Chapter Eleven

"We found two small villages with maybe a few hundred people each—and a city of several thousand. It looks like they all farm the lands together, and the crops are good. They're big, strong people, just the kind we want."

"They live well, too," Tylan said, adding to his elder brother's description of the people they'd found.

"We didn't see any weapons—or at least nothing impressive," Ragash went on. "I doubt they have anything to rival ours. We didn't see any cripples about, or any other signs that they'd been at war."

"They did have guards, though," Tylan said. "At night we saw groups of men patrolling the villages and the town. It makes me wonder if they might be expecting trouble."

That's because Gar warned them that we had returned, Shera said silently. *But it will not be enough.*

"Without rifles, they will be no match for the Walkens," Daren stated. "Even *with* rifles, we couldn't stop them from killing our people—and that was before the tas-syana."

Shera sat, contributing nothing to the discussion. She

watched Daren, noting how he was showing more emotion than she'd ever before seen in him. It was clear that he relished the prospect of making war upon these people. Or was it that he was eager to use the Walkens—to bend them to his will?

One week had passed since their wedding, and while Daren hadn't attempted to force himself upon her, it seemed that he was always watching her with a dark, brooding look, held back only by fear.

Shera was shocked at the change in Daren and the others who were part of this discussion. While it was true that they were all men she'd never liked, her dislike had stemmed from their self-righteousness, not from any sense that they could become greedy and violent. But the violence was there now, fueled by their certainty that the Bacleev were chosen to rule over all.

Furthermore, she saw the same thing, though to a lesser degree, among nearly all her people. The disdain they'd once shown toward the Trellans had now been transformed into an outright contempt for other people. Having wondered how they could justify enslaving innocent people, Shera now understood how they could do it; they truly believed that these others were little more than livestock, to be used for the benefit of Bacleev happiness.

She left off her dismal thoughts and turned her attention back to the discussion. Daren had begun to lay plans for attacking the city and villages.

"We will take these villages first because they'll be easier," he told the men around him. "And that may put enough fear into the city that they'll cooperate without force.

"I will lead the Walkens. They respond best to one commander. The gods have directed us how to handle them—and warned us that not all may respond."

"There could be trouble." Tylan frowned. Then, with a brief glance at Shera, he asked, "What about their leader?"

Shera noticed that Daren did not look at her. "We are stronger than he is. If he disobeys, we will order the others to hunt him down and kill him."

"Would they do that?" Tylan asked skeptically.

"They will do as they're told," Daren stated confidently. "Do not forget that they are now beasts—not humans. The mistake last time was in not maintaining tight control over them. This time will be different."

"I think we may have seen one of them," Ragash said. "At least, we saw a chezah that was much larger than ones we've seen previously. In fact, we saw it several times—but it has kept its distance."

"True. We must remember," Daren told him, "that we are dealing with animals that are far more intelligent than any others. We will leave in a few days—after you have rested."

"I am coming with you," Shera told her husband after the others had departed.

Daren shook his head. "It is necessary that one of us remain here; otherwise our people will be leaderless. I may be gone for some time."

"But you may need a good healer," she pointed out.

"We will have one. Seret will be going with us."

Shera said nothing. What could she do if she did go with them? She didn't even have a way to communicate with Gar and his people now. Only the priests and Daren knew the necessary spells; Daren had seen to that.

Her situation was hopeless. Marrying Daren might have assured her position as shegwa, but all that did was to allow her knowledge of their evil plans—she could not prevent the enslavement of those people. Perhaps she could see to it that they weren't mistreated once they were brought here.

She shuddered inwardly as she thought about Gar, and Daren's statement that he could force the others to kill Gar if he refused to cooperate. Could he really do that—or was he simply trying to make her believe that? Gar had seemed so strong, so completely invulnerable to her—and yet twice she'd had to rescue him from the Dark Ones.

During their last night together, Gar had told her that the Dark Ones could capture him because they appealed to the chezah in him—not to the man. But now the chezah side had gained the upper hand. Perhaps it had claimed him completely.

How she missed him. She could never accept the fact that she would never see him again—at least not as a man. Guiltily, she thought that it would have been better for her if he'd died than for him to be out there somewhere but beyond her reach forever.

Concealed by the forest, Daren and his men watched the village closest to the mountains. People were just now returning from the day's work in the fields. Daren smiled. The others had been right: these were big, strong men who could easily do the work of creating a proper home for the Bacleev. And they would bring women as well, to take over the drudgery to which his people were presently condemned. The old people and the children would be left behind, of course. He had no use for them.

Daren's body sang with power. He could feel it coursing through his veins. And he had only to turn and scan the forest behind him to see the chezahs waiting for his signal.

What a magnificent troop of warriors he had! Even he had been awed by the sight of the tawny creatures—at least until he reminded himself that he controlled them.

Not knowing how many Walkens there were, he couldn't know for certain if all had responded to his call. But he suspected that some had managed to stay beyond his reach—and that probably included their leader, Gar.

He'd walked among them, his hands glowing with the sacred fire. And as he walked, he'd studied their eyes. In none of them had he seen rebellion or hatred. That was why he believed that Gar was not among them. He'd seen the hatred in Gar's eyes that night at the castle; he would recognize it if he saw it again.

He continued to watch the village. They would attack just after dusk, and by tomorrow they would be on their way back to the valley with the workers they needed. Then, once they'd been organized, he and his men and the chezahs would return and take the others.

* * *

Shera walked tiredly through the Bacleev village. Her hands ached, as they sometimes did when she'd overused her healing talents. The spotted disease had struck among the children, and had now infected nearly all of them and a few adults as well. There was nothing she could do about the ugly little sores, but she knew they would heal in time. The danger wasn't the spots, but the accompanying high fevers—and somehow it was even worse for the adults. So, as the parents bathed their children in the herbal solution that brought relief from the itching, she had worked to bring down the fevers.

They'd lost only one child so far, though a few more were in danger. The healers among them were working in shifts, staying with the sickest, who were generally the youngest children and the adults. Her shift had now ended and she could get some much-needed sleep.

Two weeks had passed since Daren and the others had gone to attack the villages, and their return was anticipated any day now. Shera thought about the gratitude of the parents whose children she'd saved and wondered if that gratitude could help her in her quest to prevent the incoming slaves from being mistreated.

Tired and lost in her thoughts, she walked right past the house she shared with Daren. She'd never thought of it as being her home. Instead she walked on to the edge of the village, realizing what she'd done only when her own little cottage came into view.

I'll stay here tonight, she decided—or at least I'll rest here for a time before I go to check on the children. The little cottage was mostly bare, but her bed was still there, and at the moment it was all she needed.

She lit the one remaining lamp, then fell upon the bed fully clothed. Within seconds she was fast asleep.

It seemed that her eyes had been closed only moments when she awoke to hear her name being called urgently, followed by the sound of the door being slammed shut. Before she could drag herself from the bed, a little girl—the older sister of one of her patients—was standing in the doorway.

"What is it, Teera?" she asked, fearing the worst. Her brother was the sickest of all, and Shera had left another healer with him. "Has he gotten worse?"

The child nodded, but she kept glancing behind her, as though fearing that she was about to be attacked. "I saw a chezah! It was just outside, but it ran off into the woods when I came."

Gar! Shera was sure of it. Her heart thudded noisily in her chest as she got out of bed and put on her shoes. Her hands were shaking as she followed the girl to her family's cottage.

"I thought it would attack me!" the girl continued. "Maybe it didn't know that I don't have any powers yet."

"That's probably it," Shera agreed, though she didn't believe it. Gar wouldn't harm a child, even if she were Bacleev. "Don't worry. It's probably run off by now."

She spent the next hour trying to curb her impatience to return to the cottage as she also struggled to bring down the child's raging fever. Finally, with her hands pressed to the little boy's brow, she felt the heat begin to drain away as the telltale sheen of perspiration covered him.

"I think he will be fine now," she told the child's parents, who were hovering about helplessly. "Let him rest for a time; then try to get him to take some broth. I'll return in a few hours to check on him."

Then, after acknowledging their thanks, she rushed back to her cottage. It was probably less than an hour before dawn, and if Gar had been there, he would want to be gone by then. With Daren due to return any day now, this might be her only opportunity to see him.

But you won't be seeing him, she reminded herself. *You will be seeing what he has become. Do you really want that?*

Her steps faltered. Maybe she should go back to the house she shared with Daren. It was in the center of the village, and Gar would never come there—if indeed it *was* Gar. But even though her heart remained unsure, her feet carried her on to the cottage.

She stopped on the doorstep and peered into the darkness. Then, before she could stop herself, she called his name softly, her voice half-strangled by the sudden lump in her throat.

Saranne Dawson

Something moved in the shadows beneath the trees—and then he was there. Shera drew in a sharp breath. The chezah was by far the largest she'd yet seen. It stood before her for a moment, perhaps twenty feet from her, then began to walk slowly toward her, its amber eyes never leaving hers.

"It *is* you!" she whispered, so overwhelmed by its beauty and leashed power that for a moment she forgot her horror at what he'd become.

The chezah nodded its huge head, and Shera was overcome with shock and grief and sank back against the door. Tears streamed down her cheeks as she stared at it.

It came closer, still watching her intently. She reached out a hand to it, and it lowered its head, then rubbed against her palm. Suddenly her hand began to glow! She withdrew it quickly, fearing that she might hurt him. The chezah looked up at her, seemingly puzzled.

And then the animal began to change! At first, it seemed to be surrounded by a strange, pale light. Then, within that light, she saw a form: arms and legs, as though a man were rising from the ground. She gasped and blinked, thinking that her eyes were playing tricks on her.

And perhaps, after all, they were, because the strange form and the light died away again—and at that moment she became aware of the sound of footsteps approaching.

It was the father of one of her small patients. Shera could see him now as he came around a slight turn in the path. And when she looked from him to the chezah, it was gone. As the man approached, Shera's eyes darted wildly about, searching the woods in vain for any sign of the huge cat.

The man apparently hadn't seen it, because he launched quickly into his plea for her help. His daughter was burning with fever and shaking badly. With one last glance around, Shera followed him back to his cottage.

She saved the child—but just barely. And she knew that the task had been made much more difficult because she could not rid herself of the image of the chezah that must have been Gar. If it hadn't been for the fact that her earlier visitor had also seen

208

Thrill to the most sensual, adventure-filled Romances on the market today...

FROM ✦ LOVE SPELL BOOKS

As a home subscriber to the Love Spell Romance Book Club, you'll enjoy the best in today's BRAND-NEW Time Travel, Futuristic, Legendary Lovers, Perfect Heroes and other genre romance fiction. For five years, Love Spell has brought you the award-winning, high-quality authors you know and love to read. Each Love Spell romance will sweep you away to a world of high adventure...and intimate romance. Discover for yourself all the passion and excitement millions of readers thrill to each and every month.

Save $5.00 Each Time You Buy!

Every other month, the Love Spell Romance Book Club brings you four brand-new titles from Love Spell Books. EACH PACKAGE WILL SAVE YOU AT LEAST $5.00 FROM THE BOOK-STORE PRICE! And you'll never miss a new title with our convenient home delivery service.

Here's how we do it: Each package will carry a FREE 10-DAY EXAMINATION privilege. At the end of that time, if you decide to keep your books, simply pay the low invoice price of $17.96, no shipping or handling charges added. HOME DELIVERY IS ALWAYS FREE. With today's top romance novels selling for $5.99 and higher, our price SAVES YOU AT LEAST $5.00 with each shipment.

AND YOUR FIRST TWO-BOOK SHIP-MENT IS TOTALLY FREE!

IT'S A BARGAIN YOU CAN'T BEAT! A SUPER $11.48 Value!

Love Spell ✦ A Division of Dorchester Publishing Co., Inc.

a chezah near her cottage, Shera would have dismissed the entire thing as being the product of an overly tired mind.

It was daylight by the time she left the child, and this time she went to the cottage she shared with Daren. When she fell into bed, exhausted, she expected sleep to come quickly. But instead she lay there thinking about that moment when the light had surrounded Gar and she thought she'd seen the form of a man. She raised her aching hand and studied it, recalling how the fire had come unbidden.

Was it possible that she had the power to return Gar to his human form? What would have happened if she hadn't withdrawn her hand?

Gar climbed the stairs to his old home. The village was deserted, but some of the others would be returning soon. He was tired—not physically tired, but mentally. The effort required to fight off the mind of the other drained him, and so, for a time, he had given in to it and roamed the mountains as a chezah. It had seemed safe enough, since the Bacleev had gained their first objective and wouldn't be needing his people for a time.

He could taste the bitterness of failure. Too many of his people had failed to fight the call of the Bacleev. It was impossible to be sure, but at this point he thought that he had only a few dozen allies—those like him who had managed to control the other with their human minds.

As he waited for them to arrive, he thought back to his brief encounter with Shera. For three nights he'd prowled around the edges of the Bacleev village, hoping to catch a glimpse of her after his discovery that she no longer lived in her little cottage.

And then she'd come. He knew the moment she called his name that whatever her reason for marrying Daren, she still belonged to him. She was wary—but the love was still there, and he'd felt warmed by it, touched in a strange way that he had never felt before.

If only the child hadn't come—and the man. He couldn't have talked to Shera—but she would have told him why she'd done what she'd done.

His thoughts lingered on that last moment before the man had appeared when Shera had reached out to him. Something had happened, though he didn't know what it was. He'd felt the human part of him begin to grow stronger—the opposite of what he'd felt during the tas-syana.

As he waited for the others to return, the question he hardly dared ask himself whispered through his mind: Could she possibly have the power to restore him to his human self?

Shera forced herself to walk among their captives, hoping that she would see in their eyes the seeds of rebellion. But all she encountered was fear. They drew back from her, their eyes fixed upon her hands even though the fire was absent.

She knew now that she would encounter no spark of hatred that might be secretly nourished. Their terror of her people was palpable. Daren had seen to that by loosing the fire upon some of them and by setting the chezahs on others. She didn't know what sort of people they had been before being brought here, but if they had once had courage, they had lost it during the long journey over the mountains.

Her purpose in being among them now was to select a woman to take over her household chores. She had hoped she might find one who could help her bring an end to this slavery, but she saw no such person.

Finally she stopped before a young woman of about her own age whose face she could not see because her head was lowered. Shera could feel her misery and she started to reach out to her, but an older woman next to her grabbed the lass quickly and pulled her away. She turned to Shera with a beseeching look.

"Please, lady. She will work hard. She is just tired because she gave birth only days before . . . before we were brought here."

Shera stared at the two women, horrified. "Where is the child?" The question was out before she could stop herself, but she already knew the answer. Daren had ordered that children and those too old to work be left behind. The woman's halting response confirmed that, and the young mother still did not look up at her.

"Come with me, both of you," Shera said. "You will work in my household."

Finally the younger woman raised her eyes to Shera. Shera had never seen such anguish in a face before—but for one brief moment she thought she saw something else as well: not the anger she'd wanted to see, but determination. It would have to do. This woman wanted her child back. Her husband was perhaps here as well, and if Shera were lucky, perhaps he, too, shared that determination.

The men had been taken away to the castle, where they were already at work, and Daren was making plans for yet another expedition to the other small village, which lay near the quarry that provided the stones for the castle. Winter was not far away, and when it came, the mountain passes might be closed, so he wanted to bring more men and stones as quickly as possible. There were already huge piles of stone at the castle site, but since they intended to enlarge the original plans, more would be needed.

Shera led the two women back to the village, passing others of her tribe who were on their way to make their own selections. They were all laughing and chattering among themselves, eagerly looking forward to their newfound leisure and enjoying the treasures Daren and his men had looted from their captives' homes.

The two women stopped in the doorway to Shera's home and stared silently. Daren had appropriated for himself the best of the furniture and rugs that had been brought back, and Shera wondered if the women recognized them as being from the homes of friends or neighbors.

"Come this way," she told them, then led them back down the hallway to a small room behind the kitchen. "This will be your room. I will see to it that another bed is brought in. What are your names?"

"I'm Danna," the older woman told her. "This is my daughter, Tenia."

Shera nodded, then gestured to the narrow bed. "Tenia, I want you to rest."

The young woman looked from her to the bed uncertainly. Now that Shera got a better look at her, she wondered how the girl had managed to make the long journey. She was very pale and her hands trembled slightly.

"Are you sick?" Shera asked.

Tenia nodded. "There is blood. It was a hard birth."

"Lie down," Shera ordered her. Then, when the woman complied, she asked if they knew of the healing powers of the Bacleev. Both women nodded, once more looking at her hands.

"I am a healer," she told them. "Will you let me help you?"

They continued to stare at her hands uncertainly. Shera raised them. "I will not raise the fire against you—and I *can* help you. If you don't let me help you, you could die, Tenia—and then you will never see your child again."

The woman burst into tears, but she didn't flinch when Shera sat down carefully on the narrow cot and placed her hands on her stomach. Immediately she felt the heat of the infection. It was well advanced, but Shera was determined to save her.

The mother, Danna, hovered about anxiously until Shera told her to go to the kitchen and brew an herbal tea. "Do you know which herbs to use?" she asked.

Danna nodded. "I am an herbalist." She even gave Shera a tentative smile as she backed out of the room.

Shera stayed with Tenia for more than an hour, until she drank a full cup of tea and then fell asleep. By then the heat emanating from her had lessened and Shera was satisfied that she had done all she could.

She found Danna sweeping the new rug in the large front room, and told her that her daughter was resting comfortably and would be well soon if she rested and ate good meals.

"Thank you, lady," Danna said, blinking back tears.

"Are your husbands here?" Shera asked.

"Hers is—but mine was left behind. He is crippled with the stiffness."

"Danna, please sit down for a moment," Shera said, indicating one of the new chairs. "I don't think my husband will be coming home now, but if he does, this is not for his ears. You know who he is, don't you?"

Danna nodded, and for the first time Shera saw a glimpse of the anger she had so hoped to find.

"Ours is a marriage in name only," she told the woman. "We were chosen to be shegwas—leaders—and I agreed to marry him only because my failure to do so might have meant that another woman would have been chosen.

"I did not want this to happen, but I was unable to stop it. Alone among my people, I resist what is happening. There is . . . was a man who tried to stop it as well. His name is Gar."

Danna, who had been staring at her in shock, suddenly spoke. "He came to our village. He said he was coming to warn us that the Bacleev had returned. He wanted us to fight—but how could we? Besides, no one trusted him." She shuddered. "We fear the Walkens even more than we fear the Bacleev."

"You should not fear him," Shera said, hoping that was still true. "He will help you if he can—just as I will. But there is nothing we can do now. We must wait until the time is right."

Danna nodded, but Shera saw the hopelessness in her eyes, and she wondered if the woman saw the fear in her own.

For the past week, ever since Daren had announced his intention to lead a raiding party to capture the second village, Shera had been eagerly awaiting his departure. She had long since decided that it was no coincidence that Gar had shown up that night at her old cottage. He must have known that Daren was gone and that she might come back there.

Now the day had arrived, and the men were setting out on their long journey—possibly the last trip they would be able to make through the mountains until spring. The group was gathered in the meadow to be blessed by the priests on this frosty morning that held a hint of the winter to come. Their horses were stamping their feet, and steam poured from their nostrils as they whinnied impatiently.

The men were nearly as impatient, eager to be off and then return with more booty and more slaves. Shera had extracted a grudging promise from Daren to stop in the village that had been home to Danna and Tenia to inquire after the health of Danna's husband and Tenia's baby boy. She hadn't told the two women about this, however, because she couldn't be certain that Daren would keep his promise.

She thought, though, that there was at least a chance that he would do as she'd asked. Savoring his victory and his power, Daren seemed recently inclined to be indulgent toward her. In truth, they rarely saw each other, because he was spending all his time supervising the work at the castle. He would leave at dawn and return for the evening ceremonies and a meal, and then go back to the castle, often not coming back home until after she had retired for the night.

She, on the other hand, was preoccupied with the welfare of the women who were working as servants in the village. Toward this end, she had recruited both Danna and Tenia to keep in contact with their fellow servants and report to her if any problems existed. Already she had had to deal with several cases where women were being mistreated or being forced to work overly long hours. And just yesterday she had confronted a man who had been making unwanted advances toward a young woman in his household.

Shera wasn't surprised when she heard the report from Danna. The man in question, Dagon, was one of Daren's friends. He visited their own home on occasion, and she'd already seen how he looked at Tenia.

Dagon was in charge of the orchards, where a small crew of slaves were now picking the apples and pears that had ripened, while also clearing away the weeds that had taken over portions of the orchards. Shera went there and asked to speak to him privately. Because she was shegwa, he could not refuse her, though it was plain that he would have liked to do so.

Wasting no time on niceties, she told him what she knew of his activities. He, of course, denied it, saying that the girl couldn't be trusted and was a troublemaker.

"Very well, then," Shera told him. "In that case you should have no objections if I move her to another household and replace her. I was thinking of switching her with your mother's servant. She's strong and a very good worker who is being wasted there."

She smiled inwardly at his annoyance. The other servant was a large and singularly unattractive woman, though she was indeed a hard worker.

"That won't be necessary," he stated.

"But I think it *is* necessary, Dagon. Of course, if you disagree, I could discuss the matter with your wife."

This time she couldn't quite hide her smile. Dagon's wife was, if anything, even more unpleasant than he was, and had the reputation of having the sharpest tongue in the village. Furthermore, Jawan, the high priest, was her father, and Shera had no doubt that she would carry her grievance to him. Marriage vows were sacred among the Bacleev, and those few who broke them were treated harshly. Of course, since the servants were considered to be something less than human, Shera wasn't at all sure that such behavior would in fact be considered sinful.

Dagon's face grew red and he sputtered and proclaimed his innocence—but in the end, he had capitulated and the switch was made.

As she stood now beside Daren while the priests blessed their evil mission, Shera thought sadly that she was reduced to taking pleasure from such small victories while the larger one of stopping this horror continued to elude her.

Several times in the past few weeks, she had sneaked out at night to visit the sacred bowl, where the gods' flame continued to burn low. On each occasion, she'd felt that wondrous warmth—but she'd received no messages. It seemed to her that their presence here was all but gone, while the power of the Dark Ones grew steadily stronger over the rest of her people.

After the men had departed, Shera decided to pay a visit to the castle, where supervision was now in the hands of others as Daren and his henchmen went off into the mountains.

As long as Daren was present, Shera had stayed away from

the castle, but with him gone, there was no one to question her reason for being there.

She was surprised to see how much had been accomplished. The progress of the work when viewed from the village hadn't seemed all that great, but she saw now that interior walls were beginning to take shape.

She walked among the workers, taking stock of their physical conditions. Most were lean, but they didn't appear to be malnourished. Only in their eyes when they glanced her way did she see the haunted look of men whose lives had become hollow.

Most of them wore clothing that seemed inadequate for the cold morning, and that brought to Shera's mind the subject of housing them for the coming winter. They were still sleeping outdoors at this point, but that would have to change. She would speak to Daren about it when he returned.

Many of the walls were already high enough to create the impression of a maze. They reminded Shera of the shrubbery labyrinth at the old duke's palace, and the memory brought on a wave of longing for those far simpler times. She wondered if she were given the choice once again to become part of his household whether she would reject it this time.

She turned a corner to find a man working alone and immediately recognized him as being Tenia's husband. She hadn't met him, but she'd seen the two of them together one day in the forest below the castle. Daren forbade the men to come into the village, but he'd allowed himself to be persuaded that they should have a day of rest every ten days, and that the women should be permitted to visit them.

She recognized Garet because of his size and his hair. She'd never seen hair that color before: a very bright orange-red. He was both tall and broad, and Tenia had told her that he'd been a blacksmith in their village.

He apparently heard her approach, because he turned toward her after fitting one of the large stones in place. Shera immediately thought of Gar. Garet bore no real resemblance to Gar, except that both men were big with rugged features, but with the possibility of seeing Gar again much on her mind, the comparison came easily.

She smiled at him, not knowing if he knew who she was. "Hello, Garet. I'm Shera. Tenia and Danna live with me." She could not bring herself to say that she was their mistress, but a small twist of his wide mouth told her that he saw through her attempt to hide the truth from herself.

"I thank you for your kindnesses to them, lady," he said in that deep voice that only big men seemed to have. She felt another wave of longing for Gar.

Shera cast a quick glance behind her to be certain they were alone. Then she gave him a level look. "Tell me, Garet, are you being treated well? Is there enough to eat?"

He stared at her in silence for a moment, as though taking her measure. She noticed that he was the only man she'd seen up here who was unafraid to meet her eyes.

"Well enough. We aren't concerned for ourselves, lady."

"You mean that you worry about those you left behind?"

He nodded. "Winter is coming, and there aren't enough left to bring in the crops and cut the firewood. But maybe there'll be help from Yaslava."

"Is that the other village nearby?" she asked.

He confirmed that it was, and Shera wondered if Daren would leave enough able-bodied people behind to take care of that. She wished that she'd asked Daren about it, but she talked with him as little as possible.

"Rumor has it that your husband's gone to raid Yaslava," Garet said, his gray eyes watchful.

"Yes, they have. Garet, please believe me when I say that if I could stop this, I would. But I promise you now that I will see to it that no one is left hungry and cold this winter."

It was a rash promise, and she had no idea how she would keep it, but she was determined to do so. He thanked her politely, but she thought that he, too, doubted her ability, if not her intentions.

All the way back to the village, Shera thought about the confrontation that was sure to come with Daren if, as she suspected, he did nothing to assure that these people would make it through the winter. It was clear to her that the brittle peace between them was likely to be shattered.

I do what I can, she told herself— *More, I will do what I must.*

Shera waited that night until both Tenia and Danna had retired to their little room, then crept quietly past their door and out the back of the cottage. She doubted very much that Daren was still having her watched—especially since most of his erstwhile spies were with him—but she did not want to risk being followed to her old home, especially if Gar should appear.

The night was cold, and she wrapped her shawl more tightly around her as she made her way through the woods that surrounded the village. A bright, cold, and nearly full moon hung in the heavens, and the stars glittered like ice. She wondered if there was any firewood left at her old cottage. If not, it would be a long, cold wait.

She reached the secluded cottage and peered into the darkness as her heart thudded noisily in her chest. She didn't call his name because if he were there, he would surely see her in the moonlight. But nothing moved in the shadows, so she finally went inside and lit a lamp, then built a fire with the few remaining logs.

When that did little to drive away the chill, she remembered that there had been a small stack of firewood out back near the tree line. Since the tiny cottage had no back door, she went out front and then made her way toward the rear. Pines and hemlocks grew close to the cottage along both sides and in the back, so it was very dark, despite the bright moon. She had just found the firewood and loaded her arms with as many logs as she could manage, when suddenly she sensed something in the darkness of the forest beyond the woodpile.

She froze, peering into the deep shadows. "Gar?" she asked softly, realizing too late that it could be one of Daren's spies.

The chezah emerged slowly from the woods until it stood in a patch of moonlight. Her arms laden with firewood, Shera could not brush away the tears that began to trickle down her cheeks as the beast that was Gar moved closer.

"Come inside with me," she said. "Daren is gone. No one will bother us."

She turned and began to walk back around the house. Halfway to the door, she cast a quick glance behind her and saw the chezah following. She hurried on, trying not to think about his other visit and that moment when it seemed that he'd been about to become Gar again.

She'd left the door open, and now she walked through it and over to the fireplace, where she dropped the pile of logs, then picked up two of them and put them onto the fire. After that she turned, half fearing that he'd gone.

But he'd followed her inside and was now nudging the door shut with his large paw. The gesture both frightened her and made her unbearably sad. She realized that she'd given more thought to her own feelings about the transformation than she had to his. Now that she did, she found she could not imagine what it would be like to find herself in a different body, one incapable of doing so many things.

But she recalled how he'd told her once that the desire to assume chezah form lay in all his people, and she wondered if perhaps that made this all easier for him.

She sank to the old rug at the hearth as he came over to stand near her. There was so much she wanted to say to him, but she found that she could not bring herself to speak. And she could not rid her mind of the possibility that she might be able to return him to his human form. But if she tried and failed, wouldn't it be worse than not trying at all?

She looked into his amber eyes, which were now level with her own, and she saw that he was staring at her hands. He knew! He must have felt something, even though he couldn't have seen the glow around her hands as she'd touched his head.

He made a low, growling sound deep in his throat and began to push at her hand with his cold nose. It was the same motion house cats made when they wanted to be petted, and she wondered if perhaps she had been wrong. Maybe this wasn't Gar, after all. Maybe it was an ordinary chezah.

But she lifted her hand and touched his head, her fingers sinking into the thick, tawny fur. And immediately her hand began to glow softly. He remained very still, his amber eyes boring into hers.

Then that strange light she'd seen the other time spread around him, flickering at first, and then glowing ever brighter, until she had to close her eyes against the blinding glare. This time she did not withdraw her hand.

Suddenly she could feel strange movements, as though the chezah were shifting about restlessly beneath her fingers. When she opened her eyes, the light was still dazzling, but it contained within its center dark, writhing shadows. Frozen with horror, she watched as the shadows once again took on a vaguely human form. Her arm was still outstretched, but now, instead of thick fur, her fingers were touching firm human flesh and thick, coarse hair.

And then, abruptly, the light was gone, dying away rapidly to nothing more than the firelight.

"Gar!" she whispered, blinking rapidly several times, unable to believe what she was seeing.

He was crouched on the floor, one knee drawn up as though he were about to stand, his muscular arms trembling slightly as they supported his weight. He said nothing as he continued to stare at her from the same amber eyes that reflected the light from the fire in golden sparks.

Her hand now rested on his forehead, just where his tousled golden hair spilled down nearly to his straight eyebrows. Still not certain that he was real, she began to trace the familiar features of his face, until her shaking fingers reached his lips.

He raised one hand in a stiff, awkward movement and cupped her hand, then pressed his lips to her palm. Finally, she knew that he was real.

Chapter Twelve

He released her hand and sat back heavily, his movements like those of an old man—or a child newly born. The distinctive scent that she associated with him was heavy now. He was gloriously nude, and it brought back memories of their passion.

"A . . . few . . . minutes," he said in a hoarse, rusty voice she barely recognized.

She waited impatiently, unable to take her eyes off him as he sat there, his head lowered and propped up by his hands. So much had happened—so many strange things—and yet Shera was more awed by this transformation than by anything else she'd witnessed. Even though it was she who had brought him back, she felt as though he had moved far beyond her reach—and certainly beyond her understanding.

How many times, since that other night, had she dreamed of being able to do this—to bring him back and know once more the passion they shared? And yet what she felt now was a huge, yawning abyss between them, though they were only inches apart in reality. Reality itself had become a concept she could no longer grasp so easily.

"Water," he said, raising his head briefly. "And clothes."

She got up, swaying a bit before she could steady herself, and went to fetch what he required. She had to have something he could wear. When she returned with the items, he was standing, leaning heavily against the fireplace mantel as he shook first one leg and then the other. She handed him the mug and he wrapped his hands clumsily around it, spilling a bit before he drained the rest quickly.

"Do you want more?" she asked when he handed her the empty mug.

He shook his head, then swept a hand up to fling back his hair. "It . . . feels strange," he said in a voice that was now nearly normal.

"Sit down," she suggested, but he shook his head again, then began to walk slowly around the empty room. He was wobbling a bit at first, but then seemed to regain at least some of his normal grace.

"Is there pain?" she asked, thinking that perhaps she could help him.

"No. I just feel different, walking on two feet. How did you learn to . . . save me?"

"I didn't. It just happened. When you were here before, I thought it was happening—or starting to—but I took my hand away and then someone came. I wasn't sure."

"Neither was I. I felt something, but I didn't know for sure."

He had stopped his pacing and now stood facing her from across the room. "You married Daren. I saw the procession. You went to the Dark Ones."

Although his words were devoid of emotion, they still felt like a slap in the face. "It is a marriage in name only. It was the only way I could continue to be shegwa. Daren and the priests were already talking about choosing someone else."

"But you're *living* with him," he said in the same tone.

"We share a house," she replied, a hint of anger beginning to burn in her. This was no time for him to be developing a streak of possessiveness. "He has no interest in me that way. He considers me to be dirty because I slept with you."

She flung the final words at him, perversely wanting to see him show some emotion, even if it was anger. He merely regarded her impassively.

"So he knows about us."

"Yes. I don't want him, Gar. I detest him—even more now, since he has become obsessed with his power. He's gone to attack the other village—to get more slaves."

"I know. I watched them leave. Tonight or tomorrow night, he will call my people to aid him."

"Did you . . . answer that call the last time?"

He shook his head. "I was able to resist. It wasn't as difficult as I thought it might be. But many did answer—enough for them to terrorize that village."

"He hates you, Gar—and he would hate you even more if he knew that you resisted his call."

"He knows that already."

"Are you sure? How can you know?"

He shrugged. "I can't explain it—but he knows. Even after he'd gotten the others, I could feel him reaching out to me. I think he will try to set the others on me at some point, when he feels that he's gained enough control over them."

She stared at him in shock. "W-would they do that—your own people?"

"I don't know. It depends on how strong the other has become in them. But I'm not alone. There are those who have resisted."

Shera felt tears welling up. "Daren will win, won't he? He already has. And those people won't fight. They've given up. I can see it in their eyes."

The tears began to spill down her cheeks. Gar stared at her for a moment, then came and drew her into his arms, pressing her to his chest and stroking her gently. "*We* haven't given up, Shera. That's what is important now."

Shera wrapped her arms around him, touched beyond measure. How could it be that he'd found this tenderness within himself now, when he'd spent weeks as an animal? Or was that the answer? Did he now feel the need to be human more than he'd ever felt it before?

He hooked a finger beneath her chin and drew her face up, then gently wiped away her tears. If it was possible to see tenderness in such a rugged face, Shera saw it now. It was in his eyes, a new awareness and an understanding she'd never before seen there.

His kiss was soft and tentative, a first delicate expression of these new emotions. And when he drew his lips from hers, he held her face in his hands and kissed it all over: her forehead, her eyelids, her nose, her cheeks, the line of her jaw.

"It is different now," he said in a tone of wonder that ended in a bitter smile. "At least we can thank Daren for that."

She smiled, too, and their smiles ended with another kiss—one, this time, that slowly grew deeper and stronger and more demanding. Then Gar drew her down to the rug, his eyes glowing with desire.

"It is more than wanting, Shera. I love you—and I need you."

She touched his lips with her fingers. "And I love you, Gar—now more than ever."

There was no wildness this time, though it hovered around them, a dark shadow that added its own unique sensuality. They shed their clothing slowly, giving themselves to each other bit by bit, revealing flesh that ached to be touched, yearned to be kissed.

Gar's great gentleness reached deep into her, melting away the weeks of pain and frustration, healing her and making her whole again. But no sooner had she become whole than she willingly surrendered that wholeness to him, and received in return all that he could give.

They lingered for a long time on the byways of love, exploring every path, savoring every nuance. She gloried in the feel of him: strong and powerful and human. But always in the dark whispers of her mind there remained the knowledge that he was *not* human and that a part of him remained beyond her understanding.

Only at the end, when desire had become a pounding, driving force within them both, did they succumb to the dark wildness, rushing toward ecstasy, all tenderness cast aside. Flesh shuddered violently against flesh, bringing them perfect oneness.

Shera told him all that had happened, and discovered that he'd been visiting the valley regularly, regardless of the risk. She told him of her promise to Tenia's husband, Garet—and her fear that the people remaining in the villages would go cold and hungry this winter.

"Daren will leave them nothing," Gar said. "It happened before. The children and the old people are of no use to him."

"But he said there is a city, too. Won't its inhabitants help those who remain?"

Gar shook his head. "The city is far away. They'll know what is happening, and they will stay within their walls and hope it doesn't happen to them. But by spring, Daren will be ready to attack them as well."

He paused for a moment, then went on. "The Dark Ones will be even stronger by then. They feed off the Bacleev just as the Bacleev draw power from them. It happened that way before."

"We must see that the people in the villages have food for the winter," Shera said determinedly. "There must be a way."

"Perhaps there is," he said thoughtfully. "Wait until Daren returns and then demand to go to the villages yourself, to see that they are provided for."

"What good would that do?" she demanded. "I would only see what we already know."

"Perhaps we can return some food to them. Daren will insist upon sending some men with you. You have great powers, my love—and we already know they work against your own people. If you were to cast a spell on Daren's men, then perhaps get some help from this man Garet and a few others . . ."

They parted in the hour before dawn, when the night seemed at its coldest. She worried that he wasn't dressed warmly enough and wanted him to take her heavy shawl. But he told her that he would go up the mountain to his village, where warmer clothing and all the other items from his former life awaited him. The climb would keep him warm, and would also help him in his readjustment to his human form.

She wanted to go with him, at least to the beginning of the path that led to his village. She worried about the Dark Ones. But he said he would stay away from the lake and the waterfall, as he'd done before. He was gentle and patient with her fears, where before he'd barely acknowledged them.

The parting was painful, even though they promised to meet again the next night at the cottage. When he had vanished into the darkness, Shera knew a moment of pure terror, certain she would never see him again. Then she wrapped the shawl more tightly around herself, as though to preserve the touch of his hands and his lips upon her—to retain the feel of him inside her, driving deeply and slowly within her molten core.

Gar walked easily up the steep path, the graceful athleticism that had always been part of his nature returning with each long stride. He felt like a man who had just been released from a long imprisonment—but he was aware of the fact that after the tas-syana, when he'd assumed the chezah form, he'd felt the same way.

He thought about Shera—about their lovemaking and the aftermath, when they'd simply held each other, sometimes talking and sometimes not. He knew he was different, though he'd been reluctant to talk about that change.

Always, before the tas-syana, a part of him had been chezah. But only when Shera had come into his life had he realized that. How could he have known it before, when everyone around him was just as he was?

Then, during the past few weeks, as he roamed the mountains as a cat, he'd had to struggle hard to retain that part of him that was human—and sometimes he'd had to let it go for a while.

Now, thanks to her magic, he was human again—and more truly human than he'd ever been. He felt her pain and her joy and her love, and took them into himself. Filled with the pure happiness of it all, he threw back his head and laughed, then ran the remaining distance to his old home.

Shera went again to the castle, this time to find Garet. When she spotted him, he wasn't alone, and she was about to turn away when he caught her eye and gave her an almost imperceptible nod toward the far side of the outer wall.

She moved with seeming casualness, examining the work and speaking briefly with those who were supervising, then made her way out of the maze to a spot where two high outer walls came together. Garet was already there, making a pretense of selecting some stones.

"Is it Tenia—or Danna?" he asked urgently.

"No, they're fine," she assured him. Then she told him that she was nearly certain that Daren and his men would leave nothing behind for his people. He nodded grimly, obviously having already guessed that. So she told him what she planned to do, for the moment leaving Gar out of it. She knew how Garet and his people feared the Walkens.

"There are big storehouses not far from the village," she told him. "They're built into the sides of the mountain. That's where everything will be taken. I will need help getting packhorses and then loading up the food supplies. Are there men here you can trust—men who would help me?"

He nodded. "But he won't let you go alone to the villages. I don't understand how you can hope to do this."

"I have powers, Garet—powers far greater than the others."

He stared at her in openmouthed amazement. "You mean you can do to other Bacleev what they did to us?"

"You mean rob them of their free will? Yes, I can. I've done it once already—to Daren."

"But then that means you could force him to stop all this," he stammered eagerly.

She shook her head sadly. "That's not possible, Garet. If I were to control Daren's mind, I would eventually have to let him go—and I can't control all of them."

"I see," he said, trying unsuccessfully to hide his disappointment. "But what about the Walkens? What if Daren sends some of them along?"

"I can control them as well," she assured him. "Do not concern yourself about that. All I want from you is help getting the stores loaded. Before Daren returns, see if you can find some help and then try to figure out how you can escape the guards for a time. If you don't think you can, then I will put a spell on them. But it would be easier if you could slip away on your own."

She saw the plea in his eyes and knew what was coming next. "I'm sorry, Garet, but you can't come with me. It's my hope that we can accomplish this without Daren's knowledge. The storehouses will be very full and we can probably rearrange things so that no one will notice what is missing. But if *you* were to go missing, then he would know—and I think he would hunt you down and kill you."

She paused, then decided to confide in him her other hope. "I am going to try to take Tenia with me, so that she can see your baby. I'm not sure if that will be possible—but I'll try."

He nodded. "I will speak to a few of the others and we'll start to make our plans."

Shera returned to the village, her thoughts already on the night ahead—and the many nights beyond that to be spent in Gar's arms. They were being selfish, she knew, to think only of their own pleasure when Garet and Tenia and so many others were so unhappy. But the pleasure was stolen and very tenuous.

Lost in that selfish ecstasy, she was unprepared for the information with which Danna greeted her, and her happiness turned swiftly to rage. It seemed to frighten Danna, who stared at her wide-eyed.

Danna and Tenia, at her instruction, had been discreetly checking on the welfare of the other household servants. Once before, Danna had told her about a woman who was being harshly treated by the mistress of her household. Shera had already gone to the woman in question, a cousin who was her least favorite relative, and asked her to be more patient and understanding. But apparently her carefully chosen words had had the opposite effect.

Now, instead of simply berating the poor servant and slapping her, Shera's cousin was actually beating her. Danna had seen the swollen eye and the bruises for herself, and feared that some bones had been broken as well. Apparently the woman had accused the servant of having run to Shera with her complaints.

"It will not happen again!" Shera stated to Danna. "I can assure you of that."

Angry beyond reason, Shera headed toward her cousin Rella's house, which was not far away. When Rella herself responded to Shera's loud knock at the door, Shera pushed past her and demanded to see the servant.

"Why? What business do you have with her? She's mine!"

Shera fixed her cousin with an icy glare. Her hands began to glow, and Rella backed away, gasping. "What are you . . . ?"

"Bring her now, Rella!"

For a moment Shera thought she would refuse, but then the woman turned and fled down the hallway. A moment later she returned with the battered servant in tow.

"How did this happen?" Shera demanded of Rella.

"She's clumsy," Rella said, giving the cowering woman a contemptuous glance. "She's—"

"*You* did this to her, Rella!" She raised her hands. Both of them were now glowing brightly. The slave scurried into a corner, while Rella stood her ground.

"You can't turn your fire on me, Shera. No Bacleev can do that!"

"You're wrong, Rella," Shera said with deadly softness. "It's true that no *other* Bacleev can do it—but *I* can. I could kill you if I wanted to—but instead, I'll just teach you a lesson."

Shera flung the fire at her and Rella was thrown backward, crashing against a heavy wooden chair. Then Shera summoned her to her feet and flung her again, this time causing her to land in a bucket of ashes near the fireplace.

"Please, stop!" Rella cried.

"Did *she* ask you to stop, Rella?" Shera demanded, pointing briefly to the terrified servant. "Did you care that you were hurting her?"

"I won't do it again—I promise! Please! My arm—it's broken!"

Shera closed her fist on the green fire, then turned to the servant. "Go next door and fetch the woman who lives there. She is a healer. Tell her that her services are required."

When the servant had gone, Shera turned her attention back to her weeping cousin. "I've decided to make an example of you, Rella. We both know that Casima is one of the village's biggest gossips. I will tell her that I am responsible for what happened to you. It may prevent others from being as cruel as you've been."

"Daren won't let you get away with this," Rella cried.

"Daren can do *nothing*! My power works against him as well."

The servant returned with the healer, Casima, who stared in dismay at the sooty, crying mistress of the house, and then looked in confusion at Shera. "What happened? Why does she need me if you're here?"

"Because I'm the one who is responsible for what happened to her," Shera replied calmly. "And I have no intention of healing her. Rella was warned before about mistreating her servant, but she chose to ignore my warning." She gave Casima a cold smile.

"I know you carry tales, Casima—so be sure to carry this one to everyone in the village. My powers work against even the Bacleev—and I will use them on anyone who mistreats a servant. Is that clear?"

Casima's mouth hung open, but she managed to nod before she went to Rella.

"I am taking her with me," Shera said, indicating the injured servant. "After she is healed, I will find another home for her. Rella can take care of her own house for a while. In a month or so, I might give her someone again."

Trailed by the shocked servant, Shera returned to her home. Only after she had tended to the woman's injuries and then turned her over to Danna and Tenia did the full import of what she'd just done strike her. She sank into a chair, shocked at her own behavior.

But then, after a time, she began to smile. She was fairly certain that no one else would mistreat a servant. Within hours the entire village would know what she'd done.

She wondered what would happen when the news reached the priests. Daren's reaction didn't concern her. He would certainly hear about it when he returned. Rella's husband was one of his friends and was with Daren now. But there was nothing Daren could do—and he knew that.

The priests, though, that was a different matter altogether. This would not be a matter that would concern them under normal circumstances. But she had used the fire—and the high priest might well claim that as a reason to step in.

She sighed. Sooner or later she would have to face them and find out just how great her powers were. But it was a confrontation she would prefer to avoid.

Shera attended the evening ceremonies only in part because she had promised Daren she would do so in his absence. Her chief reason for putting in an appearance was to find out if Casima had done her usual excellent job of spreading rumors.

As she walked through the assembled crowd to the first circle, it quickly became apparent to her that Casima's reputation was well deserved. Those who met her eyes did so with an uneasiness that sometimes bordered on outright fear. Others looked away quickly, no doubt worrying about their own treatment of their servants.

She chose to stand in the first circle because it was closest to the priests and she wanted to see if they, too, knew what she'd done. Jawan's cold, dark eyes met hers. She arched a brow in challenge, but he merely nodded, then turned away. The others seemed to be avoiding her.

There was no doubt in her mind that Jawan and the others knew what had happened, but she suspected that they would wait for Daren's return before taking action. If they confronted her, Shera was prepared to declare that the matter fell within the province of the shegwas, not the priests. Furthermore, the gods had obviously given her this power for just such a purpose.

As the ceremony proceeded, Shera's thoughts turned to Gar, who would later be meeting her at the cottage. She was more eager than ever to see him, and she grew warm just thinking about their stolen time together.

Because she had so easily fended off the Dark Ones in the past, Shera was unprepared for the assault this time. Their voices whispered in her mind, but when she tried to brush them away, they persisted. Their dark, cold power flowed through her, touching every part of her, and the voices seduced her.

She felt what Daren and the others must have felt: the absolute certainty that this was good and right, that her people were destined to rule all those around them.

No! she cried silently, summoning up the will to fight them off. Gar's image flooded her mind, and then, for a moment, it faded to the face of a chezah. But she called it back, then held on to it as she fought off the Dark Ones. To succumb to their power meant she would lose Gar forever!

When it was over, Shera had won. But she was left trembling with the certainty that she had come very close to giving herself over to them. But why? Gar had said that they would become stronger, but how could it have happened so quickly?

The ceremony ended, and as the circles broke up and people began to disperse, Shera saw the high priest's gaze once again on her. This time it was he who issued the silent challenge—and she who turned away, hurrying back to her cottage as fast as she could.

While she waited for the village to settle down for the night, Shera tried to understand what had happened—and how much Jawan knew of her struggle. Perhaps she'd underestimated his power. If so, it was a mistake she would not make again.

There were still a few scattered lights burning in the village when Shera slipped out to make her way to her old cottage, but no one was out and about. The ceremony had given her even more reason to hasten to Gar. All that had saved her from the

Dark Ones this night was her love for him. The gods certainly hadn't protected her.

As she came around the final bend in the path, the breeze carried to her the scent of wood smoke. Gar must already be there. Building a fire in a supposedly deserted cottage was not without risks, but the night was cold and the cottage was set well away from its nearest neighbor. Ever since the tas-syana had eliminated any threat from the Walkens or the chezahs, Daren had withdrawn the guards that had once patrolled the perimeter of the village and the hills surrounding the valley.

Gar rose to greet her when she opened the door, and she flung herself into his arms, clutching him tightly and only now admitting to herself a fear that he might not be here, or that he might be a chezah again.

"What is wrong?" he asked, holding her slightly away from him and frowning down at her with concern.

She told him what had happened at the ceremony, and his frown deepened. He drew her down to the rug at the hearth, then wrapped his arms around her once again.

"You said they would grow stronger, but I didn't expect it to happen so quickly," she finished, shuddering.

"Neither did I," he replied. "And I felt nothing myself."

"You can feel them?" she asked. He'd never spoken of that before.

He nodded. "I stay away from the lake and the waterfall, but I can feel them as soon as I enter the valley."

"Then you shouldn't be coming here," she cried, though she couldn't face the prospect of his leaving. "They could—"

He kissed her softly. "They keep their distance, but I know they're there. It's just that if they are growing stronger, I should have felt it, too."

"Perhaps they *weren't* stronger," she said, though she was sure they were. "Maybe it was just because I'd had a difficult day and wasn't prepared to deal with them."

Then she went on to tell him about her cousin's abuse of her servant, and the action she'd taken. Gar was holding her in his arms as they sat by the fire, and she couldn't see his face, but as

233

she told him what she'd done, she could feel him become very still. She twisted around so that she could see his face.

"What is it, Gar?"

He searched her face solemnly and silently for a long moment before speaking. "Now I think I understand what happened at the ceremony," he said, his amber eyes dark with worry.

"What do you mean?" she asked. A chill ran through her.

"My love, the gods may have given you this power over your own people—but the Dark Ones may be influencing how you use it. You struck out in anger, Shera—not to save a life, but to seek revenge."

"That's not true!" she cried, edging away from him.

"It *is* true," he said calmly. "It wasn't necessary for you to use so much force on your cousin. I can understand that you were angry, but when you give in to that anger, you are opening yourself to the Dark Ones."

Shera swallowed hard. "But I didn't use as much force as I could have. I didn't *kill* her!"

"That's true. I'm not saying that the Dark Ones were controlling you completely—only that they may have had a hand in it."

Shera remained silent, remembering how shocked she'd been afterward at her own behavior. Gar was right. She *had* used more force than was really necessary. She had *wanted* to hurt her cousin, and in so doing, she'd stooped to Rella's level.

"There is always a dark side to such magic," Gar said, reaching out to draw her back into his arms. "You must guard against it, Shera."

"I'm frightened, Gar," she whispered, shivering.

He kissed the top of her head. "Maybe now you can understand how I feel about . . . the other. That is *my* power—and it frightens me, too."

They were quiet as they held each other for a long time, kissing and caressing, but content for now to let their desire build slowly. Shera was still deeply troubled by Gar's revelations, but she felt safe and peaceful here with him. When the voice inside her whispered that this couldn't last, she ignored it.

They made love as they had the night before: slowly and gently and with a rare sureness and understanding of each other's needs.

The glow of the fire illuminated their two bodies, one pale and smooth and the other bronzed and hair-roughened, but so entwined that only those physical differences distinguished one from the other. Both now knew all the ways to please, all the secret places that produced a gasp or a shudder of erotic pleasure.

Afterward, still wrapped in each other's arms, they dozed in the lingering warmth of their lovemaking and the heat from the fire. Shera was nearly asleep when she felt him begin to move restlessly against her, then begin to clutch her painfully.

Even as she struggled to sit up, she felt something brushing against her mind—and then she saw the light!

"No!" she cried as the light grew brighter, nearly hiding Gar from her. She didn't understand how this could be happening now. Was it because of what she'd done earlier?

Gar was still holding on to her arms tightly, and his hands were all she could see of him as he continued to writhe and groan. She reached deep into herself for her own power, determined to prevent what was happening—and then the vision came.

She saw Daren standing on a bare hilltop, his arms raised and great arcs of green fire pouring from his fingertips. Suddenly she knew what was happening. Daren was calling the Walkens, to aid him in his attack on the village.

"No! You cannot have him!" Shera shouted as Gar continued to cling to her.

Then she no longer felt Gar's touch—and she was no longer in the cottage. Instead she was there on the hilltop with Daren, a cold wind blowing over her naked skin. Her hands were glowing brightly.

"You cannot have him, Daren!" she shouted again.

He had been half-turned away from her and seemed not to have known she was there—but now he turned to face her, and even in the dark she could see his shock.

Saranne Dawson

"I will kill you if you try to take him, Daren!"

The arcs of green fire faded and he lowered his hands, still staring at her in disbelief.

"I *can* kill you, Daren—and I will if you harm him."

Her words seemed to be echoing down a long tunnel, and when they ended, she was back in the cottage and Gar was enfolding her in his arms. His skin burned against hers.

"You're so cold," he said, curving himself around her to bring her warmth.

"I was there," she said in a wondering tone. "It was Daren. He was calling your people."

"I know," he said, gently rubbing warmth into her body. "I was fighting him, but I think being here in his valley made it more difficult."

"He almost got you," she said, choking back a sob.

"No, he didn't. He might have succeeded in turning me into a chezah again—but I would never have followed him."

His response made her realize that no matter how close they'd become, there were still things he couldn't understand. She hadn't been frightened that Gar would follow Daren so much as she was terrified that he would no longer be human.

Gar held and soothed her, and before long, their caresses turned to lovemaking again. And when their passion was once more sated and she had fallen asleep in his arms, he thought about Daren.

He knows we're together now, Gar thought. *And despite what she thinks he does want her.* Gar had felt—for just a moment—a hatred so fierce and deep coming from Daren that it could exist for no other reason.

Only the nights were real for Shera now. She drifted through her days, tending to her duties, but she lived for the nights in Gar's arms.

A week after the night when Daren had called the chezahs, Gar told her that the village had been attacked and many people had been killed, either by chezahs or by Bacleev fire. Only about a dozen of his people were now resisting the call, and he knew that most of them were weakening.

Shera heard the bleakness in his voice and wondered how long it would be before he stood alone against Daren. What would he do then?

"We could leave here," she suggested. "We could return to the Trellans, where I lived before. The duke would welcome me back, and no one would know about you there."

He shook his head. "I cannot leave these mountains, my love—even if I must live here alone. And you must stay here as well. You alone can protect the people who've been enslaved. They *need* you."

She knew he was right, but she could not so easily let go of her dream. She understood that he would miss his mountains, and she knew she would miss this lovely valley—but they could be together and safe.

The days turned into weeks, and Shera knew that their time together was swiftly coming to an end. Through Gar's mind-talk with the chezahs, she learned that Daren and the others were already making their way back through the mountains with new slaves and more spoils, including great quantities of food.

She returned to the castle and managed to speak to Garet again. He told her that he had found three other men he trusted to help him steal food from the storehouses, and that they would be able to slip past the guards.

"Most of the time the guards sleep through the night," he told her. "Danna said she would give me some herbs to add to their tea that will guarantee they sleep well."

"Do you think you can manage that?" she asked, impressed by his resourcefulness.

He nodded. "We must fix their meals for them, and prepare their tea as well. It will not be too difficult."

They made their final plans, since Shera didn't want to risk being seen with him too often. Garet suggested that she should leave as soon as possible after Daren returned, explaining that with many more new slaves at the camp near the castle, there would be much confusion for a time.

That night she told Gar of her conversation with Garet, and he informed her that Daren would arrive within two days. Then, seeing the look on her face, he smiled.

"I am going with you. We'll be able to be together night and day for the journey."

"But what about the guards Daren will send along with me?"

"You can cast a spell on them, my love. They will do what they are told—and they will remember only what you allow them to remember."

She frowned at him. "You have more faith in my magic than I do. I'm not sure I can do that."

"Yes, you can," he assured her. "When the time comes, you will know what to do."

Two days later, as Shera was leaving the home of an elderly man whose passage into the afterlife she had helped to ease, she looked up and saw a long line of men and horses wending their way down into the valley. Moments later, everyone but Shera was running to meet them.

More than an hour passed before Daren flung open the door. Guessing that there might be trouble, Shera had sent both Danna and Tenia out to the orchard to gather more of the sweet red apples that were the last to be harvested.

"Where is he?" Daren demanded, glaring at her and then peering around the room as though expecting to find Gar lurking in a corner.

She considered annoying him further by pretending not to know who he meant, but instead she merely said that he had gone back into the mountains.

"You have broken our marriage vows!" Daren thundered.

"The marriage is a sham, Daren."

"I will find him and kill him!"

Shera kept her voice very quiet. "If you harm him, I will kill *you*, Daren. I already told you that. No matter how much power you think you have now, I have *more*. You would do well to remember that."

But he started toward her, his dark eyes blazing. Shera was shocked at his rage, but not afraid. She raised her hand, and it began to glow. Daren hesitated, then rushed at her. He succeeded only in pushing her against a table before she struck at him and sent him flying across the room, where he crashed into a wall and then fell heavily to the floor.

Then there was a knock at the door, and Shera heard one of his men calling him. She gave him a cold smile. "Shall I invite him in? Would you like to have him see what I've done to you?"

Daren scrambled to his feet and hurried to the door, but not before she saw the explosive mixture of fear and hatred in his eyes.

Instead of inviting the man in, he left with him, and several hours passed before she saw Daren again.

In the meantime she went to see for herself how much food had been stolen from the villagers. As she watched it being unloaded and carried into the storehouses, she became certain that nothing at all could have been left for the people who remained.

And there were now many more packhorses as well, which meant that she should be able to take as many as she needed without their being missed. After they were unloaded, they were being set free in a large pasture not far from the storehouses. It was perfect for her plan, as was the mass confusion that reigned in the village, especially with so many new people and such a huge quantity of goods.

Shera returned home to wait for Daren. He came just before dusk and the evening ceremonies. She saw that he had managed to hide his fear, but his anger had turned into a dark sullenness.

"You left no food in the villages," she stated.

"We left them some. They can forage for what they need."

"I am going there, Daren—to see for myself that they have enough for the winter."

"I forbid it!"

"She arched a brow. "You *forbid* it?" she asked mockingly. "You can forbid me nothing, Daren. I will go—with or without your blessing. And I am taking Tenia with me, so that she can see her baby."

"Are you taking your savage with you as well?" he taunted.

"No. I told you that he has returned to the mountains. I expect you to send guards with me, so that will keep him away."

"I don't trust you," he said petulantly.

"I don't trust you, either. If I did, I wouldn't be making this journey."

"I know what you did to Rella," he went on.

"She got no less than she deserved. I will do the same to anyone else who mistreats their servants."

"You go too far, Shera."

"No, Daren, it is you and the others who have gone too far. And while I am gone, you will see to it that housing is provided for everyone over the winter. The work on the castle will have to stop until that is taken care of."

"Jawan says that you must be stopped," he announced.

"Oh? And did he tell you how to do that? Or does he intend to stop me himself?" she asked. Her voice held much more confidence than she actually felt at the moment.

"The *gods* will stop you," Daren proclaimed.

"What you call the gods have already tried to stop me. They've failed. Go to the ceremony, Daren, and worship them."

He stalked out of the house, slamming the door behind him, and leaving Shera to wonder about his threat. It was entirely possible that his gods would stop her at some point—but that time had not yet come.

Chapter Thirteen

Shera lay on her bed, fully clothed, waiting to be certain that Daren had fallen asleep. He'd returned only a short time ago—later than she'd expected. She hated this waiting because it gave her too much time to think about everything that could go wrong.

Garet and his men might be caught. Daren could have posted guards at the storehouses. Someone might discover the supplies or the horses missing before she left in the morning. Daren might somehow become aware of Gar's presence in the valley and try to kill him.

She pushed aside those fears and thought instead about Tenia's joy when Shera had told her that she would be going along on the journey. What she hadn't told her was that they would bring her baby back with her. Daren didn't know that, either, of course—but Shera had decided to give them her old cottage. There were other women who'd been forced to leave children behind, but there was only so much she could do.

Finally she decided that she had waited long enough. She got quietly out of bed and opened her door, then smiled when she heard the snores coming from Daren's room. How fortunate that he wasn't a quiet sleeper.

The night was cold and still, with a bright, nearly full moon. Nowhere in the village did she see any lights. Still, she took the long route to the storehouses, traveling through the woods rather than along the streets and the path that led to the stables. Beyond that lay open fields where the additional horses were being kept, and past that were the three storehouses.

Staying close to the tree line, Shera studied the old stone buildings. From this vantage point they seemed rather small, but that was because they'd been built against natural caverns that were many times larger than the structures themselves.

She breathed a sigh of relief when she saw no evidence of guards. It wasn't likely that Daren would have bothered with them, but she hadn't been sure. She hurried across the fields, wondering if Gar could be there, and how soon Garet and his men would arrive. She was counting on the urgency of their task to keep them from being too shocked by Gar's presence.

She was less than twenty feet from the big door to the first of the storehouses when she saw, in her peripheral vision, movements in the shadows alongside the structure.

"It's Garet," said a quiet voice as four men came forward. "Do you have a key?"

"A key?" she echoed, turning to stare at the big door. To her dismay, she saw that a padlock had been placed on it. "Are the others locked as well?"

Garet nodded. Shera stared at it. Would Daren have the key? Could she go back and find it?

"You can open it," said a very familiar voice.

Shera whirled around, and as she did she heard the gasps from the four men. Gar walked toward them. "Use your magic."

He nodded casually at the gaping men, then frowned slightly. "I know you," he said to Garet. "I got my horse from you when I went to warn your people."

Garet nodded, and when Gar extended his hand, he took it after only a moment's hesitation. The other men backed away, still staring in shock at this Walken.

"You weren't with them when they attacked us, were you?" Garet said.

Gar shook his head. "I told you that I would have no part of it, but I was unable to stop all my people."

"Gar is here to help us," Shera explained. "He will take the packhorses into the mountains after we load them, then meet me tomorrow."

"Open the door," Gar said, gesturing.

Shera summoned her magic, ignoring the frightened reactions of the men with Garet. She reached out to touch the padlock, and it fell open in her hand.

With Gar helping, they made short work of loading the packhorses he'd already tethered in the nearby woods. Then Shera opened the other two storehouses and they redistributed the supplies so that the missing items were less likely to be noticed. As Gar relocked the storehouses, Shera turned to Garet and told him that Tenia would be going with her.

"You will be seeing your son soon, Garet, because we're going to bring him back here."

Tears sprang to his eyes. "May the gods keep you safe, Shera." Then he summoned the others and they vanished into the woods, heading back to their camp near the castle.

Gar came up beside Shera. "He is a brave man—and a good one as well. It took courage for him to overcome his hatred of my people and give me a horse when I went there. After he did that, the others were at least willing to listen—for all the good it did." His voice was bitter.

"We do what we can do," Shera said, thinking not only of his situation, but her own as well. "His wife is my servant and I am taking her with us. I intend to bring back their baby as well."

Gar asked about Daren's reaction to her plans, and she told him all that had happened. "He threatens me, but they are empty threats."

"Do not be too confident, my love. He is dangerous. You cannot afford to become careless."

His warning lingered along with his parting kiss as she watched him lead the line of packhorses off into the mountains.

How she wished that the two of them could leave this valley forever. But she had come to understand that Gar was right: they couldn't run away. As long as there was life in either of them, they had to stay here and try to bring change.

Shera held the reins tightly as her mare shifted restlessly, eager to be off on this clear, cold morning. She sympathized with the animal. At any moment she expected someone to come running from the fields or the storehouses to say that food and animals were missing.

But she waited with outward calm as Daren strutted about, issuing redundant orders to the two of his men whom he had sent to accompany her. Somehow he had managed to make it seem that her journey was his idea, though why anyone would believe that, she couldn't imagine. Still, she was learning to choose her battles with him carefully and avoid public confrontations.

"If you encounter any renegade chezahs, kill them!" Daren told the two men, turning to be certain that she had heard him. "You know by now how to tell the Walkens from other chezahs, and I want that savage, Gar, dead!"

Interesting, Shera thought, betraying no emotion at his harangue. So he didn't know that she had changed Gar back to human form.

Daren strode over to her. "May the gods go with you, Shera."

Acting on a wicked impulse, Shera leaned down from the saddle and pretended to kiss his cheek. "The gods *are* with me, Daren," she whispered into his ear. "And if you mistreat Danna or anyone else while I'm gone, I'll prove it to you."

She was rewarded by a dark flush of anger that belied his attempt to smile. She kicked her mare into action, and they set off.

As they rode through the woods toward the trail that would take them out of the valley and into the mountains, Shera cast a glance at Tenia. The woman's face was flushed with happiness at the prospect of seeing her baby again, though Shera hadn't yet told her that they would be bringing the child back with them. Neither had she had an opportunity to explain about Gar and what she intended to do to the two guards. She would simply have to trust that Tenia's faith in her would allow her to accept Shera's use of such dark magic.

Shera was unfamiliar with this trail, which wound along the mountains at the far end of the valley until it reached a narrow pass that then continued through the other mountains until it finally reached the broad valley that was home to Tenia's people. But Gar knew it, of course, and he had told her he would meet her at a place he had described—just before they reached the pass.

She kept her eyes on her two guards, who rode together ahead of Tenia and her, with their four packhorses trailing behind. When Gar had told her that she could control the men, she'd at first doubted him. But then, recalling how easily she'd gotten information from Daren that time, she understood that she *could* do it. She had only to *want* to do it, to reach down into that deep pool of strength within her.

The question was when she should do it. If she did it now, before Gar appeared, how could she be certain that she'd succeeded? She wouldn't see any change in their behavior. But if she waited until they met Gar, there was always the chance that one of them could attack him before she could act.

She decided that she had to do it now, and then be prepared to act again if they showed any sign of violence. She'd countered Daren's fire easily enough that time, but she wasn't sure she could handle two men, instead of just one.

She was uneasy, and because of her discomfort, it took her some time to find that calm, deep center from which her powers arose. It was very different from using the fire, which was an instinctive reaction requiring nothing more than anger or fear. At last, she found and sank into it gratefully, losing awareness of everything but her goal.

She had fixed her gaze steadily on the back of the one man, and now she reached out to him with her mind. She felt his sudden awareness and saw him suddenly jerk his head around, twisting in the saddle to face her. Her concentration nearly slipped as she saw the shock in his eyes and felt him trying to fight her. But his companion was already staring at him, and she knew she had to act quickly.

Turn around, she ordered silently—and he did, facing front again. Then she issued the orders. He would accept the man Gar, he would do nothing to harm him.

The other man was now speaking, asking his companion what was wrong. Shera couldn't hear his reply, but it didn't matter. She had now shifted her attention to the other. He reacted somewhat more violently, pulling sharply on the reins and causing his horse to rear, nearly unseating himself in the process. But she repeated the spell with him, and within minutes both men were calm and paying her no attention at all as they continued their journey.

Shera turned to Tenia and found her staring ahead, wide-eyed. Her gaze moved from the men to her. After asking the two guards to move farther ahead, Shera quietly told her what she'd done and why.

"Gar," Tenia echoed. "He is the Walken who came to our village to warn us. Garet spoke to him and lent him a horse."

"Yes, and he has taken no part in the attacks on the villages."

Tenia shivered. "He frightened me, even though he did nothing to us. My people have always feared the Walkens—even more than they feared the Bacleev."

"I understand that, Tenia—but they're wrong to do so. The Walkens hurt your people only when the Bacleev were directing them."

Tenia nodded, but Shera could tell that she wasn't convinced. She was struck by how easily Tenia had accepted what she'd done to the two men, yet remained terrified of the Walkens. It reminded her once again that for all their terrible powers, the Bacleev were still human—and the Walkens were not.

As they drew near the spot where Gar had said he would meet them, Shera watched the two guards closely, still not certain they would obey her directive. The terrain here was hilly, and suddenly the two men reined in their horses sharply as they reached the top of a rise.

Shera urged her mare forward, at the same time watching the hands of her two foes for any sign of hostility. But after bringing their mounts to a halt, they simply sat, staring at the trail ahead. As she rode up to them, she saw that their expressions were quizzical.

Gar was nowhere to be seen. Instead she saw their pack-horses. They were laden with large bags of food, and they stood there placidly, one tied to the other, with the lead animal tethered to a tree beside the trail.

Shera rode toward them, suddenly fearful. She scanned the woods and the ravine on one side of the trail with increasing desperation as she moved closer to the pack animals.

Then her mare began to shy and whinny with fear. Shera reined the beast in tightly, wondering why the packhorses would frighten her mount. A moment later, she saw the source of the mare's fear.

Gar was sitting on a heavy limb, some thirty feet above the ground, nearly concealed by the tree's thick clusters of needles. Struggling to keep her mare under control, Shera could understand why the animal was frightened. From head to toe, Gar was now the exact color of a chezah, dressed as he was in heavily furred clothing. And he was crouched on the limb with all the agility of that creature as well.

As she watched, he climbed down from the tree, displaying a singular grace that no ordinary human could hope to attain. She drew in a breath, fighting down a brief burst of fear that told her she was really no less prejudiced than Tenia.

She turned briefly to look at Tenia and the two guards. Daren's men were exactly where she'd left them, and though it was obvious that they'd seen Gar by now, they still wore the same confused expressions. Tenia, however, was staring wide-eyed, her body rigid.

Shera's mare shied again as Gar approached it, but he reached out and seized its bridle, then spoke quietly into the steed's ear. Within seconds the animal had quieted down again. He nodded toward the two men.

"They seem well under control."

"They are," she assured him. She laughed. "Though Daren's last words to them were to kill you on sight."

He reached up and curved a hand around her head, then drew her face down for a quick, hard kiss. Mindful of Tenia's presence, Shera pulled back, though not before his lips had left their indelible print on hers.

"Tenia doesn't know about us," she told him when he frowned at her.

"Then it is time she does," Gar said. "I don't intend to sleep alone on this journey."

Before she could stop him, he was walking back toward Tenia, who looked as though she were about to wheel her horse around and flee. Her mount behaved much as Shera's had, until Gar took its bridle and stroked it and talked to it quietly. Shera rode to join them as Gar turned his attention to Tenia.

She listened as he explained to her that he meant her and her people no harm, and how he regretted what had been done to them. Tenia's eyes were still wide, but she seemed somewhat less frightened, and even managed a smile when Gar mentioned that she would soon be seeing her baby.

After that, Gar walked around the two men, who turned their heads to watch him with vacant expressions. Shera saw the cold look in his eyes and held her breath, fearing that he might do something violent. Instead he turned to her and saw the look on her face.

"Don't worry, my love, I enjoy seeing them like this. Enslaved. Killing them would have been a pleasure—but this is better."

Then he began to assemble their convoy, untying the lead packhorse and bringing them all into line on the trail. Shera saw that his own mount was a beast of burden as well. She was sure that he would have preferred a better animal, but if he'd taken one from the stables, its absence would have been noticed.

A short time later they were on their way again, with the two men riding in front, followed by Tenia, then Gar and Shera. The long line of pack animals trailed behind.

The day's end brought them to a wide place in the trail, where Shera saw the remains of earlier campfires, and flattened bushes and weeds that showed that earlier convoys had also chosen this place. Beneath the trees that ringed the clearing there were bales of hay that had apparently been left there from previous journeys. Together with the two guards, who spoke only when addressed by either Gar or Shera, they tended to the horses while Tenia built a fire and prepared their evening meal.

Both men were carrying rifles and plenty of powder, though it was by now in short supply—for they had only brought so much from the duke. Gar took the rifles and powder, then swung one of the weapons against a tree trunk. It shattered into several pieces. The other one he carried over to his saddle, together with the supply of powder. Shera watched him, but said nothing. She knew he was fascinated by the weapons, and in truth, the Bacleev had little need of them anymore—except perhaps to keep her in line.

"I can use it for hunting," Gar said when he rejoined her.

Shera concealed her discomfort with his carnivorous nature.

The guards joined them for dinner, but they sat some distance away and remained silent. They watched Gar with wary, fascinated gazes, even though the Walken ignored them. Tenia watched him in the same manner, though she seemed less frightened of him now. Shera decided that even if she had been able to persuade Gar to leave the mountains and return to Trella with her, he never would have blended in. Gar was simply too different.

After dinner, as Gar made sure to check on the horses, Shera followed him with her eyes, trying to see him as others did. He had already regained his uncommonly graceful movement, and it never failed to be startling considering his size.

How much of what I feel for him is fascination—and how much is love? she wondered, knowing it was a question without an answer. It seemed that she was always veering wildly from feeling closer to him than she ever had to anyone, to a sad certainty that she would never truly understand him.

They all settled down to sleep around the campfire. Shera lay with Gar, on a quilt, another one covering them from the chill night air.

Saranne Dawson

At first Gar simply held her close, but soon his hand began to find its way beneath her clothing. The fire inside her was already burning brightly, threatening to melt away her ability to think clearly.

"Gar," she whispered. "We can't."

"Yes, we can," he murmured close to her ear. His roving fingers found her moist heat. She gasped.

She was excited but wary, and the combination brought a wholly new dimension to their lovemaking. The others weren't far away, but the firelight barely reached them. It became an erotic game: finding subtle ways to please each other, swallowing their cries and groans, prolonging the moment, then rushing headlong into silent ecstasy.

They had been on the trail for three days and three nights of furtive passion. Shera wished they could be alone, but even so, it was the most happiness she'd known in her life. Gar wasn't talkative, but she had only to glance his way to see the light of love in his eyes and feel his need for her.

She was talking to Tenia about her village when she saw Gar, who was riding a short distance ahead of them, suddenly rein in his horse and stare off up the steep slope to their left. She followed his gaze, but saw nothing. She'd nearly forgotten her concern that Daren would discover the missing food or animals, but now that fear came flooding back to her.

"What is it?" she asked as she rode up to where he'd stopped.

He got off his horse and handed her the reins. "Take my horse and keep moving. I'll rejoin you later."

"Where are you going?" she asked as he started to climb the slope.

"I won't be far. Someone wants to speak to me."

She looked up again, but still saw nothing. "Why can't they come here?"

"Because they would frighten the horses," he replied. With a meaningful glance, he turned and climbed the nearly vertical slope with amazing speed.

Shera watched until he had vanished into the trees, then

250

urged her mare on to catch up with the others, bringing Gar's horse with her. Tenia asked if there was trouble. She, at least, had never lost her fear that they would be followed.

"I don't know," Shera said in exasperation, then softened her tone so Tenia wouldn't think she was the object of her wrath. "Gar doesn't seem to feel the need to explain himself. He'll rejoin us farther on."

"He loves you very much," Tenia said.

Shera sighed. "Yes, I know, but this is one of those times when I wish he were more like other men."

"He isn't, though," Tenia replied. "He's been very kind to me, but it's hard not to fear him."

"I think he understands that." *As much as he understands any human emotion,* she added to herself, really annoyed that he would just go off without an explanation.

She wondered who wanted to speak to him: chezahs or one of his people. She supposed it didn't matter; they were all beasts now.

They rode on, with Shera expecting Gar to return any moment. Holding on to his horse's reins became difficult after a time, so she stopped and untied the lead packhorse, then secured Gar's behind it. She continued to scan the mountains above them. Gar wouldn't have left if there'd been any danger, but she knew by now that the chezahs might have spotted someone following them at some distance.

He'd been gone for more than an hour when Daren's guards, who were in the lead, suddenly stopped at a bend in the trail. Shera rode up to join them and saw Gar standing there. He paid her no attention at all; instead, his gaze was fixed firmly and coldly on the Bacleev.

"We're being followed by two men," he said, still staring at Daren's men.

"Then Daren must have found out about the missing food and horses."

Gar shook his head. "I don't think so. They left the village not long after we did, and I don't think there was time for them to find out that we took anything."

251

"But then why would they be following us?"

Gar shifted his gaze from the two men to her. "Either Daren has decided that you require extra protection—or he's planning to use this journey as an excuse to get rid of you."

Shera gasped. "He wouldn't do that. Not when he knows that I could easily kill these men."

The possibility that Daren would actually try to have her murdered was one that she'd simply never considered—and wouldn't have even if she didn't have a way to protect herself. Gar must have seen the disbelief on her face.

"I've suspected for some time that he might try this, to have you killed. You're all that stands between him and everything he wants."

"But even if he succeeded, he would gain nothing. He'd lose his position as shegwa."

"Would he? What if the priests declared that the gods approved of his taking another mate?"

Shera was silent for a moment, thinking. As far as she knew, nothing like this had ever happened. The couple who were shegwas before her parents had relinquished their positions when their advanced ages made it difficult to carry out their many duties. "I don't know."

"Exactly," Gar said, nodding. Then he gestured to the guards. "If there *is* a plot to kill you, these two probably know about it. Make them talk."

Shera turned toward the two men, who sat astride their horses a short distance away, as always, watching Gar warily. Trying to stifle the revulsion she felt at doing such a thing, she walked over to them.

"Is Daren planning to kill me?" she asked, pushing the question at them with her mind as she spoke. They stared at her blankly, saying nothing. It had been so easy that time with Daren, but that was before awareness of her powers made her reluctant.

"Answer me!" she commanded, pushing still harder.

Both men drew back, and one of them clutched his head with a hand, as though in pain. "No!" they cried, almost in unison.

Shera stared at them, wondering if they could possibly be lying. She turned to Gar questioningly.

"You forced information from Daren, so perhaps he kept any scheme from them, in case you became suspicious and used your powers on them."

"It's hard for me to believe that Daren would do such a thing," Shera confessed. "He surely hates me, but enough to kill me? We have never been killers. . . ."

Gar gave her a look that spoke eloquently of her foolishness. "How can you say that?"

"That's different," she insisted lamely. "I meant that one Bacleev would never hurt another unless it were the direst circumstance."

Of course, the moment the words were said and couldn't be taken back, an image of her violence toward Rella flooded her mind. Gar said nothing, clearly knowing that he didn't have to.

"All right," she said angrily. "Maybe it *is* possible. But why haven't they already tried? You said that these others left soon after we did, so they've had time. And how would they do it, anyway?"

"If I were Daren, I would wait until we reach the village—and then I'd have you killed in your sleep." He spoke matter-of-factly. "That way he could claim that you were killed by the villagers, which would only fuel people's hatred of them. No doubt he plans to have these two back him up." He looked at the bemused guards. "The killers would work with them, and then return alone to report to Daren."

Listening to him, Shera could all too easily imagine Gar himself hatching such a plan if the circumstances were different. Killing had always come far too easily to him, she thought sadly.

Gar apparently mistook her shudder for a fear of being killed. He drew her into his arms.

"Don't worry, my love. They will be watched, and I'll know if they come any closer."

"But what about when we get to the village?" she asked.

"I'll see to it that we're well guarded at night."

She looked up at him. "Isn't it just as likely that it's *you* he wants to have killed?"

But Gar shook his head. "Oh, he wants me dead, all right—but I think he would want to do that himself. Besides, he doesn't know that I'm with you. Although I think he knows that I'm human again."

"How could he know that?"

"We must give him credit for some intelligence, Shera. When you suddenly appeared before him that night he was calling the chezahs, he surely guessed you were with me."

"But that doesn't mean that he knew you were human again." She frowned.

Gar smiled, and then began to chuckle. "I don't think you would have been naked if I were still a chezah."

"Oh." She hadn't thought of that.

"Killing you would accomplish two things for him: you won't stand in his way, and I would become a chezah again." Gar paused. "He's desperate, my love. And in spite of what you believe, he *does* want you. Though I think he has finally realized that he can't hope to have you. And the priests may be pressuring him as well. You said they told him that you must be stopped, and I think they know they can't do it themselves."

On the sixth night of their journey, a series of ferocious thunderstorms swept through the mountains. Winds stronger than anything Shera had ever seen uprooted small trees and tore limbs from the large ones. Gar had sensed the coming of the storms somehow, and he'd led them off the trail to a high mountain meadow.

When they reached it just before dusk, and she began to see the dark clouds piling up on the horizon, she looked around in dismay. "There's no shelter here."

"Yes, there is," Gar replied as they rode across the meadow toward a rocky area. "Remember that I know these mountains."

A few minutes later she saw that he was right. In the rocky area was a series of caves concealed behind huge boulders. None of the caves was very large, but by the time the wind had begun to pick up, Gar had moved all of the horses and people into them. Shera made to follow Tenia, but Gar stopped her. He tugged on her hand.

"Where are we going?" she asked, having assumed they would have to share a cave with the horses or with the others.

"Up there," Gar said, pointing up the steep, rocky slope. He turned to her with a smile. "I have saved the best one for us."

"The best one?" she echoed quizzically. Looking up the rock face, she thought she'd be lucky if she could even get up there.

Big raindrops, driven by the ever-rising winds, had begun to fall by the time they were halfway up the slope. Gar was in the lead, and he'd tied a rope around her waist, then secured it to his belt. Twice she slipped, and only the rope prevented her from falling back down the nearly vertical rock face. She would have told him that whatever was so special about his cave couldn't be worth this, but he wouldn't have heard her in the howling wind that was now punctuated by low, deep rumbles of thunder.

Finally they were there. As she followed Gar through the narrow opening, the first thing she noticed was the smell. It was familiar, but she couldn't place it. She sniffed. "What is that?"

"A hot spring. It's back there."

"Oh." Now she knew why the smell was familiar. It was the same as the bath in Gar's village. She sighed with pleasure, deciding that it *had* been worth the effort, after all.

But her pleasure was short-lived as her eyes gradually adjusted to the cavern. The walls and ceiling were glowing much like the cave of the Dark Ones, though not quite as brightly.

"Gar!" she cried. "This can't be safe! It's lit like the cave behind the waterfall—where the Dark Ones live!"

"Come here," he said calmly. "It's not magic."

She walked over to a wall with him and he showed her the tiny, gnarled growths that covered much of the wall.

"They're a plant that glows," he said. "I've seen them in other caverns, but they make more light here because of the diamonds."

"Diamonds?" she echoed in disbelief, then peered more closely. He was right. Scattered about among the ugly, glowing things he called plants were thousands of glittering stones. She'd never seen diamonds that hadn't been cut, but they certainly reflected the light in much the same way.

"A fortune in them, I imagine," he said with a shrug. "I've heard that people value them greatly. My grandfather said that the Bacleev were always looking for them—or stealing them from those who had them."

"How did you first find this place?" she asked in amazement.

"I didn't. It was discovered by my people. Some of my ancestors used these caves as winter dens."

He took her hand. "Come. Let's bathe before we eat."

The corridor that led from the front part of the cave was so narrow that they had to walk single file. But here, too, the walls glowed and glittered. The storm struck, but as they moved deeper into the mountain, they could no longer hear its ferocity.

After some minutes they reached another, smaller room that was wonderfully warm, since the bubbling pool at its center filled most of the floor space. The water reflected the light from the walls, and its restless movement cast flickering shadows over the scene.

"This is wonderful!" Shera proclaimed with a sigh.

"It was worth the climb, then?" Gar asked, arching a brow.

"It may even be worth the climb back down," she admitted with a smile. "Thank you for bringing me here."

"Why thank me? I brought you here as much for my own pleasure as for yours."

Shera smiled as she began to undress. She wondered if Gar would ever learn the polite manners of society. And then she wondered if she even wanted that to happen. Part of her love for him was his honesty, his lack of artifice. But it was still disconcerting that he was so different.

The pool was not deep, coming only to her waist at its greatest depth. But the water was pleasantly warm, almost hot, and as before, the more she was immersed in the unusual scent, the more she grew to like it.

"Why do these warm pools smell this way?" she asked.

He shrugged. "I don't know. Why does it matter?"

"Aren't you ever simply curious about things?"

"Only if there may be a need to change it. Otherwise I accept it." He paused. "Do you find that strange?"

"Yes, I suppose I do, though my people are much like you in that regard. They tend to accept what is, without giving it much thought. But I spent much time among the Trellans, and they question everything. They're a very curious people—which is probably how they came to invent those rifles you seem to like."

He was silent for a moment. "I see. I must think about that." He reached for her. "But not just now."

It began as a pretense at bathing each other, but the charade didn't last long. Their nights on the trail, while having a certain piquant sensuality, had left them both unsatisfied. Now, at last, they were free again to set loose the wildness.

Hands and lips glided over slick, heated bodies, seeking all that had been denied them these past nights. Then Gar lifted her and she wrapped herself around him, crying out with pleasure as he entered her with a deep groan that echoed off the ancient stone walls.

Afterward, they climbed out of the pool to lie on a thick quilt, talking little as they simply held each other. Shera was thinking how perfect their times together were—and how very precious. How could she possibly return to the valley, and to Daren? If he was trying to kill her, he would not just quit.

She wrapped her arms more tightly around Gar, not wanting to think about Daren. But it seemed that he was on Gar's mind as well.

"He won't stop, you know," Gar said after a long silence, startling her because it seemed that he'd been reading her thoughts. "But there may be a way to stop him."

"What is that?" she asked.

"Since he intends to make it appear that it's the villagers who want to kill you, that gives us an advantage."

"I don't understand," she said, wishing that they weren't having this conversation—certainly not now, when she wanted nothing more than to linger in the soft afterglow of their lovemaking.

"He will have to make it appear that one of the slaves has killed you—and who better to guard you against them than the chezahs, whom they fear the most?"

Shera sat up and stared at him as a smile tugged at the corners of her mouth. Gar shrugged. "And of course, since the chezahs are under Daren's control, it would be unlikely that one of them would kill you."

She laughed, loving the rich irony of it all. Daren would be enraged, but how could he refuse?

"The chezah I have in mind would only anger him further," Gar said with a smile of his own.

"You? But . . ."

"I know. I would prefer to remain human, but this way we could be together, and we might find opportunities for me to change back."

"But what if Daren tries to . . . influence you?"

"It won't work," he swore. "You will be there to prevent it. Besides, he wouldn't dare try to use *me* to kill you—just as he couldn't use any other chezah without casting suspicion upon himself as their master."

She was silent. Everything he said made sense, except that she didn't want him to be an animal again.

"Do you really want that?" she asked. "To be a chezah again?"

"It is not as bad as you think," he said, kissing her. "And we will be together."

"But you won't even be able to talk to me," she protested.

"I think it's possible that I can," he replied thoughtfully. "Mind-talking is easy enough among my people, and you have greater powers than ours, my love."

Chapter Fourteen

Two days later, they rode down out of the mountains onto a flat, broad plain that reminded Shera of the land of the Trellans. Tenia's village was more than a day's ride across the seemingly endless expanse.

They had ridden only a short distance through the treeless, grass-covered plain when Shera began to feel nervous. Immediately she turned to look behind them, fearing that perhaps Daren's assassins had managed to elude the watchful chezahs. But no one was there, and there was no conceivable place for them to hide.

She tried to ignore the feeling, but it persisted, and as the day passed it seemed to grow stronger. It was a strange sensation, totally unlike anything she'd ever felt before: a sort of diffuse anxiety that seemed to have no source. Unwilling to say anything to Gar until she could pinpoint its cause, she rode on, unconsciously turning every few minutes to scan the empty fields behind them.

"It's the absence of mountains," Gar said, breaking a long silence between them.

"What?" She'd just turned to look behind them once again, and now she swiveled back to stare at him.

"You feel uneasy because we're no longer in the mountains," he said.

"I do? But I lived most of my life in land like this." She was beginning to sense the truth behind his words, but was as yet unwilling to believe that the answer could be so simple.

"Nevertheless, that is what's troubling you," he declared. "You've grown accustomed to the mountains around you all the time; without them, you feel vulnerable and exposed. I know this because I, too, feel it."

Shera was dumbfounded. As she thought about it, she realized that if she hadn't become so accustomed to the presence of danger in her life as well, she might have guessed the truth immediately.

That evening they were forced to set up camp in the open, near a swift-running stream that flowed down from the mountains. Gar explained that they had only to follow the stream to where it emptied into a larger river. There they would find the village.

Even though she now understood the reason for her uneasiness, Shera could not set it aside. When Gar took the rifle from his saddle and said that he was going to find some game for dinner, she very nearly asked him not to go. But she managed to hold her tongue, knowing that both Gar and Tenia were finding their diet inadequate. And they didn't want to cut into the stores for the helpless villagers.

Before long she heard several shots, and soon after, Gar returned with two rabbits. Shera managed to be elsewhere while he and Tenia cleaned and prepared their feast, then stayed carefully upwind of the campfire as they cooked the rabbits.

Their two guards sat off by themselves, as they always did, and Shera began to worry about them. She'd had no idea how long her control would last, but it now appeared that it would continue until she released them. Not once had she seen any sign of incipient rebellion in either one of them. They did what they were told, spoke only when spoken to, and the rest of the time remained silent.

Shera shuddered to think that Daren might plan to do this to the people he'd enslaved. She suspected that at the first sign of rebellion, he would try.

Though he might not yet trust his powers sufficiently to undertake such a huge task. But if those powers grew stronger, as Gar had said they would, then Daren might very well decide that he could work the men harder if he took away their minds.

They were still seated around the campfire as dusk fell over the land, when Gar suddenly turned his head sharply to look behind them. Still nervous, Shera turned, too, her hands already beginning to glow with fire. Gar reached out to take hold of them both.

"No one is there. I've just received a message. Your clever assassins are remaining in the mountains for now."

"Then perhaps they don't plan to attack me in the village after all," she said, wanting to be relieved.

"No, I think they will. Once we reach the village, they will ride hard, day and night, to get there. They stay in the mountains now because otherwise we might see them."

"I wish I didn't have this power," she said, staring down at the hands he still held. There remained only a very faint glow and it vanished even as she watched.

"Be glad that you do," Gar said. "You may have to save us both one day."

"Will it ever end, Gar?" she asked plaintively.

"I don't know," he replied. "I don't know."

They reached the first village the following afternoon. At first glance it seemed to be deserted. Although the day was pleasantly warm, there were no children playing and no old people gathered in the market square. Shera became increasingly uneasy, fearing that Daren might have left no one alive. Had she brought Tenia here, only to have her confronted with the massacre of her child and village?

Gar, however, seemed unperturbed. He turned in the saddle to call out to Tenia, who was riding behind them. "Take us to the home of the village elder, Tenia, and tell him that we come in peace."

Tenia led them to a large house just off the market square, then dismounted and went to the door. She knocked loudly several times and called out a name, but she got no response. When she returned to Shera and Gar, she was pale with fear.

"No one is here! Could they all have been—"

"Where would they go to hide?" Gar asked, cutting her off. "There must be a place."

At his words, Tenia's face grew hopeful. "Yes! There is a tunnel beneath the meeting house. It was dug many years ago—after the Bacleev attacked us before. I think they will be there."

"But why didn't you go there when Daren and his men came?" Shera asked.

"Because they came at night—and it was the chezahs that came first. They killed the guards we had set up around the village. And then your husband and his men sent the magic fire through the village. No one could resist."

Shera frowned. "Do you mean they cast a spell on the entire village?" She'd never asked Tenia for the details before, and now she was stunned to think that Daren could have such power. He'd had only half a dozen men with him.

Tenia nodded. "It didn't last long, but by the time we were free of the spell, they had captured us." She pointed west. "The meeting house is over there. I will go to talk to them."

She walked across the square to the largest building in the village, then vanished inside. Shera turned to Gar.

"I didn't think that Daren could have such power," she said nervously.

"He wasn't acting alone," Gar reminded her. "And the spell didn't last."

His words did little to calm her fears. She was beginning to realize that Daren had a great advantage over her, one she'd never before considered. She was forced to learn for herself

what her magic could do, but it was possible—even likely—
that the priests, or even the Dark Ones themselves, were teaching Daren.

Tenia was gone for some time, but finally she returned—with
a long line of people trailing rather uncertainly after her. In
Tenia's arms was her son, a robust infant whose downy hair was
a darker shade of red than his father's. Walking beside her were
two men. One of them was a white-haired but vigorous-looking
man who was probably the village elder. The other man was
somewhat younger, but badly crippled and walking with the aid
of crutches. Shera guessed immediately that he must be Tenia's
father and Danna's husband—and she saw an opportunity to do
something more for this family.

The people stopped and stared in amazement at the long line
of packhorses, their faces hopeful but not quite believing. Most
of them kept slanting nervous glances at Gar, as did the elder,
who barely acknowledged his presence when Tenia introduced
them. It was mute testimony to the fear these people had of the
Walkens.

Shera dismounted and went to admire Tenia's baby, while
Gar told the elder that they could use the help of any who were
able to get the foodstuffs unloaded. She saw the elder turn his
attention back to the Bacleev guards.

"Don't worry about them," Shera told him, speaking slowly
and clearly, as she'd done at first with Tenia and Danna. "I've
cast a spell on them. They will cause no trouble."

For the first time, the elder studied her. "You have cast a spell
on your own people?" he asked. "Why?"

Gar spoke up. "She has cast a spell on them and returned me
to my human form. The gods have shown her great favor—and
the Dark Ones cannot capture her."

By now others had crowded around, and a great silence fell
on everyone as they all stared at Shera.

"The gods have not yet shown me a way to end this and get
my people away from the Dark Ones, but I do what I can."

"You would go against your own people?" the elder asked.

Saranne Dawson

Shera met his gaze and nodded firmly. "My people have become evil. Until I can end the reign of the Dark Ones, I will fight them."

He said nothing, but Shera could see in his eyes a sad certainty that the day of reckoning would never come.

The packhorses were led off, with Gar and the guards going with them. Shera followed Tenia and her father to a house several streets away. A stout older woman went with them, and Tenia introduced her as her aunt, her father's sister. It was she who had been caring for Tenia's son, Dakin.

Behind the well-kept house was a large stable and another building that Shera assumed was Garet's blacksmith shop. She saw Tenia cast a sad look at it, and knew she must be wishing that her husband could be with her now.

Shera hadn't yet told Tenia that she could bring little Dakin back with her, and she wondered if perhaps Tenia would prefer to stay here. But that would mean a separation from her husband—perhaps for a very long time. It was a terrible choice.

She saw tears in Tenia's dark eyes as she looked around her home. It was nearly bare now, though Shera guessed it had once been quite pleasantly furnished. The floors were uncovered and only large pieces of furniture remained: beautifully carved and well-tended reminders of what had once been a lovely home.

Wanting to divert Tenia's attention from it, and her own attention from Daren's cruelty, Shera spoke to Masik, Tenia's father. "I am the greatest healer among my people, Masik, and if you will permit me, I think I can restore you to health. It will take some time, though, so we should begin now."

Tenia's eyes widened and Shera saw one of her rare and beautiful smiles. "Say yes, Father. I have seen Shera heal. I was very sick when I arrived in the valley, and she cured me."

Masik looked from his daughter to Shera, then gave her a smile of his own. "It would be a help, lady. There is so much to do here now, and I can do little."

For the next hour, as Masik lay on his bed, Shera worked her magic on him. Tenia and her aunt were in and out of the room, speaking words of encouragement. Masik's initial nervousness when he saw her hands begin to glow faded quickly—and then, of course, he wanted to be cured immediately.

Shera smiled. "I think I can restore all that you've lost, but I cannot do it all at once."

"Can you stay long enough?" he asked hopefully.

She assured him that she could, and that she would try to help as many others as she could, too—both here and in the other village. They had food to deliver there as well, though it appeared that Daren had taken less from the others.

By the time she called a halt to his treatment, her own hands were aching, but Masik was now hobbling about with the aid of only a cane, eagerly showing everyone how he could now grasp things with his hands, as he hadn't been able to do for several years.

Others had begun showing up at Tenia's house while Shera was working on Masik, and by the time she stopped, it seemed that nearly half those remaining in the village were waiting to see her. Then Gar arrived. People quickly backed away, giving him a wide berth, but they did not leave.

Sizing up the situation quickly, Gar turned to the elder, who was still with him. "You must talk to these people and explain that Shera cannot cure them all now. You must decide who needs her help most."

The elder, whose gaze was fixed on Masik, nodded. "There are several others like Masik, who could help cut firewood for the winter if they can be cured. They should be first."

"Thank you," Shera murmured as Gar guided her to a chair. "It's very hard for me to say no. Sometimes, when I went out to the far villages in Trella, I would be so tired that I had to be tied to my horse to make it home."

Gar bent to kiss her softly, and Shera heard gasps of shock from those who saw it. "It may help for them to know about us. Maybe they'll be less afraid of me," he murmured.

Then he straightened up again. "I am going to ride just beyond the village, so that I can try to find out where those men are. It's difficult for me to hear any messages in this place. There are too many people."

Saranne Dawson

"Be careful, Gar! If they find you . . ."

"It's not likely that they've gotten this far yet."

"Perhaps I should come with you."

"No. You rest. I'll be back soon."

When Gar returned an hour later, Shera was just accepting the thanks of a man who was eagerly flexing his right arm, which she had restored to use.

"There's no way I can repay you, lady," he said shamefacedly.

"Of course you can't. How could you, when my people stole everything of value? Consider this to be a small payment for what was taken."

Startled at her words, the man nodded, thanked her again, and then cast a wary glance at Gar before departing.

Gar took both her hands gently. "And who is going to heal the healer?" he asked wryly.

"I'll be fine by morning," she assured him, though it wasn't likely that she would be. "Are our enemies coming across the plain?"

"Yes, but they won't reach here until tomorrow, and I'm sure they'll wait until dark before trying anything."

"Well, at least that means I can get some sleep," she said with a sigh. "Tenia's aunt has offered us the use of her cottage. She's been staying here to care for the baby and her brother."

The line outside the door wasn't quite so long when Shera returned to Tenia's house in the morning. Obviously the elder had imposed some sort of order on the villagers.

Before she set to work on those waiting outside, she turned her magic once again on Masik, Tenia's father. By the time she had finished, he was no longer bent over and could walk easily without a cane. She was as surprised as he was delighted. It seemed to her that her powers were greater than ever before. Furthermore, she suffered no lingering effects from all that she had done the day before.

Gar had gone off to watch for Daren's assassins, taking with him a spyglass that he'd borrowed from someone in the village.

266

He'd never seen such a device before, though Shera was familiar with them from her years among the Trellans.

As she set to work on her other patients, she smiled with the memory of last night's lovemaking. Never had Gar been so gentle with her. She knew that it was, at least in part, because he knew she was tired and aching from her work—but she was sure that it was also because he was changing. Day by day, she could sense him losing that primitive side to his nature that she knew now was his chezah heritage. A part of her missed that, but not very much. The more she saw of his gentle, loving nature, the more she decided it was for the better.

He returned just as Tenia was setting out the noon meal. Shera was holding little Dakin, and when she saw Gar, she found herself wishing that they could one day have a child together.

A foolish hope, she thought bitterly. That time would never come. But she could not help wondering what the child of a Bacleev and a Walken would be like, and what it might be like to have Gar's child growing inside of her.

"I have men posted all around the village," Gar told her as the day ended.

"But they'll be killed," Shera protested.

"No, they won't," he assured her. "I've told them not to try to stop them, but instead to come let us know."

"I can't kill them, Gar. I know I should, but . . ."

"They would kill you without giving it a thought," he reminded her.

"I know that, but I still can't. I'll just cast a spell on them."

They settled down before the fire to wait. They were still waiting hours later. Finally Gar got up. "I'm going out to check on the guards."

She got up, too. "Let me come with you."

"You wait here. I don't want to put you in danger. I'll be back soon."

She started to protest, then sat down again. Maybe Gar chafed at his inability to protect them both; maybe he resented the powers she had. It was likely that, to his mind, for the woman to be the more powerful disturbed the natural order of things.

He'd been gone only a short time when Shera felt something. She wasn't quite sure what it was, however. Her entire body tingled slightly, as it had that time when she'd loosed the fire on Daren. She got to her feet, suddenly nervous. Was it possible that she was reacting to the use of the fire by one of her would-be assassins? Could they be trying to cast a spell on the entire village again? Without Daren, it seemed unlikely, but she knew she had to find out what was happening.

She left the house and ran through the dark streets, heading toward the side of the village where the men were likely to appear. Then, just as she turned the corner onto a street that led to the edge of the village, she saw two dark figures ahead, coming her way. The hands of both men were glowing: Bacleev! But they seemed to be running away from something, since both of them kept casting glances behind them.

Shera tried to hide in the shadows, but one of the men saw her, and immediately an arc of green flame hurtled in her direction. She raised her hand and conjured fire of her own. For one brief moment, the entire street was lit by an eerie green light, and in its glow, she saw one man drop heavily to the ground.

The other man turned and began to run back the way he'd come, but then a third figure appeared: Gar. Shera raised her arm to hurl the fire at her foe before he could harm Gar, but the man fell with a cry of pain.

Confused, Shera ran to where Gar stood over the second man. There was a knife in her lover's hand, and blood, blackened by the moonlight, dripped to the ground.

"What happened?" she asked, trying not to look at the body.

Gar didn't answer immediately. Instead he reached down and cleaned the blood from his knife upon the clothing of one of the dead men, then replaced it in the sheath at his belt.

"Gar?" she asked, frightened by his silence.

"It didn't work," he said in a strange tone of voice.

"What didn't work?"

He turned his attention from the dead men to her, and now she could see the shock on his face. "They both turned their fire on me—and it didn't work. I felt nothing."

"What? Are you sure?" Shera was stunned.

"They were only a few feet away. When I reached the guard, they'd already killed him, and they must have heard me coming. They stepped out from behind a house together, and they both attacked me."

Gar and Shera stared at each other, neither of them willing to say aloud what they were thinking.

Finally, Gar spoke. "I must go to the elder and tell him about his man's death. After that, I will see to these two." He tied the bodies of the assassins.

Shera flinched.

She returned to their borrowed cottage, but by the time Gar joined her, she was no closer to accepting what had happened.

"Maybe their powers weren't all that great," she suggested.

"They killed the guard," Gar reminded her. "And even if neither one of them was individually powerful, the two of them together should have been able to kill me."

"But you felt nothing at all?"

"Nothing," he confirmed.

"Then perhaps you are safe from them as long as you remain in human form. That means you should find someone else to guard me when we return."

But Gar shook his head. "There is no one else I trust, my love."

"But surely your friends . . ."

"Not even them."

Shera heard the stubbornness in his voice and decided to drop the subject. What Gar surely knew, but perhaps had temporarily forgotten, was that he could not become a chezah again unless she cooperated. And despite the danger to her, she would not transform him if he was safe from Daren and the others as a human.

Two days later they left for the other village, leaving Tenia behind with her family. Before they left, Shera told her that she could either remain there or bring the baby back to the valley with her.

"I know it is a terrible choice you must make, Tenia," she'd told her. "But you must think about it while we're gone."

They took with them two men from Tenia's village who had relatives in the other village, and when they arrived there, the men were quickly able to convince the villagers that they would not be harmed.

They spent two days and nights in the second village, during which time Shera did her best to cure the illnesses and afflictions of those who remained. Gar cut firewood and hunted game and otherwise helped to prepare the village for the coming winter. He suggested that Shera order the two spellbound guards to help as well, then took obvious pleasure from seeing them engage in the physical labor so disdained by the Bacleev—especially since their labors were on behalf of the villagers they'd murdered and robbed.

For her part, Shera was eager to remove the spell, though she was far from eager to return to the valley and the confrontation that was sure to come when she refused to change Gar into a chezah.

Her own situation, she reflected, was not so different from Tenia's. Neither choice was a good one. By refusing to transform Gar, she could be risking her life—but to do so meant risking his. In the valley, with the power of the Dark Ones growing so great, he might not be able to resist Daren's spells, even if he had done so up to now.

They reached Tenia's village late in the day, and they were greeted warmly by everyone. Those Shera had helped were among them, and she cast off her bleak thoughts to smile with pleasure at the good that could be accomplished with Bacleev magic.

Tenia, with Dakin in her arms, welcomed them with a smile. "We will come with you," she told Shera, answering her question before it could be asked. "I know that Garet would understand if we chose to stay here—and if he were asked, I think he would want that. But our place is with him, and I know you will keep us safe."

Unfortunately, word of Tenia's choice had spread throughout the village, and there were many others who begged to come as well: husbands or wives who had been left behind, young children longing to be with their parents. Listening to them, Shera felt sick all over again at what her people had done.

"I cannot take any others," she told them. "But I promise you that I will return your loved ones to you in the spring, and I will keep them safe until then."

After the people had drifted away and she was alone with Gar in their borrowed cottage, she wondered aloud what had prompted her to make such a promise.

"I know I can't do that," she cried. "It was wrong of me to make a promise I can't hope to keep."

Gar drew her into his arms. "You made the promise because you want it to happen—and maybe it will."

When Shera drew back and looked up at him doubtfully, he went on. "So far you have accomplished everything you've tried to do—and more. The gods truly favor you, Shera. And now I think perhaps they favor me as well."

Shera felt anything but favored as they set out on the long journey back to the valley. The weather had turned cold, and once or twice a few snowflakes fell from the dark, wintry sky. When they reached the mountains, they found pockets of snow many inches deep in certain places that never saw sunlight. Gar said that within a month, or perhaps less, the trail would be impassable. The valley, though, would be spared the worst of the winter storms.

On their third afternoon on the trail, a heavier snow began to fall. Still unfamiliar with these mountains, Shera didn't realize that they were once more near the caverns where they'd been sheltered against the thunderstorms on their previous trip.

"We'll go there again," Gar said. "It will provide good warm shelter for the baby."

They left the trail and climbed the already slippery hillside.

Saranne Dawson

After leaving the two men and their horses in the lower caverns, Gar suggested that Tenia and the baby join them in the cavern with the warm spring. Clutching little Dakin, Tenia stared doubtfully at the steep, snow-covered slope.

"I will strap Dakin on my back, and then tie the two of you so that you can't fall," Gar told them. "Just follow in my footsteps."

So, with the bitter wind and stinging snow in their faces, they began to climb. It took longer than it had before, but finally they reached the entrance to the cave. As before, Shera tried not to think about the journey back down—this time on snow and ice.

Gar led Tenia, and Dakin back to the warm pool, then left them there and came back to start a fire for their evening meal. He'd gathered firewood on their first stop here, replacing the small supply that they'd used then.

Later, after they had eaten their meal and Tenia and the child were asleep, Gar and Shera went to the bathing pool. There they shed their dusty trail clothes and stepped gratefully into the warm water.

"We will have only one more night together," Gar said as he held her close. "I think it would be best if I become a chezah before we return to the valley."

"Why must you change?" she asked. "If you can resist the spell as a man, then why not remain a man?"

"Because I wish to protect you—and I can't do that as a man." He kissed her. "I don't want this, either, my love—but I've thought it over very carefully, and this is the best way."

"No," she replied firmly. "It may be the safest way for me—but it's more dangerous for you. What if you can't resist Daren and the priests?"

"I *can*," he said confidently.

"I won't do it, Gar. I'm not going to change you back into an animal."

Gar stared at her for a long moment, saying nothing. Then he seemed to let it go. They bathed each other, then climbed out to make love in the warm, misty cavern.

* * *

272

In the morning they stood at the entrance to the cave and stared at the newly white world around them. Shera had never seen so much snow, though it was probably no more than six inches. It was a wondrous sight, but she could scarcely enjoy it as she wondered how they could safely return to the trail.

Once more Gar strapped the baby to his back and tied the two women to each other and then to himself. "You will have to go first," he told them. "That way I can prevent you from falling."

Shera and Tenia began their slow, cautious descent through the snow. At first they seemed to be managing well enough, but then Tenia began to slip, dragging Shera with her.

Shera fought down her panic as she felt the rope that connected her to Gar grow taut. It caught on a rock outcropping. He stood on the ledge above them, the rope in his hands also tied to his waist. But as she raised her head to look up at him, Tenia, who had been trying to maneuver back up, slipped again, sending Shera tumbling over backward.

Both women were sliding ever closer to a ledge that dropped off steeply. She heard Gar's cry just as she felt the rope connecting them go limp. Looking up, she saw that it had broken. Now both she and Tenia were sliding helplessly toward the yawning abyss!

"No!" she cried. At the same time, she lunged for Tenia's outstretched hand.

What followed was a moment when time itself seemed to stop. She saw the deep abyss, and she saw Tenia's terrified face—and then they were both lying on the wide ledge in front of the lower caverns.

Stunned, Shera could only sit, staring at Tenia as she stared back. Then she remembered Gar and looked up to see him climbing down toward them, the torn rope still dangling from his waist and the baby safely on his back. He detoured past the place where the line in the snow showed they had begun to slide, and a few moments later he reached them without difficulty.

Tenia jumped up and helped Gar untie Dakin, then clutched him to her. Shera didn't move. "Wh-what happened?" she asked.

Gar knelt beside her and took Shera's hands. For the first time she saw that they were glowing faintly. She hadn't felt the telltale warmth because of the cold.

"Your hands began to glow as you reached for Tenia," he said. "Then there was a glow around both of you—and suddenly you were here."

"How could it happen?" she asked, watching the last of the green glow dissipate. "I didn't *do* anything."

"But you did. You used your magic to save you both."

She stared back up the hillside in disbelief. The distance was probably at least a hundred feet—perhaps more. And the only prints in the snow were those left by Gar. Between them and where the two women had slipped was an unbroken expanse of white.

"Did you know I could do that?" she asked, annoyed that he wasn't at all shocked.

"No, and I've never heard of anything like it. But I told you before, my love. I think you can do whatever you must."

Shera continued to think about the incident as they followed the winding trail, drawing ever closer to the valley. Gar had accepted her feat so easily. Even Tenia, once she'd recovered from their brush with death, seemed to find nothing strange about the fact that they had moved from one place to another without touching the space in between.

But Shera no longer trusted herself—a very strange and frightening situation. It was as though some other being lived inside her body, quietly most of the time, but capable of making its presence felt at any moment.

What else was she capable of? she wondered. When would she next encounter a situation that called for desperate measures—and find that the answer lay within her? Instead of feeling powerful, as one might expect, Shera felt more and more helpless. She felt like a pawn.

The weather perversely turned warm again, melting most of the snow and making their journey much easier. Baby Dakin was holding up well to the rigors of their journey, and Tenia spoke happily about the upcoming reunion with her husband, and the cottage Shera had promised them.

In thinking it over, Shera realized that she would not have to give them her old cottage. Instead they could use the cottage near the stables, where there was also an old blacksmith's shop that Garet could use. The Bacleev had need of a blacksmith, and he had the skills. She was certain she could convince Daren of the wisdom of such an action; that would keep her old cottage as a haven for Gar and her.

All of this, of course, presupposed some minimal cooperation from Daren, but Gar had pointed out that Daren was unlikely to give her too much trouble—at least on the surface—because he feared her.

And he would fear her even more when he discovered that his scheme to kill her hadn't worked. About the only pleasure Shera hoped to find when they reached the valley was the look on Daren's face when he realized that his scheme had failed.

Strangely enough, Gar had not brought up the matter of her refusal to change him into a chezah, even though they were nearing the end of their journey. Shera wasn't exactly comfortable with her decision, but she remained adamant, even though she knew that at least in part, she was refusing because of purely personal reasons. She wanted *Gar* with her—not some great animal that had Gar's mind.

On their final full day on the trail, they were resting after a light meal taken in the early afternoon when Gar left them, saying that he would return soon. He'd done this several times before and had always returned to say that the way ahead was clear, Daren had sent no one else out from the village.

Shera was playing with the baby when suddenly Tenia's eyes grew wide. The girl stared at something behind Shera. Before her scream cut through the silence of the forest, Shera had already thrust the baby back at her and was turning, the fire aglow around her hands.

Some twenty or thirty feet away, a chezah stood staring at them. Shera got to her feet, her hands blazing. A wave of shock washed over her as she recognized that familiar amber gaze.

"Gar?"

The creature nodded.

"What happened?" she asked, horrified. Shera shook her head, denying the vision before her.

Yes, my love. Gar's words spoke into her mind. *I can change myself at will now. And it's much easier than when you did it. I will show you.*

In the next instant, the cat suddenly grew indistinct, blurring at the edges and then vanishing completely. In its place stood Gar.

"And now we know, too, that I *can* communicate with you," he said aloud.

"How did you learn to do this?" she demanded.

He shrugged and gave her a slight smile. "Like you, I do what I must. If it happens that Daren can influence me when I'm in chezah form, I will simply change back again."

Behind him, Shera saw Daren's men staring, their mouths open and their eyes wide with fear.

"Your husband is not going to be a happy man," Gar said with a decidedly evil grin.

It was not the grin, but the look in his eyes that Shera thought about as they started out again. Gar hated Daren—and now Daren could not harm him. She knew Gar had no qualms about killing when he deemed it necessary.

Suddenly, she knew it. Even though Gar had changed and become much gentler in many ways, the chezah side of his nature would always be there.

Chapter Fifteen

The sun had just dropped behind the mountains when they reached the valley. Gar brought them to a halt, then climbed off his horse and removed its saddle and bridle.

"Daren doesn't need to know just yet that I can shape-change," he said. He hid the saddle in the midst of some bushes, then set the horse free in the pasture.

"Won't he know it's you?" she asked, still fearing that despite Gar's confidence, Daren could harm him.

"He will know. It is time to release those two from their spell," he told her, nodding to the silent guards.

Shera turned to the two men. She ordered them silently to forget that they had seen Gar transform himself, and not to harm him. They hadn't seen the other two who'd been sent to kill Shera, so there was no reason for her to deal with that. She would tell Daren herself what had happened.

When she had finished issuing her orders, the two men continued to wear the slightly puzzled expressions they'd been wearing all along. Then she saw their eyes narrow, and she turned to see that Gar had once more become a chezah. She watched the two men for a moment to satisfy herself that they wouldn't harm him.

Both men seemed slightly disoriented, but finally one of them looked around and then spoke up. "Why have we stopped?" he demanded, trying for a voice of authority, but not quite succeeding.

"We're moving on now," Shera stated. She climbed back onto her mare.

They passed the padlocked food warehouses and then the stables, with Gar trotting alongside her and the two men trailing along behind Tenia and the baby. Then they rode into the village.

People literally stopped in their tracks as the procession passed by. It was enough to make Shera wonder if she'd unconsciously cast a spell on them. But she realized that few of her people had actually seen a chezah, though there was no doubt they knew what Gar was. She kept her eyes on their hands, ready to thwart them if anyone dared to raise magic against Gar. No one did, but she didn't know if it was because they were too shocked, or because they feared *her*. There surely was no one in the village who didn't know by now that she could use the fire against them.

She was thankful the priests were nowhere to be seen. Someone must have run to warn Daren, though, because soon after she reached their house and witnessed Danna's reunion with her daughter and new grandson, her husband appeared.

He entered the house cautiously, then stopped when he saw Gar lying on the rug in front of the fire. Gar didn't move either, although his long tail twitched and his amber eyes immediately locked onto the shegwa.

Shera stepped between them as she saw the telltale glow surround Daren's hands. "Don't, Daren! If you try to harm him, I *will* kill you!"

"What is the meaning of this?" he demanded. "How dare you bring him here?"

278

Shera gave him a cold smile. "It seems that I require protection, and I can think of no one better able to provide that."

"Wh-what are you talking about? Protection from what?"

Shera clenched her fists to keep from striking him. "Don't try to play the innocent with me, Daren! You sent two men to kill me. Instead they are dead."

His face grew visibly pale, and he tried to bluster his way out of it. "I don't know what you're talking about."

"Namos and Setta are dead. They followed us to the village and intended to kill me in my sleep, no doubt planning to blame the villagers for my death.

"It seemed likely to me that you would attempt the same thing here, but I'm afraid that will be impossible with Gar to protect me. And I'll credit you with enough sense to know that you can't use Gar or any other chezah to carry out your plan."

"I refuse to have this . . . this *animal* here!" Daren sputtered.

"Then move out—because he stays!"

"You won't get away with this, Shera! You have gone too far!"

"Oh? And what exactly do you intend to do, Daren? If you run to the priests or complain to anyone else, I will be forced to tell everyone about your scheme to kill me. As it is, *you* will be forced to account somehow for the deaths of Namos and Setta."

His face now flushed with rage, Daren turned and stormed out of the house. Shera heard a strangled laugh and turned to see Gar actually grinning—if the feline face could be said to grin.

No doubt he's off to seek the sympathy of the priests, Gar's mind-voice said dryly.

Shera laughed. She would certainly rather have Gar as a man, but she was glad to have him present in any form.

He won't realize that we can communicate like this, Gar said. *We should keep it that way.*

* * *

Daren did not return, and Tenia was soon asking shyly if she could see Garet.

"Of course," Shera told her. "You take Dakin and go to the cottage by the stable. You'll want to see it anyway, to know what must be done to make it livable. I will go to the castle and fetch your man and send him there to meet you."

She set off, with Gar at her side. As they walked through the village, people greeted her, but gave her a wide berth. When they had left the village behind, she asked Gar if he felt any different being here, so close to the Dark Ones.

I am aware of them, he said silently. *And they are aware of me as well. But they can't touch me now.*

"Over confidence can be a dangerous thing," she told him. "You said yourself that they will grow stronger."

But so have we, his voice whispered.

Could it be true? she wondered. He was certainly right that the two of them had become more powerful—but could they possibly challenge the Dark Ones directly?

When they reached the castle, they encountered much the same reaction as they had in the village. Shera approached the men who were supervising the work and asked where Garet was.

"Is he the big redheaded man?" one of the men asked her.

"Yes," she replied, tempted to tell him that the least he could do was to learn the names of the slaves. No doubt anonymity made it easier for the Bacleev to pretend their workers weren't human.

"He's over there," the man said, gesturing. "Beyond that wall."

"He will be coming with me," Shera told him. "He is a skilled blacksmith and we have need of one. He will be living with his family in the cottage by the stables."

"But . . ."

The man's protest went no further as Shera arched a brow questioningly, daring him to protest her order. Once again, though, she didn't know if it was her he feared, or Gar, whom he watched nervously.

"Hello, Garet," she said when they found him working on the wall. His back was to them.

He turned, a smile on his face. But it faded quickly when he saw Gar.

"Tenia and Dakin are waiting for you at the little cottage next to the stables."

"D-Dakin? You mean he's *here?*"

Shera nodded. "A very healthy young boy, too. And you won't be working here anymore. We have need of a blacksmith and there's a shop you can set up next to the cottage. It's not what I would like for you—but it is the best I can do for now."

Tears glistened in Garet's eyes. "I don't know how to thank you. Were you able to deliver the food to my village?"

Shera nodded, and then, as they walked back down the hill, she told him everything that had happened. When she mentioned Gar, she saw Garet cast a questioning glance toward the cat, and she realized that he couldn't know this was Gar.

"Gar can transform himself at will now," she told him. "But you must not tell anyone that."

Garet's eyes grew wide with shock. "You mean that's him?"

"That's right. And I'm discovering that I can do things I can't quite believe as well. I'm sure Tenia will tell you all about it."

"Then Gar will be able to protect you if Daren tries to kill you again?"

"Yes, but I don't think he'll try."

Gar's response to this was a low growl.

"I agree with him," Garet said. "As long as there is breath in that man, he will try again."

"Did anyone discover that you and the others were missing—or that there were horses and food gone?"

Garet shook his head. "Not as far as I know, and I've kept my ears open."

"Good. I intend to tell Daren that one of the storehouses must be turned into housing for your people, so it's possible that the missing food could yet be discovered. But if it is, I will tell Daren what I've done."

"We need housing," Garet confirmed. "Some of the men are already sick from sleeping out in the cold."

"Has a healer seen them?"

Garet shook his head. "I asked, but Daren said that he wasn't going to waste healing on the likes of us."

Shera stopped. "In that case I will return to the castle now. Tenia and Dakin will stay at my house. We will get the cottage ready for you."

"I told the others what you've done," Garet said. "If you need our help in any way, you will have it."

She took his hand. "Thank you, Garet. I will remember. But I don't intend to put any of you in danger."

It begins again, Gar said silently as they watched Garet hurry through the meadow to his reunion with his family.

"But what about the chezahs?" she asked.

I think they will follow me, he replied.

"I don't want to drive my people from the valley, Gar. What I want is to rid the valley of the Dark Ones."

Then that is what we will do, his voice whispered in her mind.

She started back to the castle, wanting to believe it could be done. But as she listened to the distant roar of the waterfall and thought about what lay behind it, Shera knew that what Gar said was no more than a hope—and a faint one at that. Perhaps they could continue to resist the Dark Ones, but if not even the gods could get rid of them, how could they?

The men supervising the work at the castle were no happier to see her this time than they had been earlier—and they were no less wary of the large, silent beast at her side. Shera realized that Gar had been right to have chosen to remain a chezah. Even her own people—who believed they controlled the great cats—were frightened of them.

It's the eyes, she thought, glancing at Gar as he watched the men with whom she was speaking. They weren't the eyes of an animal, but the intelligent and aware eyes of a human

282

being. In that moment, she realized something else as well: the Dark Ones had made a mistake. It was they who had given the Bacleev the power to turn the Walkens into chezahs. The gods had given the Walkens only the ability to communicate with chezahs. And the Walkens could make the Dark Ones pay.

"I am here to heal the men who are sick," she told the supervisors.

"No one is sick," one man insisted. "Some just don't want to work, that's all."

Shera stared at him. "Perhaps, Josev, *you* would like to find out what it is like to work in pain."

As she spoke, she allowed a small glimmer of green fire to suffuse her fingers. He backed off hastily, his eyes locked on her hands even though they remained at her sides. Gar gave the strangled laughter she'd heard him give before, and when she looked his way, he was grinning again. She, too, found it amusing, though it was clear that the men didn't share her sense of humor.

What a pair we are, she thought as they began to seek out the men who needed her services. *Was it only a few months ago that I lived in a world that was real?*

She found six men who needed healing, and many more whose illnesses would respond just as easily to herbal remedies that they'd apparently been denied.

At first the men were very uneasy because of Gar, but she discovered that the moment she said his name, their fear vanished. Garet had told them about Gar's role in getting food to their people. One man asked her if Gar could understand what they were saying, and when she said that he could, the man turned to the huge cat and thanked him very politely.

She left them after promising that she would send Danna to them with some herbal potions. Then she told the supervisors that she would be sending her servant up here, and that she was to be allowed to give the potions to the men.

It was dusk by the time they left the castle, and as they walked down the hillside, Shera could hear the faint sounds of chanting. Her people were at the evening ceremonies.

When they reached the forest, Shera suddenly caught movement out of the corner of her eye, and by the time she turned, Gar had once again transformed himself. He reached out and drew her into his arms.

"Let's stay here for a while," he murmured as his hands slid down over her body and his lips claimed hers.

Shera didn't protest. Everyone was either at the castle or at the ceremonies. With a sigh of pleasure, she let Gar draw her down onto a soft bed of pine needles. There, for a time, she forgot about everything and reveled in the feel of his body against hers and the driving force of his need.

Because the day's warmth had rapidly vanished, they dressed again quickly, but lingered, wrapped in each other's arms. Far in the distance, the chanting rose and fell, nearly lost beneath the roar of the waterfall.

Suddenly they both tensed, sensing the Dark Ones' presence at the same time. Gar's fingers dug into her soft flesh as he clasped her to him more tightly.

Then it seemed that a wind sprang up from nowhere, chill and dank. And before either of them could move, they were spinning helplessly in a dark void, a place so black that they couldn't even see each other.

The wind tore at them like a living thing, trying to separate them. But they held on to each other somehow. That voice that wasn't a voice invaded her mind, whispering darkly, promising her anything she could want if she would only give him up.

"No!" she cried. "No! You can't have him!"

The howling wind continued for what seemed an eternity—and then it was gone as quickly as it had come. They were once more lying on the forest floor. But in that last moment, Shera had glimpsed something far worse than her darkest dreams.

They were still clutching each other tightly, their hearts beating rapidly in unison. Gar loosened his hold slightly, and then so did she.

"We beat them," he said, though his voice was somewhat shaky.

She nodded. "For now. I think they must have been drawing power from the chants. We must be careful, Gar. I think we have to be certain that we always stay together during the ceremonies."

He nodded and was silent for a moment as he caressed her. "Did you see anything?"

"Yes, but only for a moment. I . . . I think it was *them*." She shuddered.

"I think so, too. They want to draw us into their world, Shera, because there they will have the advantage."

"Their world?" She frowned. "What do you mean: the cavern?"

"No, I think it is more than that. Beneath the pool, perhaps—or maybe someplace else entirely." He paused. "If we are to defeat them, perhaps we must go there."

"No! Gar, we can't! They will destroy us!"

He kissed her. "I don't mean right now, but I think if we are to rid the valley of them, we will have to go to the place where they truly live."

"I think you have entirely too much faith in us," she said doubtfully.

"Or you have too little," he pronounced. "Think about it, my love. First we were given each other—and we were each given powers that no one else has. That makes this time different from before."

"If the gods intend to fight the Dark Ones, then why don't they do it themselves?" she demanded.

"This valley and these mountains belong to our people. If we want them, we must fight for them. I think our two people have always viewed the gods very differently. The Bacleev worship them—or they did once—and believe that the gods take an active interest in their lives. My people have never believed that. We think that when the gods withdrew from this world, they left it to us to preserve, and they pay very little attention to us."

"But if that's true, then how do you account for our powers?" she asked. At the same time, she was thinking that her own beliefs had always been closer to that of the Walkens.

"I didn't say that they don't pay *any* attention to us—just that they aren't going to do everything for us, which is what your people have always believed."

"That's true," she admitted. "All our ceremonies and chants have to do with asking the gods to protect us and give us signs."

"The Bacleev are naturally greedy," Gar stated. "They want everything given to them; that's why they fall prey to the Dark Ones."

Shera sighed. "You're right. But how can we hope to change them?"

"We can't. All we can do is get rid of the Dark Ones, and then hope the Bacleev will change themselves. If they don't, then they will have to be driven from the valley once and for all."

"These are my people we're talking about, Gar. I may not like most of them very much, but they're still my people."

"I know that—and I really don't want the Bacleev to go—if they can be turned from evil. Besides, the Bacleev belong in this valley, just as my people belong in the mountains."

He stood up, then drew her to her feet and into his arms. "The chanting has stopped. We should go home and see if Daren intends to show up."

She tilted back her head and looked up at him. "You want to kill him, don't you?"

"Yes—and I think it will be necessary." He looked hurt at her censure. "You've threatened to kill him as well."

"That's true—but those were only threats intended to make him behave. I don't *want* to kill him—or anyone else."

Gar smiled, then kissed her softly. "You have a kinder heart than I do—or ever will."

"Just remember: if you kill him, then I will no longer be shegwa, and I will lose control over my people."

"That's the only reason he's still alive now," Gar replied.

He kissed her again, then released her. A scant second later, he was a chezah again.

"I can't get used to this," she muttered, more to herself than to the great cat that moved ahead of her through the forest.

It is who I am, he said.

By the time they reached the village, everyone had returned from the ceremonies. People were gathered in small groups in front of their houses, but all conversations ceased as the two of them passed by. Shera wondered what they were thinking, and what Daren and the priests might have told them. Obviously they'd been given some explanation for Gar's presence.

Danna was alone in the house when Shera and Gar arrived. Shera asked her to prepare some herbal potions and take them to the men who needed them tomorrow, and she promised to do so. Then she said that Tenia and Garet would be spending the night in their new home. It wasn't really ready for them, but they wanted to be together as a family again.

Impulsively Danna reached out to take Shera's hands. "Thank you for all you've done for us—and for my husband. I feel so much better knowing that he is well again."

Shera hugged her. "It is little enough. Danna, what do you hear from the other servants? Is everyone being treated well?"

"Oh, yes," she said with a smile. "Things are much better. Your people really fear you—especially since your return.

"We gather each evening when the Bacleev are at their ceremonies, and everyone says that people fear doing anything that would make you angry—especially now that Gar is with you. I think that many are secretly happy. I think many of them were just obeying the dictates of the holy men. And they say that even the priests are afraid of you now."

"Good. That fear is the greatest weapon we have right now."

"There also isn't much respect for Daren," Danna confided. "People are saying that he is shegwa in name only—that *you* are the real leader."

They both turned to Gar, who was now grinning at them.

"You may find it amusing, Gar—but it could mean that Daren will be even more desperate to kill me."

Let him try, was his reply.

"Daren has told people that Gar is here because my people tried to kill you, and he summoned Gar to protect you," Danna told them. "But I have heard that the families of the two men who died are saying that Daren sent them to kill you."

"Do you think people believe that?" Shera asked.

"Some do. I think there is much confusion right now. Some people have asked the priests if Daren tried to have you killed, and the priests say they don't know—that this is not a matter for them."

Gar growled again. Amused, Shera was beginning to think that he didn't need to speak to her mind. He was doing a very good job of letting his thoughts be known without speech.

"The priests are trying to distance themselves from Daren," she said, glancing at Gar, who nodded. "They must fear me more than I'd thought."

At that moment there was a sound at the door, and Daren walked in. Shera motioned for Danna to leave them, and the woman went to her room. Daren paused as he had before, just inside the door. Gar walked over to the hearth and settled down, then yawned, in the process showing his vicious fangs. As if that weren't enough, he stretched, displaying his long, curved claws. His amber eyes never left the shegwa.

Shera took a seat near the hearth—and Gar. "Daren, I want you to get a crew working immediately to prepare one of the storehouses as winter housing for the slaves. Tenia's husband Garet is a blacksmith and I have given them the old cottage near the stables."

"You do not give orders!" Daren scowled. "We are to issue orders together."

She gave him a look of wide-eyed innocence. "But you will be the one issuing the orders to prepare the storehouses—or are you saying that you disagree?"

"There isn't enough room. The storehouses are full," he said petulantly, his gaze constantly shifting back and forth from her to Gar.

"Oh, there's more room now. I took some of the food back to the two villages."

"You did *what?*" His face darkened with rage. "You lie! The storehouses are locked, and my men said nothing about it."

She shrugged. "I had no trouble opening the padlocks, and neither did I have any problem controlling your men."

Daren stared at her, speechless. His hands were glowing, but she ignored them. Gar, however, made a low sound of displeasure.

"It is time you understand and accept the situation, Daren. I do not fear you or the priests—or the Dark Ones. Them, we intend to destroy."

"The priests will stop you, Shera!"

"I don't think so. Of course, they *could* stop me, if they stop worshiping the Dark Ones."

"This talk of evil came from *him!*" Daren cried, gesturing at Gar. "He has poisoned your mind. How can you believe him when he isn't even human?"

Shera was facing Daren, but she caught a sudden movement in her peripheral vision. By the time she had turned toward Gar, he had shape-shifted. She turned back to Daren as she heard his cry.

He had staggered back a few feet and was now leaning against the door, his eyes wide as Gar advanced slowly toward him.

"Sooner or later, I am going to kill you, Daren," Gar said in a deadly soft voice. "Your only hope of staying alive is to do exactly as you're told."

Gar was blocking Shera's view of the man, so she didn't see

him loose the fire until the green light arced from his hands. She cried out, already summoning her own fire, but Gar simply stood there, only a few feet from Daren. The fire struck him— and vanished.

Daren made a strangled sound, then turned and fled into the night.

"Was it wise to let him know you can change yourself?" Shera asked as Gar closed the door behind Daren.

"He can't harm me. He needs to know what he's dealing with. The more terrified he is, the less likely he is to cause trouble."

Shera said nothing, but privately she disagreed. It seemed likely to her that Daren would become even more desperate now. Perhaps, she thought, that was exactly what Gar wanted. He wanted Daren to do something that would justify killing him.

"Why do you hate him so?" she asked. "I think he's more to be pitied than hated."

Gar's eyes locked onto hers. "He stands between us."

"He doesn't! He is my husband in name only."

"Nevertheless, he *is* your husband."

Long after Gar had fallen asleep beside her, Shera remained awake, half fearing that Daren would return. Gar had told her not to worry, that he slept lightly and would hear their enemy if he came back. But her real reason for remaining awake had little to do with fear of Daren. Instead she thought about Gar's earlier words—and about her reluctance now to have him here in her bed.

Marriage was sacred among the Bacleev, a lifetime bond. And while her marriage was a sham, it was still a marriage. And Gar knew that as well. That was why he hated Daren so much. Her own dislike of Daren stemmed from what he was; for Gar it was different. His own people felt about marriage as hers did, and he'd once told her that even the chezahs mated for a lifetime.

He will kill Daren, she thought, no matter what the man does or doesn't do.

She wondered what would happen if she could persuade

Daren to come with her to the priests and end their marriage. She'd never heard of such a thing happening, but that didn't necessarily mean it couldn't be done.

It would mean that she would no longer be shegwa—but how important was that now, when everyone knew of her extraordinary powers? She would willingly relinquish the position if she could end this mockery of a marriage. And even if Daren remained shegwa, she could control him, prevent him from harming anyone.

She moved closer to Gar, breathing in his scent, feeling his heat. Tomorrow she would find Daren and talk to him—without Gar. Gar's presence would surely only enrage him all over again.

The following day Shera searched discreetly for Daren as she roamed about the village. At first she'd assumed that he was up at the castle, but when Danna returned from her visit to the sick, she reported that Daren wasn't there. Several others were inquiring after him, she said, so they must have been expecting him.

As shegwa, it was easy for Shera to make rounds of the village, and that was expected, particularly since she'd been away. She asked Gar to remain at home because she knew that his presence would discourage people from talking to her. She didn't really require his protection, and by being seen without him, she was discrediting her husband's lies.

Somewhat to her surprise, Gar agreed, saying that he would seek a quiet spot in the woods where he could communicate with his people. If she needed him, he said, she had only to call out with her mind.

Even without Gar shadowing her, people were uneasy around her, though some took great pains to hide that nervousness. It occurred to her that the Bacleev seemed no happier than they had been before the capture of slaves to do the work, yet she could not seem to find the source of their unhappiness. Was it only their unease around her—or was it something more?

One of her stops was to visit the oldest woman in the village, who had now seen eighty-eight winters and was facing her eighty-ninth. Shera had always liked her; she bore her great age and the infirmities that came with it with dignity and grace.

"Come in, come in!" Eltea said when she opened the door. Then she peered behind her. "And where is your chezah that I've heard so much about?"

Shera smiled, thinking that Eltea was the first person yet to *want* to see Gar. All she'd seen on the others' faces today was relief when they realized she was alone.

"I didn't bring him with me because he disturbs people," she said. "Though that doesn't seem to be the case where you're concerned."

"No, I'd like very much to see your chezah," the old woman said, her dark eyes bright as she perched on the edge of a chair, both hands clasped around the top of her cane. "I've never seen one, you know."

"Well, perhaps he'll come," Shera said, at the same time reaching out with her mind to find Gar. It was something she'd never done, but it didn't surprise her when she felt his presence. She asked him to come if he could, making certain he understood it wasn't an emergency. But since she wasn't sure just how easily she could get a message across to him, she could only hope that he wouldn't rush in and frighten Eltea.

"People are saying that this beast is the Walken who captured you," Eltea said, the question in her eyes.

"Yes, he is, but he would never harm me or anyone else—unless they tried to harm him."

"Or unless they tried to harm *you*."

"Yes, that is true," Shera acknowledged.

"But you don't require his protection, despite what Daren has said? I am told you have great powers, my child."

"Yes, olesha, I do," Shera replied, using the term of honor for the elderly.

"I am not surprised."

"You're not? You don't find it strange that the gods would favor me when I've never worshiped them properly?"

"Neither did I, child, and yet I, too, have been blessed with a long and pleasant life—and in my younger days, with great healing talents."

"I always thought you were very devout," Shera said.

"Oh, I always attended the ceremonies. I lacked the courage you have shown to flout tradition. But I have always fought—and continue to fight—the darker powers."

Shera stared at her in shock. Eltea obviously misinterpreted the reason.

"Have you never even felt them? You must be far more powerful than I've heard."

Shera shook her head. "No. I mean, yes, I've felt them. That's why I never wanted to attend the ceremonies. But you're the first person I've heard acknowledge that they exist—besides, Gar, of course. He's the Walken we were speaking of."

"There are others, child, but no one will speak up—especially since we came here, where they live. They drew us back here, and now they have us to do their work again."

"But how can I get people to see that they're evil?" Shera asked.

"I don't know the answer to that—but I will tell you a secret. One night, not long after we came here, I went very late to the place where the sacred bowl is kept. It was wrong, of course, but what could that nephew of mine do about it?"

She paused briefly with a self-satisfied smile, and Shera had to smile as well. Jawan, the high priest, was her nephew.

"The sacred fire was burning low," she said, shaking her head sadly. "But the gods spoke to me. They said that I would live to see the dark powers banished from our lives."

Shera was wondering if that were true, or if it had been nothing more than an old woman's mad dream, when there was a scratching sound at the door. She got up quickly.

"I hope you meant it when you said that you wanted to meet a chezah," she told Eltea. She opened the door.

Gar walked in and stopped, his gaze going from Shera to Eltea and back again. Shera explained why she'd called him.

"What a handsome creature!" Eltea exclaimed, not at all afraid as she leaned forward to peer closely at Gar. "But then, it is wrong to call you a creature, isn't it? You are neither creature nor man, but a little of both. I am sorry that Daren changed you into a chezah, because I would have enjoyed meeting a Walken as well."

Gar looked up at Shera, the question in his eyes.

"He can become a Walken again, if you wish—if you're sure that it won't frighten you."

"Of course it won't frighten me. I've lived too many years to be frightened of anyone or anything."

Still, when it was suddenly a Walken standing before her, the old woman cried out in surprise. But as Gar stood there rather uncertainly, she extended one of her gnarled hands to him.

"I am very pleased to meet you, Gar."

Gar took her hand and smiled. "And I am pleased to meet *you*, olesha."

"Well," said Eltea, her hands once more propped on her cane. "What do the two of you plan to do to rid us of the dark powers?"

Gar turned in surprise to Shera, who then repeated what Eltea had told her.

"We don't know yet," Shera told her.

"I think we may have to fight them in their own world," Gar said.

Eltea fixed her bright eyes on him, then nodded slowly. "Yes, I am afraid that is the only way. May the gods go with you when you do."

They left the old woman a short time later, with Gar once again in chezah form. Shera kept thinking about what Eltea had said: that the Dark Ones would be banished within her lifetime. Had the gods really told her that?

The Bacleev had always believed that the elderly were closer to the gods than the young, which was why no one was accepted into the priesthood until they had reached an advanced age and had studied long years under the tutelage of the priests.

She wondered too, if Eltea had spoken of her beliefs to Jawan, her nephew. She obviously hadn't told him of her clandestine trip to the sacred bowl, but she might well have spoken out about her belief in the Dark Ones. If so, the high priest must have been disconcerted, to say the least.

They returned home to learn that Daren had still not shown up there, and Shera began to worry about just where he was and what he might be up to. It was possible that he'd just taken himself off somewhere to sulk, but she thought that unlikely. Instead he was almost certainly plotting something—but what could it be?

Once inside the house, Gar reverted to human form again, and told her that he'd informed his people that he could accomplish these shape-changes easily and without assistance.

"I sensed great surprise among them," he told her with considerable satisfaction. "And I told them as well that we are going to fight the Dark Ones."

"How did they react to that?" Shera asked.

"It is difficult to know for sure. Mind-talk isn't always clear. I think they are confused. Some would probably be happy to remain chezahs, but many more have grown tired of it and want to be human again. Those who want to be human will help us, I think."

"If Eltea is right, there could be some of my people also who would help us. Maybe even Jawan," she added after a brief pause.

"Jawan? The high priest?" Gar asked skeptically.

"Eltea is his aunt—his mother's only living sister. He's quite fond of her, I think."

"That doesn't mean he would listen to her."

"No, and I don't trust him, either—but I must go to talk to him."

"I will come with you."

She shook her head. "No. I want to see him alone. Your presence would only disturb him." *And Daren might be there as well,* she added silently.

"If I need you, I will call you," she told him.

"I will go with you, then wait in the woods near the priests' homes," he stated firmly. "That way, I will be close by if you do need me. Don't underestimate the power of the priests, Shera—especially those of the high priest."

Shera nodded. She understood that. Jawan had resisted her powers before, so she wasn't about to underestimate him. But neither did she want to underestimate Eltea's influence over the man.

"Daren could be there as well," Gar said as they left the house.

"If so, that is even more reason why you shouldn't come with me," Shera told him. "I can handle my husband."

Chapter Sixteen

Shera watched Gar lope off into the woods beyond the priests' homes. For just a moment she was tempted to call him back, though she wasn't sure why. She didn't really fear Jawan, and she certainly wasn't afraid of Daren.

Shrugging off the vague feeling of uneasiness, she walked into the circle, then crossed to Jawan's home, staying away from the sacred bowl in order not to offend Jawan or the others. But she did glance that way, and she thought that the fire seemed not to have changed since she'd last visited it. It was still low and burning dimly.

The woman Jawan had selected to be his servant answered the door. Unbeknownst to Jawan, she was Danna's sister. Shera had hoped that she might become a source of information regarding the priests' activities, but so far, at least, she'd had nothing to report except that she was being treated well.

She smiled shyly at Shera, then, after casting a quick glance behind her, whispered a thanks to Shera for all her kindnesses to their family.

"Would you ask the high priest if he has time to speak to

me?" Shera said, after acknowleding her gratitude. She spoke loudly enough that Jawan could certainly hear her, and she was hoping that her formal request would counter any resistance on Jawan's part.

The woman disappeared, then returned a moment later and ushered Shera to a small room at the back of the cottage, where the high priest sat in a big, comfortable chair, staring out the window that faced the woods. She hoped that Gar was staying carefully out of view, though it was possible that the high priest had sensed his presence.

He turned to Shera as she entered the room, then gestured to the other chair. His expression was neutral, but Shera thought she detected a certain wariness.

"He is out there somewhere, is he not?" Jawan asked, gesturing to the woods.

"Yes. He insisted upon accompanying me, but I asked him not to come in here."

"Why have you come to see me, Shera?" he asked. His tone betrayed nothing.

"I've come for several reasons. First of all, I thought that perhaps Daren might be here. I've not seen him since yesterday."

"Nor have I—not since the evening ceremonies. I assumed he must be busy at the castle."

Shera thought that Jawan seemed surprised when she said that he wasn't at the castle, but it was hard to tell. She'd never met anyone better at concealing his feelings than this man, except Gar.

"Jawan, I want to end our marriage. As I think you know, it has been one in name only."

"That's not possible, child. Only the gods can end a marriage, by calling home one of the partners." He stared at her curiously. "Do you wish to end your marriage so that you can marry the Walken?"

"No. I wish to end it because it may be the only way I can save Daren's life. Gar wants to kill him, even though he knows our marriage is a sham. And Daren would like to kill Gar as well."

"But he can't."

"No, he can't and he knows that. But I think that Gar *could* kill Daren. Gar is a good man, but he is still part chezah, and sometimes it is difficult for him to control that side of himself. Did Daren tell you that Gar can transform himself at will?"

The high priest went pale. "No, he did not."

"We believe that we have both been given great powers for a reason, Jawan—that reason is to rid our people of the Dark Ones."

She expected a protest at the very least, if not an outright condemnation for blasphemy. But instead Jawan said nothing. His gaze seemed far away. She continued.

"Eltea told me today that she has always believed as I do: that the Dark Ones exist, and that they control our people— especially since we returned to the valley."

The high priest waved a hand in dismissal of her words. "My aunt has never been devout, and she has become even less so over the years."

"She says that there are others who feel as she does—and as I do."

"That is probably true—but that does not mean you are right."

"We *are* right, Jawan! Furthermore, I think you know that— or you're beginning to consider it." When he said nothing, she continued. "How can you, of all people, not feel the difference? I've always thought you were arrogant, Jawan—but I have never believed you to be cruel. And yet it is you who led our people to the Dark Ones, and then led the tas-syana that resulted in innocent people being enslaved and killed."

"This is our destiny," he replied coldly.

Shera got up. "Then I have nothing more to say to you— except to tell you that Gar and I are going to destroy the Dark Ones."

"And how will you do that?" he asked. His dark eyes bored into her.

"As you yourself might have once said, the gods will show us the way."

Saranne Dawson

* * *

"I think he is troubled," Shera said after relating her conversation with Jawan to Gar.

Of course he's troubled, Gar said silently to her mind. *He fears us.*

"No, I think it is more than that. This was the first time he didn't condemn me for declaring that the Dark Ones exist. I know him well, Gar, and believe me, he never loses an opportunity to tell me— or anyone else—when they are wrong."

She waved a hand in dismissal of the subject. "But what really worries me now is Daren's absence. Where can he be?"

Then she thought about her old cottage. Daren knew it was now empty and at least partially furnished. Furthermore, it was the only uninhabited cottage in the village that could be lived in. Several others were empty, but only because they required major repairs.

But when they checked, the cottage was empty and there were no signs that Daren had been there. They returned home, with Shera hoping that Danna might have some news. Danna was turning out to be a perfect spy. She knew everyone well because of her work as an herbalist, and everyone trusted her.

When they reached the house, they found Tenia, Garet, and baby Dakin visiting. Garet informed her that the old blacksmith's shop could easily be made usable again, but he would require some assistance.

"I will help you," Gar said, after transforming himself before their shocked eyes. Shera suspected that he was enjoying his newfound power and didn't realize how unsettling it could be. But Garet recovered quickly and thanked him for his offer.

Danna had nothing to report, saying that by now she had spoken to nearly every servant, and none of them had seen Daren in the past day. Somewhere in the midst of all her spy work, she had still managed to prepare a meal, and they all sat down together.

"Has anyone come to question you about not going back to work at the castle?" Shera asked Garet.

"Two men came early this afternoon, but they seemed more

300

interested in finding out if I'd seen Daren than in what I was doing."

Garet described the men to her; they were Daren's closest allies. Apparently not even they knew what had happened to him.

After they had eaten, Gar said that this would be a good time for him to help Garet. It was time for the evening ceremonies, and neither the priests nor Daren were likely to cause any trouble now.

"I'm going to the ceremonies," Shera announced. "Daren will surely be there. He'd never miss service."

Before she left, Gar drew her aside. "Do you think it's wise for you to go there?"

"What could happen? Daren would never try anything with so many people present."

"I wasn't thinking about Daren."

"I'm safe from the Dark Ones as well," Shera told him with somewhat more confidence than she felt. She still recalled what had happened the last time she'd gone to the ceremonies. This time, through, she would be more careful and not let her thoughts drift.

Gar bent to kiss her. "Call me if you meed me. As a chezah, I will there within minutes."

Shera didn't doubt that at all. Gar had told her once that chezahs were the fastest creatures alive, able to cover great distances at many times the speed of humans. It was yet another reason they were so fearsome.

She joined the parade of people headed toward the meadow near the lake, already searching for her husband. When she arrived, the first circle was already forming, but Daren was nowhere to be found. She joined them, and several people asked where the other shegwa was, obviously perplexed at his failure to appear. A few of them cast suspicious glances in her direction, and it occurred to Shera that if he didn't turn up soon, people might think she had killed him.

Suddenly she wondered if that could be what Daren had in mind. It could be that some of Daren's allies knew where he was, but were keeping his whereabouts secret while they planted the seeds of suspicion that *she* was responsible for his disappearance.

It makes sense, she thought angrily as the ceremonies began. *He knows that he can't harm me directly, but he could turn people against me.*

He's hiding somewhere, she decided. Tomorrow she would find him if she had to search the entire valley. Or perhaps, instead, she should confront one of his close allies.

Then she realized that she was doing exactly what she'd said she *wouldn't* do: letting her thoughts wander. She focused on the chants of the priests. Her gaze met Jawan's and she held it for a long moment as she responded, together with the others, to the priests' ancient litany to the gods.

When the assault came this time, it was both sooner and far more powerful. Shera actually staggered a bit as the dark coldness filled her, though no one noticed because by this time, they were all swaying with the rhythm of the chants.

There were no voices, no whispered promises, none of the seductiveness of the past. Instead Shera felt herself spinning away into a dark, unimaginably cold void. It never occurred to her to call out to Gar; she was too busy fighting the onslaught.

She could feel her feet still firmly planted on the grass even as she spun about sickeningly, and she could feel as well the hands of those on either side of her. It was as though she'd become two people, each one clamoring for individual supremacy.

Then the spinning stopped abruptly, but instead of seeing the priests before her and the lake and waterfall behind them, she saw a dark and terrible place: a landscape littered with twisted, stunted trees and shifting shadows that were vaguely human and totally frightening.

She closed her eyes and willed into her mind what she should see; then suddenly she became aware of cries from those around her and her hands were free. She opened her eyes to see the priests and the lake and the waterfall—and Jawan lying on the ground!

Shera rushed forward, pushing her way through the other

clerics who crowded around him. She knelt beside him and felt for the pulse of life at his throat. It was there, but very faint and irregular.

Her hands glowed as she called upon her healing talents. They would allow her to pinpoint the source of his illness. Within seconds she knew it was his heart. She pressed her hands against his chest, using the rhythm of her own heart to help his. But long moments passed, and nothing changed.

Then she saw that he was trying to speak. One hand came up and drew her close. His eyes were closed and she couldn't tell if he knew it was her—but then he whispered her name.

"Shera, child, you were right," he said, his voice so soft that she could barely hear it.

She felt his heart slowing still more, and she bent even closer as his lips moved again. "Do not trust . . ."

His faint whisper trailed off with a sigh. Then his body shuddered several times, and he was gone. Shera looked up at the circle of anxious priests who had moved back to give her some space.

"I couldn't save him," she said. Tears of frustration filled her eyes. "It was his heart."

"What did he say?" one of them asked her.

"He said that I was right," she replied honestly. "We had talked only hours ago."

She got up and pushed her way through the stunned crowd. But before she had gone very far, a hand reached out to grasp her arm. Suddenly fearing that she might be blamed for Jawan's death, Shera whirled angrily—only to find Nabli, a fellow healer, standing there.

"What happened?" he asked.

"I don't know," she said, recalling that Nabli had attended Jawan in the past for some minor ailments. "His heart just stopped."

Nabli frowned. "That's strange. His health was quite good."

"Yes, I thought so, too. I had visited him only hours ago, and he seemed fine then. I did my best, Nabli—but it wasn't enough."

Leaving the shocked healer behind, Shera started back to the village. The shock of Jawan's sudden death had temporarily driven from her mind her encounter with the Dark Ones—but now it all came back to her. She drew in a sharp breath. Was it possible that Jawan had felt what she'd felt—and the resulting shock had killed him?

As she recalled his last words, it made sense. He'd said that she was right, which could only mean that she'd been right about the existence of the Dark Ones.

Perhaps it wasn't the shock that had killed him—but rather the Dark Ones themselves. If Jawan had seen them for what they were, they would certainly want him dead even more than they wanted her gone.

Do not trust . . . His last, barely audible words now echoed through her mind. Who did he mean? Daren was the obvious choice, but he knew she didn't trust Daren. He wouldn't have wasted his dying words telling her something she already knew.

She was still puzzling it over as she entered the village, deciding to go to Garet's shop to see Gar. She was about to reach out to him with her mind, to find out if he was still there, when she heard her name being called and saw Garet running toward her.

"It's Gar!" he cried. "Something has happened to him!"

With an image of the dead Jawan in her mind, Shera reached out frantically, seeking the reassuring touch of Gar's mind against hers. She found nothing.

"Tell me!" she gasped as they both ran through the village toward the stables and blacksmith's shop.

"We were working together. Suddenly he cried out. Then he seemed to be struggling with something, but there was nothing there." Garet paused, panting now as he tried to run and talk at the same time.

"He kept shape-changing—back and forth, back and forth. Then he was a chezah and it all stopped. He is breathing and his heart is beating—but he isn't there."

At least he's alive, Shera thought, even though she was terrified that what had happened to Jawan was about to happen to

Gar. They were still some distance from the stables, and Shera became impatient. What if she didn't reach him in time? What if he was beyond her help, like Jawan?

And then she was there, standing and then quickly kneeling beside Gar's inert body. This time she gave no thought to the magic that had closed the distance between them, or to Tenia's startled cry when she suddenly materialized out of thin air.

"Gar!" she cried, her hands already aglow as she touched his thick fur. He was still alive; she could see him breathing. She wished he were in human form. What did she know about healing chezahs?

He stirred slightly and his eyes opened briefly, but couldn't seem to focus. He was lying on his side, and Shera moved her hands until she could feel the slow, strong beat of his heart.

"Gar!" she cried again, bending close to him. "Wake up, Gar!" She could detect no sign of injury or illness, but she was still frightened, fearful that at any moment his heart might stop. She even thought about transforming him back to human shape again, but she worried that the shape-change could harm him. Tears of helpless frustration coursed down her cheeks.

Then he stirred again, and this time his eyes remained open. He didn't seem to see her, though. She lifted his head and held it cradled in her lap, turning him so that his eyes met hers. At first they seemed dull and unaware, but after a few moments the light came back to them, and a soft sigh poured from his lips.

Shera waited, neither doing nor saying anything because she sensed that he was slowly gathering his strength. In the meantime Garet arrived, obviously relieved to find her there. She held a finger to her lips to keep him quiet, then continued to stroke Gar's thick fur. Her hands still glowed faintly.

Dark Ones, whispered Gar's familiar voice in her mind. *Very powerful this time. I had to. . . . take myself away.*

"Take yourself away?" she asked aloud. "What does that mean?"

Will explain after I change, his mind-voice said slowly. *Must rest now.*

His eyes closed again, but this time Shera knew he was only

sleeping. She got up and moved away, curious to see what else Garet could tell her. Whatever had happened, she was sure that Gar was all right now, but she kept him in sight nevertheless.

"I felt a cold wind," Garet told her. "Colder than anything I've ever felt before. But there wasn't any wind. I could feel it, but I couldn't see it. The trees weren't moving and there was no sound."

Shera nodded. There was no longer any doubt that the Dark Ones had been involved—and their power was increasing.

Faintly, in the distance, Shera could hear the priests chanting. Their homes lay on this side of the village, and she knew they must be there now, chanting the prayers that would mark Jawan's passing. She thought again about the high priest's final words. Who was he warning her about?

Her gaze fell on the sleeping Gar and a terrible chill took hold of her, sending icy fingers of fear to clutch at her heart. Could it be him? Had the Dark Ones gotten him, after all—and somehow Jawan had known that? Was that what Gar meant when he said he'd taken himself away? Had he actually entered that terrible, dark world that she'd only glimpsed?

Darkness fell and then the bright moon rose, and Shera kept her vigil, accepting a blanket from Tenia to ward off the chill of the night, and a cup of tea as well. They offered to sit with her but, though she didn't want to be alone with her thoughts, she sent them home to their little cottage.

She recalled the times when she'd had to rescue Gar from the clutches of the Dark Ones. But that was before he'd gained the power to shape-change by himself, and to ward off Bacleev fire. Still, she feared that by allowing them to be separated during the ceremonies, she might have lost him.

Gar lay next to the old blacksmith's shop, and as the moon rose it limned his sleeping form. She was about to get up and check on him when suddenly he moved—and then he was human again. The change was as abrupt as before, but he got up very slowly.

She got up, too, but she didn't approach him. Instead she watched him warily as he started toward her—and then he seemed to sense something, because he stopped.

"What is it?" he asked, frowning. His voice was rusty.

"What did you mean when you said you took yourself away?" she asked, trying to keep the nervousness out of her voice.

He continued to frown, but came no closer. "I'm not sure. I just knew that I had to do something to keep them from getting me. But I don't know exactly what I did."

In the end it was his obvious confusion that convinced her. She ran into his arms. He held her for a moment, then backed off a bit and stared down at her.

"You thought they'd gotten me."

She nodded, then told him everything that had happened, including Jawan's final words. "But who could he have meant? He already knew I didn't trust Daren."

Gar nodded, his expression thoughtful. "Who will become high priest now?"

"I don't know. No one will be chosen until after Jawan's funeral. The high priest is chosen by the gods, in much the same way as the shegwas. It could be my uncle, Menan, though it's more likely that a woman will be chosen this time." She frowned at him. "Are you saying that's who he was warning me about? But Jawan couldn't have known who would be chosen after him."

"He could if he suspected that there was someone who intended to make sure that he or she was chosen."

"But how could they do that?" She paused, then answered her own question. "If they go into the cavern instead of to the sacred bowl. . . . Gar, that's what they'll do! The next high priest will be chosen by the Dark Ones—not by the gods!"

She clenched her fists against his chest. "The Dark Ones killed Jawan because they knew he was beginning to have doubts. And now *they* will choose the new high priest."

"Can you trust your uncle?"

Shera paused. "I think so. I've always liked him better than the other priests. He's far less pompous than they are."

"Then go to him and tell him what you suspect."

"I will—but I can't do that until tomorrow. They will all be spending the night praying for Jawan."

Saranne Dawson

* * *

"We can't allow ourselves to be separated again during the ceremonies," Shera said as she lay next to him, her fingers playing restlessly over his hair-roughened chest.

Gar kissed the top of her head. "We won't."

She sighed happily. It felt so good to be here with him, so warm and safe. And yet she had only to listen to the sounds outside—the roar of the waterfall and the faint rise and fall of the priests' chanting—to know that they were far from being safe. Instead they were thieves in the night, stealing a few moments of passion from a very uncertain future.

Within moments she heard Gar's breathing settle into the slow rhythm of sleep. But she remained awake, unable to find the same peace. A vague feeling of dread had crept over her, and now she had a sudden sharp image of Daren, his face dark with rage and his eyes alight with triumph. She sat up quickly, and Gar was instantly awake beside her.

"What is it?"

She shook her head as Daren's image faded. "I don't know—nothing, probably. I was just thinking about Daren." Was that all it was—or had it been a vision?

Gar drew her back down. "Sleep, love. There's time enough to think about him tomorrow."

Shera awoke to total confusion. It was dark, but there was a flickering red light somewhere. She was coughing from the acrid smoke that filled the air. And she was being jostled about, held securely in someone's arms.

Only when the smoke was gone and she was breathing in the cold night air did she realize what was happening. But by then Gar had dropped her unceremoniously on the ground and was running back toward the cottage. Shera called out to him, but her throat was still raw from the smoke, and all that came out was a faint croaking sound.

She blinked in disbelief. The darkness was lit by the flames that poured from the cottage's windows and covered the thatched roof. In the eerie light she saw Gar run back inside.

The Sorceress & the Savage

"Danna!" she cried, then coughed again.

By now others had arrived. People were asking what had happened and where Daren was. Before she could say anything, Gar reappeared, this time carrying a blanket-wrapped form. A collective gasp went up from the crowd as they saw him, and people backed away quickly as he brought Danna to her. Still coughing herself, Shera was reassured to hear Danna hacking as well.

There was a loud cracking sound, and they all turned to see the roof suddenly give way, falling into the house. Shera stared in horror. Had they taken another minute, both Gar and Danna would have died in the blaze.

The night was cold, and Shera began to shiver beneath the coverlet Gar had wrapped her in. Danna was shivering as well, and Gar knelt before them, an arm around each of them. She noticed that he was fully dressed.

A neighbor approached, steering clear of Gar, and invited Shera to her house. But it was clear that the invitation did not include Gar, so Shera shook her head, saying that they would go to her old cottage. Although the shegwa house was still engulfed in flames, people began to fade away into the darkness, and Shera knew that it was Gar who was driving them away. They hadn't even gotten used to seeing him in chezah form, let alone as a Walken—and before long they would all be wondering how he'd suddenly become a Walken again.

Danna had stopped coughing by now, and after making certain that she was all right, Shera suggested that Gar take her to Garet and Tenia. Their cottage was too far away for them to have seen or heard the fire.

"I'll go to the cottage and wait for you there," she told him.

Gar picked up Danna again and disappeared into the darkness. Shera took one last look at the ruins of the house and began to walk toward the cottage, her blanket clutched tightly around her. There were lights on in most of the houses she passed, and faces peered out at her, but no one came out or spoke.

Gar was back so quickly that she knew he must have made

309

the return journey as a chezah, though when he opened the door to the cottage, he was himself again. She had lit a fire in the hearth, and the little cottage was just beginning to warm up a bit.

"It was Daren," she said as he came to sit beside her.

Gar nodded. "Of course. But he must have had help. Something woke me, and I got dressed and went outside. I thought I saw someone at the far end of the street and went after him. But I lost him, and by the time I returned, the fire had started. Someone else was there, but I couldn't chase him. I had to get you and Danna out.

"I would have caught whoever I saw when I first went out, but I had a sudden feeling that he might be trying to draw me away from you."

"He wants to kill us both," Shera said, then shivered. "And he very nearly succeeded."

"At least now we know that he will take the coward's way, instead of directly confronting us."

Shera was thinking about her neighbors' reaction to Gar and about the faces that had peered out at her from behind curtains. At the time she'd still been too shocked to give much thought to her people's reaction to the fire, but now that she did, she realized just how little help had been offered.

"By tomorrow everyone will know that you can shape-change—and they will also guess that I have broken my marriage vows. Daren will have accomplished *something*—even if he didn't kill us."

As she walked through the village toward the priests' homes, Shera saw it in the eyes of everyone she passed. There were no words of sympathy, not even the usual greetings. Adultery was a very great sin among the Bacleev. Shera thought of a story she'd heard once years ago about a couple who'd committed that sin. They'd been publicly denounced by the priests and then shunned by everyone—including their own families. Ultimately they'd disappeared, likely going away to new lives.

All was quiet in the vicinity of the priests' houses. Shera was on her way to talk to her uncle, but she detoured instead to Jawan's house, knowing that his body would be there until the time for his burial ceremony. She knocked at the door, which was immediately answered by his daughter. Her husband was an ally of Daren's—the same man Shera had threatened over the attempted rape of a servant.

Instead of stepping back to admit her, Veta blocked the doorway.

"We don't want the likes of you here," she said coldly.

Dagon, her husband, appeared behind her. "Go away, Shera!" he ordered.

But Shera stood her ground and fixed Dagon with a challenging look.

"Were you the one who helped Daren burn my house last night? Someone saw you near there at that time." That wasn't true, of course, but Shera considered him to be the most likely suspect.

He regained his equanimity very quickly, but not before Shera saw a flicker of doubt and fear in his eyes. "I don't know what you're talking about," he blustered. "Get out of here."

"I have come to pay my respects to Jawan—and that is my right."

"Let her come in," said a low but firm voice behind them.

Both Dagon and Veta hesitated, then stepped back, and Shera entered to find Eltea sitting in a chair near the body of her nephew.

She went to the old woman and took the wizened hands that rested on her cane.

"I'm sorry, Eltea—truly sorry. I did my best to save him. I was here just a few hours before he died."

"Yes, I know. He came to see me just before the evening ceremonies," Eltea said in a voice that was barely above a whisper.

Shera turned to see more people coming in. With Veta and Dagon occupied with them, she knelt at the old woman's feet. "Why did he come to see you?"

"He told me of your conversation with him. Then he said that he'd been having doubts. 'Losing his faith' is how he put it at first, but in the end, I think he knew that we are right."

"The Dark Ones killed him, Eltea—I'm sure of it. I felt them myself at the ceremonies."

Eltea nodded. "I suspected as much. In fact, I begged him not to go. But he said it was necessary—that he had to be sure."

Shera told her about Jawan's final words. "We think he might have been referring to the person who will be chosen to replace him, except that I don't understand how he could have known who it would be."

"He told me that some of the other priests were also having doubts," Eltea said. "And if they let the dark forces choose the next high priest . . ."

She broke off as several people came up to her, and Shera moved away to stand for a moment looking down at Jawan. After murmuring a prayer for him, she added her own hope that he understood her reluctance to worship the gods and would forgive her for the many arguments they'd had.

Then she left the house, noticing that she was being pointedly ignored by everyone there. Once outside, she felt a wave of helpless anger wash over her. Jawan could have been such a powerful ally. He alone could have turned the Bacleev away from the Dark Ones—especially if some of the other priests agreed with him.

Now, thanks to Daren, she not only had to fight the Dark Ones, but she was being shunned by her own people.

She walked around the circle to her uncle's house, only two doors away. Her aunt responded to her knock, then quickly stood back for Shera to enter, but not before Shera saw the deeply troubled look on her face.

"I would have come to you last night," her aunt said. "But people told me that you had gone to your old cottage—with that Walken."

"Yes, I did. And I assume they also told you that he was there with me, and that he saved my life and that of my servant."

"Shera, how could you do such a thing? I know that you have

312

never been devout, but I cannot believe you would commit such a terrible sin."

"My marriage to Daren was a marriage in name only, Leepa—by mutual agreement."

"But that savage! He's an *animal*, Shera—not even human!"

Shera smiled. "You're right. He isn't human. Instead I think he is more than human—and I love him."

"Menan says you will be condemned and then shunned."

"If that is so, then we will leave the valley. I have no desire to remain here any longer—especially since Daren is trying to kill us."

Her aunt gasped and pressed a hand to her heart. "What are you saying, child?"

"It was Daren and Dagon who started the fire last night."

"B-but people are saying that you have killed Daren— or put a spell on him and hidden him somewhere."

Shera's lips curved in a bitter smile. "I wonder how that rumor got started. Daren has taken himself off somewhere. I've done nothing to him. But I certainly intend to do something as soon as I find him.

"I must speak to Menan. I know he's probably resting, but it's very important."

Her aunt merely nodded and then scurried from the room as though eager to put as much distance between herself and Shera as possible. She was gone for some minutes, and Shera could hear low voices coming from the bedroom, though she couldn't make out what they were saying. Presently her uncle appeared, looking both tired and wary. She apologized for having awakened him, then told him of her conversation with Jawan, and about the high priest's words to Eltea as well.

"Jawan told me as he was dying that he knew I was right. And then his final words were 'Don't trust . . . ' But he never told me who he meant. I think he meant the person who will be the next high priest."

Menan's gaze slid away from her. "The new high priest has already been chosen," he said in a strange tone.

Saranne Dawson

"Already? But I don't understand. I thought that the choice wouldn't be made until after Jawan's funeral service. Who is it?"

"Glewena."

"I should have guessed," Shera said, more to herself than to him. Of them all, Glewena was the one Shera most disliked—and she knew the feeling to be mutual. "But why so soon? And where did you hold the ceremony?"

"In the cavern," Menan said, still not looking at her.

Shera took his arm, forcing him to turn to her. "Menan, Jawan told Eltea that there were other priests who were worried. You're one of them, aren't you? You know that what's in that cavern isn't the gods."

Menan's mouth set in a grim line and he said nothing.

"Don't you see? Glewena wasn't chosen by the gods. She was chosen by the Dark Ones—the ones who killed Jawan."

Still he said nothing. Shera released his arm. She knew that he wouldn't admit it to her, but she was sure that he at least had some doubts.

"It is likely that I will leave the valley, which means that new shegwas will have to be chosen as well—or at least a new mate for Daren. And I'm sure it will be the Dark Ones who choose this time."

Then, suddenly, she understood what she should have seen a long time before. "The Dark Ones chose Daren," she said. "And the gods chose me. Now the Dark Ones will choose both."

She turned to go, then paused at the door. "I may leave the valley, Menan. But Gar and I have sworn to destroy the Dark Ones—and we will!"

Outside the door she paused, staring at the golden bowl. Then, ignoring the people who were coming and going from Jawan's house, she walked resolutely across the circle and stopped in front of the bowl.

The sacred fire was burning as low as she'd yet seen it, and she cried out in despair. Although Jawan had thrown in his lot with the Dark Ones, enough doubt had remained in him and perhaps some of the others to give the gods some power. But

314

now he was gone—and the new high priest had been chosen by the Dark Ones. Shera was certain that soon there would be no flame at all. The gods would abandon them completely.

"Please!" she begged, not even bothering with the usual prayers. "Please stay and give us strength to fight them!"

No sooner had her final words left her mouth than the fire leaped up and outward, engulfing her in its shimmering warmth. She never heard the cries of astonishment from those who had been watching her, horrified at yet another blasphemy.

"Gar!" she cried, sending her thoughts to him, wanting him to share this blessed warmth and love.

And then he was there, bursting from the woods where he'd been watching in chezah form, causing yet another gasp from the growing crowd. Surely they were certain the gods were about to exact a terrible revenge on both of them.

But before the astounded eyes of the onlookers, Gar transformed himself, then reached out to take her hand—just as a second tongue of brilliant green fire leaped from the bowl to envelop him.

Their hands clasped tightly, they stood there staring into the swirling green mists. The visions came and went so quickly that their brains could barely register them: the dark and terrible place they'd both glimpsed before, a flight through seemingly endless caverns, and then, finally, the mountain of the waterfall coming apart.

Abruptly, the flames withdrew and died away to a glow in the bowl—but one much brighter than before. She turned to Gar, wondering if he, too, had seen the visions, and she saw in his eyes that he had. He drew her into his arms, surrounding her as he kissed her.

"We will win, my love," he said softly but triumphantly.

Their arms still around each other, they turned and saw the crowd that had gathered at the edge of the circle. Shera lifted her chin defiantly and smiled proudly at them as they both started to walk back across the circle.

Before they reached its edge, she became aware of a lone figure standing in the doorway of one of the cottages: Glewena. Shera stopped and stared at her until the new high priestess retreated into her house. Gar looked at her questioningly.

"That is our new enemy: the high priestess chosen by the Dark Ones. And she chose *them*."

Chapter Seventeen

"He could be hiding in one of the caves," Gar suggested.

"I just can't see Daren staying there for long," Shera replied. "He enjoys luxuries too much."

They had spent the day combing the valley for any sign of him without success, and now, late in the afternoon, they were making their way back to the village.

"Then someone is helping him: hiding him in their home."

Shera nodded. "It could be one of his allies—or even one of the priests. And it would do no good to search houses for him, because they would simply move him elsewhere."

Gar was silent for a few moments before responding. "You said before that he would never miss the evening ceremonies."

"Yes, that's what I thought. But he did."

"Maybe he didn't. Maybe he was in the cavern behind the falls."

She gave him a startled look. "Of course! He could have sneaked around the back way."

"Exactly. So tonight we go there and wait for him."

Shera heard the grim determination in his voice. "We can't

kill him, Gar. I want to bring him back so people know that he's still alive. If we kill him we'll be just as evil as he is."

He nodded, but Shera knew he was far less concerned than she was about it.

As they drew near the village, they came first to the food storehouses, and Shera was surprised to find the place a beehive of activity. Under the directions of some guards, the villagers were moving sacks and barrels of food out of one of the buildings. Shera approached a guard.

"Who ordered that this be done?" she asked.

"Uh, Dagon said we should empty this storehouse so that the slaves can be housed here for the winter," the guard said, obviously uncomfortable. He spoke to her, but his gaze kept straying to Gar, who stood silently beside her.

"Dagon? Since when does he issue orders?"

"He said that Daren had issued the order before he, uh, disappeared."

"I see. How very kind of Daren to keep the welfare of the slaves in mind." She turned away abruptly. "It would seem that Daren is trying to create a new image for himself. Danna told me the other day that a few Bacleev had begun to express some concern for the men working at the castle. No doubt he knew that."

Gar nodded. "It's more likely that he knew he wouldn't get any work out of frozen men."

They continued on to the stables and the cottage that was now home to Tenia, Garet, and Danna. Until she saw the welcoming smiles on their faces, Shera hadn't realized just how much she'd been affected by the suspicious looks or pointed avoidance she'd been experiencing from others.

Garet greeted Gar enthusiastically as well. He alone among everyone in the valley seemed completely at ease with the Walken. Even Tenia and Danna, who had gotten to know Gar well by now, were still somewhat jumpy around him.

The two men went off to the blacksmith's shop nearby, while Tenia asked Shera to have a look at the baby. Her mother had already prepared an herbal potion for his cough, but Tenia was still concerned. Shera followed them into the tiny house, noting how her friend had somehow managed to make it comfortable with the few furnishings they'd managed to find in the damaged cottages and some things from Shera's house as well.

After she had assured the worried Tenia that Dakin's cough was nothing to worry about, and that it would respond well to the herbal poultice, Shera complimented her on the house. Tenia thanked her and smiled sadly.

"I've been wishing that I had at least one of my tapestries to hang on the wall. My father's family have been weavers for many centuries, but our hangings were all taken away. Danna has seen some of them in people's homes."

"Aye," Danna confirmed. "But the oldest of them were taken long ago, when the Bacleev first raided our village."

Shera frowned, remembering the treasure cave. Given everything that had happened, she'd quite forgotten about it. Several times Daren had demanded that she take him there, but she'd refused.

The cave wasn't all that far from here—perhaps a half hour's walk—and she recalled now that she'd seen some tapestries in one of the trunks she'd opened.

"I think I know what happened to those tapestries," she told Danna. "Come with me."

When they went to the blacksmith's shop to inform the men of their intention to go to the cave, Garet was eager to see for himself what treasures of his people might be there. So, leaving Tenia to tend to Dakin, they all set out.

"What have you heard in the village?" Shera asked Danna as they walked through the woods.

"Nothing," Danna replied grimly. "When I went to the market this morning, I was told that servants are no longer permitted to speak to each other."

"What? Who told you this?"

"A very unpleasant woman. I don't know her name."

Shera asked her to describe the woman, then knew immediately that it was Dagon's sister. "Did she say who had issued these orders?"

Danna shook her head. "And I didn't ask. I was afraid that she wouldn't let me buy any food."

"Do you still have any coins left?" Shera asked. She'd given Donna money to provide for her family.

Danna nodded. "But I'm afraid that something will happen to us. The woman said she knew who I was, and that we weren't going to 'get away with it' much longer."

Shera stared at her, realizing for the first time what a disservice her kindnesses toward them might do. She and Gar could protect themselves, but Danna and her family were vulnerable. Would Daren go so far as to try to kill them—perhaps even set fire to their little house?

She shot a look at Gar, who'd been listening to their exchange, and she knew that he was thinking the same thing. They had to get Danna and her family to safety.

Since they were coming from a different direction this time, it took Shera some time to locate the hidden entrance to the treasure cave, but finally she did locate it. It appeared to be untouched.

They all went inside. Gar and Garet had brought torches with them, and they all began to open the trunks. Then Shera and Gar stood back as Danna and Garet exclaimed over the lost treasures of their ancestors.

"What can we do to protect Danna and her family?" Shera asked quietly.

"We could take them up to my village," Gar suggested. "There's plenty of food in the storehouses there, and no one would think to look for them up there."

"When can we take them?" Shera asked.

"Tomorrow. But perhaps we'd better stay with them tonight."

"We could bring them back to our cottage."

"No, we'll stay here. I don't think Daren will try to come after us again—at least not now. And if he and his men come here, we'll be able to capture them."

"Why do you think Daren won't try to kill us again?" Shera asked curiously.

"Because I think he knows it won't work. No, he's planning

to have us banished. At some point, when he's feeling powerful enough, he'll come after us again. But he doesn't know where the Walken village is, and with the snows coming soon, I doubt that he'll try to find it until spring."

"We can't let him become more powerful," she protested.

"I know that. We'll get *them* to safety and then decide what to do."

They turned their attention back to Danna and Garet as Danna exclaimed happily over several tapestries she'd taken from the chest.

"These were made by my husband's people!" she cried. "I would know this craftsmanship anywhere."

Garet was busy trying to open a small wooden chest that he'd taken from a trunk. When he succeeded in getting the rusty hasp to open, he held up a gold necklace that glittered with precious stones. Danna stared at it, too. They both wore the expressions of happy children unwrapping gifts.

"This came from my mother's family, I think," Garet said. "Or at least it is their work. Tenia would like this."

"Then take it to her," Shera said. "And several of the tapestries as well. But we can't take more because you're going to leave the valley tomorrow."

Danna and Garet stared at her in surprise, and she told them what they planned to do. "You will be safe there, and comfortable as well."

"In the Walken village?" Danna said doubtfully.

Gar assured her that even if some of his people did return, they would not harm them. "But I think that none of them will return. They will stay in the mountains, in the dens my people used before. To return to the village now that they are chezahs again would be too painful for them—a reminder of what they have lost."

They returned to the cottage next to the stables, where the night passed quietly, with Gar and Garet taking turns staying awake to watch for intruders. In the morning Shera and Gar returned to her old cottage. He had said that if they were being watched,

Saranne Dawson

it would be better to draw attention away from the blacksmith's cottage, so that Garet could get some horses ready for the journey. They would meet in a few hours in the woods behind Shera's cottage, then depart for the Walken village.

Shera was about to make them some tea when there was a loud, insistent knocking at her door. She opened it to find one of the young priests standing there, looking very self-important.

"The high priestess sent me to ask that you accompany me back to her home. She wishes to speak with you."

Shera considered telling the young man that if Glewena wanted to speak to her, she could come here, but her curiosity got the better of her. Besides, there was a faint hope inside her that after witnessing the blessing she and Gar had received from the gods, the high priestess might be unsure of her power.

Gar started to follow her outside, but the young man stated nervously that the high priestess would not speak to Shera if Gar were with her. Gar looked down at him from his considerable height advantage and smiled ferally.

"I'll wait here," he said to Shera. "You can call me if you need me."

Then, in an act that Shera knew was for the officious young acolyte, he transformed himself into a chezah. With a flick of his long tail, he walked back into the cottage.

"Come along, then," Shera said, thoroughly enjoying the man's awestruck expression. She smiled some more as he kept turning to look over his shoulder, likely expecting Gar to pounce on him at any moment.

Glewena's houseservant opened the door to her and ushered her into a small room at the rear of her cottage, where the high priestess sat in a handsome carved chair. She obviously expected Shera to offer her congratulations—and her obedience as well. Shera did neither.

"What do you want, Glewena? I cannot imagine that we have anything to say to each other—unless you intend to tell me where Daren is hiding."

The high priestess's dark eyes flashed with anger. "How

322

could you expect me to know that—when it is *you* who have killed him or hidden him away, spellbound?"

"I've done nothing to Daren—and you know it. Is that all you have to say to me?" she began to turn as if to leave.

"No. I wanted to inform you that you and that savage are to be banished from the valley for adultery. It will be announced after the evening ceremonies tonight."

"I see." Shera tilted her head, regarding the woman quizzically. "I know that you witnessed what happened out there yesterday," she said, gesturing toward the circle where the sacred bowl stood. "Just how do you explain the fact that the gods themselves have not seen fit to condemn me for my so-called 'sins'?"

"Evil has entered you, Shera—an evil so great that even the gods are powerless to stop it."

Shera stared at her in disbelief. "That is the most twisted thinking I have ever heard, Glewena. We both know where the evil lies—and it isn't in me or in Gar. Jawan understood that at the last—and that's why he died.

"We both saw visions yesterday, Glewena—visions that included the destruction of the Dark Ones. You have cast in your lot with the wrong side."

Then Shera turned abruptly and walked out, before she could give in to the impulse to strike out at this hateful woman. And as she walked quickly back to her cottage, it occurred to her that Glewena and Daren made quite a pair—and perhaps had even become one. Glewena's husband had been killed by a chezah on the journey here. Perhaps once they had gotten her out of the way, they would marry. Then Glewena could be both high priestess and shegwa: a combination that would give her unsurpassed authority.

She thought about how the Dark Ones had whispered to her about power beyond her imagining, and she knew that Glewena must have been seduced by those whispers. Daren would be the perfect mate for her. He shared her worship of the Dark Ones and her greed. Also, he was essentially weak, so he would never challenge her authority.

She wondered if she should go to the ceremony tonight and speak out on her own behalf. Would those who had witnessed the two of them being blessed by the gods believe her?

After thinking about it for a few moments, she decided her cause was hopeless. Daren's disappearance, Jawan's sudden death, and the burning of her cottage would have everyone afraid and eager to believe anything the high priestess chose to tell them. Even if she were to find Daren and drag him before their people, he would surely claim that she had put a spell on him to get him out of the way—in all likelihood, no one would question why she'd now brought him back again.

It was time to leave the valley, she thought. Perhaps when they were safe and away from all the lying and treachery, they could think of a way to counter it.

But as she drew near Dagon's house, Shera decided that she would make one final attempt to find Daren. Unless the priests themselves were hiding him, Dagon's was the most likely house; he had been issuing orders in Daren's name.

Her knock was answered by the wife, Veta, and Shera was so startled by her expression that she cast a quick look back over her shoulder, wondering if Gar had suddenly come up behind her. Veta's face was deathly pale, and her hand, which clutched at the door, was actually trembling.

"I wish to speak to Dagon," Shera stated.

"He . . . he isn't here," Veta stammered.

"Is Daren here?" Shera then inquired, adding a mental push to be sure the woman told her the truth.

"No."

"Do you know where he is, Veta?"

She shook her head, then quickly withdrew and slammed the door in Shera's face. Though reasonably certain that the woman had spoken the truth, Shera considered forcing her way into the house and demanding to know where both Dagon and Daren were, but she decided against it. She didn't have time to search for either man now, in any event. Garet and Danna and Tenia would soon be waiting for her and Gar in the woods. Getting them safely out of the valley was her first priority.

Besides, she reasoned, as soon as Daren knew she had gone, he would reappear on his own. If she were going to confront him, she could do it then. But the truth was that now that she thought she knew what Daren and Glewena had in mind, confronting Daren was far less important. He was nothing more than a minor nuisance. The high priestess would be their real problem. She would have the most power.

Shera entered the cottage, expecting to find Gar waiting for her. When he wasn't in the main room, she called out, but got no response. She frowned as her gaze fell on a mug that lay on the hearth rug, tipped over on its side. A small amount of tea had spilled from it, staining the floor.

Had Gar gone already to meet Garet and the others? Or had something happened that had taken him away? Her eyes still upon the overturned mug, she reached out to him with her mind. She encountered nothing.

Terrified now as she recalled the other time that had happened—when he'd taken himself away, as he put it, to avoid the Dark Ones—Shera tried to think what might have happened. The overturned mug bothered her.

As she tried to decide what to do, she walked over to pick up the container, and when she bent down, a familiar and terrifying odor rose from the rug. She picked up the mug and sniffed at it, then whirled around, seeking the pot of herbs he'd used for the tea.

When she discovered it on the table, her worst fears were confirmed. She recalled how she'd been about to make some tea for them when Glewena's aide had come. His timing had been perfect, though she suspected that it was nothing more than coincidental.

Someone had put trecia into the herb mixture. Gar probably wasn't familiar with it, or he certainly wouldn't have drunk the concoction. Trecia was an herb long used by her people to put someone into a deep sleep when they were ill. She and Danna had discovered it growing wild not far from the village. It had distinctive purple leaves, so anyone else might have found it, too.

Then she thought about Dagon's absence—and about Veta's

reaction when she'd shown up at their house. No wonder the woman had looked as though she were seeing a ghost!

Shera clenched her fists helplessly, ignoring the bright glow that surrounded them even so. Daren was responsible for this. Trecia didn't have a particularly strong smell or taste, especially when it was mixed with other herbs, so he must have thought she wouldn't notice. He'd undoubtedly hoped to put them both to sleep—but had gotten only Gar.

A terrible dread filled her as she knew where they must have taken him. The Dark Ones wanted him—and that was where their servants, Daren and Dagon, would have gone.

Think yourself there! she told herself. *You did it before and you can do it again.* But a part of her was resisting that place, with its dark, bubbling pit of evil. She took a deep breath, then reached deep inside herself. In an instant she was there.

The cavern was empty. The only sounds were of her indrawn breath and the faint bubbling from the pit a few feet away. Obviously she was wrong—or they hadn't gotten there yet. Now that she thought about it, she realized that it would take some doing for Daren and Dagon to carry a man Gar's size around the edge of the village and then to the rear entrance of this cavern.

She stood there for a moment, staring at the pit, and then she began to wonder why she felt nothing. Were the Dark Ones hiding from her? The thought that they might be intrigued her, but she had no time to consider that now. Not only did she have to find Gar, but she also had to think about the possible danger to Garet and his family.

She thought herself to the back entrance of the cavern, but there was no sign of them there, either. She ran along the trail until she had come back to the village, but she still saw no sign of them.

Realizing sadly that they could be hiding him anywhere—he would be asleep for many hours—Shera thought herself back to the cottage, then left it to find Garet and the others.

She breathed a sigh of relief when she saw them waiting for her. At least she could get them to safety. She told them what had happened.

"I can't go to the Walken village with you, but I will take you to the beginning of the path. Then I must return to search for Gar."

Garet offered to stay and help her, but Shera insisted that he stay with his family. She saw the looks of relief on the faces of the two women.

They got on their horses and made good time through the woods to the far side of the lake. Instead of leading them to the hidden beginning of the path, where they could be seen by anyone who happened to be at the lake, Shera led them up the steep hillside until they intersected the hidden stairs.

"Just follow it uphill, and at the end is the Walken village." She described it. "Go up to the highest level. Gar's house is there, all alone. But I don't know where their food stores are. You will have to find them yourself."

After telling them that she would join them there as soon as possible, Shera left them. She turned back toward the village, staying out of sight in the woods as she tried to think of a way to find Gar.

Shera refused to let herself believe that he could be dead, even though she knew it was possible. Instead she thought about the visions she'd seen—she was sure now he'd seen them, too. Surely the gods would not have given Gar those visions if he would not live to see it happen!

When she reached the stretch of woods behind her old cottage, she unsaddled her horse and set it loose, then sneaked back to the cottage. Fortunately its secluded location made it easy for her to return without being seen.

What could she do? Gar could be anywhere, and Daren would surely know that she'd be searching for him now. She wondered, too, about the high priestess's role in this. Though she was loath to believe that the woman could be innocent in this matter, the evidence certainly pointed to just that. If the object had been to capture them both by drugging them, then it made no sense for Glewena to have sent her aide to get her.

Shera paced around the cottage, trying to decide what to do. She continued to be certain that they would take Gar to the

Dark Ones, so the only thing that made sense was for her to wait near the rear entrance to the cavern.

The day was cold, with a raw feel to the air that probably presaged snow, so she dressed warmly, then stuffed some food into her pockets and set out through the woods, staying well away from the village.

The day passed with agonizing slowness as Shera waited near the entrance to the cavern. Twice she heard sounds, but both times it turned out to be deer, not men. And with each passing hour the fear that Gar could already be dead gnawed away at her still more.

She tortured herself further by thinking about all the times when she'd been too preoccupied with her thoughts and her problems to let him know how much she loved him. She'd hoped that their time would come one day, that they'd be safe and happy and together.

And she reminded herself that just because the gods had shown them a vision of the future, it didn't necessarily follow that both of them would live to see that future. As Jawan himself had said many times, signs from the gods were often difficult to decipher.

Darkness came early now, on the edge of winter, and still she sat, getting up from time to time to jump about and try to keep herself warm. The temperature seemed to have been dropping steadily for the past few hours, and a chill, raw wind swirled around her.

It was time for the evening ceremonies, which meant that she would have another hour or more to wait. Daren probably wasn't ready yet to show his face at the ceremonies, but the others would all be there, and he couldn't bring Gar here by himself.

No sooner had she resigned herself to a longer wait when she heard faint sounds in the distance coming from the direction of the village. And a few moments later she saw them coming! First came Glewena, followed by a double row of the priests. Peering out from her hiding place into the dim light, Shera was at first confused by what she saw. But then, as they drew nearer, she realized that the two rows of priests were carrying between them a body, wrapped in the ceremonial fashion for funerals.

Totally overcome with horror, it took her a few agonizing seconds to realize that it couldn't be Gar. Not only was the bundle far too small, but it was also encircled by the long golden chain that was used only for the burial of priests.

Jawan! She'd completely forgotten that his funeral would be today. But why were they bringing him here, instead of to the old cemetery that lay just beyond the priests' circle?

A fresh wave of horror washed over her as she understood what they were doing. Instead of burying Jawan with their ancestors, he was going to be given to the pit of the Dark Ones!

She very nearly rushed out from her hiding place to stop them, and later, when she thought about this moment, she would understand that she had not stopped herself—but had instead been stayed by an unseen hand.

The long procession of priests and the rest of the Bacleev continued below her as she waited in helpless frustration. For all that she hadn't liked Jawan, she did not want to see his body consigned for all eternity to the whims of the Dark Ones. He might have led their people back to the worship of evil, but in the end, he'd tried to turn away.

How could the gods let this happen? Were they so unforgiving that they would condemn him to such a fate?

The last of the people were now crawling through the low entrance to the cavern, and Shera got up to pace around the hilltop, flapping her arms to keep warm as she unwillingly imagined Jawan's body being tossed into that noxious, bubbling pit. She wondered if Glewena were responsible for this decision, or if she were merely following the orders of the Dark Ones.

Then it occurred to her that everyone would be in there for quite some time. They had not only the usual evening ceremonies, but the lengthy funeral service to perform as well. It was an ideal time to search the village for Gar. And with luck, she might find Daren as well. She was fairly certain that he hadn't been among that procession of clerics. Certainly she hadn't seen him with the first-circle group, which had followed directly behind the priests.

She hurried back to the village and went directly to Dagon's house. She had seen that both he and his wife were with the procession. Without bothering to knock, she pushed open the door, only to find a startled servant sitting by the fire.

"I am looking for the Walken," she told the frightened woman.

"Is he here?"

The woman shook her head.

"Has he been here?" Shera asked. "He's been drugged."

Once again the woman shook her head. Shera was fairly certain that she was telling the truth, but she still searched the house quickly, then left, asking the woman not to tell her master and mistress that she'd been there.

She then went to the homes of Daren's other allies, but found no sign of Gar or of Daren. Growing more and more frightened that Gar might have been killed and buried in an unmarked grave, Shera tried desperately to think where they might have taken him. She doubted that he would have been hidden at the priests' circle, but she set out for there anyway—only to suddenly find her path blocked by two chezahs!

Shera stopped, her hopes rising. "Gar?"

She couldn't see them that well, but they were definitely as big as Gar was in chezah form. When there was no answer in her mind, she began to approach them cautiously, wondering if their presence here could mean that they were searching for him as well.

"Do you know where Gar is?" she asked when she was only a few yards away.

They both stared at her with their amber eyes, then turned and started off on the path that led to the stables. Shera hurried after them. The stables, or even the food storehouses, would both be good hiding places for Gar. Why hadn't she thought of that?

But how did they know he was there? Had they simply been searching for him for their own reasons—or was there some special bond between them and Gar that survived even when he was unconscious?

They reached the stables and the blacksmith's cottage and shop, but the chezahs kept going, now headed toward the food storehouses. When she hesitated, thinking she should check the stable, one of them turned toward her and growled, then jerked its magnificent head in an unmistakably human gesture that said: *This way.*

She found Gar in the storehouse that was being prepared for the men working on the castle. In the dim light it was impossible to see if he was breathing, but when she ran to him and knelt beside him, she saw immediately the slow rise and fall of his chest. Taking his hand and pressing it to her lips, she sobbed with relief.

But in the next moment her relief gave way to uncertainty. How could she get him out of here before Daren or someone else came to get him? She was certain that they intended to take him to the pit of the Dark Ones—probably as soon as the services were over. Depending on the dosage of the trecia, he could well sleep for another four or five hours.

One of the chezahs nudged at her, startling her. Once again it jerked its head, this time toward the door. Reluctantly she got up and followed it outside, where it immediately set off toward the stables again. *Of course!* It was becoming apparent to her that, while her own brain wasn't working very well at the moment, the same couldn't be said for the chezahs'.

The two cats waited outside while she saddled a horse for herself, then put a bridle on another and found several lengths of rope. Trailed by the chezahs, she led the horses back to the storehouse, where another problem immediately became apparent. How could she get Gar's body onto a horse? He probably weighed twice as much as she did.

She turned to the chezahs, but quickly realized they could be of no help to her. Even if they were able somehow to use their great strength, the horses would never let them get that close. Already, even with the chezahs maintaining a distance from them, they were nervous.

As she stood there, trying to think of a solution to this latest problem, both chezahs simultaneously raised their ears and turned toward the door. Then, with a quick look at her, they both turned and ran out into the night.

Startled by their behavior, it took Shera a few seconds to realize the reason for it. Someone was coming: someone they feared. And that almost certainly meant it was Daren!

Shera ran over and concealed herself behind high piles of sacks that had yet to be moved. Through an opening in the stack she could see Gar, but could not see the door. She waited impatiently, reminding herself that the chezahs had far better hearing than humans, and he might yet be some distance away.

Minutes passed—and then she heard footsteps on the stone floor. A few seconds later Daren appeared. He stood over Gar's inert form. Still she waited, trying to see if he was alone. But when he suddenly drew his leg back and then gave Gar a vicious kick, she cried out and sprang from her hiding place.

Daren had only a few seconds to stare at her with a mixture of fear and hatred before she struck. But in that moment he managed to unleash his own fire. Shera staggered back against the pile of sacks as the storehouse was lit by brilliant green fire that temporarily blinded her.

Sprawled against the sacks and aching in every part of her body, Shera regained her vision to see Daren lying on top of Gar.

"No!" she cried. She struggled painfully to her feet. Could their battle have caught Gar in its midst? In her rage at Daren she'd given no thought to the possibility that she could be harming him.

She ran over and pushed Daren's body away, then felt for Gar's pulse. It was there, slow and steady.

She turned to Daren. Even though she could see that he wasn't breathing, she still felt for his pulse. There was none. Strangely enough, her first thought in that moment was that Gar would be disappointed. He was the one who wanted Daren dead—but she was the one who'd killed him. Even in the midst of her anger over his brutal treatment of Gar, she had tried to hold back, wanting only to stun him. She'd apparently failed.

She got slowly and painfully to her feet again and went outside to where the horses were tethered. Daren must have been expecting others to join him here, since he couldn't have moved Gar by himself. He must have seen the horses and assumed that they were already there, which meant that they probably would be soon. And she knew that in her present condition, she couldn't hope to win any fire battle against them.

She searched the darkness, wondering if the chezahs could be out there. But then she reminded herself that they couldn't help her. Somehow she had to find the strength to lift Gar onto the horse.

She went back inside and began to try to drag one of the heavy sacks off the pile, thinking that she could use several of them as makeshift steps that might allow her to get Gar onto the horse. But when she had succeeded in tugging a sack on the top loose, it fell on her, sending her tumbling to the floor.

And it was then, as she was struggling to push it off her, that the two chezahs returned. One of them went immediately to Daren's body and sniffed at it, while the other one came over to her and began to tug at the sack that was pinning her down. Its sharp teeth ripped through the fabric and the sack burst, spilling grain all over her and onto the floor. But that lightened the burden enough that she could get it off of her. She smiled her thanks to the chezah.

Tas-syana. The words came into her mind in a voice very much like Gar's: so much, in fact, that she immediately glanced over at him, thinking that he'd awakened. But he lay as inert as before. She turned back to the chezahs, both of whom were now standing before her, their amber eyes glowing with a fierce intensity.

"Oh!" she said aloud. The voice had come from one of them. "I don't know if—"

Try. Not much time, said the same voice in her mind.

She got slowly to her feet, brushing away the grain. Then she stretched out a hand to touch each of their heads. Her fingertips began to glow, and then the light brightened until it encompassed both chezahs.

333

The transformation was slow and strange, as it had been when she'd first transformed Gar. And when at last two Walkens sat on the floor in place of the cats, they were as awkward and uncertain in their movements as Gar had been. Shera recognized one of them as being the man Gar had summoned to help with the two men she'd killed on her way up to his village.

Her arms dropped to her sides and she sank onto the floor again, gritting her teeth against the pain. She could heal herself in every situation but this one: overuse of her magic.

The two Walkens got to their feet. "Get . . . two more . . . horses—and rope," the man she recognized said to the other in a hesitant, rusty voice. Then, after his companion had lurched off toward the stables, the man picked up Gar and carried him outside.

Fearing that they might leave her behind, Shera tried to get to her feet. But then she remembered that he'd said "two more horses." Since there were already horses out there for Gar and her, the other two must be meant for them.

Still, she passed the next few moments in an agony of waiting, more helpless than she'd ever been before. She knew Gar, but she didn't know his people, and she certainly couldn't blame them if they decided to leave her there to be dealt with by her own kind.

But then she heard sounds outside. A moment later the man she'd recognized came back in and lifted her into his arms.

"Thank you," she murmured as he carried her outside. "What is your name? I remember you, but Gar didn't tell me your name."

"Trega," he said, frowning at her as though he found something she'd said to be strange. "Can you not heal yourself?"

"No. Only time can do that."

He set her onto the saddle, then began to secure her to it with rope. Gar was already tied across the bare back of another horse.

"What happened to him?" Trega asked, following her glance.

She explained. "He will probably sleep for another few hours, though I can't be sure. How did you find him?"

The Sorceress & the Savage

"We came looking for him when I couldn't reach him with mind-talk," he told her as he got onto his horse. Then he gestured to his companion. "His name is Haydor. He's not quite sure yet that he wants to be human again."

"That's not true," Haydor muttered as he, too, got onto his horse.

"Well, maybe you can transform yourself now, the way Gar can. Just don't do it until we get home." He turned to Shera again.

"We're going to our village. It'll be a long ride, because we have to avoid your village and the waterfall."

"There are people there already," Shera told him, then explained who they were.

Trega nodded. "More of our people should be there now, too."

"They won't harm the others, will they?" Shera asked fearfully.

He didn't answer her immediately, and Shera's fears grew. She was about to ask again when he shook his head. "They are safe. Dossa recognized the man and the one woman because he'd seen them with you and Gar."

Shera sighed with relief; his silence had meant he was communicating with the others.

The journey through the valley and up the mountainside seemed to Shera to be as long as the journey that had brought them here. She tried to fall asleep but couldn't. Then she told Trega that she was going to will herself into a trance, which was the best way of dealing with the pain. He stopped long enough to make certain that she was still tied securely to the saddle.

"The others who are waiting in the village will want to be transformed as well," he told her. "They include my mate and my brother. But it can wait until you regain your strength. When he awakens, I'm sure Gar will let them know that."

"How many are there?" she asked, recalling that Gar had thought only a few were clinging to their human minds.

335

"There are thirty-six people at the village now—including children. But many more are coming."

"But Gar thought that most of you . . ."

He smiled at her. "Gar does not know his own powers of persuasion. He has been reaching out to us, reminding us of who we are."

Chapter Eighteen

Shera leaned back against the stone wall, breathed in the aromatic steam, and sighed as the warm water flowed over her. "I may never leave here."

Gar slipped an arm around her, and his hand cupped the underside of a breast. "I've had the same thought," he admitted. "But there are many people depending on us."

Shera thought—but didn't say—that she was tired of people depending on her, tired of fighting a battle that seemingly couldn't be won. She wondered if it was only the result of overusing her powers, or if the fight had gone out of her. The truth was that she no longer cared very much what happened to her people.

It was late in the day after their long nighttime journey up to the Walken village. Because she had willed herself into a trance, she didn't realize that Gar had awakened from his drugged sleep partway up the mountain. In the dark and with his mind still clouded by the trecia, he'd mistaken his friends for Daren and his henchmen. Then he'd seen her slumped in the saddle and appearing to be unconscious or worse, and had broken his bonds and nearly attacked Trega and Haydor before he learned the truth.

Shera had awakened from her trance only when she'd felt someone untying her, then lifting her from the saddle. Somehow, even in the hazy world between the trance and reality, she'd known instantly that it was not Trega, but Gar.

By the time they reached the village, day was breaking and Shera faced what only a few short months ago would have been a fearsome sight: at least fifty chezahs awaited them. Even knowing that she was safe in Gar's arms and that they wouldn't hurt her, she still felt a certain uneasiness. No one could look upon the great cats without thinking about those powerful muscles and terrible fangs and claws.

That had prompted thoughts of Garet and the others, but before she could even inquire about them, Garet himself had appeared, walking calmly through the pack of chezahs to greet Gar and her.

Tenia and Danna, however, were less at ease in their new home, and their greetings to Shera carried more than a hint of relief. But they acknowledged that they'd been well treated and that little Dakin was faring quite well.

"Trega told me that he thought even more would come," she said to Gar as they sat in the bathing pool now. "He said you didn't know your own powers of persuasion. I didn't know you'd been trying to persuade them."

"I didn't tell you because I wasn't sure it would work," he admitted. "But every chance I had, I talked to them about what it means to be human. It isn't something we ever talked about before. Instead we often talked about how it would feel to be a beast."

"Do you think even more will come?"

"Trega thinks there might be as many as a hundred—perhaps even more. At some point, I suppose, they began to persuade each other without my help."

"Daren is dead," she said. She feared what he would say, but she had had little choice in the situation. She hoped he would understand.

"I know. Trega told me." He kissed the top of her head. "I'm sorry you had to be the one to kill him. I know you didn't want to."

"I didn't kill him—exactly. At least I didn't intend to. He died because of the combination of our magic fire. But he wasn't our chief problem any way."

Gar nodded. "The high priestess." He lifted her away from the wall and held her suspended in the warm water as his lips trailed down across her throat into the valley between her breasts. Then, with his hands still cupping her bottom to hold her in the water, he began to tease first one nipple and then the other, drawing a soft moan from her as she arched to him.

He drew her down slowly, teasing her with the hard shaft that awaited her, then settled her onto himself with a groan. Her hands braced against the stone edge of the pool, Shera rocked against him, drawing him deep, then releasing him, only to draw him still deeper until their bodies shuddered together in release.

"This is what's best about being human," he murmured against her lips.

"Oh? Did you tell the others that?" she teased.

"Mmm-hmm. It may take them a while to learn, though, since they won't have a teacher like the one I have."

Shera smiled, thinking about how he'd changed—how his lovemaking had gone from fierce to tender without quite losing the powerfully sensual edge that the savage beast in him provided. She had grown to be quite fond of that side of him.

When at last they left the bathing pool, they found both Trega and Haydor awaiting them. Without saying a word, the men quickly transformed themselves into chezahs and then back to human form again.

"It looks as though you're not so special, after all," Trega said to Gar.

Shera laughed. Already she liked the man. She knew by now that he was Gar's closest friend, and she thought that his wry humor made a perfect counterpoint to the more serious Walken.

Gar turned to Shera. "Then it could also mean that they're

safe from the magic fire. I know that Daren's dead, but some-one else will soon take his place."

"I think they probably will be safe—but we can't know for sure. And my guess is that Glewena herself will do the calling. She won't want to share power with anyone."

Trega became serious as he turned to Shera. "We owe you a lot, Shera—more than we can ever hope to repay. And unfortu-nately we have even more to ask of you. There are nearly a hundred of us now."

They gathered in the cave meeting place that Shera had once seen in a vision. Two by two, the chezahs came to her and she touched them with her glowing hands. The fiery mist sur-rounded them—and then they were human again, clumsily relearning how to use their bodies.

Several times she had to stop and rest for a while, but the effort required seemed not as great as time went on. Still more chezahs showed up, and at some point she lost count. But when it was finally over, Gar told her that more than two hundred had appeared. Both he and Trega expected that still more would come within the next few days—especially as their friends and kin reached out to them with mind-talk and urged them to give up their animal bodies.

And more did come over the next few days; Gar said that only a dozen or so were holding out. The last days were among the happiest Shera had ever known. The simple joy of the Walkens at being human again, combined with their delight in being able to change at will, was infectious. Even Tenia and Danna gave up the last of their reservations about the cat men, and lit-tle Dakin delighted everyone by laughing whenever anyone shape-changed.

Shera kept waiting for Gar to end her happiness by remind-ing her that they still had work to do, but he said nothing. Instead he seemed to be sharing her joy, with no thought for the future. Even the weather cooperated by suddenly turning very warm. Gar told her that it usually happened at this time of year.

His people even had a name for it: dat-byar, or "lost summer." It was as though a tiny piece of summer had somehow gotten lost and then miraculously reappeared.

They made love in the bathing pool in the mornings and in front of the blazing fire at night, and they were never apart for more than a few minutes. Gar didn't even go with the other men to hunt for food.

The first reference he made to the future came one evening, after they had made love and were lying in each other's arms in front of the fire.

"Could we have children one day, do you think?" he asked suddenly, after a long silence.

Startled, she raised herself up and looked down at him, thinking about the pleasure he seemed to take in playing with little Dakin. She'd noticed that he was spending quite a bit of time with him.

"Do you *want* children?" she asked.

He nodded. "I confess that I'm very curious about what the offspring of a Bacleev and a Walken would be like."

"Is that the only reason?" she asked, knowing that it wasn't.

"No, of course not. I'd like for us to be a family, like Garet and Tenia and Dakin." He paused for a moment, then went on in his slow, thoughtful way.

"I have been watching them. There is a love and a . . . sharing that Walken families have never had. We have families, of course, and we care for each other and protect each other, but there's a difference."

"Of course we can have children," she told him, thinking that he could still surprise her when he chose to reveal his thoughts and feelings, and it was more often lately.

But what she didn't say, hung there in the silence between them. They could think about having children only when this was over. She knew, as he did, that these days were a gift, that they could never truly be safe until the Dark Ones had been destroyed. And they must be destroyed—if not for the sake of her people, then for their own sake, and that of their children.

"The high priestess will call the chezahs," Gar said, proving that their thoughts were the same. "And when she does, she may well set them on *us*."

"Would they do that—fight their own kind?"

"I don't know—and I don't want to find out, either. Glewena may be more powerful than Daren was."

"But how do we fight her?" Shera asked, feeling her happiness shatter around her.

"We don't fight *her*. Powerful as she may be, she's still nothing more than a handmaiden of the Dark Ones. We must go to the cavern—and confront them."

Shera nodded but said nothing. There was no need. They both knew that it all would end in that terrible place where the Dark Ones lived.

"I think we must go soon," Gar said after a time. "The moon will be full in a few more days. That is when she'll call us."

A long line of Walkens moved down the mountainside toward the valley beneath a bright, nearly full moon. Shera walked in the lead, hand in hand with Gar. When they reached the valley, the others would surround the village—especially the priests' circle—while Shera and Gar went to the cavern.

By the time they reached the valley, the evening ceremonies would be over and the Bacleev would have returned to their homes. Garet was with them as well, and he, together with Trega and several other Walkens, would go to the storehouse, where they knew the enslaved villagers were now staying at night. After overpowering the guards there, they would tell the men what was happening. Unlike the Walkens, the villagers could easily be killed by the Bacleev, so they needed to be kept safe. Gar and Garet had decided that the Bacleev might try to use the threat of killing the villagers to thwart the Walkens. According to Gar, that had happened the last time, and many had died.

Everyone knew that there was much that could go wrong. The Dark Ones might know they were coming and alert the high priestess before they got there. The Walkens Shera had recently restored to human form might not be protected, as Gar was, against the magic fire of the Bacleev. And Shera and Gar might fail in their quest to destroy the Dark Ones.

Still, because of the visions given to Shera and Gar by the gods, they believed they would succeed. It was, Shera thought, a strange irony that she, who had never believed in the gods, was now risking her life because of visions they had given her.

They reached the valley and began to circle around the Bacleev cottages, keeping to the woods, with men dropping off every fifty yards or so to take up positions. Then Trega, Garet, and several others broke away, heading for the storehouse. Garet would remain with his people while Trega and the others would join those surrounding the priests' circle.

Shera and Gar crept through the woods behind the priests' circle, followed by a dozen Walkens. The night was bitter cold and the aroma of wood smoke from the chimneys filled the air. Shera let herself feel some relief when she saw that the lights were out in all the houses on the circle. In the center of the circle, the sacred fire still burned, but its glow just barely reached to the top of the golden bowl. Shera wanted to go to it, but Gar had already warned her that to do so risked their discovery by the priests, who might very well sense their presence even if they didn't see them.

So they left the others there to keep watch on the priests' houses, and made their way through the woods to the path that led to the cavern's rear entrance.

They paused outside the low entrance to the cavern, and Gar drew her into his arms. "We do this for our people, our children—and their children," he said softly. "But I wish I could do it alone."

She stretched up on tiptoe to kiss him. "I know you do. But we must do it together. I love you, Gar. I haven't told you that as often as I should have."

He smiled. "No, you haven't. But we'll have a lifetime for you to make up for that."

Shera returned his smile, thinking that he was the bravest person she'd ever known, and that if she hadn't been able to draw on his great supply of courage, they wouldn't be here.

More than once over the past few days, she had wanted to call it off. Even now, only his great strength and courage could propel them into that terrible place.

It's the chezah in him that has the courage, she decided—and *the man who has the faith and love.*

With Gar in the lead, they crouched down and crawled through the narrow opening into the cavern. At first darkness surrounded them, but then their eyes adjusted and they could see the walls glowing. Out of curiosity, Shera examined the walls and discovered that they were just like the walls in the cave they'd used on their journey to and from the village. The priests had told everyone that the glow was magic provided by the gods, but Shera knew now that it wasn't true, and that gave her some satisfaction.

The rank odor from the main cavern reached them long before they got to the huge chamber, but the journey itself seemed to take forever, measured by the rapid beating of her heart, which seemed to have risen to her throat.

They both stopped as they reached the end of the corridor. Standing around the noxious, bubbling pit were Glewena and four other priests, all of them turned in their direction. As soon as she recovered from her shock at finding them there, Shera scanned the shadowed faces and breathed a quiet sigh of relief that her uncle was not among them. She had feared such a confrontation and knew that she could not harm her own kin. It was now obvious that Glewena had chosen only those who shared her dedication to the Dark Ones.

"Did you think we would not know your plans?" Glewena challenged, her voice echoing off the stone walls.

"I thought you might—but it makes no difference," Shera responded.

Her attention was focused on the high priestess, so she was late in realizing that the first attack would come from one of the others. The priest closest to Gar unleashed his fire. Gar let go of her hand as the fire struck him, but he didn't so much as move.

Immediately the cavern was filled with flashing green light as Glewena and the others loosed their fire, only to be countered by Shera's own. Out of the corner of her eye, she saw Gar stagger but remain on his feet. She herself felt nothing more than a slight prickling pain before the fire died. The priests crumpled to the floor.

"Are you all right?" she asked. She closed her fists upon her fire.

He nodded. "What about you?"

"I'm fine. I think they're all dead."

"They deserve to be," Gar said grimly as they moved into the chamber and started toward the fallen priests.

But they had gotten only a few yards before the dark, bubbling liquid in the pit rose up and spewed into the chamber, blotting out the light. Gar's hand reached for hers and managed to grasp it just as they both were lifted from their feet and sent spinning through the blackness.

The air around them became colder than the outside air as they were whirled about in the acrid mist. A great wind tore at them, clutching, trying vainly to pull them apart. But they clung to each other. Shera felt Gar's muscles trembling, and she was sure that his strength would give out and they would be torn asunder and flung to their deaths.

Abruptly the wind vanished, and they were both thrown to the ground. As the darkness gradually parted, they found themselves in the place of their earlier vision: a strange world that existed in an eerie sort of half light with no discernible sky overhead. Odd rock formations mingled with twisted and stunted dead trees in a landscape littered with rocks both large and small.

They got to their feet, assured each other that they were unharmed, then began to survey the scene.

"Are we inside the mountain, do you think?" Shera asked.

"I don't know, but this must be where they live."

"How do we find them?" Shera asked, her eyes still searching through the shadows in the strange light.

"They'll probably find us," Gar observed. He, too, studied the shadows.

Suddenly the air around them seemed to be filled with thou-

Saranne Dawson

sands of tiny insects. The sound was horrible—and so loud that they couldn't be heard above it. Shera started to run, but Gar held her back and then spoke to her mind.

Don't move! That's what they want us to do. It's just a trick.

She turned her head and stared at him, but was unable even to see his face through the swarm of tiny creatures. Still, his certainty that it was nothing more than a trick made her realize the truth: although the noise was incredible and they were completely surrounded, nothing had actually touched them.

The swarm vanished as rapidly as it had appeared, though the sound rang in their ears for some time. Gar drew her close.

"They're trying illusions first," he said. "That means they're afraid of us."

Shera nodded, pressing against him. She understood now that they truly were a team. Without her magic, the priests might have destroyed him, and without his ability to think so clearly and understand the nature of war, she might well have run away—perhaps to her death.

They didn't have to wait long to find out what their enemy would try next. A few seconds later, bright orange flames leaped up from the rocks strewn around them—and a moment after that, they had coalesced into a veritable wall of fire that surrounded them and began to inch steadily closer.

"This isn't an illusion!" Shera cried as she felt the heat from the roaring flames.

"Yes, it is," Gar stated firmly as he held on to her.

Shera believed him until she saw the tanned hides of the heavy jackets they were both wearing begin to darken. She smelled smoke. She struggled to get away, but Gar held her tightly. Suddenly, once again, it was over.

Tears streamed down her face. "I don't think I can stand much more of this."

Gar kissed her. "Yes, you can. It isn't real. Just remember your people—and that we have to destroy their enemies."

She nodded, then eased out of his arms and began to look around them, seeking the next trick—or perhaps even the presence of the Dark Ones themselves. She was totally unprepared for what happened next.

She had been holding on to Gar's hand, but suddenly she was holding nothing. She whirled around, but he was gone.

"Gar!" she screamed, and his name echoed back to her mockingly.

She fought down her panic, pretending that he was still there and telling her that it was nothing more than another illusion. But she didn't believe it. He was gone; she could *feel* his absence.

Reach out, Shera. Keep the mind-link.

She actually cried out as she heard his voice inside her head. *Where are you?* she asked silently.

I'm not sure. I think they are trying to keep us separate. Trust your instincts—as I will. Let them help you find me while I try to find you.

She looked at the blasted landscape around her, but found no clue there. So she closed her eyes and reached down into her calm, deep center—and saw something. When she opened her eyes and turned slowly, she saw the unusual rock formation behind her. She began to walk in that direction, while at the same time sending an impression of it to Gar.

Shera was terrified. At any moment she expected something to happen: another terrible illusion or an actual confrontation with their enemies. Still, she continued to walk as Gar's voice spoke soothingly to her.

Suddenly his voice was gone. She called out, both with her real voice and with her mind-voice—but there was no response. And then she saw him, bloodied and broken, lying on the ground. Screaming in rage, she ran to him—but the image moved farther away. Each time she thought she had reached him, he vanished and reappeared several hundred yards away. The landscape was dim, endless.

Finally she stopped. "I will go no farther. Show yourselves!" she cried.

"We have him, but we will let him go—if you turn the fire upon yourself."

Shera spun in horror. The voice, deep and cold, seemed to be right at her ear. She even thought she had felt its cold breath. But no one was there.

"You don't have him!" she said with more certainty than she felt.

"Over here, Shera."

She turned to her left, from where the voice had seemed to come. Once again she saw Gar's broken, bleeding body. She stared at it, willing the image away. When it didn't disappear, she started toward it, certain that it would vanish as it had before.

This time it didn't vanish—and she was suddenly kneeling beside him and reaching out tentatively—and touching cold, firm flesh. Unbidden, her healing magic came to her hands, even though she knew it was too late. She threw herself on Gar's cold, unmoving chest and cried, her tears mingling with the bloody wounds that covered him.

"You have lost him," said the voice. "Turn the fire upon yourself, and we will save him."

Shera moved away from Gar's body and looked down at her hands. They were now covered with his blood. She had never had Gar's courage to begin with—and now that he was gone, she had none. Neither did she have any reason to live.

"Do it!" the voice urged her, and it was so seductive. What had she to live for?

She started to summon the fire, tensing in expectation of the pain she would inflict upon herself—but then she stopped. Perhaps twenty feet away, the air shimmered slightly and then slowly resolved itself into an indistinct but familiar figure: Jawan.

"No, child. Do not do this," his voice said, speaking aloud but very faintly. "They are—"

The image faded and was gone—but it was enough to shake her out of her suicidal trance. She'd certainly disobeyed Jawan often enough in life, but now she knew that he had saved her.

"I will *not* destroy myself!" she shouted to the empty land. "If you want me dead, you will have to kill me yourselves. If you can!"

A few seconds passed, punctuated only by the rapid beat of her heart and her ragged breathing as she waited to see what they would do. She kept her gaze averted from Gar's body, but she knew it was still there.

And then she heard that sound again: the buzzing of thousands of angry insects. But there were no insects this time. Instead what appeared before her—just beyond Gar's lifeless body—was a swirling black mass, a darkness so dense that it seemed to devour all light. And yet she could see shapes moving within its center—and she could see dozens of pairs of red eyes, all of them staring at her.

The noise was deafening, so all-encompassing that it threatened to drive away all reason. She covered her ears, but it did no good at all. Madness seemed close at hand, a welcome relief. She tried desperately to find that calm place deep within herself, failed, and then tried again—this time for Gar, and for all they had fought for. This time she reached it.

Her hands dropped from her ears and extended toward the terrible black thing. Even before the magic fire left her fingers, she knew she had won. She knew, because she saw fear in those awful red eyes.

The green flame struck the black mass, and in its light she could see the vague forms writhing in agony. The buzzing sound grew still louder—and then began to die away. One by one the pairs of eyes winked out, and then the blackness itself was gone.

Shera stood there, her head still ringing from the horrendous noise, her arms aching from the force of the fire she'd unleashed.

Then two things happened simultaneously. Somewhere above her, she heard a deep rumbling sound, and Gar's body vanished.

"Shera!"

She just barely heard the voice over the ringing in her ears. She didn't know if it was his real voice or his mind-voice—but she knew it was Gar!

"Where are you?" she shouted.

"Right here," he said—and so he was.

He was standing where his body had been—and he was unharmed. They met in an awkward tangle of arms and bodies, trying to get closer than was possible.

"Did you see it?" she asked. "They—"

"I saw it all. I was right here. I could feel you touch me. I knew you thought I was dead—and I thought you would kill yourself. They wanted me to see it happen. Then they would have killed me—and they could have."

"Jawan saved me," she said in a shaky voice.

He kissed her brow softly. "I know. They hadn't counted on him being powerful enough to send that one last message—even in death."

During the time they stood there, the rumbling noises overhead had continued. Now they grew louder. Both of them looked up into the murky light.

"The mountain!" Shera said. "It's coming apart."

"We have to get out of here," Gar agreed.

"But how?"

"Try to think us out," he urged her. "It worked before."

The noises grew ever louder as Shera reached into herself and thought about the cavern where it had all started. Suddenly they were there, sprawled across each other near the edge of the bubbling pit. Too late, she realized that she should have thought them all the way out of the mountain. But when she tried again, this time attempting to get them back to her cottage, nothing happened.

She panicked for a moment, but Gar was already on his feet and dragging her toward the corridor that led to the rear entrance. All around them, small pieces of rock were falling; the noise was even worse than before.

Just as they reached the entrance to the corridor, a huge piece of rock broke away from the vaulted ceiling, narrowly missing them and blocking their escape.

Gar turned to stare at the other corridor, the one that led to the falls. But Shera was remembering the treasure cave and the tunnel she'd seen there.

"I think there's another way that would be safer," she told him. "But I don't know where it is."

It took them precious minutes to find it, a nightmare of a time, with the stone floor shifting beneath their feet and huge pieces of the ceiling breaking off to crash around them. But then they located the narrow opening. Shera turned back before she slipped through it: the bubbling pit was now gone. The floor had shifted to cover it completely.

They ran through the narrow tunnel, knowing they were still not safe. Cracks appeared in the walls and even in the floor, and they were forced several times to leap over newly opened crevasses. There was no conversation between them because they had to save their breath for running, and because the noise around and above them was deafening.

Shera had no idea how long they had been running before the noise began to lessen. But she did notice that there were no longer any new-forming cracks in the walls or in the floor. The glow in here was very faint, and she could just barely see Gar, only a few feet ahead of her.

Finally Gar called a halt and they both sank down onto the cold, damp floor. "I think we're safe," he said.

Shera peered down the seemingly endless tunnel. "We can't be far from the treasure cave now."

"I'm not sure, but I think we've passed it—or passed where it would be."

When she gave him a frightened look, he wrapped an arm around her. "Don't worry. It must lead somewhere. We'll find our way out sooner or later."

Her own laughter surprised Shera—and apparently surprised Gar as well, since he looked at her as though fearing that she'd lost her mind. It wasn't, she thought with a shiver, an irrational fear.

"I was just laughing because you're right," she explained. "Getting lost in a cave is a minor thing now."

Then it seemed as though she could not stop shaking and crying. She didn't understand it. It was over and they were safe, even if they were temporarily lost. Gar held her and murmured soothing words, and she loved him even more because he now understood how she needed to be held and cherished.

"They're gone, my love. The evil is gone forever. But it will take time to accept that."

Shera brushed the last tears away and nodded. "I know they probably don't deserve to live, but I hope my people are safe."

"I told Trega about our visions and said that if the mountain started to make noises, he should try to persuade the Bacleev to leave the village. He and Garet will see to it that the others all get away."

"Do you think it will all be gone?" she asked, trying to imagine outside. "The mountain and the waterfall?"

Gar shrugged, then got up and drew her to her feet. "We won't know until we get out of here."

The farther they walked, the dimmer the light became, until there was no light at all, and she couldn't even see Gar. The tunnel rose and fell and rose again, and made several sharp turns. After a time, Gar admitted that he had no idea where they were, even though he had an excellent sense of direction.

Tired and cold and hungry, they pushed on. The tunnel had become so narrow that they had to walk single file. The warm strength of Gar's hand and the promise of a new life were all that kept Shera going as her mind persisted in replaying the horror they'd left behind.

And then Gar stopped and cried, "Look! There's light up ahead!"

Shera stared past him with mounting dread, unable to believe that it could represent their gateway to a new life. Instead she feared the light that grew ever brighter as Gar half dragged her along behind him.

Long before they reached the source of the light, they could hear rushing water, and Shera's fears grew. What if the water were rushing at them? What if they'd only circled around somehow and were headed back into the collapsing mountain?

But at last, they came to the source of the light. The narrow tunnel ended at a wide and high cavern, in the midst of which flowed a stream. Off to the right, only a few hundred feet away, was an opening through which streamed bright sunshine. They turned in that direction, walking along a ledge that kept them high above the rushing water.

As they approached the mouth of the cave, a memory surfaced, and by the time they stepped into the sunshine, Shera knew where they were. She had discovered this cave the day she'd gone off to explore the valley. It lay at the base of the cliffs that formed a barrier at the far end of the valley. She turned to Gar and saw that he recognized their location as well.

They were tired, hungry, dirty, and cold, but their whoops of joy rang off the cliffs as Gar lifted her from her feet and swung her around. Whatever lay in wait for them at the other end of the valley, it could not be more than they'd already endured.

Then, as Gar was setting her back onto her feet, they both saw the chezah. It was only about twenty feet away, its head cocked curiously as it stared at them. It was a true chezah, not a Walken.

"They've all been searching for us," Gar told her after his silent communication with the animal. "There was fear that we had died inside the mountain."

They began to walk back up the valley, but before they'd gone a mile, they could see horses and riders approaching them. It was Garet! His greeting to them was one of unbridled joy, while Trega, being a Walken, was somewhat more restrained.

Both men insisted that they take the horses, then walked alongside them and gave them the news.

No lives had been lost in the cataclysm. The Bacleev had required little urging to abandon their village when the mountain began to rumble, though, as it turned out, that hadn't been necessary.

"It fell in on itself," Garet told them, shaking his head in wonder. "The waterfall is now no more than a trickle, and the lake only a large pond. The only cottage lost was the one at the end of the village."

"My cottage." Shera nodded. That had to be the one he meant. "And what about my people? How have they taken all this?"

"When we last saw them, they were all gathered around the sacred bowl with the remaining priests," Trega replied. "One of them was speaking. He said that the priests who had worshiped the Dark Ones had died in the mountain—along with the high priestess. His name was Menan. He'd been chosen to be the new high priest."

Shera smiled. "He is my uncle—and the best I could hope for."

"The winter snows have not yet come, and my people would like to go home," Garet said.

Shera nodded, and Gar said that all the slaves should leave as soon as possible. They couldn't hope for the snows to hold off much longer.

"Tenia and I thought we might wait until spring to go home," Garet continued. "It is too cold to take Dakin on such a long journey. But Danna wishes to return to her husband."

"You are welcome to stay as long as you like," Shera said.

In the bright, sunlight, with a deep blue sky overhead, it seemed impossible that they had ever been in that terrible place inside the mountain.

When they arrived at the village, they could hear the chants of the Bacleev coming from the priests' circle. Shera's lips twisted wryly. "They would do well to spend the rest of the day—and more—singing the praises of the gods," she said to Gar. "Come on. It is time they learn how things will be."

Leaving their horses behind, they walked to the priests' circle. Shera sighed with relief as she saw the sacred fire burning high in the bowl. The gods were obviously more forgiving than she was.

Menan had been leading the chant, and it was he who saw them first. He fell silent, and soon the others did as well. Still in their circles, the Bacleev turned toward Shera and Gar. She took Gar's hand, and they walked through the circles as hands fell apart to make way for them.

Shera's eyes searched their faces. What she saw was reassuring. Her people were both frightened and contrite, as they should be. As she approached Menan, he actually smiled. He was officious and self-righteous, as were all priests, but she knew he was basically a good and fair man.

Shera was about to turn and face the silent crowd when suddenly two tongues of fire poured from the bowl and enveloped Gar and her in a shimmering mist. The unique warmth flowed through them both, temporarily erasing the cold and fatigue and hunger.

When the flames had retreated, Menan spoke in a voice intended to be heard by all. "The gods have spoken. Shera and Gar will be the leaders of both the Bacleev and the Walkens."

The first cheers were tentative, but very quickly the gathering erupted into the ululating cry with which the Bacleev welcomed their new leaders.

Shera was mildly annoyed. It seemed that she had lost the opportunity to berate them for their past behavior and demand that they accept Gar as her husband.

Be kind, said Gar's mind-voice. *They already know what they have done.*

She nodded, then led him through the crowd and back to the village. There they continued on past the ruins of her cottage, which had been crushed by a huge chunk of stone. Other large boulders littered the woods and the meadow, but they soon saw that Garet's description had been accurate.

The mountain had indeed fallen in on itself, reducing its height by nearly half. From its peak now flowed a narrow stream of water that made a musical sound as it tumbled down the jagged mountainside into the much-diminished lake.

"Look!" Gar said, pointing to the far side of the meadow.

Shera blinked in disbelief. Somehow the huge rocky outcropping that had concealed the beginning of the path that led up to the Walken village had been swept away, and the stairs up were now visible to all.

Shera sighed happily as she sank into the warm, aromatic water. Even Gar permitted himself a small sound of satisfaction. She was the one who had wanted to come up to the Walkens' village, but Gar had willingly agreed.

On the ledge beside the bathing pool were the remains of their feast, together with the last of the wine that Gar now poured for them. They were both too tired to make love, but not too tired to feel that love as they sat in the water, wrapped in each other's arms.

"The fire is gone," Shera said, stretching her hands out before her and staring at them. It was, she thought, a good thing, because she had grown far too accustomed to that power.

"And I can no longer transform myself into a chezah," he said, with what she thought was a trace of regret.

But the gods have given us another gift, he added in his mind-voice.

A wedding gift, she said silently. *What will we name her?*

Epilogue

The boy and girl stood at the edge of the pond, staring at the wondrous mountain. A wild profusion of flowers contrasted boldly with the dark, jagged rock. Flowering vines tumbled down alongside the musical waterfall, and in every nook and cranny on the mountainside, something was blooming: flowers, shrubs, and even small trees.

The boy was tall for his age, with hair the color of dark fire. The girl was nearly as tall as he was. Her hair was a tawny gold, but her eyes were very dark: a striking combination that promised a great beauty to come.

"Do you think they're still in there?" Dakin asked.

Revenna shrugged. "My mother says they could be, but my father says they're gone forever. How long will you be staying?" she asked shyly.

"For a while—maybe until fall. I like it here," he added, glancing at her, then quickly looking away.

"Here they come now," Dakin said, pointing to the trail that led down the mountainside.

* * *

Shera turned in the saddle to face Garet and Tenia. "Dakin is growing so fast. I hardly recognize him from summer to summer."

"And each year, Revenna grows more beautiful," said Tenia to the accompaniment of Garet's nod.

Gar stared at the children and then at the blooming mountain. "It is through them that I realize the passage of time." He leaped down from his horse and pulled off his shirt. He stretched his lean muscles rippling in the warmth of the spring day. He moved to join the children at the pond. "Once, Dakin, you were only a baby. And Revenna—then you existed only in our hearts."

Shera smiled. There was a way in which she alone counted the passing years: each one seemed to mellow Gar still more—to make him more human. But there were still times when she could glimpse the savage he'd once been—the beast—and she liked that very much.

Starlight, Starbright

Saranne Dawson

Serena has always been curious: insatiable in her quest for knowledge and voracious in her appetite for adventure. No one understands her fascination with the heavens and the wondrous moving stars that trace the vast sky. But when one of those "stars" lands, the biggest, most handsome man she has ever seen steps off the ship and captures her heart.

His mission is simple: Bring Serena to the Sisterhood for training to harness her great mental power. Yet Darian can't stop thinking about the way she looks at him as though he is the only man in the universe. Despite all the forces that conspire to keep them apart, Darian knows that together he and Serena can tap the power of the stars.

___52346-9 $5.50 US/$6.50 CAN

THE MAGIC OF TWO
SARANNE DAWSON

Quinn knows he seems mad, deserting everything familiar to sail across the sea to search for a land that probably only existed in his grandfather's imagination. But a chance encounter with a pale-haired beauty erases any doubts he may have had. Jasmine is like no other woman he has known: She is the one he has been searching for, the one who can help him find their lost home. She, too, has heard the tales of a peaceful valley surrounded by tall snow-capped mountains and the two peoples who lived there until they were scattered across the globe. And when she looks into Quinn's soft eyes and feels his strong arms encircle her, she knows that together they can chase away the demons that plague them to find happiness in the valley, if only they can surrender to the magic of two.

___52308-6 $5.50 US/$6.50 CAN

Dorchester Publishing Co., Inc.
P.O. Box 6640
Wayne, PA 19087-8640

Prince Of Thieves

Saranne Dawson

Lord Roderic Hode, the former Earl of Varley, is Maryana's king's sworn enemy and now leads a rogue band of thieves who steals from the rich and gives to the poor. But when she looks into Roderic's blazing eyes, she sees his passion for life, for his people, for her. Deep in the forest, he takes her to the peak of ecstasy and joins their souls with a desire sanctioned only by love. Torn between her heritage and a love that knows no bounds, Maryana will gladly renounce her people if only she can forever remain in the strong arms of her prince of thieves.

____52288-8 $5.50 US/$6.50 CAN

Dorchester Publishing Co., Inc.
P.O. Box 6640
Wayne, PA 19087-8640

Please add $1.75 for shipping and handling for the first book and $.50 for each book thereafter. NY, NYC, and PA residents, please add appropriate sales tax. No cash, stamps, or C.O.D.s. All orders shipped within 6 weeks via postal service book rate. Canadian orders require $2.00 extra postage and must be paid in U.S. dollars through a U.S. banking facility.

Name_____
Address_____
City_____State_____Zip_____
I have enclosed $_____ in payment for the checked book(s).
Payment <u>must</u> accompany all orders. ☐ Please send a free catalog.

Upon A Moon-Dark Moor

Rebecca Brandewyne

From the day Draco sweeps into Highclyffe Hall, Maggie knows he is her soulmate; the two are kindred spirits, both as mysterious and untamable as the wild moors of the rocky Cornish coast. Inexplicably drawn to this son of a Gypsy girl and an English ne'er-do-well, Maggie surrenders herself to his embrace. Hand in hand, they explore the unfathomable depths of their passion. But as the seeds of their desire grow into an irrefutable love, its consequences threaten to destroy their union. Only together can Maggie and Draco overcome the whispered scandals that haunt them and carve a future for their love.

___52336-1 $5.50 US/$6.50 CAN

A DISTANT STAR

ANNE AVERY

Pride makes her run faster and longer than the others—traveling swiftly to carry her urgent messages. But hard as she tries, Nareen can never subdue her indomitable spirit—the passionate zeal all successful runners learn to suppress. And when she looks into the glittering gaze of the man called Jerrel and feels his searing touch, Nareen fears even more for her ability to maintain self-control. He is searching a distant world for his lost brother when his life is saved by the courageous messenger. Nareen's beauty and daring enchant him, but Jerrel cannot permit anyone to turn him from his mission, not even the proud and passionate woman who offers him a love capable of bridging the stars.

___52335-3 $5.50 US/$6.50 CAN

Dorchester Publishing Co., Inc.
P.O. Box 6640
Wayne, PA 19087-8640

Please add $1.75 for shipping and handling for the first book and $.50 for each book thereafter. NY, NYC, and PA residents, please add appropriate sales tax. No cash, stamps, or C.O.D.s. All orders shipped within 6 weeks via postal service book rate. Canadian orders require $2.00 extra postage and must be paid in U.S. dollars through a U.S. banking facility.

Name_____
Address_____
City_____ State_____ Zip_____
I have enclosed $_____ in payment for the checked book(s).
Payment <u>must</u> accompany all orders. ❏ Please send a free catalog.
CHECK OUT OUR WEBSITE! www.dorchesterpub.com

HEART'S Prey — JAN ZIMLICH

She is a wild woman with flowing coppery tresses and luminous emerald eyes. Yet Rayna Syn is so much more to Dax Vahnti: She is his assassin. The savage beauty's attempt on his life fails, but the Warlord cannot let his guard down for a moment, not even when the lovely creature with wild russet hair enchants his very being. His need to possess the wondrous beauty is overpowering, yet the danger she presents cannot be denied.

___52277-2 $4.99 US/$5.99 CAN

Dorchester Publishing Co., Inc.
P.O. Box 6640
Wayne, PA 19087-8640

Shielder

CATHERINE SPANGLER

Unjustly shunned by her people, Nessa dan Ranul knows she is unlovable—so when an opportunity arises for her to save her world, she leaps at the chance. Setting out for the farthest reaches of the galaxy, she has one goal: to elude capture and deliver her race from destruction. But then she finds herself at the questionable mercy of Chase McKnight, a handsome bounty hunter. Suddenly, Nessa finds that escape is the last thing she wants. In Chase's passionate embrace she finds a nirvana of which she never dared dream—with a man she never dared trust. But as her identity remains a secret and her mission incomplete, each passing day brings her nearer to oblivion.

___52304-3 $5.50 US/$6.50 CAN

The Midnight Moon

STOBIE PIEL

Dane Calydon knows there is more to the mysterious Aiyana than meets the eye, but when he removes her protective wrappings, he is unprepared for what he uncovers: a woman beautiful beyond his wildest imaginings. Though she claimed to be an amphibious creature, he was seduced by her sweet voice, and now, with her standing before him, he is powerless to resist her perfect form. Yet he knows she is more than a mere enchantress, for he has glimpsed her healing, caring side. But as secrets from her past overshadow their happiness, Dane realizes he must lift the veil of darkness surrounding her before she can surrender both body and soul to his tender kisses.

___52268-3 $5.50 US/$6.50 CAN

Dorchester Publishing Co., Inc.
P.O. Box 6640
Wayne, PA 19087-8640

Please add $1.75 for shipping and handling for the first book and $.50 for each book thereafter. NY, NYC, and PA residents, please add appropriate sales tax. No cash, stamps, or C.O.D.s. All orders shipped within 6 weeks via postal service book rate. Canadian orders require $2.00 extra postage and must be paid in U.S. dollars through a U.S. banking facility.

Name_____
Address_____
City_____ State_____ Zip_____
I have enclosed $_____ in payment for the checked book(s).
Payment <u>must</u> accompany all orders. ❑ Please send a free catalog.
CHECK OUT OUR WEBSITE! www.dorchesterpub.com

THE WHITE SUN
STOBIE PIEL

Sierra of Nirvahda has never known love. But with her long dark tresses and shining eyes she has inspired plenty of it, only to turn away with a tuneless heart. Yet when she finds herself hiding deep within a cavern on the red planet of Tseir, her heart begins to do strange things. For with her in the cave is Arnoth of Valenwood, the sound of his lyre reaching out to her through the dark and winding passageways. His song speaks to her of yearnings, an ache she will come to know when he holds her body close to his, with the rhythm of their hearts beating for the memory and melody of their souls.

___52292-6 $5.50 US/$6.50 CAN